STONE
SEEDS

STONE SEEDS

JO ELY

URBANE
Publications

urbanepublications.com

Suite 3, Brown Europe House, 33/34 Gleamingwood Drive, Chatham, Kent ME5 8RZ
Copyright © Jo Ely, 2016

ISBN 978-1-910692-87-5
EPUB 978-1-910692-88-2
KINDLE 978-1-910692-89-9

Design and Typeset by Julie Martin
Cover by Julie Martin
Cover image © Cyril Rana
Printed and bound by CPI Group (UK) Ltd, Croydon, CR0 4YY

urbanepublications.com

FOR ERIC, MAIA AND GINA

"You do not do, you do not do any more black shoe in which I have lived like a foot ..."

Sylvia Plath

"All oppression creates a state of war."

Simone De Beauvoir

"And he gave it for his opinion, that whosoever could make two ears of corn or two blades of grass to grow upon a spot of ground where only one grew before, would deserve better of mankind, and do more essential service to his country, than the whole race of politicians put together."

Jonathan Swift, Gulliver's Travels

"And it will rain so hard that night that morning will come."

Unknown songwriter, Brazil

CONTENTS

WATER

ANTEK REMEMBERS IT WAS Jengi. Jengi, the shopkeeper's
assistant, who struck a match, eyed the workers. He said they
looked thirsty. He said that the last guard had a whim to dock
their water rations. And in this heat. Might lose a few.

Jengi shrugged. Then sloped off, the way Jengi does, as
though disowning his thought. Antek remembers it was
Mamma Zeina, the general's Sinta slave-cook, who rolled
the rain barrel over toward him, careful not to spill, and
then abandoned it by his left foot. Left an ancient looking tin
cup floating on the surface of the water. No word. No eye
contact even. As if she left it there absent-mindedly. A mere
suggestion. And the rest was up to Antek.

Antek knew it was against regulations but ... Once he
knew the gem miners were thirsty, he noticed other things
too ... became aware of the rows of eyes watching his hand
as he raised his flask to his mouth. The trickle of cool water
streaming onto his wrist, blotting his sleeve. And then staring
at the water marks speckling his shirt front.

Antek was meant to be guarding the gem miners. Instead
he'd played look-out whilst they drank the clean rainwater from
the tin cup.

He was bound to be found out. The general always has a
guard to watch the guards. Ever since the rumours started.

The rumour being that an undercover Sinta infiltrated the labs before batch 47, Antek's military unit, were hatched out. The rumour that batch 47, Antek's batch, were ... different.

The bottom line is that Antek has been a suspect since birth. That's what the cameras and the listening devices, the endless testing and retesting in the labs are for ... It's to find out the truth about Antek and his batch of Egg Boys. The truth, one way or the other. Everything for Antek either is, or else might be, a test of his loyalty to the general. Including this, now.

Antek had been made to walk hot rocks all day for rehydrating the workers.

Soothing the burns on his feet with the cool mud from under the rain barrel, and when that dried in the welts on his soles, the moist waxen leaves passed to him quietly by the workers had, to his surprise, helped. Sap along the surface of the leaf almost healed his wounds.

Antek had thought at least that's the end of it. But it turns out there'd been another witness to Antek's wrongdoing. Someone more important than a second guard.

———

Sweat. The youth wing officer twitches. Metal blind snaps open. The left side of the officer's face seems to light up, silver-white with perspiration. The mirage lasts a moment. The officer blinks and grimaces, changes his mind. Yanks the blind down hard, so it snags and droops on the runner, buckles and dips softly forward. Stripes of light through the gap at the top and down one side.

Antek notices a slick of sweat is seeping from the officer's hairline, gathering in a soft sheen at the roots and then drips. One long slow trickle eases into the umbrella of the officer's thick blonde eyebrows. And then escaping down his short curved pink nose. Gathers at its round, bulbous tip.

The officers are rarely Egg Boys like Antek. The general prefers to select his own tribe, the OneFolk, for the top jobs.

The OneFolk are one hundred percent organic, not manmade like the Egg Boys. Meaning they can't stand the heat the way Antek, with his tweaks and regulation modifications, can.

Dab, dab, *dab* goes the officer with his damp rag and Antek has to look away now.

The officer eyes the door several times more, adjusts its angle. Half open and half closed, nudges it back and forth minutely. The officer never seems satisfied with that door.

Antek, who is at his happiest being ignored, is right now doing his best impression of a piece of furniture. Pulls his long and boney legs up, hugs his knees and stares at the window: rain combing down it. He's briefly mesmerised by the stripes of water. Now the officer's moving softly round Antek's room.

"Shhhh," the officer says. "Shhhh."

Who knows what it all means.

Antek's heard the stories. Many of the OneFolk senior officers were forest workers in the previous era. Charged with tracking and culling the runaways. Rewarded for their patriotic work with status positions in Bavarnica's army, the food rations to go with the promotion. They were the ones who rounded up the Sinta, hidden in the copses, undergrowth and trees when the revolution failed, and the general declared the Sinta an illegal cult. Killed those escaping, made those who couldn't run slaves to the village. Slaves to the OneFolk.

Of course there were some of the OneFolk who let Sinta go free, run into the killing forest in The Before. Some live there still, that's always been the rumour. Gradually becoming immune to the poisonous plants which the general thickened out the forest with, the nipping saplings. They've learned how to avoid the huge snakes. Evolved quickly, like the rest of the killing forest. Changed. "Into something rich and strange," that's the whisper on the Sinta farmsteads.

Fairytales, Antek thinks. The killing forest is not a home of any kind, it's just a trap. And the runaway Sinta are dead, the sooner those left behind realise it … Even guarding the fence beside the forest you can see it's just a set of manmade jaws that will lure you in and close its poisoned teeth around you.

The main thing to take home from all this is … You can't know what you're dealing with, what or who. Not in Bavarnica and not with an organic. And especially not with the OneFolk. The general's tribe. Leastways that's how Antek sees it.

Antek can hear the sound of his own heartbeat, stomach pumping. Inside sounds. The officer moving slowly through his things. Picking up this and that and eyeing its contents. Because nothing should be private in the army, for the general's Egg Boys. The youth wing, batch 47.

The officer speaks in a strange, wistful voice. As if hoping for some kind of signal from Antek. As though provoking Antek to disagree with him. Watchful for any small sign that he does.

Antek doesn't like being watched.

He looks down. He can't say what he feels at this moment. Winces as he laces up his left boot.

The officer's tone hardens. "The youth wing is ripe for exploitation by The Underground, The Sinta Resistance, ripe for their lies. Private is bad, Antek." And then in a different voice, "At least that's the drill in sector three now." He sniffs. Checks his notes. Takes a key out of his pocket, un-cuffs Antek.

There is a long pause in which the officer appears to be trying to decide something. "Village shopkeeper." He gets the words out. Low voice. "Name of Gaddys," he says. "She informed on you. You're on a list now, Egg Boy. That's bad." And then softer, "That's bad, Antek. The shopkeeper's power is growing."

The officer closes Antek's door behind him gently. Antek hears whispered voices in the corridor outside. He looks up.

Antek's digs are up in what the Egg Boys call the crow's nest, meaning the upper reaches of the soldiers' barracks. Naturally the Egg Boys' only window faces inwards. They're on the left side of the look-out towers, their view: rows and rows of brick and corrugated steel, far as eye can see. Metal pipes run across the rooftops, sliding in the cracks between the buildings, dark red as if to acknowledge they're the veins of the system.

Egg Boys like Antek don't get to see the huge industrial equipment that drives the system, but Antek with his specialised ears can hear it. Groans and clanks of the mechanism, lulling him into a fitful sleep at the end of a long job.

Yesterday was Antek's first guard duty at the gem mines. Until yesterday he's been mostly sent to guard the clean-up crews, on the edge farms. These crews are people, organics, edge farmers certified tame. The crews are untrained amateurs, mostly will accidentally kill those whom they're trying to save from the rubble. But they'll sweep up the bomb damage, the way that the general likes.

The edge farms are lands outside of Bavarnica-proper, they lie just beyond the living fence of the killing forest, which was built to keep the hungry folks out of the village. Even amongst the most hardened Egg Men, this post is known to be ... Well. Antek finds it best not to dwell on what it is, or what it isn't.

Guarding the gem mines, on the other hand, is generally considered to be a plum job for an Egg Boy. Only a handful of guards are deemed necessary to guard the edge farmers working the gem mines, on account the miners are given a slave's pay, meaning food, and only just enough to survive on. They are hand-picked by Gaddys, the village shopkeeper. Generally expected to be compliant with their guards. It's a useful way to train the newly hatched guards from batch 47. At least that's the idea.

So many different tribes in Bavarnica that it's hard to keep up. But all of them under the one tribe, the OneFolk, and the general. Under them in one way or another.
Tribes aren't s'posed to mix, but Antek's gotten to know a few edge farm faces from his guard duties.

And then there's Tomax.

Antek hears the slow throb of the energiser, watches its fitful light coming back on. Yellow. Antek thinks. Like a bad omen. There are bright yellow seams running thickly down it, texture of molten gold. Now Antek hears the long low whir and thrum of the system, cranking into gear.

The officer doesn't come back to Antek's room until the lights are dim.

"You've been called for." He says.

Antek gets up and follows him.

He wilts a little, outside the tall black door of the officers' headquarters, his hands are clenched. Sweating. Antek makes up his mind not to mention Jengi or Mamma Zeina in his interrogation. They never told him to give the workers water, at least not exactly. No sense bringing them into this. It's not in Antek's nature to take folks down with him.

"Come." Brisk, cold tone. Whoever is inside must have heard Antek's feet. He knocks, belatedly. Tries the handle. The officers' door is heavy, even for Antek. There is building sweat running down it from the vent over the door. The door handle is slick. Antek eyes the metal slats of the vent suspiciously. Thinks he saw something move inside it. A twisting, sliding motion. Sense of something heavy in the space over the door. Something big enough to shake the sides of the vent when it breathes.

He tries the door again. This time it opens. Hears the soft click as it closes behind him. Senses a hand on the other side, try the handle then wait. Whoever it was lingers for a moment. Fingers sliding over the steel surface of the door. Antek turns back toward the room. He closes his eyes.

Smooth, cold voice now, running down Antek's left and inside ear, like it comes up from Antek's own stomach. Antek realises at once this is going to be what they call a soft interrogation. He hates those the most. A seeping familiar heat passes over his face. Blink, *blink*. He looks down. And as though he expected this, the senior officer smiles. Rubs his chin. "So. We heard you made a friend, Egg Boy." The officer's voice is soft, provoking. His long yellow fringe flops down over his left eye. Pale blue, squinting. He scoops his filthy hair between his fingers, presses it all under his cap. Checks the room, eyes the vent. Then he turns and looks at Antek coldly.

"Okay, Egg Boy." He says. "Give me some names and it ends here."

Antek eyes the vent over the officer's head. Something wriggles in there, bangs the sides. Rattling against the opening and then stills. Antek can feel rather than see the huge creature watching. The officer winces. "Snake." He says. Gazing at Antek. "It's one of the general's. He can open the vents from a button in central control, any time he likes." He says it like he is apologising. The officer goes on gazing at Antek. Licks dry lips. He can't speak for a moment.

Antek knows the threat implied by the snake in the vents of the officers' quarters is a threat only to an organic like the officer. Snakes are no longer any danger to the Egg Boys, as Antek's had cause to learn once or twice in his days working the fence to the killing forest which runs between the edge farms and the OneFolks' village. He doesn't know why the general's lab technicians gave batch 47 the anti-venom feature. But the technicians will do nothing without a reason. Not even a small tweak. Maybe Antek's mission will be in the killing forest some day. Who can say for sure what the Egg Boys are being repurposed for. Certainly not the Egg Boys themselves.

Antek briefly wonders why the general's got this extra security measure in the officers' headquarters, and then tries to put the thought away. It doesn't do to ask questions, not even of himself. A thing like a question can show up in your face and that's dangerous. Batch 47 are still deemed to be an active experiment. Antek's batch can be cancelled at any time, and he doesn't want to be the reason for his friends' deaths. Although strictly speaking that emotion should be beyond the reach of an Egg Boy.

The senior officer has a window, it's north facing. The view from here is vast, looking out beyond the barracks and over Bavarnica, right up to the long mountain range of The Reach and the dark lake in its shadow. The view gives the officers a certain perspective that the Egg Boys in their inward looking crow's nest barracks are deprived of.

The skyline's broken, the sun seems to Antek strange and huge behind it. The daylight moon too, visible edge the left and lower corner of his window.

"A reliable source has told us you been fraternising with the enemy. Talking to a worker you were s'posed to be guarding?"

Antek has learned better than to answer a leading question. He never speaks before he strictly has to.

"You been seen talking to the same worker. The same edge farm boy, Antek. Talking to him on both sides of the border." Softly, "*Antek*. You know you're not supposed to talk to them. Don't try to deny it. They ... We know who he is." Pauses. Eyes the vent. "We have a name."

Antek waits.

"Tomax. It's Tomax, Antek." He leans back, rolls his shoulders, "And you just got him killed."

Antek feels a cold, sliding feeling in his chest. He hears his inside sounds now. Stomach pumping, churn of his blood. Gaddys. He thinks. It was Gaddys who told.

The room turns dark. It's sudden.

———

"Wake. Wake." The lab technician closes the door stiffly behind himself. Heat expands the doorways so the old doors don't fit their hinges in the interrogation rooms now. The second lab technician approaches the bed and fingers the strap on Antek's right arm. Secures it. Prods to check Antek for a natural reflex. There's none. Antek wakes. Antek tries to wake.

"One, two, three and wake, Antek." Says the first lab technician.

And turning toward the second lab technician, "Fellow talks in his sleep."

The two lab technicians eye each other.

"Will they keep him?"

"They'll put him in the cells. They'll reboot him."

———

It's quiet for a long time in the cell after the guard has gone. Antek's hand reaches for his chin. And then falls away, quivering.

Something is moving underneath Antek's blanket, there's a scratching, subtle but relentless tugging at the toe of his boot. It's an ominously hunched shape, he sees it moving to and fro by the crack of light under the door, from the unshaded lightbulb in the corridor outside. A gnawing sound, he kicks out at it sharply. It's a shock, feeling its small body against his boot. It bares its teeth, scowls and scatters. Back out into the light.

Antek hears a tin cup clattering, rolling. The guard outside, cursing in a broadside, kicks Antek's door. Just as if it was

Antek had sent the scurvet to knock over his stool.

Scurvets were one of the general's early experiments in tame and wild creatures, back when the general was a lowly lab assistant. Even Antek has heard the story about the scurvet, although he's never clapped eyes on the creature before now. They say that the scurvet gave the general his ideas for Bavarnica.

"Quiet." The guard outside Antek's door says. "Quiet down in there."

Tomax came to Antek in a dream that night, the field behind the village gem mines. The trees were burning, smoke rolling up from them in swathes. The wind just seemed to curl the smoke back on itself, so that it fell in strange, unnatural folds, and Antek wakes with a choking feeling.

Long gasp for air. Swallows painfully. He closes his eyes. In the moment before he wakes, believes a cat is winding slowly round his leg. There's a whirring sound, and when he opens his eyes it's just a grey scurvet. This one seems tame. Tamer than the last one. Nice and Nasty he decides on the spot to call the two. He hears Nasty scatter in the corridor outside, hiss.

Antek's heart beat gently thrums against his rib cage.

Antek notices that he has a cellmate, an organic. A slumped shape in the cell's darkest corner. The cellmate's trousers are ripped and bloodied but they're officer's trousers. Bare feet, small burn marks. The man's floored and breathing strangely. He looks briefly at Antek. And then recognising that his cellmate is an Egg Boy, looks away.

Antek guesses that the officer would rather not share a cell with an Egg Boy. A thing that isn't human.

Antek falls asleep again, waking in fits and starts all night long, but the dream he's had these past weeks, the dream still finds Antek. Even here. Tomax again. Tomax is running from the Egg Men.

It takes Antek a while, in the dream, to realise that he's one of them, the Egg Men, and that Tomax is also running from him. Just a beat ahead of him, and at first Tomax sees only Antek and he is laughing, turning toward Antek the way he used to turn toward Antek. And Tomax's smile. The one that'd make Antek feel weak suddenly. Weak on guard duty. Which has to be a feeling that's against regulations. Antek would look down or away. But when he'd look up again, Tomax would always still be looking back. And Tomax's smile then, like slow cloudburst. Soft rain.

Tribes can't mix.

That's the first and most important of the general's rules.

The running dream has lasted several weeks; it is never exactly the same dream twice but one thing never changes. The ending. Tomax eyes shift up, he sees something coming behind and then above Antek. Tomax's smile slides slowly off his face, his eyes become wide and amazed. And then blank with horror. Antek sees a shadow move across the left side of Tomax's face and then the dream ends. Blink, *blink*.

Antek wakes to his cold cell.

Scattering sound in the corridor outside. A squeal then nothing.

Antek guesses correctly that Nasty killed Nice.

Hears the sound of the small furry body, dragged unresisting along the cold tiles by two perhaps three sets of sharp jaws, scuttle of several clawed feet. Antek reflects that it might have been a different story if the prisoners had only had a few crumbs to keep the Nice population of scurvet going. They wouldn't have gotten so outnumbered in here. They would not have become food.

Antek stretches his arm out softly in the dark. Feels the cold cell floor, damp underneath his left hand, his fingers splaying. Icy floor.

Boots under the door.

It's time for Antek to be stained again. He'll be rebooted after. He feels the nick in his chin. Remember, *remember Tomax*.

The stain is in fact only a side effect of the tweaks the lab technicians regularly make to the Egg Boys' DNA. But the stain also signifies how far an Egg Boy is along to becoming pure Egg Man.

Antek knows he'll get more Egg Man and less Antek every time he comes out of the lab. That his stain will spread out until it covers most of his body.

There is no point resisting.

———

When Antek's mind collapsed toward the end of the third month in the cell, something came to Antek. The past in a tilting, skewed light, and he saw something that he'd missed. And then that thin light falling on a dark scene, the streaming damp jail wall felt to him like the insides of a stomach or a soul.

The floor is damp under Antek's hand. There's a crack in the ceiling. Water running in a long stream down the wall. Antek puts his mouth up to the filthy wall, he takes a deep drink of the cool, mottled water.

There is a long crack along the cell wall. A seam that spills a gut of bricks in the middle. Antek kicks it with his foot. He has the sudden feeling that the cell itself could clatter down on his head at any moment. One swift kick to the cell door, or one too many, and the whole room would shake and split.

There are branches running out from the crack in the middle of the wall, tendrils fingering all the corners. New seams criss and cross the ceiling. Was there a bomb above ground? It seems to Antek to be unlikely that the barracks gaol would be attacked.

An accident then. That last bomb. Maybe. Antek tries to put it out of his mind. He's trained himself since birth to put away these kinds of questions. To not accidentally show by some slow gaze, or brief shrewd glance, the little he knows, or has thought to ask himself.

He puts a hand out. Feels the dark, wet wall behind him. It's covered with a sheen of something. The damp gently tugs at his hair, pulls him stickily into it.

There's a long, deep crack in the ceiling over his head.

His officer cellmate has started whimpering in his sleep. Thrashes and flails, dreaming. And then something scurrying across the floor. A yellow scurvet dips under the door and out into the light outside the cell. Antek raises his left hand to his chin, without realising that he does so. He feels the small groove there.

Antek thinks he remembers sunshine. The old sun. It's sudden. The crack of light under the door must have triggered memory. Tomax was standing with his tin cup. Standing at the mouth of the gem mine. The light was dappling Tomax's skin then he'd shielded his eyes. Squinted up at Antek from under the shade of his hand. The sun downed softly in an arc over Tomax's head. But of course it couldn't have been like that, Antek thinks. With the sun.

And then Antek's mind goes on without him, stirred and exhausted. He should never have smiled back at the edge farmer, Tomax.

The tribes can't mix.

Antek's gently butting at the cold stone wall 'til he believes he seeps into it.

His mind is spreading into the cold damp stones of his cell.

When Antek wakes again there is a glistening seam of water, running fast down the wall. He guesses there's a split pipe above him. Antek wonders if his cell will fill up like a rain barrel, drown him at the top.

He looks down.

He notices that his cellmate's trembling. Antek reaches out a hand to rearrange the officer's blanket. He thinks for a moment. Then he gives the man his own.

Antek leans into the black cell wall. He feels disoriented.

He doesn't know what he is, what or who. For one long moment he's not anything at all.

It has taken less than three months in the dark to unravel Antek.

He draws his arm across his forehead, wiping away the seam of sweat and filth gathered in his eyebrows. He sees the guard's boots under the door again. And then he hears voices.

"Is he fully erased?" First guard.

"Yes." Says the second guard. "They did three reboots in a row. The Egg Boy is submissive now."

"Are you sure?"

Small pause. "Aye. They ... We think we can control him."

Antek hears the sound of the door being unlocked. He's pulled up to his feet.

————

The air is fetid in the stairwell. Antek feels the proximity of bodies in the cells beneath him, smell comes up through the steel grating under his feet. Somewhere in the dark, faces softly rise to gaze at his boot-soles. Blink, blink, as the light filters in. Whispers, soft sliding sounds. Then a long hiss, sshhhhhh. Antek doesn't look down. The shuffling has the quality of bodies densely packed. Small sounds of chain-metal on damp stone tile. Then the scrape and clink as one prisoner strains against his portion of chain. Sound of gentle groans. And a hissed reproach, coming up through the grating.

He knows the prisoners will assume he had bought his freedom by naming names.

For a long strange moment, Antek can't recall if he did.

He looks down at his hands.

Bound in a web of strong white tape.

The guard on Antek's left side lifts a knife and unwraps him. "You is trussed up like a critter on the general's feast table, Antek." Slow look. Antek looks away from him. Blinks.

There's a soft breeze from outside running down Antek's face. Cools the dirt-sores a little. Back of his neck, where the iron collar once bit home and doesn't now.

There are two doors. Square of light around the exit, on Antek's right side.

Antek thinks how it would be to make it to the top of the staircase, half turn. Put his hand on the latch, just once. Feel the warm, rusting metal. He cannot imagine getting any further than that, but he has a sudden longing to hold on to the handle. To feel the wind blowing hot and sharp through the key-hole, the high pitched whistle of it round the hinges. Sunlight under the door.

A hot pulse of air rattling the door in its hinges, makes the guard on Antek's left side flinch and half raise his baton. Antek flicks his eyes toward him and then back to the door. Blank-eyed prisoner stare. 'Six steps between here and the exit.' Antek thinks. 'Just three bounds.' It might as well be a hundred. Antek glimpses the possibilities of making a bolt for freedom, then rejects them, one by one. Freezes there by the bottom step. "Go." The guard on Antek's left side. Soft hiss. Then a gentle push. "Come on, Antek. Go on home."

Shove from the right.

It takes Antek a moment to understand the words. Then for his feet to reconnect with his mind. An upside whack to the head from the first guard, right side. Antek can't tell if the guard used his baton or his fist. Pain is running down Antek's right ear. He's unsteady on his feet.

The world moves soundless, strange around him.

Blink and blink.

Antek raises his shoulder. He presses it against the hurt ear. The sound comes back slowly.

"Go." The second guard says. Gripping Antek's right elbow. Holds him up. Another impatient shove from his right side. And the voice on his left. Low voice. "Before they change their minds again, Antek."

Antek puts his foot on the first stair, pauses. He doesn't know why. In a bit realises that he's waiting to be stopped. Antek glances at the white-lit corridor behind him. He's left black boot tracks down the tiles, like a child's scribble.

They had dragged him from the cell to the stairwell. Scrabbling, sliding feet and snaking long legs. He'd hit his knees in the ruts and cracks in the tiles all the way up to this spot. Convinced he was going to his death. Panicked then, in spite of himself. And then hauled to his feet by his bindings. He was pulled around like a puppet on a string, and when he was let go, teetered. Silence.

And then clanking sounds again from the cell beneath his feet. If it's a protest then it's a tired one, he thinks. Whispering seems to run up and down the wall. 'Air vent?' Antek calculates.

In the early days of the general's crackdowns the prisoners had used the air vents between the cells to communicate. But it only served to inform the prison guards in the end. This cell will learn that too, soon enough, he thinks, and Antek lets his eyes roll left to check for the vent-slats in the wall. It's an old habit. Antek has been checking for vents and cracks in things ever since he was hatched. Anything that might double as an exit, or a hiding place. It's been a useful trick, anywhere but in here.

Two doors. One dark, leading back into the system, into the tunnels of underground cells, and the second door with golden sun-lit hinges. That one leads out. If this is a test then he's failed it already. He'll take the brightly framed door. If the guards even let him get there.

The wind must have died down because the door leading

outside has stopped rattling its loose metal hinges. It seems to Antek as though everything waits for him now. For his next decision. Antek slowly lifts up his arm. Touches the scar on his chin. Tries to remember who he made the nick in his chin for. Who it was that he was trying so hard to remember. Nothing comes back to him.

BLOOD

THERE IS A DRONING sound, a long hum and it stops above Tomax. And then it feels to Tomax like he's dreaming. The window pane splits, from the bottom left of his mother's house, cloud spirals like a huge finger pointing, tracing an invisible seam upwards. Its fingers darkly stretching out then splaying. The glass in the windows expands, bricks bubbling or they seem to and then rocks flip up and the earth under the house rises, churning and heaves over. The body of the house pulsing and wrestling with the air a moment.

Everything falls then.

And there is sound, Tomax thinks. His ear drums split and bleed.

And then there is no sound.

For a moment Tomax thinks he's running. Only his feet don't touch ground. And then blown down, like that. And now raining rocks. Face against earth. He tries to raise his hands up toward his head on an instinct to protect his face, his skull, but his arms seem pinned down somehow. Tomax is curled over on the ground, flying glass shards, then dust heaves across him. Like a sand dune of dust.

His mind is washing in and out of sense.

Rocks don't rain, Tomax thinks. Rocks don't rain.

It feels to him as though the world moves slow and pained.

A little sound trickles back, on one side only.

Clattering of rubble. For a moment Tomax thinks that it's over.

There's a deep crump in the earth when the second drone hits, it's like rugs pulled out from under giants, and they fall. Elbows hit the earth first. Huge elbows then knees. The cracks are spreading out beneath him. Smaller seams grow out of the cracks and the whole split widens. It's like falling into a huge opening mouth in the ground.

Tomax falls in slow jolts and then churning up in one motion, like the earth underneath him is ploughed. Tomax has slipped into the bowels of his own house. The body of the house is lying over his head.

It occurs to Tomax this trap is his tomb, and he's fighting the sides of the tomb now, fighting for air and light, fighting for the next breath, but sand pours in and stones at all the points where Tomax pushes against the rubble. It gets worse, until his body lies immobilised in dust, sand, rubble. Tomax stops moving.

And now his right foot twitching and loosens something, sand makes a small wave from it, heaves up toward Tomax's neck, throwing his jaw up and back, sharp and hard. There's a surge of shrapnel sized rubble piling up against Tomax's chin, forcing his head up and back agonisingly.

Cracking sound, soft and sickening, running down Tomax's left ear.

He feels his neck strain with the tension.

He's not thinking anything at all for one long moment.

And then Time, he thinks. I needed more time. Knowing what's above him will move again in a moment. Swivels his eyes painfully up and left. There's a beam, saved his life. But for how long? He cannot see but he can hear the wood tremble, strain. The weight above the beam moves. Something or someone is trapped over Tomax.

The edge farm boy closes his eyes.

When he opens them there's a crack in the rocks near his face. A thin seam of light filtering in through it. Dust settles slowly out there and in a bit Tomax can see bent human shapes, and they're moving. Something or someone out there. Hoving in and out of view. Whatever it was vanishes. And now there's only steaming rubble. Light glancing off the tin roofs on the ground.

Tomax tries to stay calm. He tries to gather his thoughts. The body above him alternates between struggle and exhausted pause and there is a thick pain in Tomax's neck. Blood welling in a warm pool at his left ear. He can't tell if it's from him or from above.

Some noise is trickling back, from his left ear. Then human sounds, he thinks, only not like human sounds.

Groans and a low whirring whine.

The living thing just above him is suffering. Whatever it is, it's in pain, rocking and panicking.

The sound pulls at Tomax. And then stops, as though the creature senses him too. Small thumps of its tail. Tomax's mind is washing in and out of sense. In a little while he understands it's next door's dog. It often comes to his back door for scraps, it must have been caught in the blast. As though the dog knows it's Tomax, down there, struggles again. More dust and rubble falling on to Tomax, more sand flooding in.

Now Tomax recognises his mother's voice. Outside. He tries to orient himself, where's it coming from? And then strains toward the crack. His eye strung to the light through it. It's as though he sees her for the first time in his life. She is standing by the rubble. Orange grain sack in each hand. At first she seems bewildered. "Tomax," she says. She drops her grain sacks, and he sees them spill and drifting windward, quickly gone. "Tomax," she says. Quietly at first. And then, "TOMAX!" She screams. And there's that pained sound again. Inhuman.

You think it can't be coming from you, Tomax thinks. But it is.

The pain comes in rhythmic waves now, sending jolts to the base of his skull.

There's a different voice outside now. A man's voice. "Stop," says the voice to Tomax's mother, not unkindly. And then, "Listen."

Tomax tries to identify the voice, the man sounds familiar and unfamiliar at the same time. It takes a moment and then. Jengi. He thinks. It's Jengi out there. Now Tomax knows he stands a chance. A slim one.

Jengi is last of the Diggers tribe and the Diggers were salvage workers in the previous era. The old bomb clean up crews. The Diggers were skilful at extracting the bodies, both the living and dead, along with valuable metal pipes, and other useful things. People sometimes survived the bombs in the days when the Digger tribe still worked the clean up operations.

"Tomax?" Jengi yells. "Tomax? You alive, Boy?"

Jengi. Tomax thinks. But he can't say a word.

"Make a sound if you can!" Jengi yells. And then there's quiet.

Tomax's jaws are pinned closed by the sand, rubble. He makes a sound in the back of his throat. He knows right away that it's not loud enough.

Jengi lies stomach down on the ground. "Silence," he instructs the edge farmers milling around the rubble. And then Jengi puts his ear to the earth again, strains to hear. Tomax's mother swivels slowly around to watch the Digger do what he was trained to.

"Quiet." Jengi repeats, sterner this time. Puts his ear back to the ground. He waits.

And then "Tomax!" He raises his head, yells again. "Make a sound if you can, Boy."

Tomax tries again. Sound in the back of his throat. Tries and tries until his throat is raw.

Jengi goes on listening. Then he twitches his head. He looks up.

"Nothing." Jengi says decisively. Getting up and dusting down his trousers. "I reckon he's dead."

Tomax sees his mother feeling her way around the rubble. "He's not dead," she says. More to herself. "He's not, he's not ... *dead*. Tomax, Tomax," she whispers into the crevices in the piled up bricks. And then calling down into her ruined house.

Tomax sees the fire, small but spreading quickly. Starts in one corner of the rubble and then taking hold of a dry beam. The fire grows high quickly, just to the right of his mother.

The edge farm houses are mostly made out of wood and wattle, mud daubed. When the drones hit the edge farmhouses they light up like match-heads. But Tomax's father was a house builder in the before and made his house with Bavarnican brick and cement, nobody is quite sure how he managed to get hold of the materials but deals were sometimes struck with the last exiles. Not to mention friendships which crossed lines.

The general put a stop to all that, of course. Tomax's father was forced to make do with tin for its long roof but in that way this house looks like every other edge farm house, at least from above. What you can't see from a drone's-eye-view is that he used thick beams from the killing forest to make the rafters of his house, burying the roots of them many feet into the ground. "Those rafters will either kill us or save us some day," Tomax's father said at least once every single day, including his last one.

Tomax's mother sees the fire right away. She seems to snap out of her trance, filled with a strange life, "Tomax, Tomax." She thinks she hears something at the rock, springs away and moving quickly to the next heap, calling into every crevice she can find. Calling, waiting, calling waiting. At one point she imagines that she hears him.

Now she's moving pieces of rubble, gently, expertly. In the wrong place. "Jengi." She says, "Jengi, help me." Jengi watches her. He shakes his head. Her voice still doesn't sound like her voice, Tomax thinks. Only broken, rasping sounds. And that strange mania to her digging. She's not herself, Tomax thinks. She's too close to the fire. As though she can't feel it right now. A small corner of her scarf catches fire, burns along the seam, sparks peter out at her hair. She keeps digging.

Tomax makes another sound in the back of his throat. His throat is raw and the effort's agonising.

At first Tomax thinks that no one heard him over the fire's crackle, sound of moving rubble, swish of feet. And then Jengi's close, saying "Tomax?" Softly at first. And then it's very near, Jengi's voice, and now Tomax knows Jengi can hear him. Tomax shifts his elbow accidentally in his excitement, sand moves in, pushing his head farther back. Now Tomax's forehead is jammed hard against the boulder. His eye is close to the crack.

Suddenly Jengi's boots are right there. Just to the left of Tomax's head and just a boulder between them. Tomax makes every last sound that he can in the back of his mouth. There is a tearing, ripping feeling. Pain in his throat and he's moved his head in his urgency. Stones clatter down, the right side of his head, a small surge of gravel, more dust.

Tomax knows he can't make another sound, if he wants to or not.

And then Jengi's face. Looming close in the crack. Tomax and Jengi are eye to eye for a moment. Blink. Jengi heaves away again and disappears behind the rubble.

Now he is trying to move the debris above Tomax, gently as he can.

Jengi finds the dog before he finds Tomax.

He has to use a brick to kill it. Tomax hears the soft whine as the dog greets Jengi, soft thump of tail wagging, long pause and then a sickening thud, one low dog whine, another thud then nothing. The dog's silence swelling back to Tomax.

The fire is at Jengi's back now. His limbs are black lit against it. Tomax can't see his face.

Some edge farmers come and pull Tomax's mother back from the fire. They pin her to the ground. "Stop," they say. "Stop. Your boy's gone."

Tomax feels the heat rising around him.

There is a deep keening sound. Now he sees his mother struggle against the pinning arms, fail. She sees the flames rise. And then her mouth is thrown open like that. No sound coming out, not for one long moment. The flames go on rising. Her body bucks and heaves. Then lurching, hitting, scratching, filled with a strange life, she rolls away from her neighbour's hands, their arms and elbows. She becomes unpinned for several moments, scrabbling determinedly toward the flames. Toward the wrong spot, toward the place she imagines that her boy is. And now yelling his name, his name, his name like that, down into the flames, and dragged back again. Pinned by her limbs. Body lurches skyward. Now a large-built neighbour kindly sits down hard on her stomach to hold her. She looks up. Bomb-dust rolls across the sky and smoke, a gap forming in the cloud above her like a great set of jaws, she thinks. Opening slow.

Jengi glances behind him. "Hold her," he says. And then to himself, "We'll see what's left of him in a minute." He goes on digging. Sweat streams down the sides of Jengi's face. He stops again and listens. He gets closer to Tomax. Jengi picks up a brick. He looks back just once at Tomax's mother.

Night fell that suddenly, Tomax thinks. He thinks he hears his mother's voice, and then Jengi again. He also thinks that this is dreaming. There's a burning sensation down his left arm. Smoke seeping down from the beam above him, it's peppered with sparks. Flame lights up the whole of one end of the wood.

More shouts, hiss of water on heat and the burning slows down. Jengi used the precious water on the flames. Meaning one thing only, Tomax thinks ... Jengi knows I'm alive.

Tomax passes out.

When he wakes it's the cold that comes with the desert night, the blackness of lights out, so Tomax knows that it must be after curfew. There are scratching sounds, things move around him. Desert rats, Tomax thinks. There's a determined scrabbling, then a gnawing at the brick behind him. Something slides into the cracks, wriggles the gap wider. The rats are getting close now. Tomax is that gathered by the dark, that tightly gathered by it.

Now Tomax believes that nobody is looking for him. They think he's dead. For the first time since the bombing, he wishes he were.

Scrabbling sound but there's a different rhythm to it, not rats or mice but large brusque hands. Debris tossed in a haphazard fashion. Human sounds. And then Jengi's knuckles, thick veined and blood streaked, veering in and out of view. Moves the rock by Tomax's head and then eases both his hands in. First he makes a space around Tomax's ears. Tomax watches Jengi's fingers working. They're covered in dried blood. "There you are, Boy." Jengi says in his low voice. And then "Now," he says. "Now. Try to move something, Tomax."

Jengi hasn't called out to Tomax's mother or to her edge farm neighbours helping. For the first time Tomax sees the brick, in Jengi's right hand.

Tomax moves his head slightly.

"Good."

Jengi tests the boy's neck. "Okay," he says. "Okay." Jengi seems to need to take a moment. Tomax hears Jengi breathing in and out, in and out, rough little pants.

"You are ... fixable." Jengi says.

Jengi lets the brick fall from his hand. Tomax looks down at the weapon. The brick is dark with blood at both ends.

"He's here." Jengi shouts behind him, notifying the others

for the first time.

"I couldn't tell 'em before," he explains to Tomax. "They're ... emotional. Right now. They'd have brought the whole roof down on your head. Amateurs." He says, dismissively.

There are loud voices now. Shouts and hollers. Tomax hears his name spoken. Laughter. And then voices getting farther away. Nothing to see here. Drone strikes on the edge farms are so common since the last drought and none of Tomax's neighbours can afford to be caught in an act of rescue at a bomb site when The Egg Men arrive. That'd be a quick way to die or have your family's grain rations cancelled, which would mean death too, only a slower one. Jengi checks the sky. Calculates he has less than six minutes left before the Egg Men arrive on the scene. He starts counting down in his head.

But for Tomax's mother time will be forever divided this way: There will be who she was before this bomb. Who she was after it.

Tomax sees his mother turn, fall to her knees on the hard soil. Jengi looks briefly in her direction and then seems to forget her. He identifies the beam which has saved Tomax's life, pats it like an old friend. Admires the workmanship in the hinges and brackets. He squints down at the small opening he's made to let Tomax breathe better, relieve the strain on his neck. Now he starts slowly taking rubble from above the beam, using it to stabilise the exposed ends of the wooden beam underneath.

Bent tin roofs and stacks of broken bricks rise around Tomax. For a time there's more building than digging, it seems, and Jengi looks grim, intensely concentrating on the work. Looking in the direction the Egg Men's trucks will come.

They have three minutes.

A little further off, Tomax's mother is still on her knees, giving thanks to the baobab for Jengi.

Jengi shrugs. Looks at her from time to time and then quickly away. Wipes the dirt out of his eyes with the back of his arm, and then turning in a long swathe, casting a shrewd gaze over the rubble that lies over Tomax.

Jengi has dug down to just above Tomax's waist before he risks pulling him out hard. "We'll have to make it fast. When I pull on you then the beam will shift left sharply, all this ..." and now he indicates the pile above and behind Tomax, "it's going to come down, crush your legs. So one short heave, yeah? And if you make it out then you run as soon as your feet hit the floor." Earth falls away from Tomax. Jengi drags him back quickly before the avalanche of sand and rubble, brick. And then a sickening crump as the roof is dislodged.

"Holy dursed baobab, Tomax that was close." Jengi mops a seam of sweat from his eyebrows. Grins.

There's blood. Tomax thinks. There is too much of it. It's dribbling down from the right side of his face, clouding his vision. "Am I ...?" Tomax can't think of the word. Rubble has started sliding down from the top of the stack.

"Let's go. Move." Jengi says. Only Tomax can't move.

Jengi drags Tomax rough and fast, by his left arm and right hand.

The flames climb over the rubble behind them, the heat rises. Flames catch a hold.

Tomax sees the fire veering up behind his mother. She is still on her knees.

For a long strange moment she looks to him like a puppet

without strings, a pile of rags praying to the baobab, and then she twitches, shudders with life. She cries out then, and getting up. Staggering toward Jengi and her son.

Jengi dumps Tomax on the ground at a safe distance from the fire. "One minute," he says. "The Egg Men will be on the scene in one minute." Glancing up at Tomax's mother. And then, "He needs a doctor."

"A doctor?" She looks at him. "This is edge farm land, Jengi. There's no doctor."

"Mamma Zeina."

"Mamma Zeina?" She examines Jengi's face.

"She's a Sinta. She's in the killing forest right now. She was a doctor in the before. I can pull Tomax through the hole in the fence, the one that I just came through." He pauses. "I can do it if you help me."

They are face to face. "Jengi. The killing forest?"

"Yes."

She looks down at her son. She steels herself. And then slipping her hands underneath his armpits, then eases her arms through, makes a loop of her right hand, left wrist. Now she can feel Tomax's heart thrum against the knuckles of her right hand, and the palm of her left. He's alive, she keeps telling herself. For those who believe in miracles, there seems to be one on the edge farms every day. Jengi takes Tomax's feet.

They stagger toward the fence with Tomax's long, heavy body between them.

Tomax hears the crackle of fire, swish of the killing trees. The Egg Mens' truck wheels, getting closer.

And then the coolness of the forest. Smell of dark moss.

THE FENCE

ZORRY IS SITTING IN the nipping saplings just inside the fence.

Sees Mamma Zeina coming toward her through the dark mouth of the forest. Things move around her but Mamma Zeina trudges onward. Crackling of bracken under slow, heavy feet.

"You're late."

"I been busy child." Mamma Zeina sighs. Wipes her hand across her forehead. Leaves a palm print of blood. She seems to see Zorry for the first time. "You alright?"

"I'm alright. Why you late?" Zorry asks, a little peevishly. She'd spent several anxious hours the wrong side of the fence to the killing forest, dark things moving around her. There's an edge in her voice.

Mamma Zeina eyes her. "This your first time in the killing forest?"

"Yes."

"And you spent it alone?" Mamma Zeina appears to consider this. "That's good work, Child." And then, "You'll do, Zorry." Smiles. "Mayhap you're cut out for this work. Ever think of that?" Scratches herself. "You got bitten, Zorry?"

"No. Don't think so."

"Not bad, not bad." Mamma Zeina says. "You did well." Mamma Zeina seems to take the thought and deposit it somewhere. Rolls her eyes. "Follow me."

Zorry follows.

"I heard something," Zorry says. "When you were gone. At first I thought it was a bomb but it seemed too small. And then another one. It came from t'other side of the forest. From the Edge farmlands."

Mamma Zeina rubs her forehead, doesn't answer for a while, and when she does it's an answer to a question Zorry didn't ask.

"Good news is I found a plant on my way back. Almost tripped over it. In fact, you might say that it found me." Mamma Zeina lifts her sack to show Zorry. The sack is wriggling. Mamma Zeina holds it away from her stomach and soft parts. Zorry eyes it. "Gotta take it home and splice it to the root." Mamma Zeina says. And now, as though it heard her, the plant struggles harder. And then a gnawing sound, like it chews on the sack.

Mamma Zeina grins. "Come on, Child. The Egg Men are about to check this length of fencing. The bombings get them Egg Men jittery. We're in the wrong place at the wrong time, Zorry. C'mon, Girl. Let's go."

When they're safely at the backdoor to Mamma Zeina's cottage, the sack is dangerously quiet. Zorry eyes it, "If you're sure you're alright with that ..."

"This? Ha! I can handle this." A deep, throaty chuckle. Shakes the sack.

"Alright then. I'll be ... I'd best be ..." But Mamma Zeina holds her back by her arm. Just above the elbow. "Zorry," she says. Low voice.

"Yes?"

"The feast at the general's house ..."

"Yes?"

"Tomorrow ... is it your first time serving the feast too?" Examines the girl's face. "Are you ready?"

Zorry eyes the sack. The plant is quite still now. As though it's listening.

"Yes." She says. She thinks of something. "You didn't check my fence suture."

"No, I didn't, Zorry." Sighs. "There wasn't time. So ... Did you heal the wound in the fence good, Zorry?"

"Yes. At least ... I think so. I've not done it on my own before."

"Well, let's cross our fingers. Because they'll check it. With the bomb and all."

Zorry takes a breath. "I'm pretty sure I healed the hole in the fence."

"Good. That's good Zorry." Examines the girl's face once more. She appears to be pleased with whatever it is she sees there. "You'll do." She repeats. Long, low whistle. "You may be the assistant I've been looking for." She appears to be speaking more to herself than to Zorry. Looks up at the girl, who's a clear foot taller than the short-legged, stocky old woman. "Right then, Zorry." She says crisply. "You best be getting on your way. Stay in the copse until you're sure your way's clear."

Mamma Zeina showed Zorry just the once how to make a hole in the fence and then restitch, dab the fence with a plant concoction. The wound in it is supposed to close and grow over, if you get the mixture and the application just right. Zorry believes she has got the knack of these chemical sutures to the fence.

But she's wrong.

Closing the fence wound, Zorry had failed to notice a small hole, about the size of a pencil tip. It glows black at first. And then with the two Sinta well out of sight, the black hole turns waxen green. There is a small leaf unfurling through it.

Vine bleeding down.

Now the gap widens around the vine stem.

The leaf eases itself softly toward the dark soil beneath.

Fertile OneFolks' soil. The vine tongues the ground. Sniffs the air.

Now the hole widens to a mouth size. New vines seethe through the gap.

Zorry pauses, unsure. She thinks of something. "What were you doing in there?" Turns to Mamma Zeina. "Why did you take so long in the killing forest? We risked getting caught by the fence."

"That's always a risk, Zorry." Mamma Zeina grunts. "Tell me that you knew that, Child, or why you even come with me?" And then, as if to herself, "There was an edge farm kid." She rubs her head. Then she looks at her hand, wipes her palm on her apron. Leaves a stripe of blood down it.

"The droning sound? They were bombs?"

"Yes. Neck injury. Left arm. Busted ear drums. A few broken ribs. He's going to be alright. He is lucky." She looks thoughtful. "Too lucky. I've never seen a blast victim come out in more or less one piece the way Tomax did."

"Tomax ..." Zorry thinks the name is familiar. "And that bomb, Mamma? It was strange."

"Strange?"

"I heard the drone but it didn't sound like a strike, Mamma Zeina."

"Aye. Yes, Zorry. This was a small one I reckon. This was something new."

"A small bomb?"

"Yes, Zorry. Small and personal by the looks of it."

"Who was it aimed at?"

"As far as I can see it must'a bin' just that kid, Tomax. Can't see why they'd expend that kind of effort, ammunition, over the boy, but ... Seems to be more to it than the seeming. How things appear in Bavarnica mostly ain't ... Representative."

"Representative?"

"True, Child. Meaning iffen they wanted the boy dead then he would be. Mostly don't trust your eyes, Zorry, that's the gist of it. But this bomb seemed more like a warning to me."

"Who is Tomax?"

Mamma Zeina examines Zorry's face. She stops talking for a moment. And then, "Tomax is a kid who works in the gem mines on the edge of the OneFolks' village." She looks thoughtful. "That might be where his problem started. Mayhap some dispute with his guards." She scratches the side of her head. "He's got himself on to a list, by the looks of it." She strokes her round chin. "I'm not sure how. But I'll think on it."

"Is he going to be alright?"

"Like I said, Zorry. Tomax was warned." She scratches a mosquito bite on the back of her neck. "Or mayhap he was spared by someone. Good can infiltrate any system, that's what we Sinta say." She sniffs. "But then again it could'a been dumb luck saved him. He was under a beam. Strong beam. He got out before the building ... Before the fire took a hold and the rats and all came."

Zorry shudders.

"But mostly he was lucky because Jengi happened to be on the edge farm side of the killing forest and saw it all through the fence. Jengi has some expertise in ... That kind of rescue." She checks the girl for understanding. "Jengi is the last of the Digger tribe. Do you know what that means?"

Zorry examines her palm.

"Well young Tomax has survived today but maybe not tomorrow lest we can get him re-certified tame ..." Mamma Zeina stops talking again. She looks up. Sees something behind Zorry. "Egg boy," she hisses. "Heading this way."

Zorry whips around and tries to look behind her but Mamma Zeina yanks her arm and spins her, shoves her in the direction of the copse behind her cottage.

"Go, *go*."

She notices Zorry makes no sound at all, crossing the yard to the copse. Looks down at her sack affectionately. All in all, it's been a night of revelations.

"I've found some gems tonight, haven't I?"

Zorry is bedded down in soft, curling ferns, a thorn bush conceals her. She pulls back its mottled waxen leaves, she peers through. The lights blink off in Mamma Zeina's cottage. And in a bit, a small candle appears in the old woman's window.

REPORT 1: SEEDS

"WHAT'S YOUR NAME?"

The voice is brusque. Cold. Jengi thinks it sounds familiar. He pauses.

"This is my first report, Sir. Will it be ... Is this a secure line?"

"Go ahead."

"And you'll help us?"

Pause. "Jengi. What do you have to report?"

Jengi clears his throat. "Where shall I start?"

"Start with the Sinta."

Jengi lets out a breath. "The Sinta are a slave tribe in Bavarnica. Slaves since the last revolution failed."

"Go on, Jengi."

"Those Sinta who remain in the OneFolks' village are survivors of the purge after the revolution. They are the Sinta who didn't run. Servitude. It was the worst punishment there is for a proud tribe like the Sinta. But still not the worst the general dished out after the failed revolution."

"I see."

"There's what he did to the edge farmers."

"The edge farmers?"

Jengi sighs. "Every Bavarnican tribe but the general's own, the OneFolk, was pushed over the border in the long ago. Out there facing the heat together, the outcasts became one tribe: The Edge Farmers."

"Okay, lots of tribes, got it. But exile? Since when is that the worst punishment?"

"It's been a slow motion genocide, Sir. Leaving the edge farmers to scratch a living, starve on the edge farms which border the desert was the worst punishment the general could think up for them. With respect, Sir, you'd have to stand in that desert ten minutes to understand what it means for a Bavarnican to be exiled."

"They can't farm by the desert?"

"No. They don't get the drought resistant seeds. I mean ... A few get government approval for the drought resistant seeds. They can grow in drought season and the drought seeds confer some heat resistance iffen you consume 'em raw and by the handful. Those farmers are closely controlled and can lose their privilege at a moment's notice. And they know it. Death is all around them. They are controllable. A handful more edge farm folks work the gem mines in the OneFolks' village. As for the rest ..."

"Wait. A handful of edge farmers in the OneFolks' village you say?"

"About a hundred, all told. Men and women. Firstborns mostly. But for the rest of the Edge Farmers ... Slow death. There's no water source at the edge, unless you count the dirty puddles soaking out under the fence of the killing forest. Filled with disease and toxins from the lab plants. Not enough to get by on, even if the water doesn't kill you outright. Water ain't their only problem. The edge farms get the stone seeds, like I said."

"The stone seeds?"

"It's what the edge farmers call them. On account they

mean death. You must have seen the orange sacks, no? Well, they are the ancient seeds. Un-modified. Nothing can grow from them. Not in the heat of the edge farms."

"And yet ... Jengi. Something is growing out there. Growing from the stone seeds."

"Not much."

"Not much isn't the same thing as nothing, Jengi. Why are the stone seeds growing at all?"

"Aye. Well, that's where I come in, Sir. My work in the shop. Mixing the ancient seeds with the drought seeds, before they leave the shop. Difficult, dangerous, working under Gaddys' nose. I get some help."

"Help? Is that from the mother cupboards? I have something about them here ..." The voice seems suddenly excited. "And that's the Sinta resistance I take it?" Jengi hears the rustling of sheets of paper. "Wait ... Let me find a pen, write this down."

"We'll get to it later."

Pause. "I see, Jengi."

Jengi notes the reproachful tone and ignores it.

And then, "Do you, Sir?" He asks. "Tell me. What is it you see?"

The line goes silent. Jengi takes a deep breath. He speaks into the void. Says the whole thing just like he has practised.

"The desert is swallowing up the edge farms' rugged pastures like a great toothless mouth since the heat rose and the edge farmers' rains were reallocated by the general. Only the OneFolk and the Egg Men who protect the OneFolk, a scattering of surviving Sinta who serve tables and cook for a slave's pay, meaning food, are still allowed inside the

OneFolks' village, meaning the Sinta and the Egg Men, a few gem miners who are edge farmers Gaddys certified tame, and they all don't so much live alongside the OneFolk tribe as live underneath them. We all live underneath them."

"Take a breath, Jengi."

"Yes, Sir."

"They told me you were a storyteller, Jengi. But try to keep it to a minimum would you? It gets on my nerves. I'd like to see some simple facts in your next report. Jengi? Did you hear me? Numbers. Names. Coordinates. You might want to think about making a list, Jengi. Making a map. Do you get me?"

No answer.

"Remind me, Jengi. What are the Bavarnican tribes again?"

"Yes, Sir. There are three tribes now. Four if you count the general's OneFolk, although they don't call themselves a tribe, the OneFolks."

"But they are a tribe. According to you."

"Yes, Sir."

"Start with the non-organics. What was it you called them?"

"The Egg Men?"

"Yes, the Egg Men. You said they're the soldiers. The guards."

"Yes. Only the officers' class of the military are organics, OneFolks. The rest are made in a lab. Them's the Egg Boys. And batch 47 is the last batch of eggs. They ..."

"Hang on a bit. Slow down, Jengi. And, who were exiled? Who works the land by the desert?"

"Edge Farmers!"

Pause. "Your voice sounds impatient. Jengi."

"Sorry, Sir." Now Jengi knows he's talking too fast, "The

edge farmers were the ones banished to work the poor soil beside the desert. They ... They are not allowed into the OneFolks' village. Not unless it's to collect their grain rations. They only get those if they're certified tame."

"Right. So then there's the slaves in the OneFolks' village. The Sinta. Okay, lots of tribes," he sighs. "Holy bewildering crap, Jengi ... lots of tribes. Got it. I think I got it. Okay, look." Sound of shuffled papers again. "We'll get back to you, Jengi."

"Yes. But Sir?"

"What is it, Jengi?"

"There is just one other tribe." Jengi takes a deep breath. "There was one other tribe in Bavarnica."

"You said was?"

"I am the last of the Digger tribe. When I'm gone ..."

"You're the last?"

"We rose up against the general. It was our revolution."

"And how did that go, Jengi?"

"We tried to go it alone ..." He can't finish. There is a coughing sound.

"I see." The voice says drily. "I think I'm beginning to understand, Jengi. And that's why you want to build a coalition of all the tribes for your next revolution?" The voice becomes brusque. Hard. "Give me some names, Jengi. Who are your Seeds? I'm assuming you have at least one Thought Seed planted in each tribe or we why are we even cooking together here? Jengi?"

Pause. "I have ... three Seeds in mind."

"Names?"

"Sir. No names. At least not ... Not yet."

Sighs. "Jengi?" Pause. Low voice. "There is only the one

way for me to help you."

Longer pause. "And this line is secure?"

"Go ahead Jengi."

"The names are ..." There is a long silence. And then muffled sounds, slide and thump. The sound of Jengi kicking a tree trunk repeatedly. Something falls out of the tree.

"Jengi. I'm hanging up now."

"Antek. Egg Boy." The sound of Jengi breathing out fast. Pause again. Then his voice in a rush, "Tomax. Edge Farm boy." He says. Longest pause. "Zzz ..." He stops. There's a silence. "That's it."

"You said three. You said there were three Seeds. You said Z?"

"I said that's it."

"Jengi?"

"Yes, Sir."

"You still need a Sinta. Get recruiting."

"It's not ... It isn't ... The Sinta believe that ... They have ..." He sighs. "Yes, Sir. I'll find a Sinta."

THE GENERAL'S FEAST

ONE OF THE EGG Men by the window looks young. His skull is regular sized.

"Batch 47," Mamma Zeina whispers to Zorry. "Human." Eyes Zorry. "Mostly human. But ..." She turns. "They're putting the latest batch of Egg Boys in the general's house now?" She scratches a small insect bite on her curved chin. "Well. That's new. Guess they must'a passed the last round of tests." She looks thoughtful. Turning toward Zorry, "Him, there. That's Antek," she says. She squints, looks away. Picks up a piece of food debris by Zorry's left foot.

"He's looking at you." Zorry mouthes.

Antek watches Zeina walking heavily towards the serving table. When she reaches it she leans down hard, looks up. Holds the boy in a warm, shrewd gaze. He looks away quickly, confused.

Mamma Zeina returns to Zorry slowly with a covered plate. Slow, pained movements, edges in beside Zorry. Blocks the window with her bulk.

"Move Sinta, that's where the guards stand." An Egg Man moves to stand with his back to the window. Zorry steps aside quickly. Backs behind a curtain to one side. But Mamma Zeina pulls Zorry into the listening dead zone, between the bathrooms and the hall chandelier. Casts an expert eye around her for any new bugs or listening devices. She begins her tutelage. Quietly.

Today is Zorry's first day serving the feast at the general's great house. There's a lot to learn today and no room for mistakes. The guests are scowling at name cards, taking their places.

"The general's wife is s'posed to run the flowers fund of Bavarnica, and this is its biannual meeting, fundraiser, shindig, whatever you want to call it." Mamma Zeina rubs her head slow, absent-mindedly. "Feast." Then seems to remember herself. Readjusts her scarf. "The flowers fund used to deliver food to the edge farms but the general's wife, she's ... " opens her eyes wide, "Over pollinated now."

They both eye the general's wife from behind.

Rib bones of her spine fanning out like the long teeth of a comb.

"Gaddys the village shopkeeper has taken over." Mamma Zeina scratches her chin, then her small round nose. "Now it's just flowers they deliver."

"Flowers? To starving childur? What's the point Mamma Zeina?"

Mamma Zeina and Zorry turn as one to look at the flowers on the table. They are huge and grotesque, red petals seeping down toward the table, huge insect-like proboscis pointing skyward. Rows of black beady eyes.

"Why?"

Mamma Zeina rolls her eyes. "Who knows?"

Zorry notes the tables groan with produce. Something has escaped from the food table. Several things on the food table are, on closer examination, still alive. One clawed pink creature crawls down from the top of a stack. A small mammal with oversized lower body, tiny ears, is hopping distractedly from plate to plate.

Since disease hit the food chain, the fashion amongst the OneFolk tribe has been to select the critter they're planning on eating by its movements, its overall colour and appearance, other signs of health, and then gesture with one finger toward the apparently speechless and heartbroken Sinta butcher who stands behind the feasting table. Have him kill the food in front of the guests.

Occasionally the butcher breaks down in tears and has to be replaced by an underling, causing some tittering and rolling eyes at the feast table. The Sinta butcher used to be an animal conservationist before the failed revolution. A vegetarian. The general has been creative with his punishments.

Mamma Zeina nudges Zorry. It's hard to stay awake on the job after a night hiding out in the copse behind Mamma Zeina's house. Zorry feels tense, wired, and the back of her neck and limbs are aching. In the air conditioned general's house Zorry feels cold to the marrow. Jumps when Mamma Zeina jogs her.

"In practice, Gaddys the village shopkeeper has been in charge for the last seven years." Mamma Zeina says. "That's her over there." Zorry follows Mamma Zeina's eye. She recognises the village shopkeeper at once. "Yep, I know her."

Zorry eyes the window. From here she can see the border of the killing forest beyond the first fence. She can't see past the trees but she knows that the killing forest is also fenced off by high electrified fences on the edge farm side. Mamma Zeina seems to read Zorry's thought. "No Zorry," she says. "There's no chance for them."

"What?" Zorry blinks.

"No escapees from the edge farms have ever made it over here, Zorry. Not past the last fence. The fence on our side. Leastways not so far as I know."

"Can't we ... help them to get in the same way we got out?"

Mamma Zeina twists towards Zorry sharply. Hands her a fork. "Careful Child. Them is revolutionary words." There is a long pause whilst Mamma Zeina gathers herself.

"Every month or so, one or two of the edge farms' strongest and most resourceful men and women do make it over the first fence. The one on the edge farm side."

"Eh?"

"Yes, Zorry. The fence on the edge farm side of the killing forest has roots six foot into the earth and is topped with knives, electrified, and still ..." She chuckles. "Jengi gets in and out through that fence like it were full of holes."

Zorry's eyes widen.

"Yes, Child. Jengi showed folks the routes, the best hiding places in the killing forest." Mamma Zeina shudders. Now her voice hardens. "I have argued with him. I doesn't even want to contemplate a repeat of the last revolution. What it cost. I keep telling him that we are not ... Ready. It's too soon and he is losing his best people at the fence."

She looks at Zorry softly. "But he's young and vengeful." Pauses. "Impatient. Wakes up every morning counting his dead." Mamma Zeina raises her eyebrows gently. "Never was a faster way to get folks killed than Jengi, Zorry. But he's ... Jengi is ... We need Jengi."

Mamma Zeina hears the sound of shrill mocking laughter from the feast table. Winces. "The killing forest is the biggest hurdle after the edge farm fences of course, she says. Most will never get even that far. Leastways not without training." She pulls open her apron pocket, peers inside. Looks up. "Yes." She says. "But the fence on this side ... ah that one's really the trick." She turns back toward the dining room.

"No." She concludes. "You might survive the killing forest iffens you's lucky or skilful, trained, but ..." Sighs. Looks back at Zorry. "It will always be the last fence which kills the bravest and the best of the edge farmers. That fence is alive, as you've seen. Although, of course, every living thing can be ... turned, but that fence is mostly beyond my understanding." She screws up her face, pulls her ear. "We mostly don't get there in time, when the rebels are caught in it, but even when we do them runaways is picked up quickly by the Egg Men. It's hard for the Sinta to hide a thing as big as a living body in the OneFolks' village, Zorry." Mamma Zeina looks grave. "We ain't saved even one of them edge farm rebels so far. Not one Zorry. And we've lost twice their number in trying. Only think about that."

Zorry is still looking down at the fence. "Not one saved so far," Zorry says, almost to herself. The fence seems to her so thin, even flimsy, from all the way up here in the general's house.

She sees something moving just inside it.

"What's that?"

"What is what? Oh, what in the name of unholy weeping ... Damn it, Jengi." Mamma Zeina curses quietly, and then, "Some days it's like the boy is doing the general's work for him." Mamma Zeina stares. Sighs. Then, turning, looking up at Zorry. "The general likes to leave the edge farm rebels' bodies stuck to the inside of the fence, to be slowly absorbed by it. They will be left there until their corpses dissolve, a warning to any more potential rebels amongst the Sinta slaves inside the fence."

Zorry looks baffled.

"Look close, Zorry, that is Jengi's damned revolution. Right there. Death itself, that boy. Some days." She curses him again.

Zorry sees what look like cocoons along the inside of the fence. "Aye." Mamma Zeina tilts her head left. "Edge farmers, stuck and drowning in the fence. Turned slowly to bones." She turns away from the window. Locks her jaw. "Damn that boy Jengi to Hell." She looks at Zorry. "Oh, Child, I don't mean that." She is quiet for a while, thinking.

"Hope," she says. Catching Zorry's eye and then holding her gaze. "Hope is the mother cupboards' resistance. And our creed is *gather*." Soft hissing sound on the last word. Zorry freezes. Feels the word running down her spine. "Like a sigh, like a song, ain't it?" Mamma Zeina turns away and stumps heavily toward the kitchen to fetch more platters.

Zorry watches her go.

Zorry notices the Egg Boy Antek eyeing her, he looks away quick, and then looks back. On an instinct she can't quite explain, Zorry nods. Antek returns the nod stiffly. Looks away. Now they carefully ignore each other.

Zorry can hear the moving plants in the killing forest groaning and heaving against the thin fence beneath the window, by her right elbow. She turns a little toward it. Catches a glimpse. The fence seems to bend and strain. Moves like water. Just a cobweb-thin white mesh and rippling with plant-blows, twisting as though it's alive. Zorry's had nightmares about those cocoons along the fence. Now that she knows what they are, it's worse.

Antek looks down. Notes the Sinta girl's right hand curling and uncurling. Sees her eyes glitter. He turns his head a little. Tries to see what the Sinta girl saw down there, at the fence.

Zorry hears thumps and bumps underfoot. She has already been warned that the general's labs are built underneath his feast room. There's a small crash like something or someone falling and then, in the periphery of her vision, three white-coated Egg Men make a rush for the inner door, just beside the kitchens. Antek, pulling on his helmet, joins them. The light above the inner door's blinking on and off red.

The Sinta kitchen staff go on waiting tables around Zorry, seemingly impassive. Someone hands her another plate.

"Someone made a hole in the fence last night," Zorry hears one of the OneFolk girls at the far end of the table whispering to the girl beside her. The whispering OneFolk girls are around Zorry's age and the second girl eyes Zorry sideways. And then both girls do. Zorry suspects they intend her to overhear them.

"A Sinta, no doubt."

"Yes. No doubt."

"Things came into the village."

"Things? What things?"

"The general had the Egg Boys rounding up ... strange creatures in the village since dawn." The second girl shudders prettily.

"Oh, relax," the first girl says to her friend now. "The Sinta in the general's house are all certified tame." Eyes Zorry.

"Are you sure? Even that one?" And now the girls turn as one to look at Zorry. Giggle softly.

Zorry winces. Looks away. Notices for the first time a claw mark down the side of the face of the Egg Man by the front door. He seems to notice her watching, grunts and shifts from foot to foot. Zorry looks away quickly. Tries to press further back into the space beside the window. She feels the cold window ledge agains her arm. Hot air drifting in through the grille set into the glass.

The killing forest, just beyond the fence, seems to draw Zorry's eye toward it. She glimpses things moving, down there, just at the periphery of her vision. Zorry daren't turn. She daren't turn to look again for a long time.

From her position backed against the window, Zorry can, with a discreet and well timed eye swivel, see the green tips seeping out over the fence below. There's just a glimmer of movement in the treetops. She has to train her eye to focus, catch it. Stare hard and the dark green life seems to pulse and swell and move against the boundary fence. Zorry twitches and shifts. Looks away. Doesn't do for the kitchen staff to seem too curious about the killing forest or the fence just now. Especially not on her first day. There have been several Sinta slaves vanished already by the general's troops, just this morning. Zorry doesn't want to join them.

She can't see it from here but she knows it's there. The gaol. Like a cold shadow under Bavarnica's mountain range. The mountain's shadow and the gaol spans out for miles and it's growing, filling up with Sinta slaves no longer certified tame by the general. There's the constant sound in the OneFolks' village of prisoners building new walls to their gaols. Hammering out their new tin roofs. Forced to build with their own hands the cells which will contain them and knowing all the while that one day they'll be made to dig their own graves too, all watched over by the Egg Men.

Zorry looks back at the feast table. The food is groaning. Just a low hum, you don't hear it until you tune in, she thinks, and the tinkle and clatter of the feast table barely conceals the low continuous thrum of the creatures' fear. Zorry notices that the Sinta butcher has his eyes closed. His left eyelid twitches and his mouth trembles, just a little. He is pale, blue lipped with tension. The Egg Man to the right of the butcher eyes him carefully, keeps a hand on his electric prod (the butchers have been known to break out in strange ways, one year at the feast a table was turned over, windows broken. The Egg Men won't let that happen again).

The sound of the feasting OneFolks' chatter rises. Zorry clutches her serving plate until her knuckles ache, and she's pressed small dents into her palms.

She thinks, "Why would Mamma Zeina call that Egg Boy by name? Antek." She hardens her thoughts against Antek. "A human name when the guards aren't human. How can they be? The Egg Men don't deserve names."

Zorry lets go of the serving plate with her right hand, it curls into a fist of its own accord.

Zorry has not by any means perfected her impassive Sinta expression. The thing takes practice and years to accomplish, if you can live long enough to complete your training that is. But Zorry is in theory learning from the best, Mamma Zeina, head of the general's kitchens, and so her own mother has high hopes. At least that's what she told Zorry last night, high pitched brittle voice. But then this morning, and with deep circles from unsleep under her eyes, her mother had seemed more resigned, "No one can ever truly say what Mamma Zeina feels or doesn't," and then lifting up her voice, making the effort of hope for Zorry's sake. "But a thing like that is a gift, Child. A face that holds no expression. Times like these. You need to practice that, Zorry. Right now every single thing that passes through your heart shows up here."

She had stroked her daughter's face sadly. "The general's people are going to read you like a book, Zorry." Zorry recalls the exact tone of her mother's sigh then. The way she had shaken her head. There is no deal a Sinta mother can do to get her child out of a work rota at the general's house. Not once it's written down in red ink.

Zorry watches as the escaping dinner table critter vanishes in to the tall powdered wig of a OneFolk guest, conceals a small smile. Roots for it. She thinks she sees the flower arrangement in the centre of the feast table move slightly in the direction of the escapee. She stares. The centrepiece doesn't move again. Zorry shakes herself slightly. Mamma Zeina nudges her.

"The grotesque flower funds of Bavarnica flowers will, of course, die on their first day in the searing heat of the edge farms," she says. Eyeing Zorry severely. "Their petals begin wilting the first moments." She sniffs, scratches the back of her hand. "They take them there in refrigerated vans, so it's not like they don't ..." Mamma Zeina scratches her nose. "It doesn't make sense." Sighs. "Well, nothing is what it seems in Bavarnica, eh Zorry?"

"I've seen those vans."

"Eh?"

"I've seen them. White bullet proofed vans. Reinforced steel." She turns to Mamma Zeina. "You can recognise the flowers fund vans."

"Recognise them how?"

"Solid gold headboards in the form of small crowns."

"Aye." Mamma Zeina rolls her eyes. "Gaddys is theatrical, give her that."

Zorry turns toward the flower decoration on the table. Blinks and tries to look away from it, can't: the largest flower inclines its drooping head slightly toward her. Mamma Zeina elbows her hard.

"Bred in the general's cool moist outhouse, them things," Mamma Zeina sweeps a little debris off the serving table, into her hand and then slips it into her apron pocket. Her shoulders drop. "Aye. Cool, moist outhouse," she says. "They will start dying the moment the dry desert air of the edge farms hits them."

Zorry thinks Mamma Zeina sounds strange. "Is that your tour voice?"

"I been giving this tour for a long time, Girly." Blinks. "Your predecessor is in gaol."

"I know, Mamma Zeina."

"Do you? Then what don't you know? Let's start with that."

Several flower centrepieces adorn the feast table, they seem to move in unison when they breathe. Snake-like sniffing, wavering heads, pulsing with strange life. Zorry finds herself instinctively moving closer to Mamma Zeina's side. Mamma Zeina notices, drily hands her a cloth. "Try to look busy." Zorry mops up some crumbs ineffectually. Stares.

"When the flowers fund of Bavarnica's work is done, the edge farmers will have to stand there for an afternoon, for the privilege of watching these flowers die fairly quickly, or seem to," Mamma Zeina blinks again and turning toward Zorry. "Die in their edge farm soil." She gazes at Zorry blankly, as though she can't see her just now. Looks at something behind or just above her. "Wriggle back into the hard edge farm soil, like whelks on the shore. Leaving only cracks in the earth, a few sun dried petals."

"How do you know they die? The flowers I mean."

"Did I say die? No. No, I don't think they die."

"Then what ...?"

And now turning, and her gaze meets Zorry's, "I don't know. At least not yet."

Zorry overhears the general's wife, "Your flowers are a breath of inspiration for the poor dears on the edge farms, dear Gaddys," she intones in a wobbling voice, made more wobbling by her apparent addiction to the dried pollen from the flowers. She sniffs. Now the general's wife turns and looks at the flowers. Soft, helpless, almost loving gaze. You can't say what she sees, but the plant seems responsive to her. Soft rollback of its petals, peeling back of its proboscis, a deep puff of raspberry coloured smoking pollen into her face. The general's wife sinks a little more. Her eyes swim with tears.

Zorry turns toward the flowers, as though trying to see what the general's wife sees there. "Nasty looking things," she confides in Mamma Zeina. "Give me the creeps." She takes a discreet step backward, then tilting gently toward the view once more. Considering the flowers. They appear to consider her too.

There's something unnerving in the way the flowers turn their huge bulbous heads towards you, Zorry thinks. In a bit she notices something else. The flower breathes out pollen dust in small puffs at discreet intervals, there's a rhythm to it, and the Sinta waiting tables seem to have adapted to that too, hold their breaths when they pass, swerve and avoid, blink, blink, and Zorry realises that the scene is a dance, but only the Sinta serving seem to hear the music. The guests at the feast chatter, swallow, gulp, choke on the fumes, splutter, cough and then the OneFolks' table is getting louder. And then quieter. The OneFolk slide slowly, inexorably, underneath the table.

Gaddys the village shopkeeper seems immune to the flower pollen herself, Zorry observes. She sits stiff and straight backed at the head of the table.

Mamma Zeina heaves her large frame over toward Zorry. "She'll sit like that," Mamma Zeina says, indicating Gaddys with some bitterness, "Straight backed, alert, until the Sinta clean up crew come to shovel all these OneFolk guests on to their stretchers, pour them into their waiting cars."

"What's it all for? The feast? Food ain't never just food for the general, is it?"

Mamma Zeina considers the girl admiringly. "No it ain't. Just watch." Mamma Zeina says. "You'll see." She steps away. In a little while Gaddys disappears into a side room beside the feast table.

"That's to give her 'notes' to the general via his telecom." Mamma Zeina says in a low voice. Glances at Zorry. "Gaddys is giving him useful names." She explains. "She's telling him about soft allegiances and friendships amongst the OneFolks."

"The general's watching his own tribe?"

"Of course, Zorry." Chuckles. "He must control them most of all. Any eyes which met over the dinner table or hands which found each others under it. Gaddys misses very little, in truth. Here, take this plate."

Mamma Zeina uncovers the dish before she releases it to Zorry. They both examine its contents, stare bleakly at each other. "The general likes to understand who's connected to whom." Mamma Zeina looks up at Zorry and then down again at the contents of the plate. "Not so much to suppress a revolution, Zorry, as to stub out the thought before it starts." She sighs. "Go take your plate to him. Over there." Gestures toward an ancient looking man in a cat costume, flea collar and all. Zorry gently raises her eyes toward the ceiling.

Mamma Zeina makes her way back to check on the serving table. She appears to be having some difficulty with her right knee, just now, and she is dragging her left foot a little. Stops several times to hold the wall. When she reaches the serving table, Mamma Zeina covers the blue crabs, which are scrapping and waving their claws. She turns sideways to see how Zorry's doing. Watches the girl walking back to collect a second plate.

"Walk slower." She instructs her when she returns.

"Walk slower?"

"Yes. And don't hold your head so high. Try to ... Try to glide. Try to pass unnoticed. They like their Sinta serving girls depressed. Submissive."

Zorry seems to be considering these words.

Mamma Zeina goes on, "Of course ..."

"Of course what?"

"She doesn't catch it all." Soft knowing look.

"Who doesn't ..."

"Gaddys." Ghost of a wink. "That's where you come in, Zorry. Try to see the things that the shopkeeper Gaddys missed. Observation. That's the work here, Zorry. Go stand by the window again. I'll bring you the next plate in a minute."

Zorry hears the sound of the edge farm rain dances, washing up through the crack in the window behind her. Rain beats against the window. Rain which will not pass the border, Zorry thinks, but she can hear the edge farmers' rain dance: music rising up over the killing trees and the answering bird sound, caw of crows and jackdaws, rhythm of drums. And then the soft hollers, musical shrieks. Zorry just makes out their words: 'Give back our rain.'

The edge farmers rain dances will last all night, the Egg Men will begin the crackdown on the edge farms soon, Zorry knows that much.

Zorry can hear the sound of the Egg Mens' sirens. Starts as a low complaining whine, rises to an ear splitting mechanical shriek which can be heard even in the 'anti-noise pollution' OneFolks' houses. The chatter in the feast room rises to conceal it.

There is now the sound of small, contained explosions, she sees the trees shake a little, at the periphery of her vision. The bomb dust from the edge farm side fans out over the killing forest, drifts towards the OneFolks' village. She twitches and looks away. Now she hears the caw of crows as they rise and gather. A flock, looking like a dark cloud as it passes over. "They're starting early today." Mamma Zeina says, winces. Turns away.

The crows and rats who feed on the bomb sites on the edge

farms have grown to monstrous sizes. Zorry saw them as soon as she got to the general's house this morning. Apparently attracted here by the general's moat. Some escapees from the general's feast table make it that far, Zorry knows that much. But to a non-casual observer, the moat is teeming with life.

"The rats and scavenging birds ..." Mama Zeina pauses. "They're about the only living things to've flourished on the edge farms, the last few years. Wingspans the size of a grown man laid sideways." Her eyes widen. "Tails as thick as a child's hand." She looks sternly at Zorry.

Zorry hears the monstrous flapping. Huge wings. The cloud of crows rises, turns once in the air. Sound of cawing and scrapping. They seem to only just clear the top of the killing forest.

"They head for the edge farms when they hear the sirens?"

"Aye." Mamma Zeina says. "Crows learn fast. They're the new clean up crew on the edge farms."

Something passes over Mamma Zeina's face.

Zorry turns away from her discreetly.

The siren goes on.

Shrill, urgent sounds. The clatter of the feast table rises.

Zorry notices the general's wife mops a tear. She's weak and appears to need to rest before she speaks. Zorry despises her for one long moment. *Collaborator.* She thinks.

The general's wife was once a Sinta, at least that was always the rumour on the Sinta cabbage patch farms. Zorry watches that sparrow chest heave. And then finds herself thinking that the general's wife looks lost, bewildered, just now. It will be harder for Zorry to hate her now she's seen her up close.

The general's wife is staring at the feast table as though she sees it for the first time in her life. Wilting from the knees, drooping head. She seems to move unsteadily back towards her seat.

Gaddys taps the side of her glass and the general's wife rises again, with some difficulty. Twice during her speech she appears to forget where she is. Blinks and sits down right in the middle of a sentence.

"The general's wife looks shrunken since the first time I saw her," Mamma Zeina says.

"And when was that?"

"When I was a younger woman. In the last era. Before the revolution. She used to stand on a plinth in the centre of the village. Doing a mime act."

"A what?"

"Mime. Theatre. Such things were possible in those days." Mamma Zeina sighs.

"It was the act which first attracted the strange attentions of the general to her. He liked her human statue act best. Thought it would be fitting in a wife. He was a sorry little fellow in those days. No one thought he would amount to much. No one thought he would last through the changing times." Breathes out heavily. Eyes Zorry.

"We were blinded by our hopes. Hope itself changed. Hope shed its skin and became ..."

"Became what?"

"Something else Child, don't mither me for endless answers. I am only one hundred years old." Grins softly at the girl. Zorry notes Mamma Zeina's missing front teeth.

The village shopkeeper Gaddys pats the general's wife's

shoulder. Her boney arm looks like it could be crushed under Gaddys the shopkeeper's great hand.

Now Gaddys heaves to her feet. Medals clank against each other. Earrings jangle. Her long pendant necklace swings forward as she leans, then back and she tips it over her shoulder with a flourish. Pats the gold coils of her wig.

The village shopkeeper, Gaddys, has amassed a great deal of personal power in the show village, indicating the high esteem the general holds her in, Mamma Zeina explains. Taps the side of her round nose. "Folks come to her shop for information as well as to exchange their ration cards for grain," she checks the girls face for understanding.

"Gaddys controls the information and the rations. That's important, Zorry."

Zorry can't seem to pull her eyes away from that pendant. Gaddys' gem is the largest at the table, lapis lazuli coloured but also tinged with purple, speckled with silver coloured shards like shrapnel. She's never seen a stone like that before. Thinks they must be digging deeper into the OneFolks' mine. They must be nearing the bottom of it soon, that's certainly the rumour amongst the Sinta. She thinks about the miners who work the gem mines in the show village, wonders what will happen to them when the work is done. After all, they've lived amongst the OneFolk, they've seen things. They could map the village, list names, give coordinates and all to the edge farm rebels, if they had a mind to. The general doesn't generally let a thing like that pass. She imagines the young gem miners' lives will be short and brutal.

Zorry thinks of last night, Mamma Zeina and the killing forest. What was the name of the boy whom Mamma Zeina fixed up? The name is on the tip of her tongue then it comes to mind.

Tomax. She briefly wonders where Tomax is now.

"Zorry, wake up." Mamma Zeina hisses. "It's your turn again, Zorry." Hands her a plate, stacked with fried beetles. Jewel hued green-backs, charred lightly and their wings lifting away from their bodies, as though ready for flight. Delicious with salt.

"Gaddys will decide if the Sinta slaves like you, Zorry and your family, and those few edge farmers deemed fit for now to hold possession of border passes, will get the drought resistant seeds or the stone seeds which won't sprout." Mamma Zeina pulls her head covering a little further forwards, "Not if you turn them and tend them for a year, and so ... " She pauses. Sighs. "And so in charge of the distribution of Bavarnica's seed sacks, Gaddys holds the power of life and death in her manicured hands. Here."

Zorry looks down.

"Take this plate."

Mamma Zeina watches Zorry walking slowly toward the feast table. The girl is learning. The old woman blinks and tries to swallow. She feels as though something is stuck in her throat.

When Zorry returns she hands her some napkins to fold.

"It was Gaddys' idea to visually differentiate the sacks by colour. She is brilliant, in her own disgusting way." Zorry blinks and gently leans a little toward Mamma Zeina to hear better.

"Stand up straight Zorry." Mamma Zeina admonishes.

"Sorry."

Mamma Zeina goes on, "Gaddys has a gift for

showmanship. Left hand, yellow sack, right hand, orange. It underlines her power unless any of her 'customers' should come to doubt it, Gaddys deals in life and death." Mamma Zeina taps the curved end of her nose with one stubby finger. "Drag an orange sack home, Zorry, and with your edge farm friends and neighbours looking at you, pitying or else just plain evasive. Just like you're already dead." Mamma Zeina eyes Zorry. "That's what we're up against. It all begins and ends with Gaddys."

Mamma Zeina gathers up her skirts and slowly walks away from Zorry. Zorry notices her pull distractedly on the glove on her right hand. Zorry briefly wonders why Mamma Zeina wears it. It seems to Zorry that the old woman doesn't do much without a reason.

And now Gaddys closes her square right hand around her glass. It's crystal, delicately carved with ancient species of flowers and so fragile looking that you'd think, looking at her heavy hand, that she would crush the glass between those smooth, hard fingers. Zorry finds herself watching Gaddys' hands with a strange fascination. But they're just the regular perfumed hands of a lady of the Flowers Fund, Zorry shakes herself. A little more thick-knuckled than most, perhaps, and the nails made to mimic cat claws, extend and retract in the latest Bavarnican fashion. Zorry looks down. Her own long fingered hands are hard wearing, callused. Nails bitten down to the quick.

Exhaustion rolls over Zorry. Sound of her own heart thumping in her ears.

Her eyes close for a moment.

There's a silence in the room as Gaddys rises. The sense

of breath held. No need for Gaddys to cough or tap her glass, Zorry blinks and tries to concentrate. She notices the fabric of Gaddys' dress strain against her large muscular body. And now the table is silent. The quiet seems to emanate from Gaddys, seep upward from her skirts, Zorry thinks. Like that moment when the dust comes over the top of the killing forest, drifting westward whenever an edge farmhouse is bombed.

Gaddys' hair is shaven at the sides in the latest fashion, with a spiral starting from just over her ears and making the top of her head look like a coil pot or a nest of snakes, depending on your disposition so that even the OneFolk childur from this, Bavarnica's show village (and childur, in Bavarnica, is the loose and rather insulting name meaning young people) but they can recall her hairdo every time they look at the rusting spiral water dispenser in the school canteen. Her hair is called to mind by the caterpillar twists and turns of the yellow seams running down the outside of the general's energiser by the killing forest fences. Then there's the twisted rusting pump of the school's generator. Or the water canteen in the OneFolk childurs' playground, which the boldest of the OneFolk childur call Gaddys and throw small stones at. Gaddys' hairpiece is quite a show stopper, even by the standards of the OneFolks' show village. It's how she announces her presence. It's her brand, Zorry thinks.

Zorry sinks farther back into the space beside the window, afternoon is turning into evening. She feels the shadows slip around her. Curfew is coming for the Sinta farms beneath the great house. Everyone indoors when the general switches off his mechanised sun, and the old sun is allowed to cast its dim, last rays.

Zorry presses her back into the corner. She is clutching an empty platter. Holds it to her heart unconsciously, like a shield.

When she looks down she notices that her right hand is shaking.

Takes her a while to see that the Egg Boy Antek is back. Glances at her from underneath his helmet. Looks away again quickly.

And then she follows his eye. Notices the small escaping critter is still on the move, it pops out of the side of the powdered wig of one of the grander ladies at Gaddys' end of the table. It's looking jittery and flustered, antennae swivelling furiously, and now ducks and hops on and off the curling beard of the ancient looking man to the right of Gaddys, leaps again and finds a second home in the huge extended collar of the man on her second right.

Zorry notices Antek shut down a smile.

This confuses Zorry. Egg Boys aren't supposed to have emotions. Certainly they never show them. She looks again in the direction in which Antek looks. The small spider-like creature in his eyeline has a large wobbling head, like a hat about to topple. The man it sits on, with the strange flea collar and dressed like some over large unidentifiable feline, doesn't appear to have noticed. The top of one ear of his costume droops and the old man's own ragged ancient ear peeks out.

Now the flower arrangement softly extends its huge head towards the critter, which scurries, panicked, into the cat costume and down the back of the cat-man's ancient looking left ear, scoots into his costume, runs down his sinewy neck.

The old man's eyes roll strangely.

He gets up looking a little shaky, makes his way toward the

perfumed toilet in the corridor outside.

Zorry imagines for a moment that she saw Antek smile again. Just a shadow of movement, the right side of his mouth.

The left side of the flower arrangement gently lilts its head, watches Antek go check the window. And then head left to secure the inner door on the right.

There's a commotion then. A second OneFolk man knocks against the table, sliding his chair out and, with its heavy throne-like back, it falls and several Sinta struggle to be the first to catch it. Under cover of this unseemly jostling, the squid-like creature slides slowly off the table and onto the floor. Nows it's half hidden by the tablecloth near a OneFolk woman's right feathered shoe. The critter sniffs the shoe and leans against it. The owner of the shoe looks down. She lets out a small scream. Moves her foot. The creature slowly slides toward her.

Antek goes and secures a second door. Unreadable expression and then he bends his head toward the handle, as though checking the quality of the lock. His face is concealed. Zorry imagines she sees his shoulders vibrate softly.

She turns back slowly toward the dining table.

Zorry has not seen the like of the critter before but Mamma Zeina warned Zorry earlier not to show any alarm, no matter what happens at the feast of the flowers fund.

New foods are the very height of fashion. Most of them are made in the labs.

The squid-like creature slides around the feathered shoe once more and then makes its way across the floor toward the window. Zorry wonders if it can sense the water in the moat beneath it. She steps back, too suddenly, and then watches as it reaches its tentacles up, fingering toward the window ledge beside her, and then, gripping on, eases itself up. It seems to Zorry that the creature glances her way. Eyes her solemnly and then winks its large gloomy eye, slides sinuously through the grille so quickly after that she imagines that she might've dreamt it. There's a struggle as it fails twice to pull its huge head through the crack, soft popping sound on the third attempt. Zorry hears the soft plosh of the creature hitting the moat below.

"The flower fund of Bavarnica is doing essential work," says Gaddys, squaring her feet. Quieting the soft uproar of the feast with one of her looks. She pats her coiled hair. Gazes around the room. Now she smiles, showing all her half formed child-like teeth.

There's the tinkle of "Cheers," glasses raised and clanking silverware.

REPORT 2:
COMMUNICATION

"OPERATIVE JENGI?"

"Yes."

"Communication. We want to know how the Sinta resistance are talking to each other. We assume it's in code. Please begin."

"When the general's lab technicians found the math of voices undercover, the algorithm, they thought they had removed the Sinta's last power play: they could no longer talk to each other in their workplaces, not even in code. At least not without being monitored, but in fact as the Sinta turned it on its head and used it, even that turned out to be a chink in the general's system."

"How do you mean exactly?"

"Well, he's stopped listening. Thinking they've stopped talking. Stopped being able to reach out to each other in their work places and so forth. But ... Observation. Communication. Friendship. The general forced the Sinta to get better at all these things. And talking is still the true key to the Sinta resistance, don't doubt it."

"Alright Jengi. Though I am the doubting kind. Go on. How did these Sinta get round the listening system? And surely there's not much they can say, iffens they's bugged on all sides."

"It's the opposite. Now Sinta can talk fairly freely, even under the general's bugs and listening devices, so long as they find the right notes. It takes practice, but in the end it's less risky than their old sign language."

"They had a sign language?"

"Yes. They still do. But it has to change so often that misunderstandings are common, and not even the new language's own speakers can keep up. Does flicking a napkin to the right mean yes or no? Mopping the floor with an anticlockwise motion, Egg Boy's coming or else the coast is all clear, go ahead folks? For myself I never got my head around the ever-changing sign language. Not that it doesn't take practice to skip the algorithms too. Find the music. All Sinta secret talking takes skill. And not everyone has the knack of the new speaking yet. Sinta who're naturally musical seem to be doing the best." He pauses. Strokes the faintly curved bridge of his nose. "Mostly the Sinta now 'talk' in a kind of hybrid of both signing and musical speech. The OneFolks imagine that they do all this for the feast's entertainment."

"And Mamma Zeina?"

Jengi is silent for a long moment. Scratches his head and then he appears to have decided something. "Mamma Zeina's voice sounds like she's discussing the colour of the pretty napkins she's folding, or the sheen on the cutlery, the curve of the glassware and this is important too. For a Sinta. Being calm, lighthearted. The general's listening devices will tune into the cadence of heightened emotion. A Sinta is not allowed to be angry, no matter what happens. But you can improve on your emotional reactions with practice. As it turned out some Sinta have the nature for that sort of work and some don't. In the beginning it was the warriors in the resistance movement who were arrested first. They couldn't hide it."

"It?"

"Sorry, Sir. What did you say?"

"It. You said they couldn't hide It. What is It?"

"It's the rage, Sir. They couldn't hide their outrage. It was a blow to lose the Sinta warriors, but in the end the resistance went on without them. But the outrage lived on. That was the main thing."

"Right." Small pause. "Er ... Carry on, Jengi. So what are we left with?"

"It is a measure of the success of the resistance that the general now believes he has mostly cowed the Sinta folks who are left in the OneFolks' village. When the truth is ..."

"Yes? What is the truth Jengi?"

"The truth is he's only sent the Sinta resistance deep underground."

There's a long silence and then, "Jengi? Mamma Zeina is Z. Isn't she? Your revolution's third thought Seed?"

Jengi is calculating fast. "Yes." Jengi says.

"I thought as much. Alright. Good work, Jengi."

There's a crackle on the line. Hiss and the connection ends abruptly.

Jengi feels a cold, slithering sensation at the pit of his stomach. He's name-checked Mamma Zeina. It's a risk. That's bad. He likes to think she would understand ... Would want to protect the true third Seed. Jengi has learned to make such deals with himself. He slopes back toward the lights of the OneFolks' village, the shop.

THE GENERAL'S WIFE

"AYE," SAYS GADDYS APPROVINGLY, "That's the creed of
the ladies of the flower fund of Bavarnica, we LOVE flowers!"
She says, with a flourish of her jewelled hands and her heavy
bracelets clank together. Cattish fingernails extend and retract.
And then she says it again, raising her voice to drown out the
thumps and rhythmic hollers of the edge farmers' rain dance,
sounds rising up over the killing forest and past the fence.
Seeping in through the air vents and the narrow slats in the
windows of the general's great house, followed by the rising
shriek of the Egg Men's sirens, the low sickening rumble of the
general's drones mobilising. Scrapping and cawing of crows.

The clamour of the feast table rises.

Small puffs of raspberry coloured smoke is regularly
emitted from the flower table decorations, colouring the
OneFolks' faces a deeper and deeper pink, one cheek at a time.

The general's wife, a little drunk and over-pollinated, seated
closest of all to the grotesque table flowers, sways uneasily
to her feet and gets a little off-message, "The edge farms ..."
She begins. "The edge farmers have become paralysed by fear
since their rains were taken." She slurs the last three words,
so that they run into one and seem to lilt up at the end like the
rain dance drumbeat. Long pause as if she's listening then to
the low rumble of drones and the silent feasters listen with
her. Now she raises her huge violet eyes toward the chandelier

above the feast table. It gently shudders.

Now the general's wife teeters a little on her stilt heels.
Dips suddenly to one side. She falls off one stilt and it clatters
on to the tiles and slides out from underneath the feast table.
The man beside the general's wife catches her, only just,
supporting her by her left elbow. Now he gently entreats her to
sit down, which she does, a little bemused and rubbing at her
left ankle. Someone fetches her fallen left stilt.

Gaddys sniffs. She pats her coiled hair.

"The general's wife was once the most famous beauty
in Bavarnica," Mamma Zeina tells Zorry now. She seems to
Zorry to be describing someone other than the feeble looking
woman in front of them. "She was strong." Mamma Zeina
says, inclining her head slightly toward Zorry, "And you must
understand that I am only talking about physical strength
now, Zorry. Which must not be mistaken for real strength, for
resilience Zorry. She had athleticism. Swagger." Mamma Zeina
sniffs dismissively. "It's a surface element, not the real thing
… The Sinta who remain finally know better what true strength
is. What real resistance is." Turning gently toward Zorry.
"Strength is endurance. We bend first and break last. Above all,
we go on Zorry." Searching gaze. "We talk. We share what we
know. What we've learned. Do you understand me?"

Zorry turns away. "Tell me more about her." Flicks her eyes
discreetly toward the general's wife.

"Some Sinta claim to have witnessed the general's wife
hurdle a five bar gate, fall to the other side of it, laughing
and flushed. But she barely broke a sweat doing it. That was
in the last era of course. Before the Diggers' revolution and
the general's Reckoning which came after it. There were high

hopes in the early days of Bavarnica. Hope was the spirit of the times then, and joyful. Not the thing it has become for us now. It was a time when all manner of things seemed possible." She stops talking for a moment. "The wind of that early hope has changed direction. Leaves gather, rise gently before the storm, Zorry. And we are the coming storm." Zorry feels a shiver.

Gentle rain is spitting through the vents in the windows. Warm air. Mamma Zeina turns toward Zorry, "The general's wife ... She had these wide, amazing dark violet eyes. Don't you see? It's a mixture of all Bavarnica's colours, Zorry." She opens her own eyes wide as though to demonstrate. "A luminous complexion. Which looked like she could be any tribe, all or none, and changed depending on who was looking at her and on the quality of the light. A great ... Public speaker. Although of course all in mime." Mamma Zeina thinks for a moment. Eyes swivel left and up, she seems to be seeing the past open up in her mind's eye.

"She had long hair which she kept curled and dark rust coloured, hennaed like a Sinta some weeks." She sighs. "Most Sinta no longer believe she was ever one of us," Mamma Zeina blinks and stares wide eyed at Zorry. As if she's looking for an answer in the girl's face. Her voice becomes hard. "A true Sinta woman never caves, the way the general's wife has. A true Sinta woman would never give up, the way she has ... Take the pollen." She sighs.

"At other times she wore bright knotted head scarves like the edge farm women and once even a helmet-like hat, which the Sinta called her Egg Boy hat. We thought, by these small changes in costume, she was still doing her mime act. Doing

it from the heart of government. In our naïveté we believed ..."
Sighs again, heavily.

"You believed the general's wife was for you all. All the
tribes." Zorry peers at Mamma Zeina. Takes and folds a napkin
neatly. Adds it to the pile. Mamma Zeina is gazing softly at her,
"Zorry ..."

She can't finish. In a moment Zorry seems to see this.
"What happened?"

Mamma Zeina seems to need to steel herself just to
answer the girl's question. Holds on to the serving counter
with both hands. Zorry notices her knuckles softly darken.
"And then the Sinta mountain excavations on The Reach were
ended, all the Sinta's ... Improving projects. Our dreams. The
Sinta were rounded up." She coughs, takes a moment to clear
her throat. "The Diggers rose up when they realised what was
happening, being an ancient warrior tribe, but the Diggers led
with courage not planning, and then ... The tanks came, Zorry.
It happened fast." Mamma Zeina stops talking for a long time.
"They were the best of us. In the aftermath, while we licked
our wounds and tried to gather, Zorry, the killing forests were
replanted, changed."

"So the revolution failed and the tribes were divided then."

"That's when *she* changed." They both look back at the
general's wife, head drooping over her empty plate. Flower
girls fill up her plate but she won't eat. "She sickened with the
times."

And then Mamma Zeina turning sadly toward Zorry, "We
had high hopes of her, like I said Zorry." Breathes out heavily.
"But that was a long time ago. Another time. We were all of us
different then." Mamma Zeina examines a small nail in the wall.

"You think she tricked you?"

"Maybe." She appears to think about this. "No, I don't think so. One thing is certain ... she was used, Zorry. The general ..." She sighs. "Oh, I just stopped knowing at a certain point, Child. Your questions are undoing me."

Zorry appears to ignore this. "So if she's not a Sinta and not a OneFolk then what tribe is she?"

"No one knows, Zorry. There were rumours among us at one time that the general's wife wasn't from Bavarnica at all, but dropped like a bomb or a food parcel from clean out of the sky. That was thirty years ago. More."

"You think she's a foreign agent? You think she was a foreign weapon of some kind?"

"Maybe."

Mamma Zeina looks over toward the general's wife, notes her curled head drooping over her plate. Her bleak opaque gaze. "Maybe she was something like that once," she says. "Who knows what she is now. What or who." Turns sharply toward Zorry. "It don't do to underestimate the general. Any living thing can be turned, like I said. Any. Living. Thing." She looks up. Stares into the space just over Zorry's head. "But that's a thing that can work both ways, Zorry." Mamma Zeina eases herself up with a grim expression. Once on her feet she mops her forehead. And then leaves Zorry to her own thoughts.

Beauty has not quite done with the general's wife yet, but she seems to Zorry to have done with it. There's a carelessness about her dress, dark circles from un-sleep in rings under her eyes. Her teeth have been browned by flower pollen. As if she senses she's being examined the general's wife looks up, one brief shrewd gaze at Zorry, causing Zorry to catch her breath and hold it. Ghost of a smile and then the general's wife lets her head fall over her empty plate again. Zorry breathes out.

"We must send out our flowers," Gaddys repeats. In a warning tone. And then a cool steady eye on the general's wife, who flinches lightly, trembles. Wilts a little more under her gaze. The room of feasters raise their glasses, tinkle, clink, to cover the sound of the sirens outside. The general's wife rises, wobbling, to her feet. A small gasp at this clear breach of feast protocol. It isn't the general's wife's turn to speak.

And then it happens ...

The general's wife's glass tumbles out of her left hand, rolls and hits the wall. Splits neatly in two large parts, like a new hatched egg.

There is a long, strange moment. Silence.

Gaddys and the general's wife are locked gaze to slow, knowing gaze.

Neither stands down.

Later in the kitchen, Mamma Zeina and Zorry stand at the serving hatch, preparing the second course.

"I don't get it," Zorry says. "Why won't Gaddys let the OneFolks' talk to each other?"

"Fear." Mamma Zeina says, and a feeling in her stomach like intestines tighten and then unravel. She can't speak for one long moment on account of the pain. And then rubbing at her upper stomach. "She won't put the general's wife's old allies together."

"What?" Zorry is confused.

"She's separated the old friends of the general's wife." She rubs her nose and continues, "Friendship is deemed radical in the OneFolks' village. Power blocks can appear amongst the OneFolk overnight, the general and Gaddys know better than to allow that." Wincing again.

"What's wrong?"

"Nothing, Child."

"The two at the end on the right ..." Zorry says. Opening her eyes wide.

"What about them?"

"They're protecting each other. It's subtle but ... Watch them Mamma Zeina."

"I will, Zorry. Well observed Child. And Gaddys hasn't seen it?"

Zorry shakes her head. "Not as far as I can tell."

"Good. What else have we got?"

"Purple wig and the one with the silver studded collar, they hold their breaths when the flowers puffed pollen just now. Old man with the green embroidered corset only pretended to pass out with the pollen fumes. But he's been turning his head away from it and his cheeks ain't pinked much. Seems like trouble amongst the OneFolk, Mamma Zeina. And it'd explain why Gaddys has been acting paranoid lately. Why she's been getting ... worse." Zorry looks thoughtful. "This could help us?" Rolls and puts away a napkin.

"Yes it could, Zorry. Good work."

"And the other thing ..."

"There's another thing?" Mamma Zeina says, rubbing at her stomach, eyeing Zorry.

"Gaddys' Beloved Flowers. I mean to say ... The women. The flower girls."

"Aye, Zorry. Continue."

"Employing pretty young OneFolk women as assistants to the feast?"

Mamma Zeina raises her eyebrows. "Yes?"

Zorry speaks slowly, thoughtfully, "Can't be much fun. I mean ... for them. Might they ...?"

"The flowers won't help us, Zorry. That's been tried. They are in Gaddys' employ, Child. They won't give up their treats. At least ... Not yet."

Through the serving hatch Zorry eyes one of Gaddys' most Beloved Flowers sway gracefully over, plop herself down in a OneFolk farmer's lap, the petals around her face unfurling. Soft roll back of the leaves arranged in her hair. Gaddys smiles approvingly and then the younger woman turns her sweet head gently toward the old farmer ... Breaks into a smile of such deliciousness that the farmer is unnerved for a moment. And then quite in her palm.

Gaddys turns away, smirking.

Only Zorry catches the beloved flower girl's grimace at a second beloved flower over the old man's shoulder. The second girl's petals droop discreetly by way of response.

"Holy baobab." Zorry grins and ducks under the side serving table. "Sign language? Poor Gaddys is in more trouble than she knows."

"I'm telling you ... Gaddys' flower girls won't help us Zorry. They will be on the side that wins, when it's over. When we are counting our dead and spitting out teeth. Then they'll sashay over and tell us they were on our side all along."

"Maybe ..."

"Forget them. The last Sinta to hold your position found

out Gaddys' true weakness, Child."

"And what is that?"

"It's hard for the OneFolk tribe to be her enemy but in truth Gaddys has lately made it just as dangerous to be her friend."

"And that's a weakness?"

Zeina turns to her with surprise, "Of course it is Zorry! It means that Gaddys, unlike us, has no real alliances. No one who would die to get her out of a hole or for whom she herself would jump into one." Turning to Zorry then to check her understanding. "That's the Sinta advantage Zorry. We won't desert folks. We don't sacrifice each other. Its the only leg up that we have, Zorry. Friendship. We must never lose that." She looks softly at Zorry. "Trust, Zorry. The Sinta can count on each other. We gather."

Zorry eyes her.

"We gather." She repeats. And then turning warmly toward her favourite. "Gaddys and the general can play every card there is but that one, Zorry. Remember it." Zorry looks away.

Mamma is now clutching on to her stomach with both hands, panting a little. If Zorry turned toward Mamma Zeina now she'd see that the side of her neck ripples strangely. That she sweats.

Zorry blinks. She's been awake more than forty-eight hours now. Most of it in a cold copse, under damp leaves, her body is starting to really protest. Her eyelids feel brittle and prized open only by a supreme effort of will. Zorry's vision gently swims. She leans her head on the cold wall, feels herself tuning out, the room blurs. Mamma Zeina's elbow, sharp, in her ribs. Blink and blink.

The OneFolks at the table seem to glitter, Zorry looks

closer. Refocuses. Must be a Bavarnican mine's worth of gems just in the dining hall alone.

"That boy last night. Tomax." She thinks aloud. "Doesn't he work the gem mines by day?"

"Aye Zorry. Yes, yes. But don't make connections that do not exist. You've to look for the thread that binds it all together. The whole picture. Those gem mines? It's all for this Zorry. For this competition at the feast table."

"What do you mean?"

"The only chance the OneFolks' get to show off the jewellery," Mamma Zeina says, "is at the feasts of the flower fund of Bavarnica. And so must buy up the best pieces in the weeks beforehand. It's a signifier of power. The competition in this room is important to the future alliances and bloodlines of the OneFolks, Zorry. The gemstones are money and Gaddys is in charge of its distribution. It's as simple and as complicated as that." Mamma Zeina strokes her small chin.

Zorry tears her eyes away from the pendant.

"It's another crack in the system, Zorry. Don't you see? The gem mines nearly done. And when it is ... these folks' whole world will be built on sand, Zorry. They won't know what they are. What or who."

"Yes." Zorry lies. "Yes, I see what you mean." She has no idea what this means but she doesn't want to disappoint Zeina so early on in her work rota.

Mamma Zeina sighs, "Then you see more'n most Child. But what you don't see is I'm in pain now. Enough talk. Help me, Girl. Help me to serve these damned platters." She thrusts a large silver plate at Zorry's chest. Zorry strains to catch and hold it. Looks down, shudders. "Holy baobab," she mutters quietly to the food. "I am so sorry." She takes a deep breath and gets on with her work.

Zorry deposits her platter as skilfully as she can and whips her hand away as an elderly OneFolk farmer snaps at her gummily, semi-humorously tries to bite her arm. Then grinning with his one tooth, chuckling at his own sour joke.

Zorry smiles and bows, discretely wipes the old man's slobber off her skin, she walks away. There is a red indent from his one lower tooth left in her arm. She feels the throb of it only later.

Zorry returns to Mamma Zeina's side. She thinks of something. "I heard some childur got pizened." She says. "Last time they took flowers like these out to the edge farms."

"Aye. They were so hungry that they nibbled the leaves of the flowers."

"And the year before that the truck delivery man hit an old woman with his truck?"

"He drove too fast to get away from the hungry edge farms. Now hush, Zorry." Mamma Zeina says, giving Zorry another plate to serve. "Your tune was off just now. You've been made." Glares, wide frightened eyes. "No room for mistakes Zorry. Not here."

Zorry looks up, follows Mamma Zeina's eye and Gaddys' Most Beloved flower girl on the end of the table is watching Zorry. She looks away quickly. The flower girl makes no sign to Gaddys. Who knows why she chooses to spare Zorry. Mamma zeina looks at her, shrugs. "She might want something later or maybe she's even one of us. It's hard to tell. Only Jengi knows how many we are, how far we reach out. How many Thought Seeds that he's planted into the divided tribes. Mostly we don't know about each other. It's for our own safety, Zorry. And for theirs too. At least for now."

"For now?"

"Aye. Zorry ... Even out the notes in your voice. You need to work on your voice."

Zorry clears her throat, "Sorry."

Mamma Zeina looks shrewdly at Zorry. "And it will rain so hard that night that morning will come." Mamma Zeina stops talking. Clutches her platter and makes her way slowly back toward the feast table.

Zorry saves the question which has been nagging her most until Mamma Zeina comes back, "Why are there Egg Men guarding entrances and exits every which way you look Mamma Zeina?"

"You mean him? That's Antek's father."

Zorry looks in the direction Mamma Zeina just looked. The old Egg Man's head appears to be too large for his body, and his skull is rounded strangely at the back, giving the appearance of a skull-helmet.

"No one knows if batch 46 of the Egg Boys, Antek's father's squadron, if those big heads contained bigger brains, or just heavy skulls in case of falling. I suspect the latter. They were made for the mountain."

Zorry examines the Egg Man discreetly. His neck seems to strain at the weight of his skull.

"Batch 46 were poorly made, if you ask me." Mamma Zeina shrugs. "Clumsy looking." Sniffs.

"Who is this Antek?" Zorry rolls her eyes in the boy's direction. "The son? The young one?"

"He is ... Antek is a person of interest to the resistance,

Zorry. Let us leave it at that." Mamma Zeina sniffs again and rolls another napkin.

"But the younger one, this Antek you seem to like so much," Zorry scowls ... "He has a different shaped head. He looks ... He looks pretty human to be honest, Mamma Zeina."

Mamma Zeina eyes her. The old woman becomes cautious. "He is one of batch 47."

"The new batch?"

"Yes, Child. The new batch."

Mamma Zeina stops talking for a long time. And then, "The Egg Boys are posted here today on account of the rumour that the general himself might attend this feast of the flowers."

Zorry's eyes widen.

"Relax child, that's always the rumour and the general never does show up. I've been working this kitchen ten years, and I've never clapped an eye on him." Rolls a napkin, tips an escapee back on to its plate and then looking at it. Waving claws and curiously intelligent expression. "The general hasn't shown his face in public for the last twenty-three years. Aren't too many folks, even in this room, who would recognise him iffen he did. Probably only Jengi who ever looked the general properly in the eye. They say even the general's wife only met her husband the once." Shudders.

"But Jengi saw him you say?"

"Close enough to count the pink pores on his face. Leastways that's his story."

Zorry sniffs. "And you believe him? You believe in this Jengi, don't you?"

Mamma Zeina folds a napkin. Eyes Zorry. "He's not perfect. He'll do. You don't like him do you, Zorry? Jengi, I mean."

It's not a question as far as Zorry can make out, so she doesn't feel the need to answer it.

Mamma Zeina turns a little toward Zorry. Blinks. Quick knowing smile. "We work with Jengi, Child. He is less dangerous when we do it with love." Sighs. "Look. He's a friend. We believe he means well, although he hasn't ... We didn't ... In spite of ..."

Her shoulders droop softly. She doesn't finish any of her broken sentences. Zorry listens best to what folks don't say. "Got it. Work with him. Watch him." Mamma Zeina eyes the girl's long sloping back. Presses her forefinger against the side of her head. She has learned just now that she needs to be more careful, educating Zorry. It seems the girl misses nothing at all.

The general's wife rises slowly to her feet once more, coughs and taps the side of her glass. She looks unsteady for a moment, Gaddys appears to take the reins. Support her from behind. And then the general's wife giving obsequious slightly sickening thanks then to Gaddys, the village shopkeeper, for her stirling work in getting the best table together for the OneFolks' village, like always. "Although ..."She says, peering hazily out into the middle distance, "although ... I myself cannot eat a scrap." Eyes the plate with compassion then rather than distaste.

There's a collective intake of breath. She waves one starved limb, boney fingers passing in front of her eyes.

The general's wife sits down.

It's sudden.

One of Gaddys' beloved flower girls had pushed the old woman's chair hard into the backs of her knees, ending her

performance abruptly. "You'll be more comfortable, Dear."
Pats the older woman's emaciated arm, petals around the
flower girl's face tauten then its leaves curl around her neck,
as though the plant she wears senses something. The beloved
flower girl is softly turning blue, looks over at Gaddys with
wide reproachless eyes. Pleading, suffocating. Gaddys gazing
at her grimly. Something happens. Zorry watches the leaves
slowly slide away from the girl's neck. Now Zorry and the
beloved flower girl meet each other's eye, it's an infinitesimally
brief, knowing glance. Both turn away at the same time.

Mamma Zeina winces.

"What's wrong Mamma Zeina, you still have a pain?"

"I have a thousand pains, Child. Take this whilst I ..."

Mamma Zeina holds on to the wall for balance. Now her
face twists in agony. Zorry sees something's wrong.

"Do you have a pizen, Mamma?"

"Zorry, Child ... I believe that I do."

THE MOTHER
CUPBOARD

"LOOK AWAY FROM ME, don't make a fuss Zorry."
Mamma Zeina gazes back toward the feast. "It's nothing
I can't handle." Gaddys looks at Mamma Zeina. Gives a
surprisingly wide, doggish yawn. Showing all her strange,
child-like teeth.

Mamma Zeina smiles back through gritted teeth.

"I said turn away, Zorry. Move away from me, Child."

Zorry stares out at the feast. Anyone looking over toward
the young Sinta woman would only see impassive smiles. The
Sinta left in Bavarnica learned to hide their facial tells in the
long ago and even Zorry can call on this facial stillness if she
concentrates. In an emergency, like this one, it's essential to
be calm.

Mamma Zeina doesn't like her girls taking risks, especially
Zorry, whom she loves most of all her kitchen helpers. Taking
unnecessary risks Mamma Zeina believes to be a species of
sin. Of course, coming from a woman who risks her own life
everyday three times before sun up ...

"Damn them." Zorry says, through gritted teeth.

"Hush Zorry. Not here. You is bein' reckless, Child. Now
turn toward the room. 'Taint about the battle. Child, it's about
the war. Now. Bow, scrape and smile the way that I taught you,
Sinta girl. Now. Again." She watches her student. "That's right,

Zorry. Smile like a Sinta. Meaning with clenched teeth, use the
injustice in each bow and scrape just to power you onwards,
Zorry. That's the way. Turn it, twist it. Use your rage, Zorry. Like
I taught you. Head toward the back door. Be discreet Zorry. I'll
follow you as soon as I can."

Zorry faces the dining room with a beatific look, bows low.
Turning then with a dancer's grace, she sweeps toward the
door. Several pairs of eyes at the groaning table follow the
girl, it's a dangerous simmering atmosphere. Mamma Zeina
considers this. There is something troubling about the wake
that her favourite leaves behind her. She's going to need to
address that if she's to be useful undercover. Once again
Mamma Zeina has a worried thought about, Zorry – it don't
do for a Sinta girl to stand out the way Zorry does. She'll not
be certified tame by Gaddys at this rate. She'll be sent to work
in the sewers and she'll be no use to the resistance down
there. Zorry will need to work on herself if she's going to be a
useful undercover in the general's house.

Zorry is shoved into the door hinge by the Egg Man who
guards it. A punishment for not seeming submissive enough
just now in the feast room. Young Sinta are generally meted
out this kind of treatment, small but relentless punishments
on a daily basis, to ensure they enter full adulthood compliant.
A little broken down.

Mamma Zeina winces on Zorry's behalf.

And now The Egg Man at the door eyes Mamma Zeina.

She turns away and tries to stack the dishes. Her left hand
is trembling again.

In the corridor by the back door, a show village woman
slips away from the feast and hands Zorry a napkin with a

spewed snail in it. Zorry takes it and curtsies, thanks her. The vomited up, half-digested creature, cracked shell pieces and all, drizzles nauseatingly down the side of Zorry's hand and into her shirt sleeve. The shirt that Zorry's mother, Mamma Ezray, lovingly starched and ironed for her eldest daughter this morning. As if her shirt could protect her from this.

Zorry watches the OneFolk woman's bony back sway, she swaggers past Zorry, back toward the feast. The OneFolk' women are thin on account they vomit up their food in a deliberate manner, or consume prescription medicines which enable them to digest it faster.

The woman clomps away from Zorry unsteadily on painful looking stilt-like heels which look somewhat like weapons with the points, sharp edges and studded arrangements, but in truth mostly seem to hurt their wearer. The woman's arms are strapped down to her sides in the latest Bavarnican fashion, and on her back a painting of the leafy outline of a tree from the killing forest, nipping saplings entwined around it. The general's sun drifts up behind, like a giant pumpkin, huge and round and absurd looking, the body paint bleeding out at the edges where the woman leant on her chair. She's left orange half moons on the velvet surface of the seat-back.

Zorry finds that once again, and as if by instinct, she's backed herself into a window. She turns now and looks out. The general's sun blinks out and the last light from the old sun is rising. The understanding comes to Zorry, standing here with a woman's sour smelling vomit and the soft guts of a Bavarnican snail dripping down from her wrist to her elbow. This will be my life until I die, she thinks. This.

A line of baobab trees mark the boundary where the edge

farms cede into the desert beyond them. The baobab seem
for a moment to Zorry as though they lift their great arms and
wave. Blink, blink. And then roll their huge stomachs. For a
moment it's as though she can hear the rustle of the desert
wind in their branches.

Zorry closes her eyes. Mamma Zeina takes so long to arrive
that Zorry naps briefly, forehead against the cool wall. When
she wakes she knocks her head accidentally, blinks and whips
round. Nobody saw, apparently. Zorry wipes away a seam of
sleep-dribble. Checks behind her. Zorry's eye is drawn back
toward the window. There's something out there. Moving in
and out of view.

It's a small light.

The tiny patch of yellow dances on the farthest baobab.
When Zorry squints and looks closer it disappears. Now she
imagines that she dreamed it.

Something makes Zorry look down. She examines her
hands.

The yellow saliva trail has stained the skin of Zorry's left
palm. The oozing napkin is still clutched in her right hand.

Zorry drops the napkin.

Her damp right hand slowly curls closed.

"Zorry."

Zorry turns abruptly, sees Mamma Zeina walking
awkwardly toward her. The old woman is slow, unsteady on
her feet. When she gets closer Zorry hears Mamma Zeina
hissing a stream of barely audible foul words. It takes Zorry
a few moments to understand what she's saying. It's a long,
slow, obscene string of Sinta curses, forbidden texts from the
ancients, "You do not do, you do not," Mamma Zeina curses,

"Any more, black shoe, in which I have lived like a foot ..."

And Zorry gives the answering phrase to the funeral poem, "And one gray toe, big as a frisco seal and a head in the freakish Atlantic." Mamma Zeina stares at her. "Where it pours bean green over blue." Zorry finishes with a flourish and then, "Mamma Zeina why are we saying death poems now, this ain't a funeral. Is it?"

Mamma Zeina stops. She leans heavily on the wall.

"What's wrong Mamma Zeina? You're really sick?"

Mamma Zeina can't answer for a moment. And then turning, gripping Zorry's arm just to stay upright.

REPORT 3: MEDICINE

"WHAT DO YOU HAVE for me *Special* Operative Jengi?"

"Sarcasm?"

"Not at all, it's Promotion, Jengi. You *are* very special to us. What do you have?"

"That depends what you want."

"Don't play games, Jengi."

"Okay." Sighs.

"Tell me about the greening."

"The greening, eh? So you know about that?"

"We have a few friends inside Bavarnica, Jengi. Are you jealous?"

Jengi takes a long breath. He begins. "The general's latest idea to defeat the Sinta's tendency to insubordination is ... memory erasures. Any slave who refuses the government 'medicine', refuses to forget the past, is deemed an enemy of the state. The Greening, the new policy's called."

"And how does the greening work, exactly? I mean ... According to you, Jengi."

"The greening issue divides Sinta families. It's not unusual to have one parent take their medicine, and the other parent refuse to. Forcing him or her to boil plant roots every night and scrub the green discoloration offen they selves or else be found out, greened, in the morning. It takes hours and their raw, plant-itched, complaining skin is as much of a clue to their medicine intake as turning softly lime coloured would have been."

"I see. That it Jengi? That all you got for me today? The greening? Something I already knew?"

"Well of course there's your hair, and the whites of your eyes. Not everything can be scrubbed with a hard brush or boiled, rubbed with plant roots."

"I reckon not, Jengi. Is this important at all?"

"The Sinta have not yet figured out how the general's lab technicians have achieved the spores which effect this green discoloration only in the Sinta, and only in those not taking their government meds, but you can be sure that those Sinta who remember there's a problem at all are working on the solution to it."

"And these Sinta not taking their meds ... are they the Mother Cupboards whom you spake of afore? Are they the Sinta resistance?"

"No, there are only a handful of mother cupboards fully operational in Bavarnica now. It's fairly specialised work and not too many have the disposition for it."

"I see. I heard they're calling them witches, Jengi."

"Aye. The general is always looking for the mother cupboards, his biggest problem is that the mother cupboards reseed themselves, that's what they call it. Meaning: they're fearless and up to ten more will spring up when you mow down the one. An ancient cult of scientists, doctors, gardeners, cooks and teachers. The general has found them impossible to eradicate entirely."

"I see. But it's a hopeless cause, that's what you reckon, Jengi? These mother Cupboards?"

"I never said that." Jengi thinks for a moment. "Hopeless isn't the word I'd use. The mother cupboards might save us all. In about a hundred years."

"I see. And that's too long for you, Jengi?"

"Yes. That's too long. The edge farms will be buried in the desert by then."

"And, tell me, how is it that they plan to save anyone Jengi?"

"If they can turn the drought resistant predatory plants in the killing forest to some good use on the edge farms. Well then ..."

"The killing forest? They're messing with that ungodly strip of hell. Holy Baobab, Jengi. How they even get in there, let alone come out in one piece?"

"Aye. It's dangerous. The mother cupboards ain't cowards. Cowardice weren't never their problem."

"You don't see eye to eye with them Jengi?"

"Well. Look ... Think about the killing forest for a moment. What is it? The general's man made border? Most of us just see a long, vicious, breeding, living forest-fence, but the mother cupboards see ... Drought resistant plants. Mostly predatory, mind. The plants. But if the plants can be turned, is their thinking ... Well then."

"Well then what? I don't see your point Jengi."

"If the drought resistant plants in the killing forest can be changed, turned, so they don't try to grab your throat or stop your veins flowing, pizen you in a thousand ways and can be turned into ... Food. Then the edge farms can break free of Gaddys and the village shop, tend their own crops then ..."

"I see."

"Do you see? With respect ... It's the key to their freedom, Sir. Food. An irony that if they pull it off the mother cupboards will be turning the general's best weapon, his damned killing forest, against him. Even killing plants can be farmed, turned, that's the creed of the mother cupboards." He sighs. "Everything can be its own opposite. That's what the mother cupboards say and believe. But the science of turning killing things into the means for living, turning pizen into food and water ... It's difficult, deadly work, Sir."

"Again with the deadly. I sometimes wonder if you exaggerate Jengi." There's a cough. "And what is it exactly Jengi? This ... Work that you speak of?"

"The mother cupboards like Mamma Zeina have learned to get through the fence and brave the killing forest. They dig up any promising looking new plants by the roots and take them home to breed the pizen and killing out of em, make em fit to eat. Remember that they test the plants on themselves, Sir. That's important. They do tend to die younger, even if they ain't uncovered by the Egg Boys. Pizen." He sniffs. "The thing can creep up on you."

"So what are they after? Eating plants?"

"Right now, no. They are looking for most about any plants that are good for storing water. It is Mamma Zeina life's mission, to find such a plant. One which would supply water to the edge farmers. She may die 'afore she sees the thing out, she's near a hundred years old and I've had my doubts she will pull it off before the edge farmers are dried bones, under six feet of desert."

"I see. Mamma Zeina you say. She comes up quite a bit don't she? So. She getting anywhere with this ... Work?"

Jengi feels his stomach drop. On an instinct, "Nope." He says. Realises at once that he's answered too quickly, now he hesitatingly qualifies his answer. "Leastways I kindly doubt it, Sir. Sure I'd have heard something by now."

"Relax, Jengi. Okay. You said these are women. Old women."

"Gaddys and the OneFolks call them witches but we call them mother cupboards."

"Yes. You said that already. And it's dangerous work you say? This bloody gardening that these witches are undertaking. Clattering about in the killing forests at night, risking meeting the Egg Men at the fence, or being greened so much they are arrested for not taking their medicine. Even on a good day, tasting pizens like they were sweeties. Testing them out on they own selves. These women sound pretty hard boiled to me, Jengi. All that sounds pretty ... extremist."

Jengi doesn't answer.

"Okay Jengi. Why am I here iffen you're not talking. Why call me at all? Are you sulking?"

Jengi clears his throat. "It is dangerous work that they're doing. If one of the modified forest creatures don't get them, or the leaches, then the too-many-small-bites from the nipping saplings will bring them down slow. Worse, if one of the general's Egg Men catch a mother cupboard illegally keeping and meddling with the nature of the plants, that will be it ... They'll be dragged half alive to the long gaol in the mountain's shadow or, worse, the government laboratories under the general's great house with the moat around it. He catches about two out of three active mother cupboards, even with the mother cupboards' best efforts. There ain't no crime worser'n gardening, in the OneFolks' village."

"I see." Scratch of an ancient pen, scrabbling over a scroll.

"Do you? Do you, Sir? What is it you see?"

HUNGER

MAMMA ZEINA HAS BEEN cooking in the general's kitchen all morning. She's not been paid this week and her food-ration cards are three days overdue meaning that, between the one thing and another, including an unforeseeable Egg Mens' raid of her food stores last month, the hunger almost took Mamma Zeina yesterday at the feast of the flowers fund. The general's wife will pay Mamma Zeina eventually. When she gets around to the thing, meaning whenever she happens to wake up from her pollinated stupor and finish her duties. Then, and only then, will Mamma Zeina get to eat.

The general's wife is a busy woman. She has at least three things left on her official To Do list, before she gets around to paying her slave Sinta workers their food rations. Firstly, she's to tend to the waxen flowers in the vast entrance hall, secondly, to count the heads of OneFolk babies born to the village, pat their mothers' arms serenely, coo absentmindedly and smile for the photos, and thirdly she's to choose three frocks for coronation day. This will take at least two days, without accessorising, and last of all she's to oversee the making of a new jewel encrusted bullet proof jacket which has been ordered for her by Jengi, the shopkeeper's assistant.

The general keeps his wife's schedule chocked full with things that don't matter a scrap. She works hard to keep up.

So ... There's no knowing when Mamma Zeina will next eat.

This is the third day without food for Mamma Zeina, which on a regular sort of day for her means porridge made with water and sprinkled with seeds grown on her allotment, or else the root vegetables rejected from the general's wife's own kitchen as being too rough-looking, mangled or pitted with holes. Boiled by the Sinta woman until they're soupy and digestible and then eaten with the hard dry leftover oat-bread, herbs and spices, chilli peppers from Mamma Zeina's own allotment, a pinch of bartered-for salt.

This morning the general's wife, looking frail after her latest pollen over-dose, and wobbly on her stilts, had stumbled down three steps to the kitchen below stairs. Kindly insisted on throwing the kitchen's misshapen vegetables away. Pizens, she called them, slurring her words. Promising, in her over-pollinated state, to replace them with the heart shaped oranges from her own garden.

Of course the general's wife forgets these kinds of promises by morning, sneezing and waking in a haze of pollen dust. Meantime her kitchen workers have been starved for a day, Mamma Zeina for three. They'd been counting on the vegetable soup.

The rejected vegetables were immediately dragged away from the moat, pulled to the edge by giant desert rats and eaten right there on the banks.

"How those damned things got as far as the moat in the first place beats me," Mamma Zeina wonders aloud. She examines the rat nearest to the window. Sniffs.

"These desert rat scavengers are the only creatures which seem to be able to sneak around the border fences." She gazes at Zorry. Scratches her chin thoughtfully. "Them and the oversized, fattened up edge farm crows." She points upward with her short, square index finger. "They fly over the fences just as t'other goes under it." She muses. "The only two sets of critters that can work on both sides of the fence. Lest you count Jengi, of course." She scratches her head. She's thinking.

Mamma Zeina and Zorry eye the critters through the kitchen window. There's a desert edge farm rat the size of a large domestic cat or a medium sized dog. The rat is squinting at the kitchen window in a quite unnerving manner just now. Zorry notices that it has huge jaws and long fanged grey-tipped teeth, an extra long pointed nose which droops a little at the tip. Apparently old and slow, a little mangy, distracted by gnawing at the tough root vegetable between its front paws, the critter allows itself to be cornered by two wild dogs.

The carrot is being stuffed into the rat's pouched cheeks when it's pounced on. And then dragged in two opposing directions, twists and scuffles, objects, and is torn into two still-wriggling pieces by the OneFolk village pets. Zorry notes that the larger dog is more scratched and bitten up than its small ally, which stops and swallows down its half of the rat's body, in just two or three struggling gulps. Now it's moving forward menacingly toward the second dog. The second great curling-haired beast of a dog ends up with just the giant rat tail, which it grips gormlessly by the end, and the huge tail goes on waving slowly in its pug mouth. The smaller dog comes back in a bit, takes that off him too. Like an afterthought. "These 'show' pets are pretty useless." Zorry turns.

"Zorry." Mamma Zeina says gently. Pulling the girl away

from the kitchen window.

Zorry looks up. She finds herself shocked by Mamma Zeina's appearance. She looks deathly. Her mouth is a blueish grey line, her eyes set deeper into her skull and the overall appearance is gargoyle-like, "Mamma." Zorry catches Mamma Zeina before she falls. Supports her and then lets a wooden chair by the sink take the strain.

"Mamma Zeina, take my ration," hisses Zorry, "You're faint with hunger." She struggles to pull some oat bread from her left front apron pocket.

Mamma Zeina looks down at the dry bread wryly. She doesn't move to take the girl's food ration from her. "I haven't come to that. You can kindly strangle me your own self," she says fiercely, "before I'll take food from a growing youngster."

"Mamma Zeina ..."

Mamma Zeina rises to her feet. Winces.

Mamma Zeina has had nothing but a squirt of milk stolen from a cow's teat this morning. Crossing the Egg Mens' land on her way to work in the early light of the old sun, even the Egg Mens' steel trap farms can be beautiful before curfew breaks. Curfew when the general's luminous sun takes away the shadows, the soft filtered light through the branches of the border trees.

The cows aren't afeared of Mamma Zeina, on account of she sings harmonious Sinta curses as she goes. Poems of the dead. Mostly the cows prefer rhythms and lilts, she advises her Sinta neighbours. Soft, bewildering upturns in the word-music. But you have to be pretty hungry to risk it nonetheless. One missed note and the cow could take your head clean off at the neck, such eating isn't for the faint hearted.

Mamma Zeina has learned that predictable patterns sooth the cows' reptile brains best. Makes the cows peaceable enough to milk. No mean feat since the reckoning era, when the cows were injected with DNA from an ancient and more savage strain of cow, combined with a Komodo dragon. The cows are now meat eaters since last season. Wide sharpened teeth, claws for hooves, milking them by hand is no joke, as the general intended. The modification coming after a rash of hungry Sinta thieves had diminished the OneFolks' milk supplies. Mamma Zeina has, of course, found a way around the problem, but drinking milk in the reckoning era comes with a health warning.

And there was that piece of fruit Mamma Zeina stole last night too. The heart shaped novelty blood orange which the general's wife was always promising to share with her kitchen workers and somehow never quite did. Being caught in the orange garden could have been trouble for Mamma Zeina.

"What's that on your ankle?" Zorry asks.

Mamma Zeina looks down.

There are sores on Mamma Zeina's ankles from the nipping saplings in the killing forest last night. Gnaw marks around her bulging ankle veins.

Mamma Zeina was so excited last night by a new find, another plant which can hold enough water in its leaves to quench the thirst of a child for one day, before replenishing itself overnight, that stooping in the darkness to uproot it, she'd taken about a hundred small nips to her left ankle from the nipping saplings which grew protectively around it. And that was just whilst examining the thing, pulling it up by its roots before it closed up its leaf claws and took a hold of her wrist. She had got it into her gauze sack and heard it wrestling with the thick cloth, held it away from her body's soft parts.

Mamma Zeina hadn't even felt the large, and extremely poisonous, killing forest leech which dropped softly from a mossy branch above her and, as she struggled with the water storing plant, the leech had secreted itself down the back of Mamma Zeina's collar, on the left side. Dangerously close to her jugular vein. It has been using its liquid sap to thin her blood all day.

Mamma Zeina would have noticed both the plant-itch and the stinging sensation at her throat if she hadn't been already so distracted by the pain of her hunger, and last night's stomach churning pizen experiments on herself. She briefly glanced down at the small sore developing on her left ankle this morning, promised herself she would tend to it later then ... The old woman simply forgot. At one hundred years old, Mamma Zeina has so many aches and pains that it was easy to miss something that was important.

Looking down now, Mamma Zeina sees that the red sore that she barely noticed this morning has grown darker and is spreading out black roots from the point of 'infection'. One root just above the sore is already thick as a thumb and moving up slow and steady, in its vine-like way, along the back of her leg. Making its way toward her carotid artery, sniffing out essential organs, following a trail to the heart where it's evolved to cut off her blood supply, stop her heart. It will use her remains then for compost. A small but highly predatory plant.

Mamma Zeina feels her legs rolling under her. Shoots a hand out, takes a hold of the handle of her steel serving trolley.

On an instinct puts the other hand to the side of her throat
and pulling away the swelling leech. Then, with the expertise
of a woman whose spent every single night of the last year
navigating the killing forest in darkness, she examines its
underside. Sees at once that the creature's poison sacs are
depleted.

Mamma Zeina, with her knowledge of plants and insects,
understands her situation right away. She might've been able
to handle the plant or the pizen but not both. Not together.

She's got three minutes, maybe two and maybe less.

She has two things to do first:

Give the root of the promising plant to her immediate
underling, and that's Zorry.

And then get outside as fast as she can.

———

THE PLANTING

MAMMA ZEINA MUST DIE outdoors, under the sky. The laws of Mamma Zeina's religion are quite clear on this matter. More importantly, it's what she wants most.

"Last work, Mother Cupboard. Finish the job." Mamma Zeina mutters softly to herself, under her breath. Grits her teeth and tries to move. Her left arm is paralysed for one long moment, grips the cage enclosing the vent and holds her there, vine like. As if her curled hand has a mind of its own.

"Holy baobab," she says to herself, "give me strength."

"Strength." She says again. Throwing herself away from the wall and then staggering forwards, three steps, four, and now she's falling. Slaps the palm of her left hand on the wall for support as she goes down. Saves herself, only just.

And now, sweat steaming from her brow and face twisted, hauling herself along by the pipes on the wall. Staggers against the air conditioning system, grips it with both hands. Rests for a moment. Satisfied that she's stayed on her feet. Now she eyes the door handle, lunges and grips it. Right hand. Left hand. Pulling herself along slowly.

Zorry stands watching her come with a rising sense of panic. She feels strangely unable to move.

"Zorry Child, help me. Don't stand there looking at me with wide eyes, help me, damn it."

When she gets as far as Zorry, Mamma Zeina grips the

girl's wrist hard. Pushes her pained face up and into Zorry's. "It's you." She hisses. Struggling to speak now.

"What do you mean?"

"I'm passing you the baton. I pick you. I am reseeding."

"What? Holy baobab, Mamma ..." Zorry wants to object but the words seem to stop in her throat, choke her.

"I ain't got long so I hereby reseed myself and name you Mother Cupboard Zorry, henceforth Mamma Zorry."

"Mamma ..."

Mamma Zeina then thrusts her hand into her apron pocket. Pulls out a small cup with a lid. Lifts it slightly, checks behind her. Zorry looks down at the plant root nestling inside. It's rippling gently.

"This has been my life Zorry. This here. It's a water plant. I entrust it to you."

Zorry's eyes become round and afraid, she is bursting with questions. "Mamma ... Mamma Zeina ..."

"Hush! There's no time now, don't be mithering me with questions. You've seen the work." Mamma Zeina looks at the girl, sternly and warm at the same time, as the best kind of general can be sometimes with her troops. "Do not slow me down now, Child."

"Why'd you pick me?"

"You picked yourself, Zorry. Your nature picked you. I've lived a hundred years and I've seen the likes of you, Zorry, borned and died many times over, and I know it to be a mistake to over protect young women like you. You will die of *that* sooner. You need the resistance as much as the resistance needs you, submission is pizen to a ..." Zeina smiles sadly. "I wouldn't be able to put you in harm's way iffen I didn't believe

..." She peers into Zorry's face. "Bavarnica won't change and nor will you. The double life, Zorry. It's the only way for a Sinta girl like you." She grips Zorry's wrist.

"I need more time."

"There is no more time, Zorry."

Pain overcomes Mamma Zeina. It's like a wave of contractions in her legs and stomach. As her body resists the plant inside her, the long roots and vines growing up and outward. She grips her throat, groans, there's a larger contraction in her stomach that feels to her like birthing. She curses. Spits up a drizzle of poison. Yellow sap runs down her chin. And then blood. She doubles over with pain, "Take this cup from me ..." The cup is tipping from her fingers. Zorry reaches out to catch it before it falls.

Mamma Zeina rises. Her face seems gargoyle-like once more, and strange. Haggard. She's sweating, panting, Zorry thinks she sees death moving underneath Mamma Zeina's skin. A snaking shadow and then it's gone. The old woman is gritting her teeth. Holding on.

"Mamma ..." Zorry says. Now her eyes fill. "You are in pain."

Mamma Zeina gathers herself. Her colour returns for a moment. She looks the girl in the eye, a shrewd direct stare, "This next thing will ..." Her voice falters again. She holds on to the wall.

"What do I do?"

Without looking up, "You got to take the water plant to Jengi, Zorry. He's the only one who can get it to the other side, over and under both fences, through the killing forest and to the right person on the edge farms." She grits her teeth again.

"I don't trust him."

"Zorry. We have to trust him."

"Why?"

"Because there's no-one else."

Zorry catches her breath. "Jengi ... Mamma Zeina ..." Zorry wavers. "Jengi's in the heart of the village. In the shop, Mamma Zeina." Zorry casts about in a panic. "If I'm caught they will kill me. Or take me to the labs, the long gaol, there's no worse fate for a Sinta woman."

"No. There isn't." Mamma Zeina says heavily. She goes on gazing at Zorry. "You think that I don't know what it is I'm asking?"

The girl sets her jaw, "Yes." She says. Not remembering the question, if there even was one.

The old woman looks around her, eyes the window. Sighs. Then looks toward the door to outside. The corridor leading toward the exit seems longer to her just now. The door seems to her to glow with strange life.

Wind rattles the hinges. Desert sand beats against it.

"Help me outside?"

"Yes."

Zorry takes Mamma Zeina's elbow.

They walk the white-lit corridor together, Mamma Zeina's strong right arm thrown over the young girl's slender shoulders. They walk a little zig-zag at first, find a pace.

"Nearly there." Mamma Zeina says. Looking grim, determined. Stops and groans. Zorry waits until Mamma Zeina is steady enough to go on. The girl looks down, examines the root of the water plant. It has one leaf unfurling from it already.

"I'm dying."

"Aye."

They both appear to consider this. Neither speaks.

And in a bit, "That plant has great promise, Child. It might save many lives someday. As far as I can make out ... It attracts rain," she says. Stops again and grimaces, holds her stomach. "And pulls moisture from deep in the earth. Its roots grow a hundred feet, more. Stores what it collects in the leaves and roots, vines. It might bring back the rains. It needs more work but ... Jengi." She says. "Jengi. He'll know what to do with it. Who's the best ... *gardener* to give it to. And if he can't find no-one to finish the work on it then he'll see it's planted out by the baobab. At least that. On the fertile soil of the Sinta graves there. Let the water plant do what it will then, out by the baobab."

At the exit, Mamma Zeina easing down the door handle, steps outside and then pushing Zorry back over the door jamb, inside the house. "Don't be seen with me here, Zorry. I am done now, dangerous to know. Don't speak of me. All of Bavarnica will be watching now. Tell them you barely knew me, Child."

A squeeze of the old woman's hand.

Mamma Zeina closes the door firmly on Zorry. Then she leans against its hinges.

Clutching at the ivy strewn outer wall, Mamma Zeina makes her way over the drawbridge and beyond the garden lights to the outside.

Mother cupboards like, if they can, to die in the natural sunlight, the last lights of the old sun, when it's time. She is just in time, night's not fallen yet. Mamma Zeina just catches the moments after curfew, *blink*, and the general's sun is switched off. Mamma Zeina will have less than two minutes of natural light, and she knows this too.

Last light, she thinks. Breathes out. She'd never even hoped as far as to end her days cast in natural sunlight, and yet ... Here it is. The old sun. She remembers it from when she was a girl. Normally the punishment for being here, now, under the last rays of the old sun after curfew, Well. The punishment for this would be death. Mamma Zeina smiles wryly. And then a grimace of pain.

The sun dips and then glows behind the row of baobab trees on the long horizon, it's like an invitation, she thinks. Gives her the strength to take more steps toward it, to get clean of the shadows by the general's back door before she stumbles. Catches herself, only just, then holds there for a moment longer.

Two of the general's worst killing organisms, the slug poison and a nipping sapling, are working their way through her one hundred year old system.

Mamma Zeina is still standing. At least for now.

And then turning slowly toward the baobab.

Sees the line of the trees.

She is considering the baobab.

These great trees with roots upturned and swelling, arms outstretched toward the sky, strange limbs making curving silhouettes against the last light. Splay-fingered branches, raised up. The baobab which cannot be stopped by the desert. The baobab endures. What better plant for the Sinta mother cupboards to hold on to. We were right to choose it for our sign in The Before, Mamma Zeina tells herself. We were right about some things. You can't be sure of it all. Crosses herself, whispers 'Downbutnotout.'

The mother cupboards have endured more than most, the last one hundred years.

'Down but not out' is The Last Prayer and also the first one of the mother cupboards.

Nobody can remember what it means now, if anything, but run the words together, add strange intonations, quirks, according to the aspect of your particular congregation or family, the way they turn toward the light when they pray to the baobab, to the left or the right. Forwards or back.

There is the down bet ... Not owt

The downbutt ... Net art, the

DownbutnotOw ... Tttttttttt, sounded out at the end by a long stutter, emphasised by the swishing of birch leaves. It doesn't matter, she thinks. It ain't about how you say it, it only matters that you say it: We are down but not out.

But no matter what their creed or origin story, the mother cupboards in both tribes, the Sinta and the edge farmers, have the same singular aim of keeping the childur safe and fed through the crackdowns, the riots, the droughts, by way of a thousand ingenious small schemes. There ain't nothin' else to the mother cupboards' religion, and nor should there be if you ask a true mother cupboard. That's all, that's it, that's everything. The whole of Bavarnica ranged, it seems, against the edge farm childur. The sinta childur. And only the mother cupboards on both sides of the fence standing between the childur and long death. There's nothing simpler or more complicated than a mother cupboard's work.

Mamma Zeina looks down at her right hand. She pulls her

glove off, with some difficulty. The skin of her hand is reptilian-looking. She's been greened.

The goal of the general's greening programme has been to make the Sinta mother cupboards and other rememberers seem inhuman. Dehumanising is usually stage one before a purge, a crackdown on the rememberers on the Sinta farms. The ones who aren't taking their medicine. There aren't too many folks in Bavarnica, the general has learned, who'll risk much to defend the rights of a thing they believe isn't 'truly' human. A witch.

The greening makes the rememberers look a little reptilian, strange. Not entirely inhuman, but 'off' just enough that they make a natural target in the country lanes, where they're often stoned by a passing farmer, or on the streets of the capital city where, they say, the OneFolks might simply take a potshot at them from a high storey window. OneFolk children are told terrifying bedtime stories about witches, just to prepare their minds. They are taught to scream, 'Witch!' If they spot a little patch of green behind their nursemaid's ear or on the family gardener's thumb, a tendril of green hair twisting out from under their slave Sinta cook's headwear. There have been even worse things. Unimaginable cruelties since the greening began.

Mamma Zeina has a moss coloured tongue, which she dyes red using beetroot, whenever she can get some, and the white of her right iris, underneath her black eyepatch, is emerald coloured, crystallised and quite blind. And with the glove on her right hand, sewn so tight to prevent any slippage that she generally struggles to remove it at nightfall, it seems amazing even to her that she's remained undiscovered so far.

A Sinta rememberer, member of the mother cupboard cult here in the general's own kitchen, and for all these years. It's enough to give Gaddys the village shopkeeper a heart attack.

It has been Mamma Zeina's greatest triumph, hiding her greening. But she understands that her corpse may be a problem for those left behind her. Once the Egg Men discover she's greened, they'll try to rout anyone who has helped her. They will look for her friends. The general's paranoia has been deadly to his people many times over, and he has been obsessed with outing the mother cupboards ever since he took power.

A new pain enters her eardrum, right side. Mamma Zeina thinks about Zorry. She regrets what she's done to Zorry. No mother Cupboard relishes reseeding herself. It cannot be helped.

Mamma Zeina breathes deep on the desert air. Lifts her head up, for the last time. Her past one hundred years seem to tumble inward, memories jostling up against each other. She remembers her children's faces, every one of them, many of whom she didn't happen to have borned. There will be no tears, at the end. She tells herself. Not one. She will not allow the general any manner of victory over her, not even in dying.

Mamma Zeina asks the baobab for one last thing. At least ... she opens her mouth to speak and "Zz ..." She says. "Zz ..." Something seems to take her voice away.

She falls. Crashes heavily onto her knees, and then her chin hits the earth. She groans.

I have led with my chin all my long life. She tells herself. This thought lessens the pain that encases her skull from the impact. Her jaw is thrust forward and up. There's a slash in her tongue where she bit, there are several cracked teeth, but Mamma Zeina's borned twelve childur, including three sets of twins. Alone in a birthing hut, severed the cord with her teeth. Most of her childur were lost when the Sinta fled after the last revolution, caught hiding out in the forest or running toward the mountain. One lasted three days longer than the others, he was her youngest. Hid in the sewers and then dragged out by his heels, right in front of his mother. The others were gaoled or taken by the desert.

There has been nowhere to put the grief. The rage. Nowhere but the work.

At some point in the years after her losses, Mamma Zeina decided to go on living. To go on with her food experiments, to go on spending her nights scouring the killing forest, getting each night deeper and deeper into its dark mouth and spending her evenings with a mortar and pestle, testing pizens on herself, getting the roots and bulbs to Jengi of the plants she believes can be changed. He'll promise to plant them out by the baobab for the edge farm mother cupboards to garden. Mamma Zeina decided that as long as her body held out then she would hold out too.

Inching forwards, relentless as the desert, slow and sure as it. The mother cupboard pushes it back, death, as it comes. Push for push, step for step. The vines are winding through her and she resists them, every one.

It was in these last few years of nights spent in the mouth of the killing forest that Mamma Zeina discovered something important.

She came to understand that whilst she feels pain, she no longer fears it.

It's the single quality which has made Mamma Zeina the most dangerous mother cupboard Bavarnica has ever known. Dangerous to the general. Her light comes in at her wound.

Holding her eye toward the baobab now and the soft natural light glowing behind it, Mamma Ezray shimmies on her stomach, slow and sure toward that last light. When her legs give out then she uses her elbows. Her left elbow and right hand give up last and then she uses her chin for leverage, to get another few inches forward. These efforts get her just far enough away from the general's house that she gets to die without the sound of Gaddys in her ears, her high pitched mindless chatter, the nervous laughter of the OneFolk guests and the general's wife, who just broke out in over-pollinated great sobs and will not be consoled. The explosions of mirth and the tinkling of crystal glasses vanish.

And then Gaddys' shrill voice washing in and out like a tuneless instrument. Fading.

The desert's sound rises.

Sand dunes are moving. Spreading up and out beyond the killing forest. The desert's silence seems to expand. Cicada, rustle of spider, slow slide of snake.

One thing left to do.

One thing.

Last thing.

Mamma Zeina strains her ears toward the sound of the great nothing before her. There is the slow creak of the baobab, in time with the wind. Small rushes of sand, like a chorus.

There's a small light. At first like it's tangled in the briar, but then rising in slow uncertain movements up one branch of the lowest baobab.

At first it drifts gently up and down, the light, and then seems to pull free, the small beacon dancing down one branch, bounces to another branch below it and then drops softly. Fizzles out on the earth beneath the tree. Her mind is washing in and out of sense.

She feels the tightening spread to her throat. Soon now. She thinks.

"Did it take long to find me?" She asks the nothing.

And then rising as much as she can rise now.

Her right elbow goes from under her, cheek against the soil now. Hard soil.

Green jewel coloured beetle runs across her splayed left hand and scurries onwards, and now her left eye swivelling upward, following its line of flight. She loses sight of it quickly. And then the small light again, just at the periphery of her vision. Gently up and down. A little above the lowest branch of the smallest baobab. A new small light dances. Smoke.

I said, "Did it take long to find me?"

Now the pain gets worse.

Something comes up from Mamma Zeina's stomach, her spine ripples and arches, gargling in the back of her throat....."Zz ..." She says ... And then, "*Listen.*"

The last word comes out like a sigh, like a song.

Eyelashes clutch, unclutch the last light.

She closes her eyes.

She seems to give a shudder and then she relaxes.

The small light in the baobab blinks out. There's the sound of tinny buzzing, distant, and then someone scrabbling down the side of the baobab tree, leaping from the lowest branch,

THE PLANTING

hits the earth and then takes off, running, in the direction of the village shop.

"Damn it, Jengi." Mamma Zeina's last words.

A small green leaf is growing out of Mamma Zeina's mouth now.

The leaf seems to twitch then look up toward the sound of Zorry stumbling and hitting her shin in the shadow by the window. Nearly catching herself on the upturned row of nails along the wooden frame. She climbs down from the window ledge with skill. Narrowly avoids the edge of the moat and slips across the drawbridge quickly, into the garden. Veers right.

Zorry doesn't see the slump of Mamma Zeina's body in the shadow. She leaves her behind.

Now there's only the sound of Zorry's feet, scramble of small stones. Rhythmic beat of her running. Getting fainter. The vine twists slowly around the slumped shape of Mamma Zeina on the ground.

———

SMOKE

ZORRY IS MAKING HER way toward Jengi, now before the
feast is over. She figures it's safer to give the plant to Jengi
whilst Gaddys is safely ensconced at the feast table. Zorry
reckons she may have a chance to be minutes ahead of the
village shopkeeper. It's a bold plan, perhaps motivated in large
part by Zorry's instinct not to take such a revolutionary plant
home to the house she shares with her Mamma Ezray and
infant sister Zettie. Doesn't want to take that kind of trouble
to her own front door. Aims to get rid of the water plant as
quickly as she can.

When Zorry reaches the village shop, Jengi is waiting
in the alleyway beside it, as if expectantly. He's panting
slightly, as though he'd just been running, she thinks. And
then dismissing the thought. He is pretending to inhale on
his government smoker. Jengi has clearly been waiting for
someone.

Jengi's regulation smoker is a useful alibi as he's found
on more than one occasion when caught out after curfew by
the Egg Men. He never inhales but can do a good enough
impression of passing out with the effects of the fumes. He
has carefully cultivated his reputation as an addict, all the
better to be sure he's underestimated, passed over. Zorry
notes that he holds it well away from his face now. Drops it
and wipes his right hand on the side of his trousers, crushes

it under his foot. It goes on giving off a small light. Jengi lights another. Holds it away from him.

Zorry makes her way towards him by its small light, which lights up one side of his face. His right hand.

Jengi leans against the shop wall at an angle. Cap pulled low.

"Where is Mamma Zeina?"

Jengi has a way of asking you a question as though to test what you know. Zorry finds that sly. She sighs. She has no time for Jengi's games.

"Do you want this or not? She holds out the cup with the plant root in it.

Jengi doesn't move to touch it. "I see." He says.

"Do you, Jengi? What do you see?" And then, "Look ... I don't know why she trusts you but ..." Zorry thrusts out her hand. "Look, just take this cup from me, would you Jengi?"

Jengi conceals a small smile. Takes the cup. Touches her hand for a fleeting moment, runs his index finger down her palm.

Zorry pulls back.

Now Jengi examines Zorry by the thin light, seems to see her for the first time. Blink. "Oh! You're a bit young for a mother cupboard." Jengi looks disappointed.

"Guess I just happened to be in the wrong place when she was reseeding."

"No." Jengi gazes at Zorry, the look is more brotherly now. "Mamma Zeina must've chosen you for a reason." He looks up and seems to glance something behind her. "Now, get out of here. Scramble!" He says.

They both hear Gaddys' car pull up at the front of the shop.

Jengi thumbs toward the fence at the back of the shop, hisses, "That way!" But then catches her upper arm as she leaves. "Zorry." He says. They are eye to eye for a moment. "She's never been wrong Zorry. You are a mother cupboard now. Welcome to the resistance."

Zorry examines his face. She is thinking. It's a long, strangely unnerving moment for Jengi, the girl seems shrewd beyond her years. He blinks and she moves, sliding into the shadow beside the shop.

"Wait." He says. "Don't move yet."

Now Jengi moves toward the front of the shop, greets Gaddys with a deep bow. Takes her jewelled hand in his own as she steps from the car and doffing his hat at the same time, one sinuous motion with more than a hint of swagger to it.

"What were you doing back there?"

"Smoking, Madam. My apologies."

Gaddys smirks. Jengi kisses the shopkeeper's thick, ringed fingers.

Zorry slips noiselessly toward the fence which blocks the other end of the alleyway. She is distracted by Jengi's strange performance with Gaddys, catches her hand on the top of the fence by mistake. Curses in silence.

Zorry considers that Jengi might have mentioned the broken glass at the top of the fence.

She leaves her blood at the scene.

THE LIGHTNING BOX

ZETTIE QUIETLY SLIPPED OUT of the yard and meandered toward the schoolhouse, the way she does whenever Mamma Ezray's too exhausted from her night work, collecting plants in the killing forest, to notice that the small child playing out in the yard is too quiet, that Zettie's singing has stopped, and Ezray allows herself to drift asleep a little, head face down on the hard kitchen table. She tries to hold her eyes open for as long as she can, but then there is only the soft clucking sound of the chickens, shuffling of the wind in the pear tree in the yard, morning light filtering in through the blinds, and the half open back door, and all of it no reason at all for alarm.

Mamma Ezray's last waking thought is to tell herself that she'll only sleep for a moment. Just for a moment, before her work rota starts. And then her eyes closing softly against the smooth circles and knots in the sanded down wood. Blink, blink, and the vegetable scraps, chopping-knife scars in the wood and the hinges and joints of the table vanish. Eyelashes clutch the light, flutter and close. Her breaths get deeper and less hurried. Eyeballs twitch and move underneath her eyelids.

Zettie had, like always, climbed on to the rain barrel outside the kitchen window, to check Mamma Ezray was fully asleep before she started out on her daily expedition. If Zettie had a plan at all, then it was to be home just before Mamma wakes.

There is an transparent cage around the OneFolks'
schoolhouse now, a faraday box made of thin but strong mesh,
to protect the children from lightning strike. The OneFolk
childur inside the protective box call it Furdy. They have been
banned from going outside the Furdy during school hours
and especially when it's storming outside. But Zettie is a
Sinta. A slave girl. She is not allowed in. Not inside the Furdy,
not inside the schoolhouse. Girl. Slave. They are the most
important words in Zettie's life, coming only after the word
'Mamma', in order of importance to the child.

Zettie is only small but she knows what 'Girl' means, more
or less, but not yet what a 'Slave' is. The word seems to her to
carry a great physical weight. It has the power to darken the
kitchen, she thinks, to press down on her parents' shoulders,
eyebrows and the corners of their mouths. Even the back of
her mother's neck, so that Mamma Ezray's head sinks a little,
under its weight. Some days the word seems to have more
power over Mamma Ezray than other days, so Zettie knows
that it can rise or sink and bide its time. It is a word which
cannot be said at home, not once the evening fire's lit. A
taboo. As if the home fire protects them all from the word, for
a while.

"I will not have that word in this house." Mamma Ezray
intones daily. But the word is always waiting for them, outside,
the way Zettie sees it. It's the shadow beside the front door,
it crosses the mat and zigzags the front porch. Zettie has
also noticed that the OneFolk childur use it freely. The word
seems to Zettie to relate to the fact that she is not allowed
inside the protection of the Furdy now. Not even when the
thunder seems to roll right underneath her, shake the bushes.

The word has great power, she knows it keeps the Furdy gate closed.

Zettie watches the gate. Feels the first rumbles of thunder. And then a cracking sound, like the earth splits behind her. Sound of heavy rainfall, her own heartbeat in her ears.

The OneFolk childur huddle underneath the sheltered area, in the inner section of the Furdy which butts against the schoolhouse. The childur watch Zettie. They have been told not to open the gate and it does not occur to any of them to break the most important school rule. Not even for a small girl in a lightning strike. After all ... She's a slave. Isn't she?

Zettie squats on her heels outside the mesh cage of the Furdy, hugging on to its dripping sides with her small, gently pudgy infant arms when the lightning cracks and cracks again behind her. She shivers so much that her vision blurs a little, rain beats against the small curve of her back.

The word has not yet filtered under Zettie's skin, but she feels it close by. And in the way that even a small child can understand the thing, Zettie has understood this. Even when she's playing alone outside, she senses the word is there playing close by also. Like something dangerous and obscene in the shadow. When the word becomes quite silent, then it's worse. That's when Zettie is most afraid that in an absentminded moment she has somehow allowed the word to slip inside her. She imagines that it would enter in the same way that the poisonous plants in the killing forest, the ones that Mamma Ezray talks about over supper, slow plants that seem only to nip your ankles just a little, but their vines thicken and grow in your bloodstream. Trace their way, slow, to your heart.

Other days Zettie imagines that the word would get into her when she breathes, and so be more like the smoke from Gaddys' furnace, which Mamma Ezray informs Zettie is pure pizen, so don't ever breath in, if you happen to be passing it when Jengi's cooking back there. Zettie holds her breath when she thinks about the furnace, without quite realising that she does so. One thing the child knows for sure, the word must never be allowed in, the way it has gotten into some of the older Sinta children already. Like they've weights in their limbs, and small weights running over their bodies, from ear tips down to elbows, spine, knees, feet.

The child wiggles her fingers and toes each morning, checks the palms of her hands, and even her tiny right thumb before she pops it into her mouth. Checks it's free of the word. Understands without being told that the word might seem innocent enough in your mouth, but once there it might kill, maim, or worse. Just like any pizen. For herself, she has only ever said the word once. She had asked the question of Mamma Ezray, 'What's a slave?' But Mamma Ezray hadn't found a way to answer. Simply turned and gazed at her child.

The OneFolk childur huddle together in the sheltered area inside the Furdy. Watch Zettie shiver outside the lightning box. The childur's eyes are as wide Zettie's, watching her outside the Furdy. Clinging on through the storm. "Slave." Zettie hears, and she turns her head toward the word. "Don't let It in," she hears the small OneFolk boy say. Zettie, meeting the small boy's eye, believes she knows just what he means. She thinks it's nice that the boy understands too. What *it* is. That *it* is dangerous.

The Furdy looks invisible from the inside, but from the

outside, where Zettie sits, seems like a black box. All corners and angles. Small. She can see inside only when she presses her small face against the sides or the roof.

Zettie feels sorry for the childur playing inside when the wind is up and nature moves around her, bugs fly past. And yet the children in the black box fascinate the infant, draw her to the box every morning when Mamma Ezray thinks she's playing with the chickens in the yard.

When the rain has slowed to a stop, Zettie watches a lizard crawling up the inside of the mesh sides of the Furdy, there's one on the outside of the box too. Both lizards pause a moment, seem to eye each other sideways. And then, *blink*, the smaller lizard vanishes.

Now Zettie notices tiny water droplets hanging through the surface of the lightning cage. Zettie is thirsty and she puts her lips against the mesh, tasting the water. Tastes of metal, now, and tin. Something else you can't describe, the something that all things appear to taste of lately. The lizard on the inside of the mesh watches Zettie curiously as she drinks, and so do the OneFolk childur.

Zettie doesn't see the smaller lizard has come back until it scatters from a large drop of water, falling from a palm leaf just to her left. She follows its trail, finds it concealed under a fallen palm leaf. The tiny creature has scootered into the gentle rot near the stem, which now leans against Zettie's small left foot. She looks at the lizard for a while, doesn't move. Just once she wiggles her toes, to gauge the lizard's reaction. Nothing. The little lizard tilting its small head up first left and then, swivelling a little, tips it right. As though it watches her too, fearless. Zettie blinks at it, smiles.

The last scattering of rain makes a map of lines down the leaves around Zettie's face, drips out of the ringlets in her hennaed hair. Some trickles down over her forehead. She wipes the clean sleeve of her dress across her eyes. And now Zettie is tilting her small round face up first left and then right, she's mimicking the lizard. And then pushing back her straggle of rust coloured hair to see the small critter better. Carefully lifts the leaf stem and one corner of the dark waxen leaf, peers underneath it.

All Sinta have eyes that change colour, but Zettie's mostly stay the same, she reckons. When Zettie looked into the cracked hallway mirror this morning, before breakfast, her eyes were brown with a small patch of sky-blue. From the small lizard's eye-view, Zettie's huge eyes appearing in the gap, seem to grow. Two wide, amazed, tawny-coloured eyes with one blue patch in the left eye. Never blinking, or never seeming to blink.

The lizard blinks first. Shifts slightly, whips its small tale. It's a tiny gesture that only a child as observant as Zettie would have noticed. And then its throat looping in and out like a small red flag about the size of a copper coin, or a large coffee bean. She waits until the small throat-flag has stopped flashing.

"Is you a pizen lickle lickle?" Soft clucking sounds, nonsense words and rhythmic, the child has learned to make certain noises when creeping up on small creatures. Senses how to sooth their minds. Now she gently reaches her small left hand out. Strokes one tiny index finger along the underside of the lizard's chin. The tiny reptile eyes her. Now she remembers its teeth. Pulls back her hand and holds it close to her shirt.

"You oughta scurry." She gently admonishes the lizard now. And then, "Is you a pizen or ain'tcha?" She asks it, soft, small, reasonable voice. The reptile makes no reply. Swivelling its eyes in her direction. Eyes her beadily for a long time.

Something happens. It's as though Zettie feels her hunger only then, all of it, at once, hunger screwed to the sticking point when it's pain and before it's quite starvation. Her small hand shoots out. Catches the tiny lizard expertly, wriggle, wriggle, squeeze, and then she squeezes harder. Before she's had time to think about it, she's stuffed the small lizard into her mouth, bit down hard, spat out its head, one more wriggle, crunch, crunch, the child kills the creature quick and mercifully, the way her sister Zorry taught her. And then she chews it slow. Careful, she thinks. Feeling small claws on her tongue, spitting them.

It tastes not unlike dried meat. Although not quite so salty, she thinks. Once she breaks through its small tough hide. A bit like chewing down hard on a leather shoe, and with just a small drop of moisture, that's the guts, which Zettie also spits, and she gags then forces herself to swallow the rest of the lizard.

She leaves the tail in her cheek, feels it alongside her teeth, briefly, before she opens her mouth, lets it drop into her hand. She examines her teeth with her tongue. Zettie herself can't quite comprehend what just happened, as though the thing happened to her instead of because of her, as though she had played no part in it.

"Zettie ate a whole lizard from head to tail root." A small freckled boy pulls a face.

"Aye. I saw that. Good one, Zettie. How was that?" Asks

a droll little girl with one long black plait, trying to climb the inside of the lightning box and failing. Squashes her nose against the mesh. The children are pretty impressed.

Zettie is still feeling her teeth with her tongue, doesn't speak and in a bit the curious girl flicks her black plait over her shoulder, turns away. Not bad at all, Zettie is thinking. "Not nearly as bad as you might think," she tells the girl, mimicking the words of her older sister Zorry. The words she's so fond of saying whenever trying to persuade her small sister Zettie to eat some unspeakable food item which the family have been allocated. One second, two, and Zettie's hunger is gone.

"You can't say if things are pizen right away." The girl with the long black plait advises her.

"I know that." Zettie says. Pushing out her chin slightly. That much Zettie's Mamma Ezray has already taught her. Zettie waits. "Nothing." She says to the girl, who smiles shyly. And in a bit Zettie pads around, looking under the leaves for another one.

"Oh, that's hunger," says a voice that seems to come from above and behind the lightning cage, and both at the same time. Big voice, Zettie thinks. There's a deep rumbling chuckle. Zettie identifies an older edge farm boy whom she thinks she's seen before. She looks down at his large, boney feet and then up at his protruding collar bone which, apart from his face and hair, are the only parts of the boy which are not covered by his shiny black edge farm uniform. He looks as though he works the mines from the state of his bare feet and neck and the sides of his hands which are all dust encrusted. She notices the patched up wound one side of his head and the homemade sling on his left arm. When he slides, one armed, down from the top of the lightning cage, Zettie looks briefly panicked.

Looking down through the mesh, Tomax had seen the whole thing. The trail, the hunt, the capture. Seen Zettie eating the forbidden creature.

"You were pretty nifty, catching that critter." He says.

For the first time it occurs to Zettie to feel proud of her action. The OneFolk childur had mostly looked grossed out, apart from the girl with the long black plait, who was kind.

"Don't worry," he says, getting caught briefly on a corner edge of the cage by the batwing sleeve of his edge farm uniform, and then sitting himself down cross-legged beside Zettie. Getting comfortable. Looking at her expectantly then, as though he waits for her to continue the conversation.

Zettie pulls out the lizard tail to show him. Neither speak at first. And then, "Generally 'taint advisable to eat a lizard, Sinta, but I guess you know what you're doing."

He adds, "Hope you don't get a pizen in your stomick. Eating escapees from the killing forest ain't a great plan, little Sinta. Leastways cook it first next time, eh?"

Zettie doesn't respond. She feels strangely offended. The boy seems to understand this and he's quiet for a while. And in a bit, Zettie says, "My name ain't Sinta, and I ain't 'little' neither, Edge Farm." She feels confident enough in him that it feels safe to be cross.

That low, rumbling chuckle again. "Well my name ain't Edge Farm, Sinta." Grins. Puts out his hand to shake hers. "I'm Tomax," he says, and Zettie notices that he puffs himself up just a little, when he says his own name. And then thumbing toward his chest, as though to underline himself in her mind. She decides right away that she likes him.

Thunder growls behind Tomax, then a lightning crack and the rain stops. Zettie puts the two things together in her mind, the thunder and Tomax. She notices that he doesn't seem to be afraid of lightning. "What's your name, Sinta?"

Little Zettie grins shyly. Doesn't speak now. She has so far always clung to the Furdy when the lightning cracks. She decides now that she will never do so again, but just sit calm and cross legged in the shrubs, the way that the boy does.

Zettie holds out the lizard tail toward him now and lets him take it from her. Tomax examines it, as though with admiration, hands it back. "If you don't get a pizen then reckon you ought to tell your folks about that critter. Oughta spread the word. I mean ... There are plenty of them critters, see 'em everywhere."

And then, "I ain't never gotten a pizen," Zettie says proudly. "I can digestify most about anything I reckon." Zettie thinks she feels something small moving beneath her feet. Something burrowing. She peers down at the shrub. It seems to shake a little.

"You'll be alright then," Tomax says.

"Yes." She says. "I will." Looking up. And then seems to remember something. "I'm Zettie." She says. Now Zettie pops the lizard tail into her apron pocket. Rubs her tummy. "My stomick feels just fine." Zettie stretches out the last two words, soft upturn at the end, like a rhyme, like a song, like a question. She has learned to speak musically, like all of Mamma Ezray's bedtime stories. Giggles.

"My Mamma Ezray is teaching me to talk like music."

"Is that so?"

"Yep. Tiz."

"Ah well, there's still time to get a pizen, Zettie." Tomax says, concern in his voice. "Be careful not to get a pizen. For myself, I don't eat nothing what scuttles." He looks at her, to check her understanding. "It's by way of a personal rule."

"What do you eat then?" Zettie looks at Tomax with interest.

"Crows eggs. Other scavenging birds. Vulture's eggs taste sour and rotten, even when they ain't. I don't eat those unless I'm clean 'bout starving."

"Aren't you afraid of the crows ..."

"Yep. I am kindly afraid of the egg's mamma, Zettie. But not so afraid of a crow so much as I am afraid of starving to death." Grins again.

Zettie thinks for a moment. "You is a good climber then?"

"Yep. I suppose."

Zettie thinks about the taloned feet of the giant crows, the vultures, and the other scurvy, hybrid scavenging birds that come after the general's drones hit. They have been known to roof on the busted up top of the school house, in the peaceful periods when there are no bombs or drones, no riots and smoking piles of human bodies for them to feast on. In the peaceful times between the rain dances, the crows watch the OneFolk children inside the Furdy.

Zettie tells Tomax about the day when she only just got away in time and was saved by the school security manager, thrusting out a hand, gripping her collar and pushing her into the shed which held the spare generator. This story seems to surprise Tomax. Especially when Zettie then goes on to tell him that the school security manager had used his club on the birds, which is technically speaking illegal, as the birds are government property. Now that she has his full attention, she tells Tomax how the school security manager had said, "You hold my life in your hands now, Child, so what's it to be?"

"And what did you say to that, Zettie?"

"Mmmm. Can't remember." Zettie pops her thumb in her mouth. She is remembering that there was a cobweb in the corner of the cupboard that the school security manager had shoved her into. That she'd been as scared of the spider she couldn't see as much as she'd been 'fraid of the cawing and scrapping birds outside.

Zettie has not told anyone but Tomax about all this. Not even Zorry knows, but there is something about the boy that makes you want to confide. She smiles up at Tomax.

Now her small face darkens. She is thinking about the birds' hard curved toes. The sharp tipping end of their beaks. Their squawking, flapping, scrapping. She had thought, that day, that she glimpsed rows of small teeth in their beaks. She decides to ask Tomax about this, seeing as he is a good listener, seems to know some useful things.

"Birds don't have teeth. Do they?" She asks Tomax. Shudders. And then, "Reckon the birds might eat me iffen I tried to get eggs like you do."

Tomax looks into the child's wide, amazed eyes. He thinks quickly. "Yes. Second thoughts, Zettie, you stick to lizards. Leave them crow eggs 'til you've growed a bit. Then I'll teach you to catch 'em." Grins again.

Zettie decides right away that Tomax is good. Or rather, she has decided that she really likes him, which amounts to about the same thing in the small girl's mind. She breathes out. Maybe she won't dream about the crows again tonight, or wake up in a sweat the way she has every night since that close shave.

Zettie thinks she hears a rustling underneath her again, as though something in the shrub still insists on being noticed. She gets up slowly from her crouched position, pads around, looking. The child has learned to move without making the bushes come alive and the ground crackle with the sound of her. "Nothing." She says. She can't see what's making the sound. Tomax shrugs, shows her his palms. He doesn't know either. He seems to be getting up to go, only Zettie isn't done conversing with him.

"Watch this." Zettie says. Trying to hold his attention for a little longer.

"Okay."

Zettie makes it a point of honour now, in front of Tomax, to climb the side of the Furdy without making the bushes beside it tremble. Her face is pressed so close to the mesh that the changing light makes patterns running down her, making her seem strange, even a little alarming to the children inside. Her shadow appears on the dusty floor of the playground underneath the Furdy.

"That one. She bit down on a lizard just now," an older girl says, pointing Zettie out to the girl with the long plait, and, had she only known it, using her own mother's best disapproving voice. Shudders. "That Sinta creature." She says.

"That's Zettie." The girl with the long plait replies. It's a small reproach. "She's hungry." She pauses, examines the first girl's face. "She's just a hungry little girl, that's all, ain't you ever been hungry, Cinda?"

"No. I ain't never." The first girl scowls, as though the question itself were an insult.

A stone flies pasts the girls' ears.

"Stop it, Luco."

The small boy inside the Furdy throws another stone now. This one hits its target, the mesh near Zettie's head but Zettie, for now at least, still holds firm to the belief that all folks are more or less friendly. This is something that the Sinta like to teach their childur when they're small. Zettie smiles sweetly now. As if the OneFolk boy played a neat joke. She smiles so sweetly at him, eager to join in this game too, any game, that the girl who'd called Zettie 'Creature' just now, becomes ashamed. "You can't throw stones at little folks," she says. Yanking the boy's arm quite hard at the shoulder. "Let her alone." She says now, shifting her outrage toward him. She smoothes her apron, glares. "Ain't cha ... Zettie?"

Zettie thinks for a moment, and then, "No." Zettie says. Squashes her button nose flat against the mesh. Eyeing the older girl. "I'm very extremely big."

"Oh. Hmmm. That so." The big girl pulls her knitting out of her pocket.

"What's that?"

"Finger knitting." Says the girl. "Now don't mither me, Sinta."

The girl with the long plait sits down cross legged beside her friend, watches her thread and loop.

"I ain't mithering." Zettie says quietly, but the two OneFolk girls are ignoring her now, not unkindly.

"Who taught you that?"

"My Sinta nursemaid."

"Teach it to me."

Zettie is pleased at how things are turning out today. Her stomach is full and various things seem less frightening than they did. Birds. Lightning. Big girls. Lizards. And she's made at least one new friend, maybe more. She turns and suns herself, lying flat on her back on the roof of the Furdy. Her arms are outstretched. The world seems to her to swim above her. The general's sun rolls across the sky like an absurdly giant pumpkin, luminous pink lines scribbling up the sky right behind. She turns onto her stomach. Taps the cage softly, one small finger.

The children inside the Furdy blink. Look up at Zettie, and in a bit jumping in and out of her shadow, giggling. She hears someone start calling her name. And then someone else is gently rattling the sides of the lightning cage, at first it's just to encourage Zettie to come down. Zettie notices that Tomax looks worried. She looks away quickly.

"Come down before the teacher sees you, Zettie." But then, as more children join in, the rattling gets a little harder, a little less gentle.

Something happens.

The stone-throwing boy, humiliated about his yanked arm, rattles the cage hard and then, taking a run up at it, throws his small body into the side of the Furdy. Zettie slips down a little. She hears someone say Stop and then, squinting, sees the two big girls put down their knitting and get up quickly, they lock arms and hold themselves against the side of the Furdy, saying Stop, stop, but the rattling grows worse. Now it's impossible to tell who in the crowd is shaking the sides, and who's trying to hold the Furdy steady. Zettie's holding onto its edge, by small fingers slippy with mud, Tomax is getting up to help her but he's still too far and one-armed with his sling, and now Zettie's grip is slipping. There are yells of "Do it, do it!" and more screams of "Stop, stop, the baby's falling, STOP!" Zettie slips three inches, grabs a foothold. She looks down and sees the children's faces upturned. The girl with the plaited hair is splayed against the inside of the Furdy, gripping the earthen floor of the playground with her toes. Her body is stiff, face dark red with her effort to hold the Furdy steady. Two small boys are banging her fingers with stones. She is crying loud, full-bodied, despairing sobs. Cinda is throwing herself against a wall of shaven headed boys to reach her friend, punching heads and taking blows, making the Furdy shake dangerously.

Zettie looks down at the long drop beneath her. The world seems to her to be moving slow and strange. She feels herself hovering somewhere outside of herself. Zettie freezes. She holds on.

Someone is calling her name. She doesn't dare turn toward the sound.

Tomax is stumbling through the scrubby bushes at the base of the Furdy, getting his left foot tangled in thorns, cursing quietly, catching his batwing sleeve on the corner of the Furdy again. Zettie, paralysed by fear, is making no attempt to climb to a safer position. She just hangs on, waiting for Tomax. The trusting and amazed expression never leaves her face. The child waits patiently for everything to be alright. Tomax curses, rips his sleeve, and tears his skin on the wire edge. Reaches out his one good arm as far as he can toward her. He can't get a hold of anything but her foot. For a moment Zettie is fully exposed. "Hold," he tells her sharply, "Hold fast."

The children have stopped moving. Some watch the edge farm boy as though they're openly rooting for him. The playground is completely silent.

The small boy who started the rattling gets a strange look on his face. A muscle in his jaw moves, grits his teeth. His little sister beside him, having seen this look before, seems to understand what he's about to do before the boy knows it himself. She moves quickly, pulls his hair and his ear, twists the fingers of his left hand, and now digging her stubby fingernails into the soft flesh under his chin and by his left ear, holds him back from throwing himself into the side of the Furdy. He's bigger, stronger, and it takes every single thing she has to stop him. The boy flails his fists at his sister, strains toward the side of the box.

Now the two small siblings roll and scrap on the floor, creating a distraction long enough for Tomax to get a foothold in a branch by the Furdy, take a hold of Zettie's right elbow. By the time the small boy is sitting on his sister's stomach, throwing punches at her face, Tomax has got a hold of Zettie underneath one armpit, helped her painfully down.

The knitting girl, Cinda, pulls the boy off his sister, "Don't. Hit." She says. He looks down at her bruised, scuffed up knuckles. Blood under several of her fingernails. "No, ma'am."

She takes a hold of his left ear, twists it hard.

Tomax takes a breath. He turns to Zettie. "Don't climb that thing again."

"I won't." Zettie gets the words out, sounding shocked.

"Now go home, Zettie. Might see you tomorrow, iffen I'm passing." Tomax looks up toward the school security manager, heading toward him around the outside of the Furdy. He scratches his shaven head, smiles. For an edge farm boy in the wrong part of the village, Tomax doesn't seem unduly alarmed.

Zettie stands up, looks in the direction of home. She still feels strangely detached from herself, looking down at her feet. Wonders if her feet will know the route without her.

The small rattling boy slopes off to a corner of the Furdy to sulk. Hold his pinched ear with both hands and gazing menacingly at his younger sister, who, sitting down cross legged now, between the two knitting girls, pokes out the tip of her tongue.

Zettie trails her fingertips along the mesh side of the Furdy, behind the three girls, tap, tap, *tap* on their cage. Very gently. The small girl squints up at her, smiles shyly.

"Bye, Zettie." Says the girl with the long plait. "See you tomorrow." The big girl doesn't look up from her knitting. Threads and loops. The colours slowly merge, fan out under her hands.

"You're quicker than me. What you making, Mezan?"

"Dunno, Cinda. S'gonna be good though." Sniffs. There's a soft knot in the wool. She rubs her round nose. And then examining Zettie's footprints by the gate.

CAT

"BE CAREFUL, CAT." SOMEONE says. Sliding in through the Furdy gate beside her and then shutting it carefully behind.

"I'm Zettie."

"Cat."

Zettie visited the Furdy twice yesterday, just after first light and then again in the last light of evening, when it was cool enough to venture outdoors. When Zettie appears again this morning, first she carefully eyes the beribboned plait nailed to the gate of the Furdy. And then she peers in.

"Cat, cat." She hears.

At first Zettie can't imagine they can mean her. She checks the grass behind her. But some of the OneFolk childur have, as it turns out, decided that Zettie is due for a name-change. Hence 'Cat'.

Zettie, who is just four droughts old this season, by no means buys into the Bavarnican idea that cats are vermin, and she likes the flying caracal cat most of all. Mamma Ezray had to chase one away from the chickens only last night and Zettie had examined the creature with pleasure. The long stripes running down the cat's body, its huge pointed ears. And yet ... something about being called Cat bothers the child. Zettie thinks about this.

The mood here is different this morning, that's clear. Last night Zettie had most about convinced herself that the thing didn't happen. She'd spent the night, hands over her ears, and in the morning she told herself she'd forgot. Zettie shook herself and put it all away like that.

But Zettie does remember.

She presses her face against the mesh of the Furdy, peers in. She looks down at the playground. Zettie notices the scorched ground where the flat rocks were lit and heated. Leaving a black trail in the dust after it was all cleared away. The rain makes rivulets now, in the scorched ground and looking across the small covered yard, Zettie finally understands that what happened yesterday evening underneath the Furdy was real. Yesterday seems to get realer the longer she looks. There is a cold feeling spreading out from the base of Zettie's stomach. It seems to seep up toward her throat.

Yesterday a small group of the older OneFolk children inside the Furdy had tried to poke Zettie food through the gaps at supper time, even though sharing food is strictly against Bavarnica's most important regulations. No one could quite remember who had the banned thought first or who it was decided to act on the thing, but like they looked down at their supper together, saw Zettie watching them eat. Three children had the same thought at the same time, 'Let's share.'

Anyway, the gaps in the mesh were too small to pass anything through, as it happened. Zettie watched the OneFolk childur try with the strange amazed expression she is known for. She had appreciated their intention, though it seemed like a shame, she had thought then, to waste it. Zettie had seen from the start that their efforts were doomed. The size of the food and the holes in the mesh. But she'd gotten caught up like the childur in the intensity of the game, the way they'd worked together, some playing look out. The boy who had rattled the fence yesterday morning was, by the evening, a turncoat. Threatening to tell on his schoolmates at the mesh, and he was pinned down and sat on by his younger sister and two small friends. Other childur had joined in, taking sides. It had been a small playground insurrection. It was only just before playtime ended that the OneFolk childur trying to share had admitted defeat. The Furdy itself stood between them.

"I can't do it. I can't get the food through. She's going to starve." Said the girl with the long plait. A tall thin boy with white hair examined the gate, kicked the side of the cage.

That last act was what had brought the school's security manager and the class teacher outside, the teacher was holding her clipboard, taking names. "What are you children doing with your food?" Zettie had crept into the shrubs just outside the Furdy and watched.

"It's just ... It's just decoration." Said the girl with the long plait, suddenly inspired.

The teacher took a pair of scissors out, hacked off her plait at the base of her neck.

"Don't lie, Mezan."

Apparently the class teacher and the school's security manager had seen the whole thing from an upstairs window. They'd not even missed the boy with the over-tight uniform collar and the anxious face who appeared to have assigned himself the post of look-out. He'd looked at every window, every shadow and leafy corner, looking for a face or a camera. Only he hadn't looked up.

"That's a lesson you won't forget in a hurry, eh Zinko?" The school security manager said, somewhat ambiguously. And then seemed to point at the brim of his hat. The boy blinked. And then noticed it.

Behind the school security manager was the school security camera, like a blinking red-lit eye on a stilt. Blended with the small red flowers on the vine which crept along the school wall, you wouldn't see it at all, unless you knew where to look.

The security manager's office window is just above the camera. He decides what camera footage to keep and what's safe to delete, according to the general's instructions. Ghost of a wink. The boy had examined the security manager's face with a soft, amazed expression. Blinked.

When the children had all gone in, Zettie had stared at the mushed splats of food on the mesh. She looked to sharpen a twig small enough to poke through the mesh, grab back bits of the wasted food, but nothing worked. She did not expect it to. Eyed the forlorn shiny plait pinned to the gate. The ribbon still in it.

Zettie had stayed hidden in the scrubby plants beside the Furdy when three of the schoolchildren were made an example of about an hour later: Mezan, the girl with the long plait hacked off and black hair falling into her face, looked sullen, tear stained. Clinging to her side was the tiny freckled girl, Ezmay, who'd taken on her own older brother in order to save Zettie from falling off the Furdy and was now, in Zettie's mind and her own, a firm and lifelong friend of Zettie's. Joined by blood, scratched up knees and their matching bruises.

The tall, white-haired boy, Zetan, stood apart from the two OneFolk girls. Zettie remembered his grim determined face when he'd tried to help get the food through, help as though his own life somehow depended on it. The playground leader looked younger now, beaten in the presence of the teacher.

"What is *she*?"

"A slave. A nothing. A wild critter." The three OneFolk childur repeated robotically, looking down.

"And?"

"Sharing is dangerous." That toneless chorus again. The white haired boy had glanced up.

The two older children were punished the worst.

Later, the teacher had reminded all the OneFolk childur of the punishments involved in sharing food. The childur with an instinct to share food with a small hungry girl, and the courage to do something about it, were made an example out of. Were made to walk a line of hot rocks in front of their classmates. Not so hot they'd break the skin but enough to cause pain. The humiliation of tears.

"You've got to breed the sharing out of 'em early," the teacher had whispered to the school security manager who'd nodded sternly. "Yes." He'd said, turning toward her, seeming to take her in with a glance, "You must remind children that mercy is wrong." And then eyed the teacher cautiously to see how she took this. She didn't appear to have heard what he meant, only what he said. Scratch of her pen across her clipboard. Taking down the names of the three scapegoats.

The school security manager had taken down names also, Zettie had noticed this much. Well, not so much names as faces. He seemed to carefully note the girl with the hacked off hair, the white haired boy, tiny freckled girl. And then shifted his eyes gently left, as though he takes his thoughts and deposits them somewhere inside. Zettie has seen Mamma

Ezray do this trick many times. Sinta cannot write
things down, it's not safe. But there are other ways to
remember.

Zettie is still staring at the fence, the seared ground from
yesterday, food still stuck to the fence, dried out now, she is
letting herself remember. Trying to think what it means. She
tries to find the words to frame the feeling. Thinks for a while.

When Tomax appears at Zettie's left elbow, without making
her startle, it's as though he simply grew from the bush. The
first thing Zettie tells him is surreal, as far as he's concerned,
"I ain't a cat, I am a little girl." She says.

Tomax blinks. And then leaning forward intently, as though
he is trying to figure it. All of it. He grins. "What sort of cat
aren't you?"

Zettie draws herself up to her full height. "I aren't *any* sort."

Tomax sniffs. And then, with a sudden intuition, "I like
caracals best." He checks Zettie's face for a sign. "Those cats
can fly."

Zettie looks sour. "Mamma Ezray says they only jump."

"Oh. But still ..." Tomax smiles. And then eyes her, nodding
as though he believes in everything that Zettie said and even
the things she didn't find a way to say yet. Somehow conveys
to her that these unsaid things will also be good. This seems
to help Zettie to contain what she's feeling. She's quiet for a
while. Sucks her thumb.

And in a bit, "Yep, caracals are the best sort of jumping cat,
I reckon." Tomax stares down at the palms of his hands.

Zettie feels her indignation rising, checks his face. He's still
examining his hands intently. And then, "Look, Edge Farm."
She says, cheering up. "Loooooook!" Shows him the soft lined

palm of her tiny hand. Zettie wriggles her fingers. "Hum-ing bean," she says.

Tomax pulls a face. "That's ... Disappointing."

Zettie giggles.

"Nah, you is a ... Cat." Tomax teases her now. "A little girl would have fell offen the Furdy that morning, fell offen and clean died. You must've held on with your claws."

The infant examines her own hand again, just as though she's checking. And then looking up at the edge farm boy with a wide eyed amazed expression. Scowls suddenly. "I ain't a cat. Edge boy." She says. Bursts into tears.

Tomax is sorry right away. "I was teasing, I'm ... The OneFolks' teacher is half-crazed, Zettie. You can't ..."

Zettie's sister Zorry is coming up behind them. When Zettie sees Zorry she stops. Now she smirks at Tomax as if to say, 'You're in trouble now, Edge Boy.' Tomax puts his hands up, mock surrender. Zettie has stopped crying just as suddenly as she started. She's looking up expectantly at Zorry. Wipes her face. It takes her a moment to realise how much trouble she's in.

"What the hell are you doing here, Zettie? And who in the damned unholy is *he*?" Zorry says, indicating Tomax with an angry flourish. Zettie ignores the question. She has noticed that her sister Zorry's hand is bandaged and that she holds it to her chest defensively, as though she's in pain. There is a little blood at the edge of the home made bandage. The child frowns.

Now Zorry's voice becomes harder. The child's not even listening to me, she thinks. This seems worse. "Tribes ain't to s'posed to mix," Zorry addresses this to Tomax. "Aren't you on a list already? Are you trying to get this little child in trouble, Edge Farm?"

"Sorry." Tomax says. Meaning it. "I didn't think."

Zorry relents a little. "Tribes don't mix," she says again, and this time she means it as a warning.

"Got it." Tomax says wryly. Meets Zorry's eye. Now Zorry tries not to notice Tomax's white toothed grin, his warm irisless eyes or the way that his black eyelashes curl up at the corners. Blinks. Zorry turns away, scooping up Zettie and in one sinuous motion plopping her small sister on to her shoulders. Zettie looks unsurprised, holds on tightly, expertly. Smiling weakly at Tomax, "Goodbye."

Tomax nods. Doesn't speak.

Zettie is still watching Tomax as they're turning the corner of the schoolhouse. At the last moment, before they pass out of sight, Tomax gives Zettie a wave. She waves back happily.

"Ignore that edge farm boy." Zorry reproaches. "And stop talking to the OneFolk childur whilst you're at it, Holy Baobab Zettie, kindly stop conversing with folks outside your own tribe. "

Zettie pulls her thumb out long enough to ask the question. "Why?"

"Why? Oh, I give up on you. Because the general said so, and because it can only end in trouble, Zettie. Even for a littl'un like you, and you wouldn't want Mamma to be punished for it, would you? Mamma or me?"

"No." The child furrows her brow. Checks her nose is still there with the wet end of her thumb.

"No. I wouldn't."

"Well then."

Zettie watches the hedgerows bobbing past her. The fences and wires and the bullet riddled farm buildings. It's as though the child sees the scene for the first time in her life. Things blur and change. Now she hears voices behind her. Something that sounds to her like singing.

And now, taking a hold of Zettie firmly, Zorry shifts her. "Sit up straight, Child, you are a weight on my shoulders."

"Sorry." Says Zettie absent-mindly. Doesn't move.

It is only minutes before the whistle will go for curfew and Bavarnica's childur are coming out of their schools and workplaces. Zettie turns, watches them trickle out from the buildings around her.

The children are all headed most about the same way, as far as Zettie can see. Toward the egg farms and the Sinta cabbage patch-sized allotments, the copses and cottages at the edge of the fence and the steel trap farms beside them. Some toward the OneFolk houses in the heart of the village.

"Stop turning to look at the childur, Zettie. You're plain hurting me now."

Zettie feels bad. She's already wondering if Zorry's bandaged hand is her fault. On account of the way she's been making friends all over. Now she tries to only face forwards on Zorry's shoulders, but she's too curious, can't. She keeps shifting to look. Zorry doesn't set her down, she wants to get home fast to deliver Zettie. Zorry has somewhere else to be after the whistle goes. Some place which occupies her mind fully just now.

The Egg Boys from their training grounds, Zettie thinks, barefooted Sinta from the OneFolks' kitchens, the dirt encrusted edge farm childur who work the gem mines, let out

now with the OneFolk schoolchildren, all to beat the curfew.
Zettie takes a careful note of their different uniforms, she
looks down at her own dress. It's mossy and covered in grass
streaks and dust from her playing. Now she thinks she hears
her name being called, "Zzz ..." Zettie turns toward the sound.
Can't see where it came from.

Zettie is an eye-catching child, and the childur behind
her get a closer look at small Zettie whenever she turns. She
certainly has an appealing but unusual appearance. Expansive,
wild ringlets of hennaed hair, button nose and huge amazed
eyes. A skin so luminous she could be any tribe in Bavarnica or
none.

Those who've worked a rota or two at the general's house
say Zettie looks like the general's wife. A small Sinta girl
comes close enough to note Zettie's quite mismatched eyes,
tawny coloured with a hint of yellow-green when you look
closer, on the left side, and so dark that the right eye seems
almost irisless. But then there's the blue patch, the small girl
thinks, in the upper right hand corner of it. It's like the break
in Autumn trees, like a patch of sky. Zettie and the small Sinta
girl grin sheepishly at each other.

Zettie is near to sleep now, with the lolloping and hypnotic
rhythm of Zorry's striding. She's hunched over Zorry's head
and legs tipping slightly over the back of Zorry's shoulders, so
that Zorry has to reach out her right hand to catch her when
sleep finally takes her. Supports the child from behind now,
with both hands. Zettie is washing in and out of sleep, she is
close to dreaming.

Even though Zorry says the tribes don't mix, Zettie can
feel the mixing, rhythm and notes of the childur's movements

behind her, ghostly winks and soft evasions, nudges and averted gazes, squabbles and scraps, scratching heads and grinning. Zettie can feel the dance, hear the music. Smiling softly in her near-sleep now. Blink and blink. Now Zorry feels the child's head droop, loll against the top of her head. Zettie's sleep-dribble dampens Zorry's left ear.

Zorry slips Zettie off her shoulders and secures her in the knotted loop of her shawl. Now Zettie's small dark head dips and slides against her older sister's shoulder. Zorry supports the child's head with her bandaged left hand.

"You hungry Zettie?" Zorry asks when Zettie wakes a little. There's a small indent in the side of Zettie's face from Zorry's apron strap. Zorry laughs at her.

"You got stripes."

"Nah ... umm," Zettie says. Still too sleepy to make real words. And then, "No I haven't." Quite indignant. She looks down at the hand gripping her under her right arm now. Zettie can't take her eyes off her sister's bandage. Zorry's hurt hand still troubles the infant. She stares down at the hand.

"Make it all better," she says.

"Ah, that's nice. Yes, Mamma Ezray will have a nice potion for my hand, won't she?"

"Yes," Zettie says, pleased at the thought. And then, small worried frown, "Do it hurt some?"

Zorry gazes down at Zettie's small upturned face. "No, not at all." Zorry lies and Zettie notices Zorry wince when she moves the shawl to readjust Zettie's position.

Zorry thinks of something.

"How come you ain't never hungry when I ask you, Zettie?"

Zettie reaches down and pulls a lizard tail out of her apron pocket, thrusts it at Zorry's face to show her.

"Zettie!" her sister is shocked. Reprimands the child now. "You ate a lizard again? You can't eat lizards!"

"Yes, I can. I did it." Zettie answers accurately rather than diplomatically.

The children in the line behind Zettie chuckle at this exchange and Zettie turns back to look behind her again. Now Zettie's grinning properly.

"Zettie can eat lizards," an older Sinta girl says, somewhat admiring, encouraging the child to act out a little more, as far as Zorry's concerned. Zorry sighs, rolls her eyes. Zettie is known for being a small entertainer amongst the Sinta families who pass her yard on their way to work.

Zettie grins and holds up the lizard's tail again, to show the childur behind.

And then leaning low over her sister Zorry's shoulder, dropping the tail in the dust. She counts three of Zorry's dust footprints away from the lizard tail before somebody leans over to pluck it up. It's one of the older Sinta girls, raises her hand briefly in thanks, and then examines the lizard tail thoughtfully. Pops it into her own apron pocket, to show mother at home. "I've seen them lizards before," she catches up to Zorry to tell her. "They's new and they is multiplying. Don't nobody know how they got through the killing fence but they're breeding faster than anything else. Can't think why the lab technicians would've bothered making a thing like that for the killing forest, they're not dangerous at all, my mother says." And then turning toward Zettie, "Does you have a pizen in your tummy, Zettie? Tummy ache?"

The child shakes her head and rubs her tummy happily, grins.

"She don't never get a pizen, Zorry confirms wryly. I can't digest half the things Zettie lives on."

The Sinta girl examines Zettie's face with interest. "No pizen. You're sure?"

When they're within sight of their small mossy cottage, just behind the copse of trees, they've barely reached the stone wall their father built around the yard when Zorry and Zettie's mother, Mamma Ezray, runs out. She's holding on to her hat and her skirts are flapping. "Mamma Zeina is dead." She says. Catches her breath. Holds her throat, leans down hard on the gate. And then staring hard at Zorry. Her eldest daughter does not seem to her to be surprised enough by this information. She squints, "Zorry, you were there last night. Tell me, did you know about this?"

"Yes Mamma. I was going to tell you tonight. But now I've got somewhere to be."

"Have you now, Zorry?" Mamma Ezray eyes her eldest daughter sceptically. "Mamma Zeina's dead, we're ten minutes, less, from curfew, and you've got somewhere to be? Well." She sniffs. "Just be quick. And ... We'll talk about this later, Zorry." She thinks for a moment.

Zettie slides out of her sister's arms. Looks around right away for a stick to draw with. The child knows from her mother that you are supposed to draw a new food when you find it. Just as soon as you know that you ain't got a pizen.

Mamma Ezray watches her eldest daughter wrestle with the rusting gate in the cottage wall. Vanish behind the hedge beyond it. Listens until she can no longer hear the sound of Zorry's running feet.

Mamma Ezray sits down hard in the yard. It's as though

her legs go right from under her. She looks down at Zettie, her youngest. Already making patterns in the dust of the yard. A curling tail of something. Then finding stones for its eyes.

"Well, Zettie, Mamma Zeina is dead, and your sister is headed toward ... darned if I know where. And what in the durned baobab are we all going to do now, eh? When the hungry times come, without Mamma Zeina's back door bread deliveries. Gaddys will have us by the throat." She sighs. She assumes the child has not understood a thing she's said. That she's been talking to herself.

Zettie stops drawing. She pops her thumb in her mouth. Examines her mother.

Now Zettie turns back to her drawing. At speed and she's equally skilful at drawing with both hands. Mamma Ezray stares hard at the back of the child's dipping head, face hidden by her straggle of hennaed ringlets. A cold feeling passes over Mamma Ezray. Shakes herself. Puts the feeling away. And then, "That Child never listens," she tells herself, out loud. "Just plays in the dust all day." Quietly Mamma Ezray wonders to herself if the child is quite all there. Wonders if she takes in anything at all. She doesn't even know how to stay in the yard.

Mamma Ezray means to go inside but something makes her stop and look down. And again that cold, nagging feeling. Premonition. Shivers. She picks up the washing basket, rests it on her hip. She notices that Zettie has drawn the curling tail of one of the new breeds of lizard. Now she looks up at her mother with a curious expectant expression. Then again she seems so knowing sometimes, Ezray thinks. Zettie pops her thumb in her mouth. Seems to wait for an answer.

"Ah, Zettie. What will I do with you, eh?" Mamma Ezray is

exhausted from a night in the killing forest, and the last leaf she tested on herself made her irritable. There is nothing, now, for supper. Worse, she's been anxious since she heard the bad news about Zeina. A sense of slow dread. She responds sourly to the child now. "I don't have time for this. I have serious matters to ... I have to think about how to get us some damned food, Zettie."

Mamma Ezray sighs heavily. Regrets her words before they've left her lips, she didn't mean to take it out on the child. Stares at the gate. Then puts her second basket onto her head and sways inside.

She counts the steps between the gate and the front door to calm herself. She asks herself how long it'd take Zettie to get from the back door to the copse behind the cottage if she had to ... Doesn't bare thinking about but she has to think about it. Never know what you'll need to know and when. Never know what thing might save you, in Bavarnica. She sighs. It'll take more than information, it'll take a miracle to keep these childur alive through what's coming down the tracks towards them. Worse, Mamma Ezray doesn't believe in miracles.

Hesitates on the back step now. Pulls the basket off her head, stacks it on top of the first one. Pushes on inside.

Zettie watches the back door close behind her mother.

In a bit Zettie goes back to her drawing. Dust lizards fanning out round the gate. Stones for eyes.

SNAKE EGGS

GADDYS HAS SLIPPED QUIETLY from the shop's front
door, glided noiselessly around the bulging, top-heavy shelves
which line the sides of her shop and appeared behind her
brass pulpit, behind which she keeps the till. Tomax, stepping
into the cool room, thinks it's empty and then, "Hello Edge
Farm," she says. Popping up. Gaddys loves to be theatrical.
Loves managing to surprise an edge farm boy who's used to
climbing around the man-eating birds which are accumulating
on the edge farms.

Gaddys examines Tomax. The boy has been afraid of her
since childhood, since the day she tried to sell his mother
an axe. Her 'sales techniques' had alarmed him. Now, it's as
though the old woman has rewired his mind. Even the smell
of Gaddys makes Tomax's adrenaline start pumping. He's not
a coward. Tomax has never been a coward. Perhaps Gaddys
sensed that, even back then. She remembers a small boy's
upturned face, chin out slightly, stepping protectively in front
of his mother. Daring to look Gaddys right in the eye.

Bavarnica has always liked to prune its young. Cutting
them down before they're full grown is the best way, in the
end, Gaddys has found. And cheaper. The 'gardener' can
take a step back then. Watch the young branches grow out in
strange, unnatural shapes. No direct violence will be required,
most times, no unnecessary use of expensive government

ammunition on an unruly adult. Simply bend them before they're full grown, and step back. It's amazing how many creative ways a young person can find to sabotage themselves. Do your work for you, Gaddys thinks.

Gaddys, gazing at the full grown Tomax now, smiles at the memory of the small boy and the axe. She keeps the axe under her counter for boys and girls with 'That look' in their eye, Burgo and red ink, she calls it. But Gaddys has more than axe-tricks up her sleeve. The best way, she's learned, is to have the occasional 'accident', a lassoo loop which doesn't un-knot quickly, some faulty farm equipment, firing sparks during a sales pitch, or a farm gun which just goes off too soon and in the wrong direction. Oops!

Gaddys herself will conduct the necessary investigations after. Of course she'll have to heave the grieving mother out of the shop, and she finds that a drag. The way they scream, pray, hold onto the hinges of the door. But afterward ... When Bavarnica's news-shop has picked the 'story' up and put it down again, when things quiet ... All the children in Gaddys' shop will be ... Well. Different. It'll be at least a month before she'll feel the need for another 'accident'. To remind them.

"You still with us?" She asks him now, very sweetly. Smiles again. This is more terrifying to him than an axe flying past his ear, splitting the shelf behind him. He looks down at her hands, gripping on to the edge of her pulpit-counter. He's not sure if he's supposed to reply, and then, "Yes." He says. His voice jagging in his throat. The cool dry room, smell of antiseptic, a fit of coughing takes him. When the coughing slows down, he feels sputum on his lower lip. He wipes his arm across his mouth, feeling embarrassed and strangely exposed. Gaddys eyes him. "I'm still ... With us." Tomax says. And then he stops talking. Places his work card on the counter for her. "Extra rations." He says, grimly. This is the dangerous moment. Tomax knows that much.

Gaddys takes his ration card. Examines it.

"It's been stamped by the general's wife?" Gaddys squints at the stamp to confirm this. Then leans back heavily. Soft, sugary voice. "Well, now. You surely are in with the in-crowd, Tomax. Aren't you?"

This seems to Tomax more like a threat than a question and he doesn't attempt to answer it. Hides his hands behind his back. Bends his head. It doesn't do to look Gaddys in the eye. His left hand is shaking.

Tomax wishes he weren't still as terrified of Gaddys as he had been as a child. It isn't only Gaddys' obvious power. Gaddys' power over the food chain, Gaddys' influence over the general. Gaddys hand selects the officers and the special guards who guard the general, Gaddys stamps the certificates of tameness for the workers, or else Gaddys doesn't stamp them. Gaddys Beloved Flowers spy on the OneFolks and Gaddys cherry picks facts for Bavarnica's News, saying who can speak and what they can say. How they may say it. Gaddys decides who will be gagged and silenced in the back of the newsroom for the crime of twitching an eyebrow at the wrong time, or a tone of voice that doesn't suit, Gaddys decides what information the whole of Bavarnica will get, and how they'll see it. She has orchestrated several campaigns against the 'Witches' in their midst. All that is, of course, terrifying power. But there is some other indefinable frightening thing about Gaddys. Something more ancient and more savage.

Tomax doesn't know but somehow intuits that when his back is turned, even for just a moment, then her face becomes a vicious mask, a gargoyle's grimace. He senses Gaddys still misses the hands-on violence of her younger days. Tomax has heard all the stories, of course. How Gaddys came up through the ranks. Tomax feels a tightening in his stomach, throat, when she looks up. When she smiles then it's worse. He tells himself to get a grip. Collect his rations, head down, no trouble, it will be over in a minute. This thought calms him. She is just a little old woman after all. He grips the shaking hand with the still one, behind his back. He holds on.

Gaddys is stamping his card, which gives Tomax a chance to examine her briefly, unseen. Gaddys is a conventionally pretty woman, without being in any way appealing. She dresses in the latest Bavarnican fashions: bee stung blue-ish tinged lips stretched thin across her gleaming half formed baby teeth, doll-like, wide, staring eyes. The colour of road kill and other dead things: just turning from deep red into shades of silver. And then rolling back in to her head when she looks away, or when her gaze shifts sideways. A nose so small that it's close to being an indent in her face when she turns to place your ration card in its box to the left of her pulpit, and shows you her profile at the same time. Not a line or a wrinkle on her to show the years, only smooth, oiled, plumped up skin. Tomax knows that Gaddys is several years older than Mamma Zeina was when she died.

"Seen enough?" Turns her cold beady left eye toward him. The right eye takes a moment longer to catch up.

Tomax winces. "Sorry."

Now Tomax notices, with a small jolt of relief, Jengi easing in through the back door behind Gaddys' pulpit, almost imperceptible nod. Tomax dares only turn a little toward Jengi, who's sloping toward the shelves at the front of the shop now. Collects his mop and antiseptic bucket, slowly washes the aisles all the way toward Gaddys' pulpit at the back of the shop. It's a long, strange moment. When Tomax feels Jengi reach his elbow, he can't help but turn a little toward him, small checking gesture. The boy breathes out.

Gaddys is preoccupied with something under her till.

"Scurvet." She tells Jengi sharply. "Could you sort out these durned scurvets once and for all, Jengi? Burrowed under my till." And then gazing at the two young men in front of her, looking from one to the other. "Second thoughts ..." She says sharply. "Clean out the shed, Jengi." She gives this instruction without meeting his eye. Watches him until he reaches the back door again, mop in hand, and then turning her full attention back to Tomax. A smile of such terrifying sweetness at Tomax that it makes Jengi wince. He almost fumbles his mop, trying to pull on the back door handle and hold on to the mop and bucket at the same time. And then in her soft, lisping voice. "Thank you Dear Jengi. That will be all." Clipped tone.

Jengi looks at the back of her head. And then a long, slow stare at Tomax. Tomax knows it's a warning. Jengi seems to struggle with the door. Takes some effort to close it, "Sticks on the door jamb, Ma'am. I'll see to it." Mops his brow for effect. Huffs and puffs and heaves on his bucket, like it was made of lead, Tomax thinks. Jengi leaves the door open a crack. Gaddys doesn't seem to notice. Shoulders softly rise and fall.

Tomax is amazed by this performance, Jengi is like a different person in front of Gaddys. Tomax has an instinct to avert his eyes, somehow sensing Jengi's shame at being seen in this light by a friend. Servile. Submissive. Well, it's better than dead, Tomax thinks. Maybe.

The shop's front door crashes open behind Tomax. Trill of the door bell, and then the door crashing shut again, someone staggers in. Leans against the shelves. Gaddys raises one pencilled eyebrow and Tomax risks turning briefly to look, recognises his aunt before she pulls back her hood and tugs off her headscarf. She looks at her nephew briefly, and then opens and closes the shop door again, as though to check that she's not being followed. Satisfied that the dusty street outside is empty, yanks the shop door hard shut.

The bell on the door tinkles furiously. Its another warning, to Tomax's mind. The urge to run is quite strong now. Tomax is trying not to meet his aunt's eye. Her timing in being here now seems a little too much like coincidence to be one. He remembers that Gaddys did not seem surprised to see Aunt. He remembers Jengi's attempted warning. Feels his throat closing, coughs once, twice. Eyes the window, the door. Examines the vents in the walls. His aunt's body blocks the only clear exit.

Tomax's aunt regularly overdoses on her government medicine and when her mind is quite bombed enough to consider that her alibis with her edge farm neighbours is complete, she makes her way steadily and surely toward Gaddys' shop. Here she sells her information to Gaddys 'accidentally'. She always claims, if caught out, to be sorry for it after. To have been tricked and abused, all whilst under the influence of the government medicine. Her catch-all excuse for more than a decade of unspeakable behaviour. But she looks quite at home now, to her nephew Tomax. Lolling against Gaddys' counter, slurring her words.

Her plan is generally to just keep talking until she's said enough to bring home fresh meat, fresher eggs which she will then conceal and eat soberly, and alone, over the course of the following weeks. Aunt will not share a scrap of her ill gotten meat rations but she'll go through the whole rite again the next time she feels properly hungry. Meantime she avoids suspicious pointing fingers by accusing various entirely innocent women on the edge farms of doing the very thing that she herself is doing. *Collaborator.* She'll hiss. Supplying the details, the dates. She can be very convincing, with the result she inspires more than a little fear amongst the edge farm women. People try to keep her fed as much as they can, strain their meagre resources to do so. Keeping Aunt from hunger is like a second tax on the edge farms.

Most of the edge farmers have figured Aunt out, more or less, or at least they know it in their bones somehow, know that Aunt is not quite what she seems. And so, without even discussing the thing with one another, the edge farms have simply starved Tomax's aunt of information that she can sell.

Given the droughts and the impossibility of giving up any more of the children's food to her, Aunt is now pretty hungry. She's been on a meat-free diet the last six weeks and is only getting the information which is closer to home. This is unfortunate for Tomax. Aunt is the beloved younger sister of Tomax's mother. "The baby," Tomax's mother still insists on calling her, even now that both women have hair striped with silver, bellies sagging from childbirth and missing teeth.

Only Tomax has guessed the true extent of his aunt's eating

project, and only Tomax dares to voice his suspicion that there is a more or less direct link between his aunt's visits to Gaddys and his step cousins currently residing in Bavarnica's long gaol. Tomax's mother won't countenance any of that sort of talk of course. There is no point raising it with her anymore. Tomax eyes his aunt coldly. He waits.

"Goodness. You look quite grey, Dear." Aunt says. Touches Tomax's face with one long cold finger. He feels the cold burn of her hand on his cheek for several moments after. She picks at the brass swirls in Gaddys' pulpit-counter. Traces the shapes of the feathers, then the bones in the wings. "Chicken wings?" Aunt's eyes seem to gleam for a moment.

"Angel wings." Gaddys corrects her with surprising gentleness.

"What's them now? Don't suppose you'd be able to fry 'em?"

"I don't suppose so, Dear. Angels are imaginary creatures, for the most part."

Aunt peers at the brass engraving again. "You don't say." Sighs. "Thought maybe you was advertising something you had out the back. In your lovely food store." Smiles. She has two missing front teeth. Runs her tongue across the gap.

"Only Jengi back there, Dear. Jengi and some ... Bird meat." Gaddys emphasises the last two words, to get the conversation back on track again. Aunt's eyes glitter. She licks her sharpened canine, top left. And then turning toward Tomax, as though she sees her nephew standing there for the first time. Stares.

Tomax smells the medicine on his aunt's breath, recoils a little. She's clearly been getting herself slowly bombed on

the government medicine all morning, he thinks. And that
generally means she is preparing herself to tear someone
down. But who's left? Most of Tomax's relatives are already
dead or in gaol. Everyone except for Tomax's mother. And
Tomax. Surely she wouldn't go that far? He calculates fast.
Tomax's mother is Aunt's last truly reliable food source, so
Mother's probably safe for a while.

"Tomax, dear Tomax," Aunt says. She even tears up a little.
Tomax turns toward Aunt, grimaces. She recoils.

"He's so hostile toward me," Aunt says to Gaddys. There's
a whining note in her voice. "No one cares for me," she says.
Leans on the counter and sobs gently. Gaddys puts a large,
clawed hand on Aunt's shoulder. Lets her cat nails retract
slowly. Aunt looks up. Gives Gaddys a beaky stare.

"My nephew never checks in on me." Gaddys gives Aunt
a soft, encouraging look. Prods her coils suddenly, with the
sharpened end of her index finger. "Ah, the young ones," she
says. And now turning slowly toward Tomax. "The young lack
... Empathy." Gaddys says. Smiles.

This seems to be all the encouragement which Aunt needs.

"Our Tomax has been climbing for crow eggs in his
hunger," Aunt says. Sniffs. "My sister is so worried about
him." Now she won't look at Tomax, not for one long moment.
"And he's wasted his uniform." Her voice sounds shrill now
and more sober than she intended. Ruining your government
uniform is a serious crime in Bavarnica. She seems to realise
this, lolls against the counter. Tries to slur her words. "I
am alone," she reminds herself. Eyes glitter. And then, in a
different voice entirely, just as though it's another person
speaking ... "I do *worry* about him." Gesticulates toward her

nephew. Gaddys turns toward Tomax.

"Of course you do, Dear." Gaddys looks reproachfully at Tomax. Unfathomable smile.

"It's my weakness." Aunt tears up again.

"Yes, Dear."

Gaddys goes on patting Aunt's shoulder, her claws extending and retracting as she purrs saccharine words of encouragement, for which Aunt, almost girlish now, thanks her. Tomax has never seen Gaddys so friendly before, catches a glint of his aunt's huge jagged tooth. In the bottom row, left side of her jaw and sharpened, steel tipped. In the fashion of Aunt's youth.

That tooth used to give Tomax nightmares as a child. There is a cold, sliding feeling in the pit of his stomach now. The same feeling Tomax gets when he's looking for crow eggs, and suddenly gets the distinct sense he's being eyed from above. Sometimes he'll have these kind of intuitions in the moment before a drone comes, a smell perhaps, or a small sign that he hasn't consciously observed. The bombing still feels like yesterday and he was different after it. He'd looked up in the seconds before the explosion and there were crows circling. Now that memory is etched deep in his mind. A few lives have been saved on the edge farms in the last weeks, on account of Tomax letting folks know that the crows have learned to spot the drones and follow them. It's an early warning system of sorts and Tomax has become a keen bird watcher lately.

Generally Tomax scrabbles down the tree long before the mother crow returns to her eggs. But there is nowhere in the world to run from a danger that comes at you softly, like this one. A danger that seems to climb into your skin. His mother tells Tomax that he is suspicious and evil minded about his poor aunt. Perhaps he is.

"Well." And now Aunt lolls some more. Becomes expansive. "Twas on a branch he nearly hung himself on. Of course," and now she leans forward a little toward Gaddys, speaking sotto voce and making quite sure that she slurs, "The fabric tearing let Tomax drop to earth before he was strangled, was how my sister described the thing to me. Of course I was not there myself."

"Of course." Gaddys sniffs. "It's all quite illegal my dear."

Aunt strokes her own arm serenely. Now Aunt mimes the scene for Gaddys. With a flourish of her hands describes the fabric gathered up and twisted around Tomax's neck, like a noose. She gets a little excited. Gaddys lets out a snort. "Goodness dear." Gaddys says. Eyes Tomax. There is a long strange moment in which Aunt cannot meet anyone's eye, not Gaddys' and not the boy's either.

"Ah," she says. "Ah, he's such a good boy." Shudders.

Tomax hears soft clanking sounds from the food store out back. The sound of a fridge door being opened and then closed. Smoke signals from the furnace which holds the roast meats. Slide of metal against metal. Now Tomax smells toasted bird.

Jengi comes back into the shop. Pushes a covered metal tray underneath the shop counter, just by Gaddys' right hand. He looks up and meets Tomax's eye. Expressionless.

Now Gaddys slides the hot metal tray onto the counter. It doesn't burn her and she doesn't look at Jengi. Tomax notes his aunt's eyes swivel left slightly toward it. Now she seems transfixed by the tray. She gets louder and more urgent. Teeth flash and her steel capped incisors clank together.

Aunt has a wide mouth and sharp pronged molars, missing teeth at the front from a drunken fall when she was a girl. Gaddys lifts the cover slightly, examines the meat with surprise, "Jengi?"

"It was the only bird cooked today, Ma'am. Must've fallen in by mistake."

Tomax glimpses the blackened crow's feet poking out from under the cheesecloth. His aunt doesn't appear to have noticed that her chicken ration is a little ... Unusual today.

"Tell me Dear, did our Tomax here have any ... success? For myself I can't imagine eating a crow's egg." Gaddys shudders.

"Yuck, me either. Them birds smell of rot. But he gotten three crow eggs from the venture ... didn't you, Tomax?"

Tomax's mouth is dry. He tries to form a word which is both yes and no at the same time, myennoo and then nothing seems to come out of his mouth but a low groan. He closes his lips tightly. He wonders if this interrogation will be over soon.

Tomax's aunt turns away from him, "Yep, he ate one egg raw before he slipped down the tree. He shared the two he'd got stacked into his hood." Now Gaddys pushes the tray toward Aunt. Leans back and eyes Aunt shrewdly. "He shared it you say? Now that's worse even than stealing extra rations in the first place."

Tomax blinks. Tries not to shuffle his feet. There seems to be no way he can extricate himself, or none that he can see.

Aunt makes sideways eyes at him, then lolls and slurs. "Yes." She says. "He shared food. Not with me, mind." She adds bitterly, grimaces. "Shared them with a young mother on the edge farm. She'd gotten herself into a state on account of her orange grain sack, which you no doubt had your very good reasons to allocate her, Gaddys Dear, but what with her milk for the new baby drying up slowly ... Well. Tomax is a sentimental boy." She turns toward him, "Didn't you Tomax? Didn't you share with that young girl?"

Tomax squints at his aunt. He imagines for a moment that he sees a little redness in her cheeks. She's not quite without shame, he thinks. Almost. Not quite. He goes on gazing directly into her eyes. It's his only hope.

"I'm sure I've said too much." She blinks, swallows. "I think that I may have ... Overdone it." Lolls and droops against the counter, then makes a clumsy grab for the tray. Gaddys puts one manicured finger out and pins it. Wide smile. And then "Never mind, Dear." Gaddys pats Aunt's hand. She takes the cloth off the food, with a light flourish, like a magician performing a trick.

The roasted crow has been plucked roughly, feathers sprout in the pits of its wings and under its chin. Its wings have been arranged angelically across its chest, huge black clawed feet thrust out at strange angles, arranged heel to heel. The bird still has its head, eyes, beak and all. The creature looks dignified and somehow reproachful.

Aunt doesn't appear to have noticed, or else she is too hungry to object. The smell of roast bird hits Tomax. The meat smells a little rotten to him. Just a hint of sourness, and the bird is very thin which most likely means old or sick or perhaps both. Again Aunt doesn't appear to notice anything much wrong with her 'chicken', plucks the tray from the counter, glancing at Tomax briefly, almost smugly. Slides the bird into her basket, which, although large, can only hold the bird's stomach, its feet and beak thrust out at each end of the checked cloth, its wings, stubbled with patches of feathers, trail down. "*Some* people are kind." Aunt says to Tomax. "Thank you Gaddys." She sniffs. Bows.

Gaddys raises an eyebrow.

"Sorry about that chicken, Dear. You'll have a finer one next time. What about an egg for your troubles? A bonus." Smiles. She places a round egg-like object on the counter. She examines it. Appears to need to take a moment, summon her patience. "Jengi?" Jengi shrugs.

"It was the last egg we had, Ma'am." His face is opaque. If Jengi has any feelings about the egg, one way or the other, then even Tomax can't tell what it is.

Gaddys rolls her eyes. "You're a dunce, Jengi. Order more stock, why don't you?"

"Yes, ma'am." Jengi says sincerely. Humbly, even.

"It looks a bit round," Aunt says sharply. "Sure it ain't a snake egg?"

"It's just fine. It's a hen's egg." Gaddys pats Aunt's hand. Her fashionable claws retract, and then extend at the tip, just a little. It's a small warning, meaning 'Don't complain'.

Aunt looks down at the hand. She appears to remember herself. Tips sideways slightly. Lets her basket swing. "Only ..." She looks at her nephew and then back toward Gaddys. She stops talking. "Ah," she says. "Ah, well," and then turning to glance behind her. Tomax has gone. "Something or someone has spooked Tomax," she says. "He's done one of his vanishing acts." Shrugs.

"He's on a list already," Gaddys confirms. "A walking ghost. He wouldn't even be *here,* amongst the living, if the general's wife hadn't woken up enough to sign his papers personally. I don't know who got to her, but when I find them ... Anyway, with what you've told me." She smiles sweetly at Tomax's aunt. "When I find them then I'm going to be ... Cross." She enunciates the last word crisply. "Aren't I Jengi?" She says lightly. Eyes him. Jengi turns briefly toward her. "Yes." He says. He turns back to his work, stacking the Sinta's empty jars and the orange grain sacks.

Aunt looks up at Jengi on his stool, "Goodbye Dear!" Then she meets Gaddys' eye. Clutching on to her over-full basket, makes a rush for the door. When she gets to it, slows down to pass an Egg Boy in the doorway. Stops just long enough to squint at him. "The new batch look almost human," she says, "Don't they?" Turning to Gaddys. She peers closely at Antek. Something she sees in his face causes her to take a sudden step back. Rattle and squeak of the shop door as she tries to jam it into its hinges behind her and fails.

BLACK FLOWERS

JENGI EXAMINES ANTEK BRIEFLY, looks away. Lifts a jar and climbs the stool to stack it. Top shelf. But just a moment later he's teetering for a jar just out of reach. Leans far right enough that he'd take a nasty fall if he lost his footing even for a moment, especially over the meat slicer like that. It seems extraordinarily clumsy to Gaddys. But then what else can you expect from a Digger? She thinks. He's been making mistakes lately, too many and it's a pain that the general's wife goes on re-certifying him as 'tame', three times a year and year in, year out, no matter how pollinated she gets. The damned woman never seems to forget to do that one thing.

Jengi will be easy enough to replace in the shop, Gaddys calculates. With her right foot pushes the meat slicer a little closer to Jengi, moving her foot backward so casually that it appears like an absent minded gesture. She goes back to counting her ration cards. And now she's making small indecipherable marks on her clipboard in red ink, next to Sinta names on today's work rota.

"Right a bit, Jengi Dear." Smirks. Jengi, balancing on one foot only now, teeters on the edge of his small platform.

What happens next happens fast.

Antek lunges. Shoots out his right foot, secures Jengi's stool with it. Now he holds his right arm out steadily, for just long enough for Jengi to get down safely.

The two men eye each other, wide scared eyes, the significance of Antek's action is immediately apparent to them both. Now Antek feels rather than sees Gaddys' curious gaze on the back of his head. He understands his mistake. He is already on Gaddys' list. There's no room for him to make another error like the one with the rain barrel. He's only just gotten out of prison, and even that by the skin of his teeth.

Egg Men aren't supposed to help out a member of any tribe but their own, and the OneFolks of course, and even then only when following orders. But apparently the Egg Boy's right foot and right hand have decided something else without him. It's too late now, Antek thinks. Best to brazen the thing out. "Didn't want to see the jar smash." Antek says in a stilted voice. "Egg Boys must protect the rations. Them jars are fine quality foodstuffs." He says stiffly. Pauses, looking down. The smashed jar was empty. "You want to watch them foodstuffs better, Digger."

Gaddys shrugs, eyes the row of empty jars. She looks bored. There is no reason for her to doubt Antek, after all the Egg Men were bred to be incapable of deception. The Egg Boys don't lie.

"Yes. Of course." Jengi's tone is giving nothing away. "Now I'll get out of your way, Egg Man."

"Good." Antek sniffs. "You do that, Digger."

Gaddys turns away. Fixes her coils. Checks her nails and yawns again. Showing all her small white teeth. "Over there," she says. Pointing Antek toward the Egg Boys rations. But she watches Antek closely as he crosses the room. A cold, shrewd gaze.

Antek, with his ration box under his left arm and a half

rotten fish slithering out unwrapped from under his right, strides quickly toward the shop door. But when he gets to the door, something causes him to pause there. Risks a quick glance back at the room.

And then Antek is caught, eye to eye with those marbled pupil-less eyes that Gaddys wears on Tuesdays, reminding The Egg Boy of the fishes stacked in rows and piles at the front of her shop, just at the point where they're tipping softly into rot, covered with a veil of white mucous.

Gaddys examines the Egg Boy's face. And then staring down at his right foot. Nodding softly. It's a clear warning.

Jengi glances briefly at Antek then looks away. He goes back to his shelves.

Antek steps over the door jamb. Softly turns to go. The Sinta girl Zorry is entering the shop as Antek leaves it, this seems like no coincidence to Antek and he gives no indication of having seen her before. He pushes past Zorry abruptly, and then he's gone. Zorry hears the whole door frame clatter and stick fast in the frame, so that the ancient bell on the top of the door goes on tinkling and ringing after Antek. Jengi takes the broom handle. Deals with the bell roughly.

"Those clumsy Egg Boys." Gaddys says. "But the general's wife has a liking for *that* one, for some reason. Certified him all the way out of a cell. No idea why the general puts up with such sentimental nonsense. It's not as though they're human, no need to get attached to the servants. Is there Jengi?"

"No, ma'am."

"No, that's right, isn't it, Jengi?" And then, in a further unpleasant aside, "The Egg Boy will be better after he gets his staining."

"Yes, ma'am." Jengi replies, more tonelessly than Zorry has ever heard Jengi speak. He turns and stacks the shelves faster.

Gaddys turns to face Zorry now.

"Yes, Dear. What can we do for you? Don't be shy now."

Zorry is nervous, coming here. It can be tricky for a Sinta to collect their rations. They don't always leave here the way they came in and Zorry knows it. She has heard the stories. Eyes flick toward the exit. The smoke from the furnace outside, just visible through the mottled upper window of the back door.

Zorry silently places her ration cards on the counter. She moves so quickly that she scratches the palm of her hand on the edge of one of the brass angel wings which decorate Gaddys' counter-pulpit. She curls her hand closed behind her back, pressing her fingers down on the hurt.

Gaddys has her back turned toward Zorry just now, giving Zorry a chance to examine unseen the small pale lumpen head with its sheen of soft white down, like feathers, which is Gaddys' current look for Tuesdays, when she is washing her coils.

"Fetch me that jar, Girl." Gaddys says. Without turning.

"Which one?"

"Top shelf." Gaddys manages to pour as much contempt into those two words as she can.

Zorry walks around the room with an air of outraged silence. Pokes a cabbage, on the way to collect the jar. Runs a single finger over the rows of skin coloured chalks and the coiled hair pieces, the potatoes with the white roots, the softly mouldering bread. Gaddys' back is still turned.

Zorry hurts her neck looking up at the huge shelves, row upon row, tilting up as far as the eye can see. The ceiling of the shop is like an aircraft hangar. Impossibly high.

Most of what sits on the shelves are items in jars and tins, rations for the domestic workers and slaves who work in the OneFolks' village, the Sinta and the edge farm miners. The rest of the shelves are stocked with differently coloured grain sacks, meant for the edge farmers, those who still have their pass cards to the OneFolks' village. The furnace outside is for meat, which is only for the OneFolks' and those whom Gaddys considers to be useful to her.

And then there's the black shiny store shed.

Nobody knows what's in there. No-one but Gaddys and Jengi, of course.

Zorry takes in as much as she can. Tries to note any changes. Jengi watches Zorry. Cold hard knot at the base of his throat. The girl is collecting information under Gaddys' nose. Jengi's not sure if she's being naive or simply reckless. Possibly both. Mamma Zeina didn't have enough time, in the end, to train Zorry. The girl is doing fine work under the circumstances, it's just that … It takes all of a hundred years of Sinta knowledge, passed down mouth to ear, to know how to deal with the village shopkeeper. And there's no room for mistakes, not even one small one. He squeezes his eyes shut. Blinks and opens them again. Hard stare at the patch of white wall at the back of the shelf. Places an empty jar there. Takes two careful steps down from his ladder. Notices Gaddys watching the girl with her powder compact.

Taking a few extra seconds between the order and the following of the order, Well. Jengi thinks, watching Zorry's slow movements. That's about the only time of day a Sinta gets to call her own. The time between the order and the following of the order, Jengi thinks, the only form of protest left. To fall down at the work, let things rust and seize up slow in the bomb factories, sew the edge farm children's uniforms full of breathing holes and with a little slack at the throat. Be the spoke in the wheel of Bavarnica's many interconnecting systems. Weaponised slowness.

Jengi remembers that 'God Speed', is the soft, ironic Sinta goodbye. When two neighbours meet in the street. But Gaddys is not some factory guard, or an untrained Egg Boy. There is a reason the general trusts her to decipher who's 'tame' and who's not. Jengi scratches his head. What Zorry needs right now is a distraction.

Gaddys strokes her balding head. With the sproutings of white feathers in her wrinkled skin cap she looks like a too-soon-hatched chick, Zorry thinks. Gaddys pulls a silver wig out of her pocket, pulls it on slowly. Stares at the girl. Silence.

This can't end well.

Zorry puts Gaddys' jar down on the counter. Soft clink.

"What is your purpose here, Girl? What are you for?"

"I've come ... I'm here to collect funeral flowers, for Mamma Zeina's grave," Zorry says. And then lifting her chin slightly. Meeting Gaddys' eye. It is a long and dangerous moment.

"I have the ration cards." Zorry says. She speaks quietly, but there's a steeliness in the girl, Gaddys thinks. She's not afraid. Gaddys taps her tooth. Jengi takes another small step down his ladder. Plucks an empty jar. Now he finds himself gazing at the second empty jar behind it. He's listening. Holding his breath.

"That's quite a collection of ration cards." Gaddys

examines the Sinta family names on the cards. Writes them down.

"A funeral has been approved." Zorry says, objecting as much as she dares to. Her voice is just a little more shrill than she intended.

"Has it now? And who exactly was it who approved a Sinta funeral? I can guess, Child, but I would like to hear you say it."

"The general's wife."

Jengi freezes. Collects himself and then, dipping his head, takes a jar from the shelf beneath his elbow. He takes the opportunity to glance at Gaddys' face. To see how she takes this.

Gaddys snatches up the ration cards again. Examines them with a sullen expression. She's trying to find something wrong.

Feels like only seconds later, Zorry is leaning against the cool sweating wall in the alleyway beside the shop. Listening to the sound of Gaddys shrieking, making phone calls, hitting Jengi with the brush end of his own broom.

There's a sting in the sun today. Zorry has no flowers. No ration cards. And she's put a clutch of Sinta names, via their ration cards, into Gaddys' hands. This whole thing was a mistake from beginning to end. What's worse, Gaddys has noticed Zorry now. Zorry listens for a little while longer to the sound of Jengi taking a beating on her behalf. Guilt seems to take Zorry by the throat and press down. It's paralysing. She can't go home or go back.

A side window opens behind her. And then Jengi's arm, his thick bony wrist. He's clutching a black flower in his fist. "This is for you." He says, grimly. "For Zeina." Jengi hands her the flower. Zorry notices the bruising on Jengi's face, that his mouth and right ear are bloodied. He rocks one loose tooth softly side to side with his tongue. Grins wryly.

"We're alright, Zorry. It's not your fault. She's been wanting to do that for a while, damned savage. Now, go have Zeina's funeral." And turning toward a sound behind him, hisses, "Scurvets. Now, Scram!"

Zorry doesn't need to be told twice.

Levers herself over the glass topped wall at the end of the alley. One seamless, flowing motion, Zorry hurdles the fence. Not a single petal falls.

This time she knows how to avoid the glass shards.

Zorry just keeps going. Sound of her heart in her ears.

RATIONS

EGG MEN ARE TURNING over the house. Zorry notices Zettie hiding out behind the chair in the corner. The child is sucking her thumb and her eyes are closed tight. She's buried her ears under her hat, with her hair stuffed around it. Zorry throws the black flower into the sink, covers it with the dish cloth just in time. Ezray eyes the sink, small nod at Zorry, and then turns quickly away.

The Egg Men find it all. All the family's food stores, including the fresh eggs from under Mamma Ezray's hat, and the new hatched chicks in the box behind the oven, peppered with breathing holes, the red peppers under the sink, the root vegetables sunk down with stones at the bottom of the rain barrel. The perfectly formed mushrooms in the hidden pouch of Father's jacket.

Zorry's father seems to take it worse than Mamma Ezray.

Zorry's father was left with nothing this evening but a handful of dried beans because no one thought to check in the palm of his hand. Too obvious. He curls his hand around the beans until the Egg Mens' search is over.

Antek's father, the chief Egg Man for this sector, tucked a food ration card in the top left pocket of Father's jacket as he left. "Gaddys will replace it all. Don't look so sour, Sinta. Present your ration card at the shop. You are lucky we left you anything at all." Zorry rolls silence around on her tongue, the way Mamma Zeina taught her. Zorry's father looks down at the ration card.

A few dots on a ticket and his children to spend their lives begging back the half rotten leftovers of all that he raised or grew. He bangs his hand against the side of his head, once, twice. As though he's trying to remember something that won't come back.

Zorry tries to protect her father as much as she can, understanding without ever being told that he's not as strong as her mother, Mamma Ezray. And that several years of taking the government medicine has ruined what was once a fine mind. Now she tells him it's alright. What else? She tells him that Gaddys is nice and not to forget to take his medication. Pats his shoulder, sensing that what he's lost is too great for him to contemplate. If there was a time for him to confront all that he was and is now, then that time was long ago. He slowly pulls on his overalls, ready for his work in the sewers. But once they're on, he looks down at them. As though he sees them for the first time in his life. He doesn't make a move toward the door. He doesn't move at all, for one long moment.

"It will be alright, won't it?" Father gazes at Zorry opaquely.

"Yes." She lies.

Mamma Ezray grows herbs and strong spices to cover the taste of soft rot in the rationed shop food.

Their father regularly complains that Mamma Ezray's chilli burns his tongue.

"You, Woman. You woman with your bitter cooking. Trying to kill me, you are." He said last night, the way he does every night. Medicated as he is, Zorry thinks that deep down he knows.

There have been small signs. That day when he threw the cooking pot at the kitchen counter. The day he slid down the wall and then sat there. Three straight hours. His eyes blank, unreadable. He didn't get up until the bell rang, once, twice, to call the Sinta men for their work.

Zorry's father will clear the drains that run underneath and alongside the OneFolks' village. Then he'll come home and sleep through the day. Return at nightfall for his next shift.

He was a teacher in The Before. A professor of botany before the last Reckoning Era, before the mountain deaths and the Diggers' revolution. Zorry doesn't know anything about that time. It was before she was born. All she knows is that her father has been getting more distant every year since she was born. Since she was a small girl she has believed that some day he would just get up and vanish like smoke. Even his voice sounds farther away every year. As though he's leaving his family in slow pieces and parts.

"Reckon we need another Reckoning of you all. Another purge of the Sinta." Gaddys stands at the cottage door, eyes her manicure. Pats her coil of hair. And then, unfathomably, she smiles at Zorry. Just as though she's pleased to see her. Bright corporate smile, the way the shopkeepers were trained to in the long ago. As if her face betrays her, Zorry finds she smiles nervously too.

Zettie slides out from behind her chair, slipping up to her sister Zorry. Holding on to Zorry's leg and then slips in front of her. Leans. And then without taking her eyes off Gaddys, slowly lifting her small hand in the air, tiny thumb pointed upward. Puts the thumb in her mouth. Zettie gazes solemnly at Gaddys. Fails entirely to read the situation, as far as Zorry's concerned.

Gaddys takes a package from the Egg Man standing beside her, unrolls it. The rotting fish slaps on to the kitchen table. "Present," she says. "For my best slaves." Zettie looks up sharply when she hears the word. Now Gaddys is eyeing Zettie. Soft, knowing smile spreading out over her features. Zettie repeats the word, "Slaves." A gentle uptilt at the end of the word like she asks it as a question.

And then the infant turning to gaze at Mamma Ezray, quick checking gesture.

Mamma Ezray seems to slip inside herself.

Zettie eyes her mother.

Something seems to get into the child.

Zettie reaches out her small hand, prods the fish with her right index finger. It oozes a clear liquid tinged with yellow. Now she steps back. The liquid pools on the floor, around her feet. Now she gazes up at Gaddys.

"Take it. You, Child. Take it. You're a slave, ain't you?"

Zettie pulls her left thumb out of her mouth for long enough to say it. "No." She says. One word.

"I am a Sinta." She says. As politely as she's been taught to speak to adults. The child doesn't look away from Gaddys once. The most revolutionary words ever spoken to Gaddys, and they came from a child. Gaddys' face blossoms red.

Now Mamma Ezray and Zorry stand in front of Zettie. She looks through Mamma's legs.

"She's just a Chil ..." Zorry says

"She'll learn ..." Mamma Ezray says, sinking.

After Gaddys has gone, Zettie cannot be persuaded to

touch or even look at the fish. And what's more, she appears to be not speaking to either Zorry or Mamma Ezray. Maintains a dignified quiet. Neither Zorry nor Mamma Ezray object or try to break the small girl's silence. "Let her keep something." Mamma Ezray's last word on the subject.

After Gaddys' home visit, Zettie holds her tongue as much as she can.

LEECHES

"GADDYS HAS LEFT A bag of protein pearls." Zorry's fathers voice, from the cottage doorway. He glances behind him briefly to watch Gaddys moving slowly away, down their rockoned garden path. Skirt the gate and vanish behind the tumbledown stone wall. The hedge. This time she has an Egg Boy assistant, he's soft on her heels. Father turns back to his family. "So that's good news eh? Protein pearls." Holds the bag up.

"What was she doing here?" Zorry asks Mamma Ezray. "Put it outside. Why's she singling us out?"

"She's deciding whether to re-certify us or not. Did something happen in the shop? That day. When I sent you for our rations."

"What? You think this is my fault?"

"I didn't say that." Mamma Ezray gazes at her eldest daughter. "She's trying to figure out whether we're tame. There'll be a test for us somewhere now. We must be ... Cautious."

Zorry's father, disliking this kind of talk, simply acts like he doesn't hear it.

Something makes Zorry look up. She notices the small dark shadow on the back of her father's neck. Closer examination, it's curved like a half-moon. Thumbnail mark, and the purple print from an adult-sized thumb, just above it. She knows he won't remember how he got the strangulation marks. The scratch. She doesn't ask. Whatever happened to him during his last work rota, it was apparently bad enough that he was rebooted afterward. She examines his face closely. She had heard there was an escapee from last night's work rota. A runner. Is it possible that Father helped the man, or else saw something? Now she sees the small electrical burns on the sides of Father's temple. He has certainly seemed to be ... Different. Lately.

Mamma Ezray catches Zorry's eye and now they are both staring at the back of Father's head. They forget about the bag of protein pearls. The bag is on the floor by the front door and Zettie steps outside, toward it, quietly. She opens the bag. The packaging is striped pink and white and she examines it with pleasure. Two illustrated candy bars criss and cross on the front. Sweets, she thinks. She doesn't check the bag before she plunges her small right hand in. Then she feels something moving under her fingertips. Yanks out her hand. It's covered in sulphurous, sliding creatures, snails with half formed soft shells, tree slugs too, of the sucking kind. Mucous sliding out from their poison sacs underneath. She feels the first sting right away and she screams for her mother.

It takes Zorry and Mamma Ezray fully fifteen seconds to prise the leaching things off the child. They look at the tiny holes and bite marks in her hand in silence. Swelling and reddening already. One small mark streams with blood and Mamma Ezray wraps it. Both Zorry and Mamma Ezray are also covered in small stings and bites. They bathe Zettie's wounds in silence. Zettie holds out her hand patiently, quietly. Her eyes are half closed. Gritting her baby teeth against the pain. Small winces as Mamma Ezray dabs the ointment.

"Protein balls was it?" Zorry says in disgust.

"What are they?" Zorry's fathers voice sounds shrill, urgent.

"Bavarnican snails and the leaching, stinging tree slugs from the killing forest."

"What Gaddys give you that for?" Zorry's father, fish still in his hands, looks genuinely shocked.

"Gaddys put the snails and leeches in sweet packaging. It was clearly aimed at the child."

"What?" Father says, stupidly.

Zorry feels something rising in her. A sudden need to have her father pay attention to what's under his nose, to make him face what Mamma Ezray has to. She explains, as quietly as she can bear to, so as not to alert the neighbours, with the result that her words hiss, her eyes narrow, "Killing forest snails can move fast ... Father. They leave a glutinous trail behind them as thick as a finger. Look at it. *I said look at it.* If Mamma Ezray hadn't seen the trace of the last one on the back of Zettie's shirt, heading in a neat loop toward her neck, then our Zettie would have been killed." Zettie gazes softly from Zorry to Father.

"What?"

Mamma Ezray looks down. She shakes her head at Zorry. "Don't. Zorry."

But Zorry, now that she's started, cannot stop herself, "Mamma Ezray whipped Zettie round and caught it before it reached Zettie's jugular vein. One moment too late," she said, "and Zettie would have ..." Father looks shocked. He stares at Zorry.

Zorry holds the creature by its shell now, upside down. To

show Father. It curls around and tries to reach the tips of her fingers.

She drops the snail and Mamma Ezray crushes it underfoot.

Zettie looks down at the small squashed body with interest. There are thick meaty edges to its underside and yellow suckers running down it. Now Mamma Ezray sees something, screams. She spins Zettie. She finds two more snails on the back of Zettie's head, one is one of the worst kind of leaches. Now Zorry spots a stinging tree slug, on the child's wrist and slipping out from the edge of her sleeve. Zorry pulls it off. All three are pale now. Panting for breath. Now they strip the child and plunge her into the rain barrel beside the kitchen window. They turn her clothes inside out, examine the hems and the seams.

"That was the last."

Mamma Ezray pulls the child out of the rain barrel, checks her over once more. Rainwater streams from her onto the floor and they dress her quickly. Pat her head. "It's over. Zettie it's over." The child has slipped inside herself. She looks pale. Detached.

Zorry looks up now. Notices that her father seems to have tuned out even further. Shambles toward the sloping wall beside the kitchen. Takes a seat on a leaning, busted kitchen chair. And now he's staring hard at a chip on the wall. Right in the very place where he'd thrown a plate of Mamma Ezray's cooking, just last year. Zorry can't see what Father sees there. But he seems to wilt. Fade in front of her eyes.

Rallies just a little to say, "You must've done something bad, Zorry. In the shop." And then he falls silent.

"Don't blame her. It's not the child's fault. Don't talk any more. Just don't …" Mamma Ezray snaps at him. It's the first time Zorry has seen Mamma Ezray lose her patience with their father.

Zorry takes a hold of Mamma Ezray's hands and turns them softly, palms up. She looks down at the trail marks and snail bites on her mamma Ezray's fingers. Gazes into her face. Waits for her mother to speak again. Her father, behind them, goes on shaking his head. "It doesn't … I don't …" He says. Bangs the side of his head twice, hard. Now Zorry listens to the sound of him opening his medicine cupboard, squeak of the hinge, the long pause. As though he is considering the thing. Then the soft popping sound as the medicine lid is opened. Mamma Ezray's shoulders rise and fall. She gazes gently at Zettie. Zorry has never seen her mother look defeated. Until this moment now, she's not truly known what fear is. She says to her mother quietly. "Look. I got to go."

"Yes." Mamma Ezray looks up. As though she sees her daughter for the first time. Soft appraisal. She puts a hand on Zorry's shoulder. "Yes. I know."

She turns back to the sink.

Zettie is sitting on the cottage back step, looking into the middle distance. Mamma Ezray can't see what Zettie sees. The child seems to her to be exhausted in a way that's too old for her years.

"How did my children get so old? So old, on my watch." And then, heavily, "Go talk to Jengi, Zorry. There is no going back now." Shoulders rise and fall, clutches the sink. "There is only going on."

Soft sound as the door closes behind Zorry. Mamma Ezray

stares into the sink for a long time after she's gone. And when she tries to, Mamma Ezray finds that she can't move her hands. That last leech she pulled off her youngest had wrapped itself around her thumb, delivered all of its poison. She examines the large hole in her thumb. The paralysis lasts a moment. Mamma Ezray stuffs the dish cloth into her mouth when the pain rises. She bites down.

THE STAINING

ANTEK HAS BEEN PRESCRIBED two more stains before he'll be certified an Egg Man.

His next staining is tomorrow.

Bavarnica is stretched out beneath Antek but his eyes are closed. His head is face down on his arms, so he can only see the rough green linen of his sleeve, the stain on the hairless skin creeping out from under the edge of the fabric, just above his wrist. The stain has moved down since this morning.

Antek opens his eyes. He can hear the sound of hopeful OneFolk people singing karaoke in the village below him.

The village itself seems to seep out from the strange dip at the bottom of the mountain, like a chin and a throat at the stone base, he thinks. And the show village like the chin's shadow, or just a spill on the mountain's vest. Antek shakes himself. Bad songs and bad singing, he thinks.

Farther away still, somewhere to the left of the rock wall he leans on, Antek with his specialised ears can just hear the sea. Coming darkly in and out. Cicadas. The sounds seem to him to rise now. Antek puts his hands over his ears. He shifts on to his haunches. There's a gentle rock fall behind him. Then another clatter of gravel unloosed by that, small stones sliding down the mountain's sheer face, bouncing off his back and skimming to either side of him. Antek doesn't move. He goes on looking down.

Lately Antek has taken to climbing The Reach. The mountain range behind the OneFolks' village. He doesn't know why but more and more, he finds he wants to be up here alone.

Antek's hearing is acute, so much so that he's sometimes uncomfortable to the point of low level pain. No one knows why batch 47 needed that feature, but things will become clear, they say, when batch 47 grow to man size and their mission for the general is started. The lab technicians are not known to add unnecessary features to the Egg Boys.

Antek puts his hands over his ears but the sound of cicadas in the scrubby plants at the bottom of the mountain, are like a long slow chainsaw to him, slicing through Bavarnica's head. There are small stones under Antek from some long ago rock fall. Caught by the upward jut of his mountain shelf. He pushes his feet into the stones. He breathes out.

Antek is hidden by a long jag in the rock which must date, he thinks, from when the Sinta tried to fund the building of tunnels through it. Roadways to the wider world, that was the spirit of the times then. Of course everyone in Bavarnica who's heard the story also knows that those early Sinta builders were caught on the rocks. Batch 46, meaning Antek's father and his unit, were sent to finish them off. The Diggers' revolution began the next day, Antek knows that much from the whispers he's heard in the batch 47 barracks, after dark, and whatever other fragments he's caught from the edge farmers' songs during the rain dances.

All that's left to remember those long-gone Sinta are some odd dips and curves in the mountain now, they're like wide open mouths when the light hits them in a certain way, just before curfew when the general's artificial sun is dimming. The mouths darken further as the light shifts downward, at which time those Sinta who still remember will tell their childur, "Look up, Child. See how even the mountain can cry."

It was typical of the general to let the Sinta get half way with their improving plans, to let them spend all their funds and sit through a thousand hopeful meetings in which the minutes are taken and the attendants' names are listed one by one.

All the idealists amongst the Sinta were, of course, drawn to the mountain project. More lists for Gaddys. More names. Names of the dead, now, Antek guesses. He's been told more than once that there are unmarked graves just beyond the line of baobab trees, at the point where the edge farms meet the desert. The strangely ploughed-looking ground, the earth mounds and farrows appeared at the end of the Digger riots which marked the last era. The edge farms' rain dance songs tell how the soil there is fertile with the dead. Things grow there.

Antek is right now sitting in the most successful Sinta half-tunnel. He's about half way up The Reach, give or take a few handspans. Antek pads about the rock shelf to check for signs of his father, down there. Careful to make no sound.

Antek's father doesn't generally tolerate Antek being this late home, and he'll be out looking by now, Antek knows that much. Even crawling over the small rocks and gravel, Antek can accomplish this feat of silence, on account of a certain cat-like muscular control which one of the general's lab technicians apparently decided would be a useful feature in the lab batch of stained folks Antek belongs to.

There are tweaks in each generation of the Egg Men. Each

batch, the OneFolk villagers say, seems better and more life-like than the last one. Antek's batch 47 are mostly organic this time around, Gaddys the shopkeeper says. But even Antek knows there are computerised parts to him. Some things are run from central control, he can feel his limbs slowing down a few moments after curfew, so he's guessed this much. "They are run off a different system to us, that's the main thing." Gaddys likes to say often. And this in front of Antek, whenever someone happens to comment that Batch 47 seem so human. Gaddys soon puts them straight. She's commissioned several news programmes on the matter. So it's settled then. Antek is not human. That's that. He pushes out his long toes, feels the cold stones.

From his mountain shelf, Antek can see the OneFolks' village, nestled at the base of The Reach, and to the side of that, and just beyond the small Sinta farmsteads, Antek can just make out the edges and corners of his father's steel trap of a farm.

Beside the OneFolks' village, Antek can see, from up here, the long dark seam of the forest which the OneFolk villagers, Egg Men, Sinta and edge farmers alike all call the killing forest, on account these are government protected lands and experimental. "There are things in there," Gaddys the shopkeeper tells her customers with a little shudder. "There are things in there ..." What things she never quite gets around to telling, but generally the OneFolks will stay away from the fence. A few reckless youth on the edge farms have also learned in the last years to fear it. Those cocoons hanging there all night, for all to see in the morning.

It seems to Antek like just a small bound from the

OneFolks' village and the killing forest to the edge farms, arranged in lines and circles like clots in the veins at the edge of the forest.

The edge farmers work the poor soil, Antek knows that much. And, from up here, Antek can see the stark difference in colour between the fertile earth of the OneFolk villagers' farms and the poor untreated soil of the edge farmers, the long boundary fence of the killing forest twisting between the two tribes' farmlands, like a line of spite.

The killing forest looks much like regular jungle from Antek's spot, and not a man-made tangle of stinging brush, trees and scrubby bushes, developed by the general for the sole purpose of testing out his latest living weapons. Nothing gets past the fence of the killing forest, Antek has been told. Not the edge farmers and not their desert.

The desert stretches out as far as the eye can. Antek knows that no-one goes into the desert. Impossible for even the hardiest of edge farmers to survive its burning shadeless daylight heat or its freezing nights for more than minutes. You'd live for an hour at most, OneFolk children are advised in school. Same goes for the killing forest. And for all but Antek's batch 47, with their specialised climbing skills, climbing the mountain reach without equipment is a no-go also.

Triangulation, the security managers call it. The mountain, the desert, the killing forest. Protected on all sides. "We are invincible in defence in The Triangle."

That's been Bavarnica's motto ever since the Diggers' revolution was ended and the general's long reckoning era began.

The general's motto has never made much sense to Antek.

It's not even a triangle, he thinks. So that's the first untruth.

From his mountain viewpoint, Antek can't decide if 'The triangle' is a safe zone or a slow-squeezed trap. It seems to him to keep the OneFolks' in just as much as it keeps the edge farm danger out. Certainly Bavarnica seems to Antek to have shrunk since he was a child.

Antek knows that, by government diktat, he will have to stay within The Triangle until he dies. He knows that his bones will rot in the field behind The Holy, where the Egg Men are buried together in piles, under one banner, denoting their batch number and a tombstone with approximate time of death chiselled into it. No names.

When he's gone Antek knows that his family, and any batch 47 friends he's made, will be rebooted. Antek won't be remembered at all. Every 'son' his mother ever raised for the general, she named Antek. He positively doubts she remembers the difference between all her lost sons.

Antek goes on staring at the desert horizon for a long time. The light dips softly at first and then a sudden black out. He realises with a small shudder that he's broken curfew. Total blackout is rare enough in Bavarnica to take villagers by surprise, but it happens about every few weeks in truth, as Antek has observed, on his few occasions breaking curfew. It lasts for a moment, whilst one generator switches to a new one and the first one's recharged. It comes down fast, the dark. Antek thinks. When it comes.

Phosphorescent moon rises. Antek shivers.

He thinks he sees something out there. It's just for a moment. Lit up by a shaft of moonlight and then slipping out of sight again.

Antek realises that he must be looking at the government gaols. Shouts and whistles rising up from it, when he tunes into the sounds. And, from up here, the guards looking insect-like to Antek. In a little while he watches the prisoners shuffle out from their cells. Moving in droves from one side of the prison yards to the other in darkness, in patterns seeming orderly and strange. Moving together, perhaps for the comfort or warmth he thinks. And then he remembers the chains. Soft clink and rattle when he listens closely. Antek remembers what it was like to be trapped in a space so small. Boxes within boxes. He stops breathing for one long moment. Tears his eyes away.

The gaols were the first government buildings to be attacked in the Diggers' riot which marked the end of the last era. The Diggers themselves had so many family members and friends inside the gaols. After the Digger tribe were mown down in one swathe by the Egg Men of batch 46, there were crackdowns to rid Bavarnica of the 'dangerous' hungry folks on the edge farms. Every Egg Boy, and batch 47 included, is taught the history of Bavarnica in school. There were gaps in the teaching, but batch 47 were taught not to ask. The most important lesson they learned.

Stage two of the general's crackdown was, of course, the killing forest itself. A thin scrubby brush was replanted, fed and watered. It expanded quickly. It is subject to constant 'improvements'. The lab technicians are worked hard in the basement of the general's great house (Antek's seen that much, working guard duty at the feasts). But the killing forest also evolves by itself in new ways which the lab technicians hadn't necessarily foreseen.

Antek looks down at his hands. And then up. Desert sounds. Cicada, slow rattle of snake. Antek eyes what his father calls the upside-down trees, but the edge farmers call the baobab. Tree limbs like roots hanging fat and bulbous, and beyond their thick lines, only more desert scrub. The baobab make a bumpy silhouette against the desert.

The old Sinta rememberers say that the baobab used to walk but that they stopped when Bavarnica's tribes were divided. The baobab haven't moved since. But Antek knows that is only an old Sinta bedtime story, told to quiet infants on the Sinta cabbage patch farms. Storytelling's quite illegal.

The general's man-made sun comes up now, like a grotesque pumpkin or a hole in the sky. The sky around it seems to Antek as though it fills up with blood.

The OneFolks' village has just gotten through a winter without dark, which came on the heels of a summer without daylight. But this is Autumn in Bavarnica. In the OneFolks' village, at least. The climate isn't so changeable on the edge farms, there's a wet season with barely any rain, followed by a dry one which takes up more and more of the year than it once did. The desert is coming in slow but surely over the Edge Farms.

Antek understands that the rains are being redirected toward the OneFolks' village. He's not sure how it's done. But there are rumours, spreading out from the officers' quarters. Whispers in the vents.

Before the Diggers' revolution, before even the Sintas' trials on the mountain, the edge farmers had stood in a long line, hand in hand, along the border between the edge farms and the OneFolks' village, causing the OneFolk farmers to down

tools and gaze in wonder. And the edge farmers had watched
the rain come down then, over the OneFolks' village beside
their lands, not a splash coming over their side of the fence.
Silent. It seemed more like a reproach than a protest at that
time. But later the killing forest grew up and outward. Things
changed.

Only the Egg Boys who guard them know that some of
the edge farmers will still stand there for hours, hand in hand
along the fence as the dust on top of the dry soil of their
lands behind them blows up in swathes, and small dunes
rise against the backs of their heels, as sand collects against
anything standing still for long on the edge farms. And that it's
right after the rains fall over the OneFolks that the edge farms'
rain dances begin.

When the music starts up, the soft hollers, the rhythms of
feet, whoops and shrieks, then the general's sirens start up
too. Like the chorus.

Some of the senior officers, Antek knows, had thought
that banning the rain dances was an unnecessary measure as
most folks had forgotten all the steps in the ancient dances
anyway. If they even believed in the dance now that the rain
was apparently government property, just like everything else.
Antek watches the rain clouds gathering. He realises that he's
waiting for the sound of the rain dance and the sirens. Nothing
comes. Perhaps the edge farmers are too tired to protest
today, the latest drought has after all lasted several weeks now.
What food was stored has long run out and most edge farmers
are using what strength they have left to tend to their dying.

Antek considers that if he were human, some or all of this
might matter. Tries to remember he's not. He looks down at

his hands.

Antek watches the next moon rising, the second one a little bit above the first one, until they're like the two crooked eyes of the desert hyenas, or the pirates that feed on them (illegal fairy tales told to OneFolk village children, meant to keep them indoors and away from the fences). One 'moon' is an all-seeing eye which rises over the mountain and scans it, lights up Antek in its beam. Antek tries to scramble backward into the rock mouth behind him but it's too late.

Shouts from below. Antek's father saw something moving, guessed it was his son. Long pause, during which Antek turns over his hands, examines his palms. Soft pink lines running down, covered in a thin layer of rock dust. Antek starts back down the mountain. Ducks under the rock tooth of his cave and slipping down its sheer face smoothly.

Antek is face to face with his father. There is a suffusion of blood in his father's face, Antek's never seen him so red. And the veins in his father's neck and temple standing out as thick as plant roots. His overly large eyes seem to bulge in his great head. This is going to be quite bad, Antek thinks, with the inexplicable feeling of detachment he's had since his last stain.

A soft cough from above in the silence, and then the government rain falls, soaking Antek and his father. Antek can hear the rush and hiss as rain hits the ground fast and hard round his feet.

The wind gets up, and now the tree behind Antek's father is heaving and straining against its roots. Flailing its stunted, burned limbs.

"It's time for your second staining, Egg Boy." Father says. "Your human side is still making you weak, I can see that even if you can't Egg Boy. Weak is a thing you can't be in the times coming, Boy. You will need to be a man soon. A man like me, Antek."

"Yes, father." Antek says. There is no intonation in his voice.

In the shadow of the rock behind, a small light dips and rises.

Now Jengi blows smoke toward the path the boy and man took. He's examining the back of Antek's head, and then the huge strange skull of his father beside him. The rain slows and the two moons dip, one by one, behind a rain cloud. And then seem to blink out.

There is only the sound of Jengi's feet now. Trooping back to the shop.

FIRST KILL

ANTEK ISN'T CUT OUT to be a farmer. Worst, for him, is pulling the male calves away from the teat. Antek hates that above all the things he's so far listed in his mind that he hates about farm life. There is soft, curled fur between the calf's dark eyes, blank with fear now.

Antek's father puts the gun into Antek's hand. Wraps his fingers around it. "Here. Take it, Egg Boy."

Antek looks at the gun.

"An Egg Boy eventually has to learn to kill things, Antek. This calf is yours now. You know how to use it? The gun?"

"Yes." Antek doesn't look up.

There's a clunk and rattle as Antek's father slides the rusting bolt across in the door behind him. "You'll come out when you've done it, Antek. Not before."

Antek leans his forehead against the thin chipboard wall which separates the calf from the cow in the next stall. The calf is knowing. Frightened. Antek tries to calm it but this only seems to make the calf panic more, it scatters in the small space, banging itself against the walls, soft groans for its mother. Better get it done quickly, Antek thinks. Get it over with.

He's let off the gun before he's even finished that thought. It takes longer than you would have thought for the last life to leave the small body. When it's over, when he thinks it's

over, Antek puts his hand on the small tufted brown head with
the dark mottled neck still extended out softly toward him.
The Egg Boy believes he can feel the last pulse heave and tick
underneath his left hand.

There is a long and bovine groaning. You think it can't be
coming from you, Antek thinks. But it is.

He can't say what he feels. Nothing he has any words for.
He tells himself that he's a killer now. That today is Day One.
Antek stares down at his stain. It's as though he sees it for the
first time in his life.

Now Antek senses his father standing outside the stall
door. And then the slide of his huge feet. Antek turns toward
the sound. The old man's boots cast a shadow in the gap
underneath the door. There's the slide of the bolt and the
accompanying heavy feeling in Antek's stomach, the one he
gets when he's in the presence of his father. Like a cold stone
in the gut. The door opens slowly.

Antek's father appraises the situation on the ground. The
clean-killed calf and the boy soaked in snot, drenched in tears,
haggard face. Like he'd seen the worst thing that life holds.
And then done it himself. Antek's father tips back on to his
heels. He scratches his head. Can this really be a stained boy?
An egg boy? He thinks. This guilt, this suffering? Why would
the lab technicians have kept that part of his humanity? They
never did before, not in the previous 46 egg batches. They
considered humanity to be a flaw to trip a soldier up on duty.
So ... Is the boy a flawed sample? What was the plan? He
remembers the rumour that a Sinta infiltrated the labs before
Antek's batch was hatched out. The Egg Man tries to put the
thought away, can't. If the boy is flawed then he'll be cancelled

along with his batch. High treason not to inform the general on him.

Antek's father decides not to file a report on the boy, it's sudden. That decision. And he can't exactly explain it, even to himself. But the thought rattles round the Egg Man's head. Must've been tweaks in this batch, he thinks. Wasn't that always the rumour? Gaddys said it was designed to sow fear in the ranks, and that batch 47 have been rigorously tested in the labs. But now the Egg Man considers his son Antek. The boy has certainly never quite seemed like a stained boy. *He's never felt like my son.*

Antek feels the calf's mother nudging at the chipboard, bump, bump, bump and then a bovine moan which must have come from the locked stall next door, but to Antek seems to have come up from below the spiky hay floor, and even under that too, from the wooden floorboards which Antek rests his large bony knees on, further down and down still until it seems to Antek there is nothing below that long groaning sound of the calf's mother.

And one day this will be only a memory Antek has of his first kill, but it will be a memory which will seem to survive all memory reboots and erasures until the day when the past will be all stripped away, then this one scene will rise up. The calf and the cow shed.

And there will be who he thought he was before it. Who he knew he was after.

"Stop that noise, Boy."

Antek's father takes the gun out of Antek's hand.

"Get on back to the house." He pushes the calf with his boot. The soft flesh of the calf's stomach yields to his boot pressure, he slides a knife out of his back pocket.

"I'll follow you back when I'm done here, Antek." Wields his knife in the air.

Antek reaches the farm gate to his house, he pauses. He's not quite sure why. Sniffs the air. Just a few scrabble-necked chickens pecking in the yard, the occasional gloomy bellows of the cows in the field beyond the glinting farm fence. And the dog is barking. But then again, the dog is always barking.

Through the farmhouse window, Antek can see the fire burning in the fireplace. It seems huge, the fire. Even from outside. His mother must have put too many logs on it again. Antek presses on forward, pushing against his premonition. Puts his hand out toward the familiar door knob, his hand seems to him to be a mile away. I am untuned again, he thinks. Quietly wishes Central Control would address the problem.

The door knob against his palm is cold. Antek turns the knob, then he pushes. Soft clanking sound as the door opens. He presses it closed without looking behind him. Holds on to it one moment too long, noting the fingernail marks in the paintwork round the door knob, and down the hinge of the door from the day his mother tried and failed to escape with him as an infant. Antek can't remember that day, except perhaps in bits and pieces. He remembers holding on to his mother's head, while she scratched and clawed at exits. While she screamed. He remembers Father's huge boots on the door jamb, the cold light behind him and that his mother was different from that day forwards. Antek's father had voluntarily increased the number of his wife's daily reboots. Once she was assessed a flight risk.

There is a strong wind in the yard outside the farmhouse just now, a powerful enough surge that it conducts a swathe of the yard's fine gravel before it, the door shudders in its hinges. Antek's mother sits with her back to the door. Not moving.

And then a sudden wind-blast that rattles the door and threatens to tear it out of its hinges. She flinches sharply once. Then goes on softly shuddering in her chair. Her tremor lasts around a minute, and normally Antek would go to her, hold her inside the loop of his arms joined by his hands and squeeze in the way that he's learned will steady her. Although he's not quite sure why. Some unfathomable tradition from her girlhood. She used to try to 'hug' him back when he was small, but the thing unnerved him and in a little while she understood, or at least she had seemed to accept it. Antek doesn't like to touch people, not if he can help it.

Antek feels exhausted in a way he can't explain, not even to himself. When Mother reaches out one bony hand to pat him, passing, he steps around her outstretched fingers. Moves toward the kitchen drawer and slides it open. He stands there, looking down. It's a strange impulse, what am I doing here? He thinks. Antek's mother sits immobile in her chair. She waits for her son.

Something about the contents of the drawer catches Antek's eye, it's an odd arrangement. Spoons collected at the top, forks at the bottom, battered knives to the left side, then in the heart of the drawer: one spoon, one fork, one knife. Perfectly polished. It isn't like Antek's mother to clean things. She rarely moves from her chair. The cutlery on either side is dim grey with collected dirt. Tinny-looking, next to the gleaming silver in the middle. Looking closer still at the silver cutlery set in the middle, Antek sees the nick in the knife handle. Now he's thinking. Fingers the scar on his chin.

And now he notices that one prong of the fork is bent slightly left, like a listening antennae. And then there's the spoon. There's a small inky stain in the centre of the spoon's face. Antek can't say what the substance is, but it doesn't come off when he scratches at it with his thumbnail, not on his shirt neither, when he rubs at it. "What's this?" He asks. Turning softly toward his mother. She doesn't answer. Turns toward him. She begins gently rocking her chair.

It seems like paint, only paint has been forbidden for a long time in Bavarnica.

"What'd you do to the spoon?" It's a scientific question, as far as Antek is concerned. His mother never moves from her chair without a reason. And her reason is always fair-to-middling interesting to Antek. Mother and son are not entirely unalike, or so it seems and in spite of the fact that she is only an organic.

She watches her son. "Antek." She says. And then her long, dim, unblinking gaze. She seems to look right through Antek. As if to some essential thing hidden just behind the boy. Antek has the sense that she is looking toward someone else. He turns. No-one.

Now the pupils of his mother's eyes darken and change, and then the changes spread out from that centre: the coloured yellow iris of her left eye seems to shift into brown, the lapis lazuli blue of her right iris is blackening. And then the coloured irises are being swallowed by her pupils, followed by the yellowing whites of her eyes. In a minute, perhaps two, the entire area of both eyes is treacle coloured. Antek takes two sharp steps forward, toward her. He tilts her head up with his hands. Makes a quick, expert appraisal. "Reboot." He says aloud.

Mother's clearly been rebooted, and recently, Antek calculates. From the look of her, she was erased some time over the last hour. And if that's true then when did she do this with the spoon? It must have been some time before that, so she knew the reboot was coming. What was she trying to remember?

Double helpings of the erasures is a regular dose for the mothers and wives of the newly stained Egg Boys. As they transition into Egg Men, there are occasionally breakouts from the mothers and sometimes younger family members. Furniture thrown out on the streets, yelling, or the smashing of windows. For mothers to be removed and replaced is not unheard of in Bavarnica. But it seems that Antek's mother has been through a triple or even a quadruple course of reboots. It's likely that she won't know who he is.

"Antek," she says again, sharply. And then softer, "Antek." She repeats, looking at him. It's a knowing look, with a hint of triumph in it, "Antek, give me my spoon, Boy." Antek looks down at his hand. Passes the spoon over. And now she wraps her trembling hands around it, pulls it into her chest.

"Why do you never want to forget me?" Antek asks now. "I mean ... after the reboots. You always find a way to know who I am, Mother. Even when you can't rightly say what my name is."

"I know who all of you are. Antek." She says. Not making sense, or not making any sense that Antek can see.

"Antek," she says. "My sons." And then looking up at Antek sharply. "Your name is Antek?" And then gazing gratefully at the spoon-reminder. "I knew I was due for a big dose, a large reboot." She sighs. She sounds more like herself. "So I 'wrote' your name all over my kitchen."

"You can beat the reboot?"

"Yes." She says. "Sometimes." She eyes the scar on his chin.

Antek takes a step back, makes a shrewd appraisal of the room. Letters are banned but Antek's mother has been inventive at leaving herself signs and notices of all kinds that something was being lost. Something or someone. Taps the side of her nose. "I have found ways," she says. Cackling, and then falling silent. As though she forgets again. And now pressing the spoon into the tassels of the embroidered scarf around her neck, so that the spoon is hidden underneath the tassels. "I have ways to remember my sons." She says. "I take back what I can."

Her eyes glisten.

And now if you blinked then you'd think you imagined the thing, Antek thinks, as once more his mother's face takes on that lost, absent expression of the recently rebooted. Another shiver starts in her shoulders and then running down over her body, like a small wave or as though a seam of electrical points attached to the surface of her skin are triggered, one by one. She drops the spoon when the sting of it reaches her wrist.

Antek doesn't pick the spoon up, not right away. Spins gently on his heels. It's as though the scene springs into life:

he can see that the house is a body of signs, mementoes. Many of which he guesses that his mother can no longer decipher since her reboot, but leave her with only the vague sense of a disjuncture in the normal lay out of a room: a picture askew, the three lampshades in a row, heads bowed like three huge feeding birds, to remind her there should be three of us, mother, father and son. A sideboard cabinet pulled out, so that the sharp jut hits your hip as you pass the lampshades, as if to say 'Take notice. Something is changed.'

Not so much a reminder of what's lost, most of it, Antek thinks, fingering the scar on his chin, not so much a reminder of who is lost as a reminder that someone was.

"Snake." She says. Eyeing the back of Antek's head.

It's what she always says. Antek used to wonder if she meant him or maybe his stain, which can look a little scaly sometimes. And silver in the dim light of the living room. But something makes Antek look toward the vent, a moment later a small sound catches his attention. He listens.

"Snake in the vents of the house." She says. "They put it there to control me. The day you were stained, it came. Snake in the vents of a house not to control me ..." she says. "But to get me to control myself around you, Antek. Not talk too much. The latest batch is always precious to the general." She smiles. Eyes the vents. "What they don't know because they never checked is ... I ain't afeared of snakes." She smiles. Hugs herself.

Antek sighs. "And your son is a spoon." He turns toward his mother. Now Antek watches as his mother's grin spreads out slowly across her features, wrinkles her nose and the soft lines around her eyes. Blink and blink, and the colour of her eyes returns to normal. It's like a break in the cloud, a sudden and unfathomable joy, to have her fully return from the reboot. The warmth of it spreads through Antek.

There is a glimmer of light filtering in through the dusty curtains and the fern over the fireplace softly uncurls. This seems to release something in Antek's mother. "We take back what we can, Antek." Taps the side of her head. "They won't get it all, Antek." His mother seems to take some delight in repeating his name.

They hear the snake bumping hard against the side of the vents. Rattles its tail. As though it senses the change in the room's atmosphere. Mother gazes in the direction of the vent, the snake.

"It's terrified," she says. "I can't see what it sees. The poor thing, but it's trapped. Like me. It belongs in the killing forest with the other fearful things." She says.

"That snake is big, Mother. It would happily eat you."

She smiles at her son. "Of course, of course. Well, it is a snake after all. T'aint nothing personal." She shrugs, as though unconcerned. "Speaking of snakes, where did that durned Egg Man get to ...?" She stares at the front door for so long that she seems to forget again. She settles down in her chair.

Crunch and slide, Antek hears his father trudging slowly, heavily, down the gravel path toward the farmhouse. When the front door slams open, it hits the wall fast, bounces back and is caught by Antek's father's stiff right hand. Must have hurt his fingers, Antek thinks. He notices that his father doesn't react.

Father appears not to see his wife and son right away, "This room is a tip," he says. And then eyeing the rearranged lamps, the crookedly placed sideboard. Looking shrewdly at his wife, who leans and slumps in her chair. He crosses the room then. Sitting down heavily in the chair by the kitchen window. He looks out. Antek looks in the direction that his father's looking.

Beyond the kitchen window, Antek's father has a clear view of the slowly greening Sinta cottage next door. Zorry's cottage. He seems to rearrange his chair now, the better to see. Now Antek and his father watch as Jengi slips out from beyond the henhouse at the back of the Sinta cottage, crosses the dusty yard with his loping step. Three strides, he takes. Just to reach Zorry's back door.

"Some strange comings and goings, to be sure." Father says. Grunts. And now Antek catches sight of Mamma Ezray briefly, at the left, upstairs window. And then again at her kitchen window, only moments later. She is drawing all the curtains and blinds, although it's several moments before curfew and the whistle hasn't even sounded yet.

Antek's father goes on looking at the Sinta cottage for a long time. And now Antek looks too. Tries to see what his father sees there.

"Like a house in a dream, the moss covered cottage." Antek's father says. It's a strange and surprising statement, coming from Father. And after it, there's a long, strained silence in the kitchen. Antek waits for his father to speak again, but he seems to have said all that he plans to.

Once more there's the sound of heavy boots in the gravel outside. Voices. Antek turns toward his father's chair. Empty. Shape of his father' behind has slow-worn grooves in the wood. His father, having moved silently and fast across the room, is now opening the front door with some gusto. Greets his men.

Antek recognises the two soldiers only slightly. The larger Egg Man, on the left, is from batch 46, fully stained just like Antek's father, and with the same huge skull which is the most distinctive feature of his unit. The man on the right is different. Judging by his physical appearance he's a batch 47 Egg Boy. Antek believes he's never seen this one before, noting that the boy looks jittery and confused, so it seems likely that he's recently received his last stain. The Egg Boy has luminous red hair, freckled skin running down to his collar bone. Wide amazed eyes. It's a warning.

Antek notices that his mother has begun rocking her chair, rhythmically behind him. Her rocking motions begin slowly. Getting gently faster.

Antek doesn't have a choice about the last staining, as it turns out. He's taken to the labs by force. Father's hand is clapped over his mouth as he heaves him over the door jamb toward the waiting van.

Antek's mother rocks her chair in crazy rhythms now, urgent, fast and getting faster, until it seems to her son as though she'll be flung from her chair by the motion. Antek's father deposits his son in the large boot of the van, locks the door and then marches tight-lipped back to the house. He gives his wife a brief and furious stare, "You see what you did, Woman?" He opens his mouth wide, showing all his sharpened steel-capped teeth. "I had to force him to go. How does that help?"

And then raising his bitten hand to show her. "The boy bit me!"

She goes on rocking her chair back and forth, back and forth. More steadily now, but the motions still in that urgent manner. She is staring straight ahead. Antek's father explodes,

"You see what you did?" He screams. "Now the boy don't want his stain! Do you imagine for one moment, Woman, that any of this helps him? DO YOU WANT THIS SON TO BE CANCELLED TOO?" He stops, panting. Lowers his voice and spits the last words. "Along with every other Antek there's ever been."

The snake is rattling furiously through the vents now, circles the house, bangs the tinny sides of its cage, bumps the vents and flickering its huge tongue in and out of every corner. Now Antek's mother lets her eyes wander from her husband's feet to his face. She seems to see her husband standing, boots planted either side of the doorway, face turning puce and the huge stems at his neck expanding. It's a vision that would terrify most people in Bavarnica, but she closes her eyes and the ghost of a smile. Eyeballs seem to roll back in her head.

And now the life seems to go out of Antek's father. It's sudden.

"The boy doesn't want to be an Egg Man!" He slumps against the door frame. And then quieter still, "Doesn't want to be an Egg Man like me."

She stops rocking. She blinks and opens her eyes. Remains perfectly still.

Jengi, underneath the window ledge out back of the house, softly slides out and into the shadow to one side of the cowshed. He arches and stretches his limbs.

Makes his way toward the long copse out back.

PIZEN

ZORRY'S COTTAGE IS NEXT door to Antek's farmhouse. A soft landslide had left the Sintas' cottage buckling to the left, and now it was as though it tipped its hat to the steel trap egg farmhouse next door, with its razor sharp glinting fences. The cottage took a bow or stumbled, somehow couldn't get up.

A creeping moss grows over the most broken down parts of the cottage and from a distance it looks as though the whole building's growing haphazardly out of the soil.

Zorry's mind moves slowly today. She hasn't eaten in twenty-seven hours.

"You hungry?"

"Yes, Mamma," Zorry says quietly.

"Nothing to spare in the general's kitchen?"

"Nothing today." Small pause and then, "The Egg Men have started throwing the leftovers into the moat."

Mamma Ezray's shoulders droop. She looks down at her work.

"Aye. They're only following orders."

"Following orders, eh? Well ... I wouldn't mind so much, Zorry says. "Only they killed the critters first." She looks up, checks her mother's face for understanding. "Killed them for waste, Mamma."

Mamma Ezray doesn't seem to hear her daughter. She is

grinding something green with her stone mortar and wooden pestle.

Zorry untangles herself from her apron. "Did it right in front of the half-starved kitchen workers too. Were they orders too? Seemed spiteful to me." Now Zorry eyes the Egg Man's farmhouse through the kitchen window. Rubs the back of her hand against her left cheek. She shivers suddenly.

"Cold?" Mamma Ezray looks up. "Night's falling. Shut the windows, Zorry."

Zorry doesn't move. "I heard they'll start burning their food leftovers from tomorrow. Destroy what they don't need." Mamma Ezray's face takes on a strange, amazed look. Eyes widen. "The general's moat has its own ecosystem nowadays. I don't think anybody planned that." Twists at one long dusty grey curl, lets it fall across her left eye. "Now they'll have to deal with that'un too. Diseases, vermin, all sorts. And the wild dogs that feed on the vermin, multiply, some of them have rabies. Imagine that? Rabies in the general's show village. An ancient disease."

Ezray sighs. "Sometimes ... Sometimes Zorry I do wonder if they're even quite right in the head. The OneFolks." She gazes at her elder daughter.

The green substance at the curved round end of Mamma Ezray's wooden pestle is just a little off somehow. She can't say exactly what's wrong with it, but she knows something is. Tipping her head slightly toward it, sniffs. And then sticks out the tip of her tongue.

Something is stopping Mamma Ezray from testing this plant. She can't say what is yet. Sometimes these intuitions can be important, but she's not sure if this one is. Or whether she's just been rattled by Zorry's kitchen tales from the general's house. Ezray pokes her tongue out again, toward the soft green substance.

Zorry eyes her mother. "Don't. It looks like pizen, Mamma."

Zorry's hungry stomach groans and the rumbling growl goes on for several seconds. This seems to steel Mamma Ezray.

"Only one way to find out." Mamma Ezray forces herself to taste her new plant, grimaces at the first lick. Spits it up. "Sorry. Not this one. Not for eating anyway." She screws up her face, dabs the end of her tongue with her apron.

And then, "But I've not seen nothing quite like this plant here, Child." She holds it up to show Zorry. "I found it last night, growing right at the edge of the forest's mouth. Like the killing forest spat out a tooth, just for me." She smiles. Stares at the green paste still clinging to the end of the pestle, and then down at the softly wriggling root of the plant, pinned down by a small arrow head to the right.

"You going to grind that one?"

The plant seems to wriggle harder against the arrow head. Mamma Ezray eyes it. "I reckon not." She says.

There is a quivering leaf on a separate tray beside the long root, and the two parts of the plant seem to be trying to rejoin.

"What's that mottling on it? Disease?"

Mamma Ezray does not seem to hear Zorry's question. And muttering softly to herself now, "I just know that I can ... Turn this plant."

"The forest spat out a tooth, eh?" Zorry eyes the plant on the table. "You sure it weren't a fang?"

Now the plant root begins rocking softly side to side.

"Not yet edible." Mamma Ezray pronounces, watching it for a while longer. "I need more time."

"You tried cooking it?"

Mamma Ezray rolls her eyes. "Are you aiming to teach me my business, Zorry?" Mamma Ezray is irritable with hunger.

Zorry's shoulders droop a little. Her stomach hurts and her mind swims gently. She gets up and moves slowly across the room toward the sink. Stops and holds a kitchen chair back halfway. Mamma Ezray looks up, concerned.

They know at once, just from the quality of the door knock, that it's Jengi outside.

"Quick, let him in," Mamma Ezray says, getting up to close the curtains, although it's several moments before the whistle announcing curfew will be blown. Jengi knocks again. Open palmed, and rattling at the handle.

"Come in!" Mamma Ezray's voice carries gently. Jengi dips around the door. Soft click as it closes behind him. Jengi slides the rusting latch across. Glances through the blinds to the left of the door. "He saw me."

"What?"

"I think he saw me. The Egg Man next door."

"It's fine. You have a shop delivery for us, don't you? That'll cover you. Something suitably spiteful from Gaddys, something that ain't so much a gift as a threat?" She eyes him.

"I guess I might be able to think of some kind of alibis along those lines."

"Do that."

Mamma Ezray goes on watching Jengi, with a warm, shrewd gaze. Notices he does not meet either Zorry's eye, or her own. He seems to always look down. Jengi takes three careful steps toward her, pulls up a chair. Mamma Ezray feels Zorry's presence behind her now. Feels Zorry's nail-bitten right hand on the back of her chair.

"What do you want, Jengi?" She asks.

She notices Jengi's gaze swivel, as if by instinct, toward Zorry. "And you can take your eyes off my daughter, Jengi." Mamma Ezray says, warm and stern as a general can be sometimes with her troops. And then folding her arms across her chest. "Do not bring trouble to my house, Jengi. This is what I have asked you in return for my work. And yet, here you are. Explain."

The two are eye to eye, for one long moment.

Jengi shows Mamma Ezray his palms and smiles. "You and I have always seen things more or less the same way, Mamma Ezray. I came to tell you that Zorry's mission is finished. That her work is done."

"Good." Mamma Ezray smiles approvingly. "Then you may have my next promising plant. To seed out by the baobab."

"Thank you, Mamma Ezray."

Zorry winces. Turns toward the sink, with her back toward Jengi. Zorry is silent when she's angry. As though she mistrusts her own words. How dare they speak about her this way? As though she were a thing to be traded over. Zorry will never be owned, not even by Mamma Ezray trying to protect her. Zorry is wiping down the cutlery. Simmering quietly by the sink. As if they sense something, no-one looks at her.

Once more something on the floor seems to catch Jengi's eye. Now mamma Ezray rustles in her apron pocket, pulling out a second plant root. "She sticks to leaves now," Zorry says, turning at last toward Jengi. There's an edge in her voice. "Mamma Ezray nearly died this time last year, tasting berries and the new seed, gathered from the ground around the fence to the killing forest. The same pizen berries are in season now but their appearance has changed. We have to watch out." She checks Jengi's face for signs of understanding.

"I'm worried Mamma Ezray's going to catch a pizen now that she's stepped up her work, what with Mamma Zeina gone."

Mamma Ezray tuts, she goes on crushing the new plant root with her mortar and pestle. Jengi goes on examining the floor, as though he hasn't even heard Zorry. At one point he finds an excuse to move his chair, examines what's underneath its wooden limbs.

"You looking for something, Jengi?" Mamma Ezray sniffs. "I mop my floor every day, Son."

"It's ... I'm looking for ..." He looks up. Meets her eye, and then as though he catches himself, "It's nothing."

Mamma Ezray sniffs the mortar's contents. She scratches an insect bite on her arm. Grinds the pestle anticlockwise.

"And what are you looking for Mamma Ezray? Are you looking for water, like Mamma Zeina was?"

Mamma Ezray gives him a bleak look. "I am looking for food for my childur. Gaddys is starving out the Sinta, at least until she gets her some information from one of us. Haven't you heard about that, Jengi? I am looking for a plant that my family can eat." She repeats, speaking too loudly now. Her eyes fill up with fierce tears.

"And how's that going Mamma Ezray?" Jengi leans forward, asks her quietly.

She sniffs. She looks down at the half crushed plant and then seems to relent. Lean towards him a little. "You caint eat this one, not the t'other one neither. Not yet any road, so that's a wasted night's work." She stops. She rests her elbow on the kitchen table, her forehead on her hand.

"We're trying to breed the pizens out so we can eat it." She looks up at Jengi. "But we're not there yet. Won't kill you now, those two. But they'll still leave a stomach ache lie a kick in the stomick. That's bad. I guess we'll eat it when we really have to."

Zorry looks down. The plate where the first root was pinned is now empty. Zorry curses. Picks Zettie up off the floor. There's a slightly anxious moment whilst Mamma Ezray locates the escaping plant and then pins it down again.

"It's no good." She says. Skewering it.

Some days it feels as though everything gets away from Mamma Ezray. She's struggled with the plant for the last three hours, and they still can't eat it. And all this straight after a night spent in the killing forest. A night and half a day of effort and her children are still hungry. She feels her eyes closing slowly, she lets her hands fall. And then, blink, blink, and she goes back to attending to the plant.

"A mother cupboard cannot give up her work," she tells Zorry now. Sighs. "No matter what. That's the oath: hope. Hope is the resistance, Zorry. In truth, it keeps us alive as much as food or water." She scratches the insect bite on her arm once more. "Of course ..." She sighs. "Some days it's easier to hope than others, just as the food cupboard is sometimes bare, sometimes full." Mamma Ezray turns to look at Zettie. The child is playing on the floor with a stick and a pile of stones. "But what else?" Mamma Ezray says, watching the infant for a moment longer. "There is nothing else but to go on."

Jengi places a capsule on the table. It has the shop's packaging on it. Gaddys' hair-coils drawn across the plastic lid.

"What's that?"

Jengi pulls the lid off the capsule, by way of an answer. They smell the soup before they see it. "Sweet potato, peppers, chicken, white beans." Jengi reels off the list, as the aroma of herbs and spices, nourishing cooking oils from the soup hits their noses. "Made it myself."

"But ... This is a feast, Jengi?"

"Forget it," he says. "And I only got a cup for you. Lots of hungry Sinta right now, but I saved this'un for you." Jengi pushes the small plastic capsule towards them.

"Give it to them, the children," Mamma Ezray says, brusquely. Indicating Zorry leaning at the sink, Zettie playing on the kitchen floor tiles. And then, "You are taking over Mamma Zeina's work then, Jengi?" She smiles. "Feeding the Sinta in the hungry times."

"Aye." He nods. "Well I owe Mamma Zeina that much."

"Do you? Mamma Zeina never wanted anything from us in return, Jengi." The Sinta woman eyes him curiously.

"Nor do I. Truly." Jengi looks down at Mamma Ezray's mortar and pestle, the luminous green paste squelched against the side of the dish.

The Mother Cupboards often work as cooks to the OneFolk by day so it's an irony that Jengi enjoys that the mother cupboards cult is all about creating a wealth of secret eating. Keeping alive the very folks that aren't invited to the feasts in the first place. But they've been working day and night since the hungry times began on the Sinta farms, they can't last like this.

Mamma Ezray reluctantly accepts the last spoonful of the soup from Zorry, expecting little more than vegetable water, realising quickly that her daughter has loaded the spoon with chicken. Mamma Ezray's surprised and a little of the red soup dribbles down her chin. Zorry mops it.

"We're worried about you, Mamma Ezray. You have to keep going for us."

Jengi is winding his big hooked thumbs gently around each other. Watching his thumbs. He's still looking down at the floor. And then up at Zorry, sensing her watching him too, cat-like, nervous, sinking into her corner. Jengi pretends not to notice. "It's just … They need a …" He stops himself. "We have no map. What we have really always needed is a … Map of the general's house, Mamma. The general's house, the labs, the feast room and the sewers running underneath it. All of it." He's still looking down at the floor.

"My parents were mapmakers," Mamma Ezray says, after a small pause. "As I imagine you know. My father mapped the mountains for the excavation projects that got folks so excited in the last era. It was stolen from him, and helped guide the Egg Men to every last one of his friends. Got folks killed. He never made another map after that."

"Didn't he? Are you sure?" Jengi is looking at Mamma Ezray strangely.

"No. And nor will I. A map would only bring trouble to my children, Jengi. A map would bring foreign bombs, death and worse. There is a reason the general built Sinta farmsteads over his most important projects. The man's not a fool. We are ... Dispensable to him."

"Understood. But there are other ways in which a map may be useful to the resistance." Jengi smiles. And then looking up at Zorry wryly. She bows slightly.

Zettie, sensing something, examines her sister briefly. Just a glance and then gets back to her work. Zettie is making something from the contents of her apron pocket. She's perked up since she ate the soup and her work absorbs her.

Mamma Ezray had done so much food experimenting whilst pregnant that before her little sister Zettie was born, Zorry was a little worried that the new baby, when she came, would have the texture of a boiled frog, or loosely veined floppy ears like the pizen leaves which her mother munched as her belly rose. Don't talk rubbish, child. Mamma Ezray used to say, but with a nervous edge in her voice until baby Zettie came out looking exactly the way that Zorry had looked as a baby, which is to say, shiny and round, with strong little legs that curled toward her chest, trying to take the shape in which she'd been squashed into Mamma Ezray's womb. She had Zorry's huge amazed eyes, tinged with green in the first days, and then changing as the seasons shifted. Zettie now has Zorry's eyes, gold flecked irises. And like all Sinta, Zettie's eyes shift in colour with her mood, the light, and depending on what she has eaten. Also the shifts in the weather. Mamma Ezray says that this is muddle-headed talk. Eyes don't change.

Mamma Ezray gets up now, to fetch Jengi black coffee and a twist of cactus chipotle. She comes back in from the kitchen. Hands the last piece of oat bread to Zettie, who chews the end of it thoughtfully. And then trying to soften it in her tin cup of rainwater.

"You still teaching her about the edible plants and the pizens too?" Jengi raises his head, looks at Zettie. "That's a useful thing to larn the child at a time like this, Mamma Ezray. We have to pass on everything we know, that's a lesson we can all learn from the loss of Mamma Zeina. She took much of her knowing with her."

"Zettie don't listen to me overmuch," Mamma Ezray replies, "you caint tell what goes in. What doesn't. Childur go their own way. No way to know for sure what Zettie is learning, if she's learning anything. She don't communicate much. But the child's best quality is that she appears to grow up on thin air. Don'tcha, Child?" Mamma Ezray says, gently leaning down. Patting Zettie's small knees. "Don't know ... What Zettie will learn to rearrange for her own self, one day. And seeing it all differently in the entire, I shouldn't be in the least bit surprised." Mamma Ezray is squinting into the low light at the window. She thinks she sees something moving behind the Egg Man's farmhouse.

"Did you see that van?"

"No."

"I heard screaming. I thought ... I heard something next door."

"You look worried Mamma Ezray."

"Aye. Something's wrong." She says. "I can feel it."

"Wrong more'n usual?"

"Yes." She says. "Wrong more'n usual."

Jengi gets up and strides toward the back door. But something causes him to stop. Eye the latch. He turns back toward the room. He's still looking down at the floor.

Zettie gets up from drawing her lizard, pads over toward him. "Jengi." She turns toward her drawing, points.

"Ah, Zettie," he says. "I haven't time for playing lizards today."

Zettie's lizards are now in the space left by every broken floor-tile, of which there are three.

Jengi's warm smile in the gap between the door and the hinge. Click. Zorry turns back to the room. Small shock. Her mother is standing right behind her. Arms crossed across her chest.

"Zorry, your work is done. This is too dangerous now."

"Yes, Mamma."

Zorry feels her mother's scrutiny all the way to the front door.

"Where are you going now, Child?"

"Mamma ... I'm not a child."

THE SCHOOL ROOF

THE LIGHT IS FALLING gently, outside. Mottled pattern of leaves on the classroom floor and, in a bit, the edges of the pattern seem to move and change. The OneFolk childur look up to see Zettie's face upside down at the topside rim of the window. The teacher is writing at the board, has her back to the class.

Zettie's grin is warm and slow, turning her head slowly, and her friends, stuck inside, feel strangely honoured by it. Zettie vanishes. The OneFolk childur hear a clatter of bare feet on the classroom roof, and the tumbling gravel as Zettie skids, slips down and bangs herself on something, saves herself at the last minute. Soft, concealed laughter from the OneFolk childur.

And now the OneFolk childur hear the small thuds of feet overhead, the soft thunk and patter. Zettie is pretty much the leader of the Sinta children, the ones still too young to work by a year or two. And this is a testament to Zettie because Sinta childur are not easily led as a point of pride.

The large school pond is, of course, a natural attraction, to all manner of life forms, including children. Zettie and her small friends now come in small scouting troops toward the schoolyard most days, and the storms permitting. Mostly they come in the damp, baking aftermath of the storms just to see what's risen in the school pond just beyond the Furdy. Dead things mostly. And if it's worth trying to eat or not depends not so much on what it is, Zettie reckons, but on how hungry we are.

The Sinta children are always barefoot, although Zettie once had a left shoe, three sizes too big and with the sole coming clean away from the body of the shoe, so that her foot flapped like a tongue in the gap. She'd dragged that shoe along to slow herself down for three days until she'd swapped it for an old neck tie that was plucked out of the rubble of a bombed out house. Now Zettie wears that instead. No shirt, just the tie. Red silk, from the old times. The defiant gesture of the tie, and in a banned colour, seems to define Zettie's leadership. Although her followers are half-starved, mostly exhausted children, with the exception of the children of the Mother cupboards. They are a little better fed, on account of their mothers' gardening.

It's a daily struggle for food on the Sinta farms since Mamma Zeina's death. Gaddys hopes that by shrinking the rations she'll persuade somebody to come forward, name the mother cupboards. No-one has, perhaps thanks to the mother cupboards being a more reliable source of food than Gaddys herself is, perhaps due to Jengi and his back door groceries.

The Sinta childur are mostly attracted to the school roof these days by the smell of cooking food, in the school kitchens. Hanging like bats (the effect of the new Sinta uniforms, with their winged arms and pointed hoods) over the lightning box around the playground. Their newly buzz-cut hair revealing small forlorn-looking skulls atop boney necks, lower still there are protruding rib cages, strong, skinny limbs. If the crop doesn't come on time there will be swollen bellies on the Sinta Farms by the end of this month, well ... "We are not there yet." Mamma Ezray would say if you asked her. She's working day and night now on her plant experiments. And sometimes puffing herself up, just a little. Rising. "We may be hungry but we ain't starved. Least not yet."

All the Sinta childur physically struggle against the constraints of their 'uniform'. Unlike the OneFolks' childur, the Sinta know what it is to long for comfortable fabrics, t-shirts, shorts and flowered patterns, stripes and shirts and dresses printed with the silhouettes of baobab trees at sunset. Clothes patched up from the old days until they're mostly, it seems, made of patches. The government uniform is sticky and hot, restricts limbs. Worse, it's overly tight at the collar and seams, leaves the children's skin raw and complaining. Welts at the arms and wrists for their mothers to bathe after curfew, which is the only time that the uniforms are allowed to come off.

The tie around Zettie's neck is strictly speaking against regulations. She's also keeping her hair, at least for a little while longer. Worst of all, she has an officer's button, found by Jengi out beyond the baobab trees and sewn, by him, into the seam of her uniform.

Zettie has learned to twist the officer's button when she's anxious. Jengi told her it was a secret but, not understanding children, didn't realise that you can't burden a child with secrets. Of course Zettie has told all her friends.

One of Zettie's tiny followers told the school teacher about Zettie's officer button in exchange for a sandwich three days ago. And then dropping the sandwich, as if the child's own hands protested at their owner's betrayal, and the sausage and lettuce, the contents of the sandwich all over the floor and the table.

TRAINING DAY

"SO WHAT'RE WE DOING here, Jengi?"

"Hushhhh. I'm training you." Grins.

"You're training me for the killing forest?" Zorry sighs ironically. "And here I thought you liked me, Jengi."

He turns and eyes her. "I do. I do like you. But you is a mother cupboard now, Zorry. Better I teach you how not to get killed in here, since it's kindly 'bout to become a home from home, so to speak. Now. Hurry up with that fence."

Zorry gently strokes the suture in the fence, and then unpicks it. "You first," she says. Jengi rolls his eyes.

"It's dark," Zorry says to his back. And then, "I don't reckon to go right into the mouth of the forest."

"Zorry." He turns. Steels himself. "That's where Mamma Zeina got all her best plants."

Zorry doesn't answer.

"Okay. So it's slightly different every time," he explains.

"It doesn't seem so bad." Zorry lies. Things seem to move in the darkness around her.

"Don't get overconfident," he snaps. Zorry notices Jengi's teeth and eyes glitter, he's striped with moonlight. She takes a step backward from him. She can't quite say why.

"At first the forest will just try to learn you, Zorry." He says, a little softer this time. "It ain't a regular sort of jungle, Sinta. The killing forest is a single mind, with many parts to it. It will pull you in slow and then swallow you up fast. You have to learn its ways quickly. No room for mistakes. The forest can be ... Unforgiving."

Dark shapes of tree limbs and curling ferns are outlined against the moonrise. There is something sliding in the ground underneath her feet. "So ..." Jengi says, looking at her critically. "Just stay awake, okay Zorry?"

Jengi can't tell what the Sinta is thinking just now.

"As far as I can make out ..." Jengi looks around him. "Only the creatures at the edge of the killing forest, those in the low brush, are willing to come out of the killing forest. Through the fence iffen you let them, or leave a gap when you suture it. There are other things that ..." She looks where he looks. "Back there. The dark centre of the forest." He says. "Them things won't come out for love nor money, they'd rather pull you on in. They have ways. We haven't figured it all yet."

Zorry shudders.

"We'll stay on the edge of the killing forest tonight. Most mother cupboards don't never go in further than this point, not even your own Mamma Ezray. At least not since her childur were born. Mamma Zeina was ... She is a loss. We won't see her like again any time soon."

Zorry understands this to be a challenge. Steels herself. Pushes on through the leaves, just a little ahead.

"Scurvet." Zorry points to the tracks.

"Good." He says. Turning. "But which kind, Zorry? It's important to know." Zorry isn't sure.

She feels Jengi's eyes on her once more. "Stop staring," she instructs him, angered now. Blinks and scowls. Jengi, leaning forward, plucks an insect off her face. Pins it between his thumb and forefinger, turns it upside down to show Zorry its underside.

"A fast moving spider with jewelled back," he explains. "Enters your ears, nose or mouth." He points to the sharp little pincers, squeezes them expertly, and a little yellow liquid oozes. "That's the pizen."

"Oh." She says. And in a bit, "Thank you."

"What's that sound?"

"Don't worry about it."

"But Jengi." Holds his arm back. "I am worried about it. Tell me what it is. If you know."

"A creature you can hear but not see," Jengi explains. "Sounds as big as six bears but, as you've noticed, it's a strangely human groaning. Spooks you, don't it? Well don't let it, Zorry. The forest is just trying to raise your adrenaline levels. It's a kind of stress test." Looks around him. "Remember it's learning you, Zorry. Every step. Who you are. So ..."

"What do I do?" Zorry freezes again.

"So ... Let it know you, Zorry." He grins. "Push on forward like a mother cupboard. Like Zeina did. You ain't never been a coward, so far as I can make out."

He plunges on through the thicket toward the trees, by the path Mamma Zeina made with her feet over her years of trekking here. Zorry pauses briefly. Looks up. Moon through the tree bowers, creaking sounds overhead. Entwined fingers of twigs silhouetted against the old moon's singular light. No sign of the general's second moon yet, the search beam. She follows Jengi in, until she's enveloped by the dark.

Now there is only the sound of Jengi's breath, getting farther away. His feet in the bracken and the soft plant rot of the forest floor, crunch and squelch. Slow, regular steps, getting fainter.

The forest is still. Something makes her stand here, just a moment longer. Smell of waxen leaves and dark moss, something else. She can't say what it is.

Zorry catches up. "So that creature? The sound? Will it come after us?"

"I don't know. It never has so far, that's all I can say for sure. But it has established a ... pattern of behaviour, let's say. It doesn't get farther or nearer, just seems to want to stay close."

"Great. So it's stalking us."

"I don't ... I don't know."

She feels the creature beside her, sound of low, deep breaths. Not coming any closer or getting father away. Zorry feels angry suddenly. Unreasonably angry about the gaps in Jengi's understanding, why'd he bring me here? If he doesn't know his own self what it all is?

"So, I'm behind. I'm watching your back, Jengi. Who's watching mine?"

He sighs. "You're never going to trust me are you?"

She eyes him. "I don't remember you asking me to. Should I?"

"No. Absolutely not." He says sincerely. Slow smile.

"Alright then."

"So what was I saying ... We figure it's mostly been designed for general killing forest ambience." He says lightly.

"What? Is that supposed to be a joke?"

Jengi turns back in time to catch Zorry's scowl.

"I mean to say that it doesn't do much. At least not yet,

Zorry. Scares the holy baobab out of folks, that's about it. Far as I can make out." The heavy animal sounds stop, as if the creature were listening.

They go on trekking forwards, Zorry knowing to avoid the nipping saplings and leeches, learning from Mamma Zeina's downfall not to ignore the deadly small things, or to let the nips cluster on her. From time to time she picks a leach off the back of Jengi's neck, and he turns to her gratefully.

"The one eyed desert hyaena has apparently been modified again." He says. "Come on, climb."

"Where is it?" Zorry says, unalarmed, taking her cue from Jengi. And then she sees it.

"What the ...?"

It waits by the roots of the tree. Curiously human expression, gazing upward. Zorry feels a scream coming up from the base of her stomach. Now her fingers freeze and her grip on the tree becomes slippy. Now she grapples and fights to hold on to her branch. When she's found a secure hold, breathes out. Looks down, a little calmer.

The beast eyes her shrewdly. Gives a low, throaty, almost conversational snarl. There's an up-lilt at the end of its bark, like it's asking a question.

Jengi seems to Zorry to be unnaturally calm. Calmer than she's ever seen him. She sees it for the first time then, "You live for this. Don't you, Jengi? Danger, I mean."

Jengi shrugs. "I'm a Digger." He says. As if that were any kind of answer. And then, "Reminds me of Gaddys, that one," he says. Throwing sticks down at the creature. The creature tries to catch the sticks in its mouth, one hits its ear, hard, and its snarling grows louder.

"Holy baobab, Jengi. What the hell are you doing?"

"Relax. They're all noise."

The creature's pupils have narrowed into cat-like slits. A little drizzle is running down the black gums spilling out from its clumsily made jaw.

"Jengi." Zorry says sharply. "I think it understands you. Jengi, stop."

But Jengi shrugs again, doesn't seem to notice or care. Breaking off branches and throwing them down. Once again the creature dips and swerves and snaps at the air around it, several sharp branches and twigs manage to hit the sides of its head. It does not leave, but goes on dodging and whimpering, and then, when the branches stop flying, seems to take a long shrewd look at Zorry. Turning in a loop, slopes away.

"Guess it wanted to get a good look at the newest mother cupboard."

Zorry shivers.

"Anyway. It's had enough for now," Jengi says, sounding more serious suddenly. "But you showed it some fear, that's of interest to it. It'll double back with its friends. Now that will be something to worry about." Jengi slides expertly down the side of the tree. "We need to get back now." He says. A little more urgently than she's heard him speak since they arrived in the killing forest. She's noticed something else.

"What's wrong with it?" Zorry watches as the creature's vulpine nose reappears between the curling ferns to her right. Teeth and gums protrude from the hyaena's mouth, it has an immensely heavy lower jaw, and a top jaw which ends in a long, hooked, blackened tooth. Now Zorry listens to the sound of its lolloping footfall, moving away to the left. "What was wrong with it?" She asks the question again, unable to frame exactly what she's intuited. "Is it ... Fearful? A fearful creature?"

"What?" Jengi shrugs. "That's a Sinta question that I ain't equipped for." He laughs. "It's mostly just blind, Sinta. Seeing is not necessary when its sense of smell is so good. That creature sensed us long before we even got here, Zorry. It smelled our intention to come."

Zorry shivers.

"You cold?"

"No. Let's get out of here."

"The killing forest is evolving all the time Zorry. Or mutating at least."

The creature circles back in silence, puts its head back through the ferns, sniffs the air. Watches their blurred shapes moving away. And now tilting its over-large head, as though it understands their conversation. Curiously intelligent eyes.

"Why didn't it call for the others?"

"I don't know."

The creature seems to take a careful note of Zorry's outline, smaller than the first one, it thinks. But not by much. Not as strong, but more skilful at moving quietly through the forest than him, the creature notes. A thing like the girl could creep up on the nest. She's more dangerous than him. And then *Predator*. It says. Deciding. Soft, whooping, conversational-sounding calls to its mate. Danger. It says. And then Danger, *danger*.

There are several answers. Low, rasping, nuanced barks. And that soft up-lilt at the end again. Like a question.

"What does that barking mean?"

Jengi glances behind him. "We should get back. I'm ...

a little out of my depth." Jengi says, manoeuvring himself around a rotting tree stump. Zorry looks up again, listens. Seems to tune into the barks and low rasps, which are coming from several different angles now, meaning that the two of them are almost surrounded already. "This way." Zorry grabs his arm and then "Run!!"

Zorry's vision blurs slightly, launching them both, heads first, through the bracken. Zorry is faster on her feet than Jengi, she quickly lets go of his arm, gets ahead. Reaching the suture in the fence before Jengi, tearing it apart with her hands.

"You first."

Shoves Jengi through, Zorry climbs out after.

The creatures make no attempt to come through the hole in the fence and Zorry stitches the sides of the tear together slowly, carefully. Trembling tight hand. Muttering soft apologies to the fence as she goes. There is the sound of barking, snuffling as she stitches and pours the healing pizen. The fence re-grows until the stitched seam in it is hidden.

Jengi turns to Zorry, "How did you know what to do? Which way to run?"

"I don't ... I just knew."

Jengi eyes her curiously. He leans against the rain barrel by the fence, he's panting hard.

"What?"

He shrugs. "Starting to see why Zeina picked you."

Zorry notices a small gap in her suture. She finishes suturing up the fence all the way to the edges, the fence quivering under her hands and she strokes it again. Soft, soothing words. She's getting fairly expert at doing this already. The fence seems to trust her, Jengi notes. Seems to remember. It relaxes its fibres, making the stitching easier for them both.

"Good work. Now be quick," he says. "Egg Men will be here in ..." Jengi looks down. "In about six and a half minutes." Jengi is telling the time by the shadow, spreading out underneath the street lamp.

The post-curfew street lamps are timed and their light goes out in increments. This makes it possible to tell the time by them if you happen to have an observant nature. Jengi mutters a soft count-down under his breath.

"Time." Zorry thinks, watching him. "We have to keep time on our side, just like everything else."

"What?"

"Nothing. Just one of Mamma Zeina's sayings." And then, "What was that rattling underneath us?"

"Rattling?"

"When we walked by the fence just now. Hissing sounds too. Seemed to come up from under our feet."

Jengi looks down, notices Zorry's bare feet, as though for the first time.

"Prod holes or vents under the leaves." He sniffs. "It was your own Mamma Ezray who figured that for us, Zorry."

Zorry looks surprised by this information.

"Small forest things fall into the vents, can't get out again. It explains the strange noises underfoot in the playground underneath the Furdy."

"You think the trapped creatures are burrowing under the village?"

"Yes, Zorry. I know they are. The forest is spreading out roots and critters in all directions. You can't keep a living thing pinned. Only the fence knows how far it goes."

"They're burrowing under the OneFolks' village?"

"Yes."

"What the hell are they?"

"Dunno." He looks up. "Ask your father. Don't he work in the sewers? So maybe he saw something already." And then, "You got bit." Zorry looks at her hand.

"Yes."

"You should have said, Zorry. You don't want to show up at the general's feast tomorrow with that'un, Zorry." Jengi curses. "You should've been more careful." He's mostly angry with himself.

"I'm sorry. Must'a happened in the tree, when I was distracted."

He wraps her hand. "Remember next time," he says. "They're in the tree moss. They were the real danger all the time we was both looking down at that clown of a hyaena."

"I'll remember." And then, "You got bit yourself," she says. He seems to see his small wound for the first time. The colour drains out of his face. "I must have took it sliding down the killing tree. I didn't feel a thing."

"Some of them plants contain anaesthetics, precisely so you'll ignore them. Wait." She blinks. "Thought you was s'posed to be training me?"

"The forest isn't never the same way twice, Zorry. That's all you can learn. Anyone can make a mistake, you can't never really train for the killing forest on account the killing forest learns you too. Changes it up." Jengi looks at her grimly, and then down at his hand. The pizen spreads so fast that he

quickly finds it hard to move his fingers. Gently, "Help me."
He says.

Zorry examines his hand. The effect of this tree bite is
a thing she's not seen before. Black vine-like branches are
spreading out under his skin. It looks different to Mamma
Zeina's plant bite, which was mostly inflamed. Green and red.

"These kind of nipping saplings, you can catch em iffen
youz quick, and they deliver stings as you go," Jengi explains
to her now. "No one is dangerous on its own, but you gots to
figure out a way of not collecting 'em." He glances down at his
feet. His voice is weak now, drifting, "You need to tie it with
something."

She rips a strip out of the sleeve of her maid's uniform.
Makes a splint. Checks his pulse. "You'll be alright. Just keep
breathing." And then looking down at her handiwork, is
pleased with herself.

Zorry walks ahead along the fence now, back towards the
lights of the village and her mother's cottage. She's been
noticing a heavy, sliding sound for a while. It's the other side
of the fence. Zorry turns towards it. The light on the creature's
head blinks on and off. She thumbs left, points it out to Jengi.

"Is it a spy?"

"You asking me? Training day is over, Mother Cupboard. I
already told you about everything I know." Jengi is impressed,
also sulking a little. He didn't plan on being rescued twice
today.

The fence seems to undulate towards Zorry, soft webbing
breathes in and out.

It takes her a moment to realise that Jengi's stopped
walking altogether. She goes back for him. "Your hand?"

He bends his neck, looks down grimly.

There are small black veins still spreading out from Jengi's plant bite, just above the bandage. Zorry binds it tighter, making Jengi wince. "They'll turn into tree vines, if we don't stop the blood to 'em. Gotta cut off the flow for a bit, it's what them sinews need to grow I reckon." She explains. "You need to loosen it soon as you can, or you'll lose that hand."

"Thank you."

She nods. "We're even." She says.

"There is one more thing I can tell you before you go back in alone, Zorry."

"Aye. What's that?"

"If you see the shape of a man, or a woman, then drop. Hide. Get out as fast as you can."

"Who ...?"

"I ain't figured that yet. Runaway Sinta from the last era? The old forest workers, or stragglers from the old time? Egg Men sent in by the general in some new guise? One thing's for sure, the killing forest has changed them. What I saw ..." He shakes his head. He stops talking for a moment. Grimaces. "But I don't care iffen you's in a patch of evil stingers when you see that kind of a human, you just drop, Zorry. Understand me?" Eyes her. "And then you get out."

"Alright but ..."

Jengi rubs his head with his right hand. He's thinking. "You may never see even one, iffen you never go into the dark mouth of the killing forest, Zorry. Most Mother Cupboards don't go there. There was only Mamma Zeina. We won't see her like again." Jengi eyes Zorry curiously now, to see how she takes this challenge.

"You said that already. Holy baobab, Jengi. Do you ever stop trying to play folks? What has Bavarnica done to you, Digger? You might try being direct for a change."

He eyes her gently swaying back as she walks away. "Play it straight eh? Maybe I will." He says, low. Breathes out.

Zorry is looking toward the forest, looming up over the gently rippling fence. It's like a dark mouth, she thinks. On a night like this. The whole thing, a snake's body from tip to root. It seems to expand and contract at the edges. Zorry shudders. Looks away. Premonition washes over her. She can't say what it means, only a bad feeling. She tries to put it away.

THE EGG MEN

FATHER IS ON A mercy mission to his sister's house at the edge of the village. Her crop didn't come up this year, some kind of blight. Food sharing is strictly banned and getting even vegetables to her is a dangerous mission. He'll be gone all day. Zorry has gone to the allotment to see what Father has left them.

Mamma Ezray is alone in the house with Zettie when the Egg Men come. Watches their huge heads bobbing just above the hedgerow beyond the cottage. Mamma recognises the batch 47 Egg Boy, Antek. He stops to lace his boots on the path out front, forcing the two huge Egg Men to wait for him. This gives Mamma Ezray a precious moment to prepare.

"Run!" Ezray tells Zettie. "It's now, Child."

Zettie pops her thumb out of her mouth. "No." She says, firmly. And then Zettie, in her infant stubbornness, wastes crucial moments resisting being pushed toward the back door by her mother.

"I'm staying with you." Zettie starts to cry.

"Zettie." Mamma Ezray says, "Zettie, you've been trained for this. Be a Big Girl. Right now. Go and wait by the fence. Nobody will look for a child there at this time, except those who know to. Don't you want me to proud of you? Don't you want Zorry to be?"

Zettie thinks about this. Sets her mouth in a line and eyes

her mother stubbornly. "I don't rightly like to, there's a man in that forest. He's got slugs in his ears. I am going to stay here with you, Mamma." She pops her thumb back into her mouth. Now her eyes are wide.

"Run." Her mother hisses. Twists her hands. And then in her desperation, "I will be there. That's where I'll be. Zettie. By the fence. I'll be coming right behind you. You just got to wait for me. Now go, go."

Zettie examines her mother's face. Then she heads for the kitchen and the back door beyond it. Closes the kitchen door behind her just in time.

Things unravel fast.

"It's now." Ezray thinks.

She hears the back door softly open and then close. She believes Zettie's gone. Probably half way across the back yard by now, she calculates, counting down the steps. Or in the copse running around the back of the house, under the leaves. Zorry or Jengi will pick Zettie up by the fence when they hear, which will be soon, the Sinta grapevine being what it is. Mamma Ezray breathes out. She believes Zettie is safe.

Sound of boots in the gravel outside the front door now. Something comes to Ezray then, watching the door. Knowing that it will bust out of its hinges in just a moment. She has prepared for the possibility of this moment for so long that now it's here it's like a kind of dreaming feeling descends on her. She feels untuned and strange, standing here by her mother's wooden table. The door seems to her to glow with a strange life. Cold unravelling feeling in the mother cupboard's stomach. Now Ezray holds on to the wooden table with both hands.

The door bursts, just as though, she thinks, just as though it were made out of cardboard or paper.

"Witch." The Egg Man says. And then his heavy boot, crunch, across the door jamb.

Ezray looks down at his boots on her newly mopped floor. For a long, unreal moment she can't imagine what they could be doing there. On her floor tiles. She looks slowly up from the floor.

"Witch." He says again.

And then, taking two steps forward, knocking over a lamp and picking up Zettie's small doll. Looking into its face with a bemused expression and then tossing it to one side. "Look around you, Men. Look. Dirty paint-signs, voodoo dolls, smell of boiled plants. These Sinta are filthy animals, I tell you." And then, "Search this room first."

A moment later Mamma Ezray is laying cracked and broken on her tiled floor. Her mind is washing in and out. These are the tiles, she thinks, still looking at the Egg Man's huge boots on her newly mopped floor, these are the tiles my father painted and laid with love. Mixing and scraping cement carefully into the gaps between them. He finished his work so carefully, you'd think that it could last forever.

"Filthy Sinta witch." The second Egg Man says.

Mamma Ezray notices that The Egg Boy Antek eyes her, small checking gestures. Unreadable expression. She can't see what he sees.

There is no point resisting, she thinks. Mamma Ezray is still looking at the tiles.

"Dirty witches." Antek's father turns toward the second egg man and, in a conversational tone, the second Egg Man replies, "They ain't strictly speaking human, the Sinta." He says. "It's all been scientifically proven by the general."

The Egg Men are pulling patched clothes and knitting, jars of preserved cactus chipotle, woven scraps and hen eggs from the drawers and under the floorboards. Paint pots. Seeds. Smashing all that they find without looking at it. "Witches. All of 'em. We'll burn this lot after." Points to the heap on the floor. "And we'll keep this pile, in case it comes in useful. Even the scrolls."

"Burn it." Says Antek's father quickly. "Burn it all."

"It's poetry," says the Egg Boy, looking down. "You do not do ... " He reads.

"Let that Witch stuff alone, Boy."

The Egg Boy takes a step back from the pile, though signs and symbols tend to draw his eye, he looks away from the scrolls. But the boy seems to stumble around now. He gets in the way. When Mamma Ezray gets up slowly, feeling her teeth with her tongue, the second Egg Man moves swiftly toward her but Antek, seemingly clumsy, trips and staggers across his path for the second time. Causing the second Egg Man to shove him, hard. "Wake up, Dunce. You're getting under my feet."

"Yes, Sir. Sorry, Sir." The Egg Boy stands up slowly, he is rubbing his arm.

"Keep out of my way, Egg Boy." The second Egg Man says.

"He's a clumsy kid, that's all." Says Antek's father. "Batch 47 are badly made, as you know. It ain't the boy's fault." And then, "Well you heard him, Boy. Make yourself useful some way. This ain't training no longer." Rubbing the back of his huge skull. "This here is it, Boy."

It comes to Mamma Ezray some way, watching her hard-won possessions piling up around her. Her forehead against the floor and trying to feel her teeth in her mouth, Ezray remembers that she is loved. It's a curious sensation, like being washed with warm air. For a singular moment she feels sure that she is. Loved. A little light filters in at the edge of the patched curtain. The sunlit moment passes over, and is gone. Now her head throbs. There's a little blood running down the side of her temple. Vision blurring on the left side. Ezray goes on looking at the floor tiles for a long time. Up close to it, the way she hasn't been since her childhood, when she'd lain on the kitchen floor on her stomach every morning. Watching Father work. Painting the swirls and the arcs. Paint the curving feathers and the gem colours with his homemade paintbrush. Dragons with scales and fish bones, dogs, crows and rats, castle moats. And now the disjointed pictures on the blue tiles curling into a kind of slow sense. Blink, blink. It's as though Ezray sees the picture as a whole for the first time. Looks away from it quickly. No one saw what she saw.

Mamma Ezray had only seen her father cry one time in his life, although he'd lost so many loved ones in the reckoning era. He'd dug up something in the vegetable patch. Something he'd buried for safekeeping, under the slow growing root vegetables in the back yard. Whatever it was, he'd wept over it and then simply put it back. Covered it over with dark soil.

When her father had come back to the house there had been no sign in his face of what had just passed. Whatever it was he didn't ever seem to want to talk about it. Some relic, from the time before the purge, Ezray had always assumed. There were many Sinta who'd lost people in The Before and there were so many of Ezray's uncles, aunts and older siblings who'd tried to flee to the mountains. Were caught by the Egg Men in the mouths of their own half-dug tunnels. No. Whatever it was her father had buried, dug up and re-buried in his back yard, he did not plan to share it with her and Ezray had accepted that, like a good Sinta daughter. He'd started painting the floor tiles around that time. A distraction from his grief, she and her mother had assumed. But he'd painted with such intensity, such concentration. He'd painted this last thing as though their lives depended on it now or would do soon. The mapmaker's very last map.

And then smiling to herself, recalling how Jengi spends his visits looking down.

Jengi saw it first, she thinks. Bless that Digger boy. He'll have it all in his head by now, the map to the general's version of Bavarnica. Its soft interconnecting parts, all the fish bones in Bavarnica's throat. Ezray rolls painfully on to her back and she looks up at the cracked ceiling above her. When it comes, the laughter starts up in her belly. And then seems to run up toward her throat, stopping there.

That sound.

A rattling at the back of the house. Ezray freezes, and then the understanding running through her body, unravelling her in slow parts. Zettie is still in the house.

The Egg Men heard the sound too.

"I'll see to that," Antek says firmly. And then eye to eye with his father. "I need the ... Killing practice."

"Good. Make sure you do, Antek," says his father, surprised. "Whatever it is ..." He says sternly. "Whatever it is ... Deal with it decisively. It's just like the calf, Antek. Nice clean kill."

The Egg Boy makes no reply, turns to go. His face is unreadable. Antek takes three noisy steps toward the door to the kitchen then a brief pause at the door, as though he hesitates to leave the room. Catches Mamma Ezray's eye and something seems to pass between them. Antek blinks. He stares down at the door handle. Takes a breath. And then he opens the door to the kitchen. Closes it behind him softly.

Now Antek pulls off his helmet, so as not to alarm the child. Ruffles his hair and it stands up like feathers or a jumped in hay-pile. He puts his finger to his lips, smiles weakly. "Don't cry." And then, "Shhh!"

Antek pads around the room, examining the exits. And then eyeing the closed adjoining door behind him. Now he moves toward the back door quickly, intending to open it, but Zettie scatters away from him toward the far side of the room.

In the next room, Mamma Zeina is dragged up by her collar. She is pinned to the wall. Eyes swivel right toward the door to the kitchen. And then looks away quickly. Puts her right hand on the cool wall behind her. Something comes to her, as she hears what she thinks are Zettie's tiny fingers battle with that grim latch on the back door of her house, as she fights with the lock to get out and Mamma Ezray can sense without seeing it that the lock becomes slithery, sweating, invincibly shut. She believes Zettie needs more time. She needed more time than I gave her. Mamma Ezray's eyes become wide.

Something comes to her. She can't say what it is.

Antek's not sure what the child did to the lock, but he can't open it just now. He checks behind him. Zettie is leaning against the rough, hard wood of the cupboard under the kitchen sink, and now, seeing the Egg Boy stare, she puts one small arm up. She's nervously fingering the wood-knots, the curling traces of woodworm, the sharp rusting edges of the keyhole.

"The door latch is broken," she says quietly. As though understanding without being told that he's trying to help. And then, "Mamma said that I have to go."

"Yes. Yes, you have to go." Antek gazes at the window. "You have to go to the copse and then go to where she told you to wait." Puts his hands over his ears. "Don't tell me where that is. Don't. Okay?" He takes his hands away from his ears again. Smiles at the child, tries to smile. Zettie points to the latch at the top of the window. "I lost the key." Antek reaches up and rattles the lock gently, to test it. "No," he says quietly. Curses. And then he tries one more time, breathing heavily. In a bit he gives up. Turns back to face the room. He's trying to think.

Now Zettie watches Antek take the three steps back toward the kitchen door, pull the latch silently across it. Then ease the kitchen table over, quietly, skilfully, wedges it under the handle. That'll give her three seconds, he thinks. I might hold them three more. And then eyeing the window, the door, with increasing desperation. Breaking the window will be noisy, it'll bring them running. Six seconds isn't enough time for a child her size to cross the yard and dive into the copse.

The child seems to sense something. She slips underneath the table, curls herself into a ball. Closes her eyes. Hands over her ears, the way Mamma Ezray taught her to do when there are Egg Men searching for food in the cottage. Blink, *blink*. Opens her eyes again.

Antek pulls the child out gently, by her right arm. Scoops and plops her into the kitchen sink by the window. Casts about

for something to use to break the window, settles on his elbow.
Something causes him to pause. He looks down at the child.
A scrap of a chance is better than no chance but something
makes him stop here, by the window. And then it comes to
him. He looks up at the sky. The changeover of the generators
is coming. It will be dark soon. Antek briefly recalls that his
father was always very insistent about the timing of this raid.
Antek puts away the thought quickly. Now the child hears him
softly counting down in twos, just under his breath.

The wind is blasting into the valley now, and the tree just
beyond the back door is heaving at its roots and throwing
its vast arms in the air. It seems, to the small girl in the
kitchen sink, that it rolls its swelling belly knowingly, leans in
menacingly toward the window. Zettie is squinting through her
fingers at it. Waits.

Mamma Ezray spits. On the floor. Right on the Egg Man's
boot. Just like that.

Time, she thinks, and now Mamma Ezray is holding the
Egg Man's gaze with a clear cold eye.

And she could never quite work that lock, Zettie, always
locking it when she means to unlock it, dammit, Ezray thinks,
durnit, that thick sharp piece of metal, damn the thing for
always and forever. Curse it now with all the night that you can
draw toward it, burst it, rust it, ruin it, Draw Fire. Draw Fire.
Draw Fire from that child. She sends an ancient Sinta curse
toward the lock, although she hasn't believed in the Sinta
curse since childhood. She believes in it now, at the end. Ezray
rises to it.

The second Egg Man steps back a little. He's briefly
confused. "What the hell is your boy doing in there? Why is he

taking so damned long? I'll go look."

And now Ezray is looking at the second Egg Man's long back, moving toward the kitchen door, screams a Sinta curse at his back to unnerve him, "You do not do, you do not. ANYMORE." She yells, spitting. Drawing his attention back toward her, and then away from the door to the child.

The second Egg Man seems to take the bait. He turns slowly toward her, half smile. "Any more black shoe, in which I have lived like a foot," she says, and then, "Sylvia Plath," she says, picking up whatever she can and lobbing it at his huge skull. Lamps and shoes and small brass candlesticks bounce off the side of the Egg Man. He walks slowly towards her. Catches a vase, and examines it briefly. Drops it. Smiles. "You singing your death poem? How fitting, Sinta."

Draw fire, draw fire, *draw fire* from the child. It is all that Ezray is thinking now.

The huge Egg Man is standing over her. Strange empty mirthless, joyless laughing and Ezray thinks it once again, 'I'm not myself.' And that voice, she thinks. That strange voice. You think it can't be coming from you, but it is.

"You do not do ..." She falters. "Anymore black shoe in which I have lived, like a foot." And once more that unreal feeling saves her. It's as though she is a clear foot over her own head, watching her own performance with amazement. Glancing at her feet and noticing it's a blue tile that she stands on. It feels like a sign to her. "Like a foot," she says. And then looking at the Egg Man. "And one gray toe. It's as big as a frisco seal." She says. The Egg Man tilts his head left, as though he's listening to the word-music. "And a ... Head in the freakish Atlantic. Where it pours bean green over blue." She tries to gather herself. She looks down again.

Now she sees Zettie's little dust lizards, drawn in the spaces left by every missing tile and spilling out of the cracks in the wall. Where did the child even find the paint for that last one? It must be made from that missing plant root. Why does the understanding only come at the end? Time, she thinks once again. This child only needed more time. Give her mine. She thinks, rising.

"There," the Egg Man says. He shoves Ezray's shoulder.

And then pulling her face into a snarl. Ezray flies at his face but one huge knee in her stomach and she is doubled over. And then pulling herself up quickly, painfully from the floor using the wall for support now. She crawls toward the door and the second Egg Man, laughing now, lets her place herself in front of the door, failing to understand this was the tactical advantage she had aimed for.

"You can't stop me."

"No."

"Then why resist? Tell me. Why you Sinta make such a fuss about dying? Egg men are cancelled in batches every day. You don't see us complaining." He sniffs.

"Then maybe you haven't never been alive in the first place, Egg Man. Ever think about that?"

The second Egg Man shoves Ezray hard and she stumbles backwards. Gets up from the floor again.

"Now, look. Why do you have to keep getting up? You're just making it worse for yourself, Sinta."

"Where it pours green bean over blue." She says slowly. Reaches out and picks up a knife from the sideboard. Left hand. Switches it to her right hand, raises it.

"Oh my." The second Egg Man lifts his empty hands up, slowly now, in mock surrender. She meets his eye, looks away again quickly.

"This is taking too long, Man. Let's do it. We've got three more of these tonight." Antek's father objects.

Antek hears Mamma Ezray's back sliding against the other side of the kitchen door, sound of a Sinta kitchen knife unsheathing, clink, *tap*, against the hardwood door. Inside the kitchen, the boy is calculating. He looks down at the child in the sink. "Nine seconds." He tells her. "Mamma can give you three seconds more. You will have nine seconds, Zettie. To get to the copse. When I break the window." Zettie, being only four droughts old this season and not understanding what a second is or why another one more or less might matter, gazes up at Antek with a look of amazement. Pops her thumb in her mouth. The two Egg Men on the other side of the door to the kitchen, nod at each other grimly, fan out. There is one on either side of Ezray.

Draw fire, draw fire, draw fire from the child, Mamma Ezray thinks. She is fire now. Rising slowly, painfully. The knife glitters in her right hand.

"Make it quick and clean."

"Aye."

Ezray's eyes become wide. She looks up. Last light, she thinks. And then *Slow*.

Shadow sweeps over the kitchen floor.

The Government Sun is switched off, curfew. The world is plunged into a blackness so deep that the air around Mamma Ezray's head feels thick with it. Time, she thinks. And then, Now. She moves just as she hears Antek break the kitchen window. Ezray plunges forward into a darkness that's thicker than life.

Last light, thinks Antek at the window, and then the Egg Boy, without missing a beat, throws his right elbow hard once again into the kitchen window, tinkle and smash and he pushes Zettie outside at the same time, neatly avoiding the clinging glass shards and Zettie, on an instinct, reaches out her small feet toward the edge of the rain barrel. Balances expertly, the way she has every morning for this last week, when climbing to check Mamma's asleep. Zettie holds there like a tightrope walker. Perfectly balanced.

"Jump!" He says.

Zettie jumps.

"GO!" Antek yells.

Zettie, like a cork out of a bottle, goes flying into the yard. She's running before her feet hit the floor. Running into the mouth of the darkest night that she's ever seen. Just like her legs decide what to do without her. Zettie's fast and she just makes it into the copse in nine seconds, not one to spare, slams herself down and then swivels. Covers herself up with leaves. The cottage lights blink back on. Light filters into the yard, but the copse remains in darkness.

Now the search lights blink on. Zettie shuffles down deeper into her leafy bed. She covers her ears, but the sound from inside Mamma's cottage goes on and on.

She uncovers her ears slowly. What is that sound?

It's the sound of the second Egg Man's frantic, high pitched screaming. It's the sound of him crashing about the rooms and bumping into walls, falling over the sideboard. Zettie hears something clatter to the floor and roll. That's the jug, Zettie thinks. Standing up. The Egg Man's scream rises up over the village.

The child brushes the leaves off. Now that she's here in the copse, she remembers her training. She is looking out toward the small lights of the village, and then away. In the direction of the fence. The fence, Mamma said. Iffen the bad day comes.

Well this is a bad day.

This here. And if Mamma Ezray can handle two full grownved Egg Men then she, Zettie, can certainly handle a damned fence after dark. So let's go, she tells herself. Testing herself against the darkness. She's going to make Mamma proud.

Zettie sniffs the air. Smell of crow eggs, she thinks. Dank moss.

Mamma is at the fence to the killing forest right now, Zettie believes. The Egg Man's screaming seems to her to confirm it.

She's waiting for me to come, Zettie tells herself.

It goes against every instinct in the child's small body, to head toward the most fearful seeming place in Bavarnica after dark. But Mamma will be there. My mamma will be there. Isn't that what she said?

The child feels tuned out, strange. She sets off running toward her Mamma. Toward the killing forest, the slowly wavering fence.

Several miles away on the family allotment, Zorry turns, blinks, then goes back to her work. Wind's getting up, she thinks. She waits a moment for the lights to come back on. Then realising that she's out after curfew. I'd better head home quietly, she thinks.

And then Zorry hears it. Something that doesn't sound

strictly human. Shrill scream. High pitched but not a woman's scream.

She shrugs. Something from the killing forest got in to the village maybe. It's been known.

A Sinta whom Zorry only knows a little straddles the fence to the allotment with some difficulty, "Zorry ..." He says. She examines his face and then she sees it. Written across his features.

She drops her spade.

"Zorry." He says. "Zorry. The Egg Men. This ... It's your house, Zorry."

ONLY ZETTIE SAW

ZETTIE HEARS DRUMMING IN her ears, her own heartbeat. Inside sounds. The world seems to move slow and strange around her. Sometimes she can't tell if she's running or if the cottages are only moving past her. There are Egg Men fanning out into the yards behind the Sinta houses. She looks back briefly. Someone is searching the copse out back of her cottage with a torch. Kicking the leaves and shaking the bushes. Their small search lights zigzag through the branches. Zettie keeps going.

Now she remembers what she's supposed to do. She remembers it all.

Zettie follows Mamma Ezray's training. All the way to the edge of the killing forest, then she stops. Panting. Rib cage aches. Feels sweat running down the insides of her arms, pools at her inner elbows. She clenches and unclenches her hands. They're sticky, cold. The fence sways and the forest looms above Zettie. Swivels around on her right heel to look behind her. Mamma Ezray is not here but she will be soon, Zettie thinks.

Mamma Ezray never lets Zettie down.

Mamma Ezray does not lie to Zettie.

Mamma said that she would be here, by the fence, and she will.

The main problem is they'd never practised this in the dark.

When the killing forest comes to silent life, groans and pushes against the fence. Zettie puts her arms over her head and her thumb in her mouth, she folds herself into the smallest ball that she can make.

There is a huge heavy, sliding thing just inside the fence, inches to the child's right. Small red lights to either side of its long, slanted nostrils. She shifts on her small haunches. Zettie opens her eyes wide in the dark.

At night the white fence to the killing forest becomes transparent. After a few moments, whilst her eyes adjust, it is possible to see things through it. Dark shapes, moving. And a long, low moan that seems human, also not quite human.

Zettie keeps perfectly still.

Now the killing forest trees move apart in front of her eyes, Zettie tells herself that this can't be happening. But the forest roof creaks open and there are leaves unfurling, it's like a tunnel appearing in the trees. A long dark, leafy throat widening and then closing, and then ripples open again. And at the end of the tunnel, there's the small light of the old moon. Wavering from side to side, as the child dips and wobbles, almost like it's coming closer. Zettie rubs her eyes with her curled fists.

Something plops out of the rain barrel by the fence, flops wetly on to the grass by her left foot. Zettie doesn't hear it jumping onward. A frog is a bad luck sign, the child thinks.

The forest sounds rise. Clattering and squawking in the branches.

Mamma Ezray always told her that she must be brave for this part.

There's the sound of sliding again, bird shriek. Something

moving sinuously up and along the inside of the fence, the whispering of several voices, just inside the fence. And now Zettie hears the heavy clomp of footsteps coming closer. And a loud hiss, someone saying her name, "Zettie? Zettie?"

Zettie is running once more, looping away from the fence, heading back toward home and the long copse at the back of her yard. The clomping heavy feet behind get faster. When Zettie gets to the copse, the figure leaps and fells her. She's pinned by an elbow in her small back.

"Quiet child. Be still." And now Zettie is fighting, biting down hard on the hand over her mouth.

"It's me, it's Jengi." The voice says. "It's only me!"

Zettie feels the scream rising up in her throat.

Jengi covers her mouth with his hand.

LAST LIGHT

"ANYTHING OUTSIDE?"

"Nothing." Antek says.

"I thought she had childur?"

"There's no one else. Leave it."

"Do not instruct me in my duties, Egg Boy. I know you let the child go."

The second egg man strikes Antek with the handle of his cow prod. It hits the side of the Egg Boy's head, a sickening crack, thud. Antek is out cold.

"Get up from that, Boy."

Black tile, white tile Mamma Ezray thinks. Looking across at the boy. The Egg Man rolls her over with his boot. Cheek against the cold floor. Black tile, white tile. And Blue, she thinks. Red. Blood is seeping onto the painted tile around her head, making a new country out of her father's last map. It spreads out. There is no fear, she thinks. At the end. Moonlight filters in through the blinds, and then she sees it, whole, in the seam ripped through the patched up fabric. The old moon.

Like a soft gold thumb hole in the sky now.

Wind is rattling the back door.

Ezray rolls her swollen tongue along her jaw, examines the cracks in her teeth. The Egg Man seems to loll in and out of her eyeline. Now her sense of the room around her changes. She is moving in and out of consciousness, drifting. Zettie will need time to get ... She thinks. Time to get to the copse and toward the ... Toward the fence where no one would, where no one would ... Time. The child needs time. And Ezray forces herself up again.

"Witch." The second Egg Man says, sharply. Kicks her. "Stay down, Witch."

But there is fear in his voice now.

Mamma Ezray curls her tongue around a front tooth, soft tug tug with her tongue and spits it. Small bloody spray where the tooth lands. Ezray grins with her missing tooth. Eyes him.

But her head's still bleeding and the sense of things unravels in spools now, since that kick, since the boot, since the black tiles, white tiles, going on and on. And flecks of blue, she thinks. In between. There is a sound outside.

A gun is cocked. The second egg man tilts the blind to look out.

It's just the wind now. Wind in the trees. Says Antek's father, coming back in from the kitchen. And then, sternly, "I'll check it out," he says. Brief glance down at his boy on the floor. He meets the second Egg Man's gaze. Squares his jaw.

"I didn't hurt him, batch-brother. He'll wake up with a headache is all."

They are eye to eye. "You stay here and nurse your finger. I'll be outside."

"Anything?" The second egg man says to Antek's father, moments later.

"Nothing. I've checked all through the copse, there's nobody there. Just a gale getting up." He looks down at Ezray, unreadable expression.

"I thought you said you wanted to finish this quickly?"

"Did I?" The second Egg Man holds up his hand and regards the stump of his index finger.

There's no blood, but the Egg Man's pain sensors, looking gnawed at the ends, hiss and fizz.

"Well. Curiously, batch-brother, I appear to have changed my mind." He squints at Antek's father, holds his gaze. And then soft, reproachful. "Don't you want to take her alive batch-brother? Get some names out of her? That's the protocol here. In a case like this one." He flicks his thumb toward the prostrate woman. "This one has turned out to be pretty hard-boiled. Who can say what a woman like that knows?"

Antek's father seems to be trying to think of a reason to object, something that would lie within the general's regulations. Finds nothing. Sighs.

"No names," Ezray says from the floor, she's semi-conscious and her words wash up like a voice in a dream. Drifting like a sigh, like a song, into the busted-up room. "No names, no names, no names in here," she lilts. Gentle Sinta music. And then, like a harsh drum roll at the end, "Never," Ezray takes a deep breath. And now Ezray seems to be listening to another kind of music, on the inside. Something nobody else in the room can hear just now. She tilts her head from side to side in time with the hidden drum curls and the tumbling rhythms. "I'll go out like a light." She pronounces.

"Like a light, eh? You don't know Gaddys very well then. Do you?" The second Egg Man speaks whilst looking at his finger. "She'll make you hate yourself before she's done with you."

"You should know." Antek's father is looking down at the second Egg Man. Slow gaze. And now the second Egg Man is looking at his ruined finger again. "I'm going to see that she dies slowly."

Ezray looks up. It occurs to Ezray now to provoke the younger man into executing rather than arresting her. She doesn't want to die naming names in Gaddys' basement. "How's your finger?" She asks, fully lucid now. Snarls.

"Nice try. But I'm not going to kill you, Sinta. I'm going to take you to visit with Gaddys."

Ezray turns toward the old language like a blanket. She thinks of her father, teaching her the last words in the firelight after curfew, and only hold on to that thought, she tells herself. And boil that thought until it's curling back to you like oil through water. Cover me now. The ancient, long-banned Sinta words seem to find her tongue."Water." She says. Out loud. And now Ezray's surface is receding again. She is dying. "Five fathoms five my father lies." She says. Sinking. Lifting her head up from the cold tiles to say the last thing, and then looking down dreamily at the old mapmaker's last map.

Antek's father is looking where she looks.

Now he moves in closer. Examines the tiles. Hand on his holster. Moves until he's standing behind Ezray. She doesn't look up, only senses his quiet presence there.

"You do not do, you do not do anymore," she says. And then, "I can't think straight just now."

She looks tenderly over toward the Egg Boy lying on the floor. Soft purple bruise at the side of the boy's head, blood clotting slowly at his wound. "Blood." She says. And at first it's as though Ezray's speaking to no-one. And then, gazing up at Antek's father, and once more a look seems to pass between them, "Your Egg Boy is bleeding. Friend."

"Stop talking, Mother Cupboard." He says. She looks up.

"Yes." She says. Closes her eyes. She doesn't feel the last blow, when it comes.

The Egg Man can't say what he feels. Maybe he can't even feel it. Anymore.

It was over quickly, he tells himself.

The second Egg Man is eyeing Antek's father curiously. "It would have been better to take her to Gaddys alive. Wouldn't it?"

"This witch knew nothing."

And then Antek's father is gazing down at Ezray's slumped body. Blinks. Turns and strides quickly out into the yard.

The second Egg Man can just see him through the open doorway. Examines the slope of his shoulders, his lowered head. Scowls. He'll be on a list soon, he thinks. Him and his mismade boy.

And now the second Egg Man is imagining how nice that would be. He's looking down at the stripes on his shoulder. Another one would be nice, and the food rations to go with the promotion. The second Egg Man smiles slowly. And then looking down at Antek's prone body, in a heap by the fireplace.

"There was meddling on this night and that's for sure." He scratches his nose. And then staring at his ruined hand. "And somebody always pays for the meddling ... It's not going to be me."

Voices outside the front door distract him briefly. "We've got the flowers' van. We are ready for collection. Have you got them? There oughta be three?" The red haired Egg Boy looks down at his clipboard. And then up at Antek, laying curled on the floor. Blinks.

"There is only one body. Take it outside." The second Egg Man indicates Mamma Ezray's corpse. "Take her the long way. Drag her past the copse out back. If there are childur hiding out in the yard, that'll bring them to their mother in less than a heart beat. We can take the whole family to Gaddys, a job lot."

They drag the mother cupboard outside, slide her over the cool tiles, past the slumped Egg Boy and the piles of her broken things. A slow trail of blood washes out behind Ezray, making a dark swathe right across the room to the door.

The back of her head bumps twice over the stone kitchen back steps.

There is only dark.

GONE

ZORRY HOPS OVER THE cottage wall, straddling the thing with difficulty. The body of the front door is seeping away from its hinges. Eases herself in through the busted hole in the wood, fingering the splintered edges of the door, as though looking for clues. Zorry passes into the dark room.

It's empty. Scorch marks on the floor, smoking rags. The lamp is broken, the fire's out. Zorry steps over a broken egg. Notes the chips in the wall. Other small signs of a struggle.

The dark shapes of furniture are crooked, wrong side up.

The floor appears to her to tilt, she sways and the ground seems to rise up to meet her. Catches hold of the wall and slides down it. Zorry is on her knees now, getting up slowly. When she's on her feet again, leans her forehead against the cool brick. Not the in-breath, Zorry thinks, but the out-breath. That's the struggle. She concentrates really hard on breathing now. Holding her gaze to the wall. The small indent from Father's pot-throwing is still there. She looks at it for a long time. Something comes to her. Now she is moving slowly through the room, looking for clues. For some kind of trail. She is still swaying a little, but she stays on her feet.

Fingernail marks in the kitchen door, running down it. A fine red mist on the wall beside that. Small but adult-sized bloody fingertip-prints in the hinges, and another red print, of a palm, to the left. Zorry knows without looking closer they are from Mamma's hands, not Zettie's.

She looks down.

And then black tile, white tile. The curls of turquoise paint, swathes in the blue tiles, the tiny gold inscriptions. Zorry picks up the lamp. She examines the floor more closely. There are muddy footprints, crossing the kitchen in a haphazard pattern, running up to the back door. Blood is embedded in the patterns left by both sets of huge Egg Man boots.

Now she sees it. A large finger on the floor, from the knuckle up. It's still wriggling obscenely. Curling and trying to point. Zorry forces herself to step closer to the writhing object. Confirming what she already knew. It is not Mamma Ezray's but the thick boney knuckle, vein-strewn finger and curving yellow fingernail of an Egg Man. Mamma put up a fight.

It's the first sign of hope.

Whatever it was that happened here, Mamma Ezray did not go quietly. But why not? She must have had a reason for resisting. It occurs to Zorry for the first time that Zettie might be alive.

She looks up, toward the open back door in the room beyond her. Eyes the broken kitchen window.

Zorry dips her head under the low doorway to the kitchen. Smell of tin and something else, she can't say what it is.

She looks down again.

And now she's walking beside the dark trail which runs across the kitchen. Blood all the way to the back step. And then, standing over the stone back steps looking out, Zorry finds she can't move. Can't take another step forward or back. She's looking across the yard and beyond it, into the copse.

For one long moment, she has a feeling of rising up softly and away from her body. Where would Zettie have gone if she ran? Now Zorry's mind seems to tune out, thoughts rattling, colours in the yard butt against each other, things blur. She holds on to the door frame with both hands. Nausea rising.

And now, from the looted, ruined rooms behind her, something comes. At first she doesn't know what it is. But she smells Mamma Ezray's plant smell, mixed with soap, candlewax. It's like being washed by warm rain. Zorry doesn't turn. Only letting the soft presence run over the back of her head and neck. Then it's gone.

Gone as though it never were. Shakes herself.

Now the thought comes to her fully formed. Zettie would have gone to the fence.

And now Zorry knows it, knows it suddenly. With all the clarity of an intuition. Steps into the yard, sniffs the air. She needs to get to the fence. Fast. Something makes her pause, just a little longer. She can't say what it is. Her left hand is shaking.

She looks back at the broken back door to the cottage. It has strange energy to it, the darkness in the yard and the copse just beyond, the dark open door of the cottage behind her, a quality of horror to the cottage back door, the step. This can never be home again, she thinks. There is no going back. Only on.

The back door is hanging off its hinges. One sharp gust of wind and the door hits the step, tumbles into the dusty yard. No one has put the chickens into the henhouse and they scatter from the falling door, soft clucking. Gentle squawks.

The gale is picking up now. The tree out front seems to groan and complain, heaving up its leafy arms and rattling, twisting left and right, like a warning.

Zorry sees the Egg Boy, Antek, standing just beyond the back door, by the shed. It's a shock and she takes a step backward, wavers. He puts his right hand up to the side of his head. There's blood in the handkerchief, wadded up in his hand and he's pale. Paler than she has ever seen him. Blood loss, she thinks. Ripping off the long cuff of her shirt, stepping carefully toward him, as though approaching a deer, or a child.

"You gotta bind it, Egg Boy." It doesn't occur to her to be surprised that the Egg Boy is bleeding. She realises only now that she has always understood that he was … human.

Antek pulls a slightly torn document out of his left, front pocket. Zorry believes that the Egg Boy is bringing her an official death notice, but who for? The document is colour coded pink, meaning that it's for a child. She stumbles, feels rather than sees the Egg Boy moving forward fast to catch her. It is her elbow not her head which breaks her fall on the step.

When Zorry looks up she sees Zettie, standing over her. Waiting.

The child looks unreal. Shattered. Blank amazed expression. Soft button eyes.

Zorry rises, "Wake. Wake up Zettie." Zorry waves her hand in front of Zettie's eyes. Pulls the child into her arms. Zettie blinks. There's a small sign of life, a flash of recognition, and then it's gone. A kind of stiffness passes over her. The child gently resists being held.

"You're cold." Zorry takes off her scarf to warm her. The

child looks away. Zorry rubs Zettie's cool arms. "Zettie?" She says the child's name. Soft as she can. Says it twice.

Zettie had gotten all the way to the edge of the killing forest then circled back again to run from the fence and then from Jengi. To find her mamma. Jengi had caught Zettie in the copse with only moments to spare, hid them both in the leaves at the edge, pinned his elbow in Zettie's back, hand over her mouth, stopped her going to her mother just in time. Hardened as he was, even Jengi had to close his eyes when they dragged Mamma Ezray out, bloodied, by her feet, just seconds later, that sickening bump, *bump* and the soft thud of her skull hitting stone. Jengi couldn't pin Zettie and cover both her eyes and her mouth at the same time, not without three hands, three arms.

Only the child saw her mother dragged down the two hard back steps.

Mamma Ezray was hauled, feet first, toward the van with the crown for a headboard, which the red-headed Egg Boy had parked in the stoney country lane just beyond the cottage. Only the child saw them drag her mother's body over every stone, cracked rock, earth ruck and puddle in the Sinta's long front yard. Only the child saw what she imagined were small signs of life in Mamma Ezray's left hand, reaching out and sliding fingers through the yolk of a crushed hen egg, or Mamma Ezray's head turned, as though looking blindly out toward the quickening in the copse.

Only the child saw the end.

Zorry finds that she can't look at Zettie now and she can't not look.

"Zettie."

Zorry wraps her arms tighter around Zettie. The child is stiff for a little while longer, but then becomes limp, unresisting. This seems to be worse.

Zorry has forgotten about Antek. When she looks up, startles softly. Antek is now standing to one side of the Sinta cottage. He steps back, avoids her gaze, sliding into the green shadow that runs beside the house. She listens to the sound of Antek's footsteps, slipping quietly around to the front of the house and away.

Zettie gazes up at Zorry with a blank, amazed expression.

"Was the Egg Boy bad to you, Zettie?"

The child looks at Zorry in surprise.

"He ain't a Egg Boy, he is a Antek. He breaked the window." She says in her small voice. "Jengi gived him a paper. For me."

"A paper? What paper?"

Zorry looks down. There is a certificate of tameness poking out from Zettie's apron front. A little of Antek's blood is on one corner of it and it's been signed by the general's wife with her very own hand.

Zorry stares at the certificate for a long time. "You are safe. You are safe now, Zettie." And then, looking up, "It seems you have ... You have a lot of friends, Zettie. Important friends. Do you know what that means?"

Zorry looks up toward the path which Antek just took.

"No." Zettie says.

"No more do I."

Dust rising, leaves, as the wind gets up. And now Zettie is clinging to her older sister. Zorry doesn't take her into the cottage, she doesn't move from the spot.

No-one comes home, not yet. Not Zorry's father, not

Zorry's aunt in the next village. Though you'd expect them to have heard by now, the Sinta message systems are hidden and effective and the Sinta are expert at reading the signs and quiet codes in the slightest rearrangement of their surroundings, so that a child in trouble can be identified, located and swooped up quickly. There are rules in place for such times which have taken a hundred years to configure and cowardice amongst the Sinta is unusual, especially when it comes to children in danger. And yet ... no-one comes for them.

Zorry guesses it was the Egg Man's scream that did it. *We are untouchables now.*

Zorry tries to think, but again her thoughts rattle, blur, and move too fast for her to catch them. The sense of things coming undone. She looks down at the child in her arms. The night-freeze is coming, and they've no shelter but ... Goose bumps are appearing on the child's arms and legs. They must go back into the house. Where else?

Now Zorry drags Zettie into the kitchen, the child resists this at first and then seems to give up. Zorry holds her tighter now, to try to stop her shaking. The child still feels cold in her arms. The lights in the house are out. The fire is not yet lit. Zorry gets up to light it, transferring the child to her hip and going at the fire now, clumsily one-armed, with the poker. She gets a small fire going. It's mostly smoke.

Through the kitchen doorway Zorry can still see the curves and angles of things tilted in the wrong way, menacing upside-down shapes of old, familiar items. Everything's changed. There's a burning feeling in her throat, Zettie coughs and now they watch the flames lick upward. A crack and snap like gunshot, causes Zettie to startle. The hewn branches in the log-fire curl and turn quickly to ash. Zettie watches the fire waver and hiss. Wide eyes.

Zorry hears her name called twice. And then Father's nervous voice carries from the front door of the cottage. At first he doesn't come into the house. Now there is the sound of her aunt, rattling through the house, kicking at piles of rags and opening cupboard doors. "Children?" And now Father seems to find the courage to follow Aunt in.

Zorry listens to his footsteps getting louder, hesitating. And then coming closer again. Zorry can't raise her heart high enough to answer, but Aunt quickly finds the two girls by the kitchen fire. She breathes out heavily. She puts her arms around them. And then Father's voice again.

It briefly occurs to Zorry that Father might report her presence here, which could be a problem as she is no longer certified tame, as of tonight. Zorry is ashamed at once of mistrusting Father. She tries to put the thought away. Steels herself. And then looking down at Zettie.

"That's your father," Zorry says, trying to break through the child's emptiness. Zettie nods robotically. It's hard to tell if she hears the words or not. It is like someone came and sucked life out of her, Zorry thinks. Zettie presses her face into Zorry's neck.

"She's shaking," Aunt says. And then bending to peer closer. Lifting up Zettie's matted lock of russet coloured hair, examining her small face underneath. "She's in shock!" Aunt says loudly. "The child's in shock." These words seem to wake something in the children's aunt. She checks Zettie over, wraps her with every shawl she herself is wearing. And then, gently scooping her out of Zorry's arms, holds onto her tightly.

"We have to get her warm."

In a bit, Father tries to pull her clumsily out of Aunt's arms, but the child clings resolutely to her aunt. In a bit Father stops trying. "We need to get her some sugar. Fruit." Aunt says. And Father shambles outside toward the pear tree in the front yard. To see what the Egg Men have left them, knowing in advance that it will be nothing. Nothing.

"Zettie," Aunt says. And then she seems to remember something. Rustles in her basket. "Keep her warm," she says brusquely, plonking the child back into Zorry's lap. "There now, there." She pulls Zorry's shawl off her roughly and then re-wrapping it around both Zorry and the child.

"Take off your coat, Man," she barks at her brother when he reappears at the front door. Now he ignores her, stumbling a little over the door jamb. Zettie holds Aunt's oat biscuit in her mouth as though she's forgotten how to chew or swallow. And then in a bit she seems to remember. A little of her colour returns.

Father seems decisive suddenly. Yanks the child out of her coverings by one arm. Sits down and pulls her on to his lap. "Your father is here now." He says. Squaring his jaw. "Here to take a hold of this ... madhouse." Brief, cold glance at Zorry, as if she did this. All this. And now the infant is shuddering uncontrollably. Aunt rushes forwards to wrap the child again, but Father raises his right arm against her, warningly. Now he turns his back toward both women, as though to defend himself.

"At least let her under your coat, Man. Can't you see she's frozen? The child's in shock." And now the whole of Zettie's upper body is hidden by the flap at the side of her father's jacket, the fabric of which is torn open at the back now and moves like a small, boneless wing, covering the child only just, but covering her. "She's alright," Aunt breathes out. And then turning to examine Zorry briefly.

"She's alive. Zettie is alive. That's the main thing."

"She's alive," Zorry repeats her aunt's words. And then looking at Zettie's small blue-tinged, bare feet. As though she sees them for the first time in her life.

"It's a miracle." Aunt sniffs. "And no thanks to your mother. Damned radical. I told her. Bringing trouble to a house with children in it." Aunt purses her lips. And then turning back to Zorry.

"Are you alright, Zorry?"

A wave of exhaustion washes over Zorry. She can't say what she feels just now. Can't even feel it. And again that feeling of being untuned, of drifting six feet over her head.

The morning after's cold and bleak and the sky is thick and grey and heavy, rain clouds gathering. Zorry, waking just a little, watching the low light filtering in, lets herself understand it for the first time.

She's gone.

Mamma Ezray is gone and now no place is safe. Or ever will be again.

REPORT 4: PLANNING

"IS THAT YOU, JENGI?"

"Yes." Long pause. "What do you want?"

"What do I want?" Clears throat. "Well, since you mention it, Jengi ... I need the name of the last Seed."

"And why is that exactly, Sir?"

"Jengi. No games. Give me the name. Half of Bavarnica has a Z in their name. I know it wasn't Mamma Zeina. Or Mamma Ezray. I know that now."

Silence.

"Jengi?"

"I don't report to you anymore."

"Jengi!" Sharply. There's another silence. And then, in a different voice, just as though another person entirely were speaking, "Jengi, how do you expect me, us, to help your revolution, if you won't file reports."

"Well, I'll be straight with you, Sir." He stops, takes a breath. "I haven't seen enough evidence that you are the helping kind."

"Jengi!" The voice is loud now, too loud. Jengi holds his hand over the receiver and then gazing down at the roots of the baobab.

"What is it you want? What exactly are you cooking here, Sir?"

"Forget that. Are you going to stick to our plan, Jengi?"

"I may stick to a plan." Jengi says. Gently switching the receiver to Off. Replacing the excavated patch in the tree with the jigsaw piece of tree bark. He looks up. He's thinking.

"Jengi!" Muffled voice from inside the baobab.

Soft clicking sounds as the line dies slowly. Buzzing. Now Jengi hears two voices. Jengi can only just make out their words.

"What's Jengi doing?"

Sigh. "Jengi is negotiating."

THE FORGETTING
MEDICINE

NEXT MORNING THE EGG Boys come with clipboards instead of guns. The red headed Egg Boy takes off his helmet. Runs his right hand through his hair.

"Extra doses of the memory erasures today." He stops talking, gazes around him. Takes in the room. And then a small, weak smile, "For those Sinta feeling *delicate* this morning." He taps his clipboard, "Shop's orders. Special offer."

The red-headed Egg Boy points at Zettie with his pen. "Even her." He says. "We can give her the medicine a little younger than is strictly good for her brain."

"No." Says Zorry quickly.

"Yes," says Zorry's father. "We'll take it." Turns slowly toward Zorry, "After all, I am her sole remaining parent."

"It's true." The red-headed Egg Boy checks his clipboard. "Yes, it's your choice, Sir." He makes a faux-bow to the child's father, which Zorry finds humiliating on her father's behalf.

"No," she says again. "You have to ..."

"I have to what?" The red-headed Egg Boy gazes ironically at Zorry.

"We'll take it." Father glares at Zorry. Looks away.

Now Zettie looks from her father to her sister, and then

back at her aunt. Quick checking gestures. Aunt pauses. She nods.

Zorry's father takes his medicine mechanically. Zorry watches him swallow, a small shudder and then it's gone. She notes he looks calm, changed. He'll have forgotten Mamma Ezray by nightfall.

Zorry turns toward Zettie. She examines the child.

Zettie has developed a tremor in her right hand, since last night. An eye tic. There are large dark circles under her wide eyes, from lack of sleep.

"Will the medicine let her forget?" It's Zorry's aunt who asks the question, looking from her brother to her eldest niece.

Father impatiently pushes his own medicine box towards Zettie. "Wait!" The Egg Boy says, just a little too quickly. Checks behind him. "*This* one's for her."

Now he taps his clipboard again. Hands the forgetting medicine to the child's aunt. "Well?" He says. And now Aunt realises that he's waiting for the child to take it in front of him.

Father looks up, he seems to note his sister's hesitation. He yanks the child's arm abruptly, dragging her away from her aunt.

"Well after all, he is the child's father." The red-headed Egg Boy says, and bowing a little again toward Father.

Zettie is stiff in her father's arms, she tries to push away, and now Zorry's holding out her arms to take her. "This is my child," Father repeats, as though it's himself he's trying to convince.

Now Father takes the medicine capsule with Zettie's name on it, expertly flicks it open and, pinching the child's mouth open at the cheeks, squeezes the medicine down her throat. Double dose.

Zettie can't help but swallow the medicine. She looks panicked and her eyes become large. Her pupils expanding softly until they consume the coloured iris. Just a moment later and Zettie is quiet, relaxed. Her limbs seem to lose their stiffness slowly, the soft shuddering goes and her eyelid tremor with it. She gets up and starts to move around the room. "It's like she's waking up from a bad dream." Aunt says, amazed. The child stretches and yawns. The Egg Boy ticks Zettie's name off his long list of names.

Zorry refuses to take the government meds in front of the Egg Boy, claiming she will take it later, and the Egg Boy dutifully notes this down. Places her sack of capsules on the table. And then the warning, which the Egg Boy appears to be reading off his clipboard.

"If you refuse five erasures Zorry, then you will be greened and after that the general himself will wash his hands of you."

He looks up from his clipboard, points at the blood stained boot-print at the kitchen back door. "Well. You know what happens next Zorry." He looks at her. Shrugs. And then more softly, "Ain't your sister been through enough?"

It's as though something takes a hold of her throat, "So you are Batch Forty Seven." Zorry says, quite recklessly, as far as her aunt's concerned. "And ... This is your mission. Is it, Egg Boy? You're going to kill us with what you write on your clipboard. Kill us with red ink?"

There is a long, strange silence in the room.

Zorry is eye to eye with the Egg Boy. "Yes." The Egg Boy says. "This is *my* mission, Zorry. What's yours?"

Something seems to pass between them.

Zorry listens to the gentle ticking sounds of the Egg Boy's

feet walking away. She gets up from her squatting position and walks over to the window. Gazes out through the gaps in the blind. The red-headed Egg Boy pauses at the gate. And turning back, looking in the direction of the kitchen window. As though he senses her there. He pulls his head protection back on. Zorry quickly ducks beneath the kitchen sink.

In a bit, Zettie gets down from her aunt's knee. Pads over the room toward her sister. Zorry tries to read the child and, for the first time, finds that she can't.

"I have to go, Zettie. Soon. It's important. Will you remember ... Know it's me? I mean, when I come back?"

Zettie takes out her thumb.

"Here. Have this, Zettie." Zorry pulls off both her twine rings roughly. Places them, one by one, onto Zettie's thumb, where they will not be so loose. Aunt, looking down at the child's small hand, sighs, "Zorry. Don't do something stupid now. It's all I ask."

Zettie's eyes glitter.

THE REBOOT

"SHE'S TRYING TO BURN the chair." Zorry's father says.

"Who is? What chair?"

"The chair with the patchwork cushions. Zettie put the whole thing in the fireplace."

Zorry scratches her head. Gazes into the flames. And then turning toward Zettie.

"Yes, it was the ... The spare chair." Father says. Bangs his ear. Bangs it twice. And then a soft, amazed expression. He seems to tune out.

Zettie seems mesmerised by the fire. The heat rises and the fire spits out glowing ashes, landing one by one around her outstretched feet. She draws her legs up. Hugs her small knees and rests her chin there. Soft, wide eyes.

Flames slowly lick along the wooden limbs of Mamma Ezray's chair. There are sparks along the edges of Mamma Ezray's slow-patched cushions. Small fires in the seams.

"I wouldn't mind," complains Father. "But Zettie should have asked me first. I could have taken the axe to the spare chair. Busted it up into small pieces, burned it over a week."

"No!" Zettie says. Interjecting suddenly. And then, "You gotta put it in like that. Whole. Like I did. Or it ain't proper."

"It ain't proper what, Zettie?"

Zettie glances up at her sister, doesn't answer. And then

keeping her fierce, watchful gaze on the chair. On the chair and the flames.

Is the child thinking about a Sinta funeral? Zorry wonders. Burning the dead's favourite chair is an essential part of any secret mother cupboard death rite. The chair is burned whole in the absence of a corpse (a mother cupboard's dead body is stamped 'property of the general', rarely returned). But the Sinta rememberers will burn the dead's favourite armchair, cushions, patches and all. Keep watch until it's all gone, to make sure that only the fire, the smoke, the air, soil, wind can take the chair. Along with the scarves with curling patterns of turquoise and lapis lazuli blue, from the old times, the chipotle jars, the mother cupboard's mortar and pestle, the dried cactus paddles, pod-like seeds, the beads and the knitting. Detritus of plant experiments, paint pots. All the possessions of the dead, built up over a thrifty lifetime, invested with the spirit of the one who touched, made, patched up and held onto them, and will never touch or hold them again.

All but the dead's hidden books will be burned (because a book can never truly have an owner).

But so that the general and his Egg Men, Gaddys, may never confiscate, steal, or repurpose these things. Not now, and not forever.

Downbutnotout and Amen.

Zettie has only ever attended one illegal Sinta funeral, to Zorry's certain knowledge, and that was Mamma Zeina's funeral, six weeks ago, more. It's inconceivable to her that the child would remember that far back now. Zorry makes the decision to approach the matter cautiously with Zettie. If she has some memory-debris then it may be a fragile thing and she mustn't be pushed.

"Well." Zorry says. "Well it seems funny, don't it? It looks strange. The chair. Funny. With the flames licking around it that way." Now Zorry looks at Zettie sideways, she examines the child. It seems impossible that the child could remember their mother. She was given an adult-sized medicine dose and she's only four droughts old, small for her age. Zorry pauses, thinking, and then, "I wonder, Zettie. Whose chair is that now?"

"It's the spare chair." Their father says gruffly, from his corner. Bangs the side of his head. And then putting on his coat, as though he puts a coat on for the first time in his life. He staggers into the front room.

Zorry listens to the sound of Father, rattling open his medicine cupboard, the hinges stick and the handle's too heavy, falls off. Zorry turns toward her small sister again. "Is it the spare chair, Zettie? Is it nobody's chair?"

Now Zorry crouches beside Zettie. She holds the child's gaze.

Zettie looks up at her sister for a long time and then, as though the whole of Bavarnica weighs down hard on her tiny shoulders, a heavy sigh. "You don't know whose chair it is. Do you, Zorry?" And now Zettie, sounding almost comically like their mother, "Durn it, Child. Zorry you've forgot your own mother. You'd forget your own head too, your neck, elbows and arms iffen I let you. Wouldn't cha?"

Zorry blinks and sits back on her heels.

"Yes. Zettie. That there is Mamma Ezray's chair." And then, "But ... you took the meds. You took the meds and ..." Checks

Zettie's arms, and then, lifting the child's matted hair, her ears and the back of her neck. "You're not greened."

"Quit poking me about."

"You've no green on you. How did you ... do that?" Zorry stares hard at the child. "I'll fetch Jengi." She says.

Soft sucking sound of the newly mended front door as Zorry almost pulls it out of its hinges. Clanking sound as she forces it back into its too-small frame. Zettie turns away from the fire and she looks at the door Zorry closed behind her. The child watches the door for a long time, listening to the pat, crunch, lollop, sliding rhythms of her sister's running feet on the rockoned path out front of the cottage. Zettie goes on listening until she can't hear Zorry's feet anymore.

She turns back toward the fire.

Mamma's chair is slumped against the inner sides of the fireplace. Smoke rises from the patchwork cushions. The logs Zettie used were damp and the fire is going out.

"I knewn it." She says. And her small hands curling and uncurling. "You caint have a funeral iffen you ain't dead. It won't take."

Jengi pops his head around the door. "I heard you were holding a real Sinta funeral, Zettie."

Zettie looks down. Scowls.

It occurs to Jengi for the first time that if the child remembers her mother then she might also remember his own good self, pinning her down by the elbow, not letting her cry out or go to her mother, the guards. The child might very well blame him for what she saw in her yard.

"Is she a hidden rememberer? A rememberer hiding out in plain sight? Ungreened?" Zorry asks Jengi. Jengi meets

Zettie's eye. "Aye. That's what it looks like. There have been a handful lately, on the Sinta farmsteads. Most of the hidden rememberers are ... children."

Jengi seems to read Zorry then. "Now, don't start hoping, Zorry. You Sintas and your bloody hope, it's most likely just ... They're having remnant memories, Zorry. It might all be gone by morning." Jengi says, his eye caught by the child's small hands closed into two fists, her small brow furrowing. He decides to softly provoke Zettie, hoping Zettie will reveal what she knows, "The child's memory is a flash in the pan. Nope." He says. "I don't reckon this child remembers her mother, not really." Jengi eyes Zettie curiously. To see how she takes this.

Zettie scowls again, and then ... Something seems to happen. She starts singing. Babyish made-up words, but it's not the rhythm or the intonation of a Sinta funeral dirge. It's one of Mamma Ezray's nursery rhymes.

"You're singing, Zettie?" Aunt appears around the kitchen door, roiling at a tin cup with a dark red cloth. A smile spreading across her tired face.

"It's the first time the little one has said a word in weeks." And then, when Zettie's sing-song rhyme is finished, "Zettie, you will never guess where I found this hen's egg?" Aunt pulls the egg out of her apron pocket to show Zettie. "Reckon the hens were trying to save it for you. Go on. Try to guess where it was."

Zettie seems to withdraw into herself.

Aunt peers at her. "Now then. Now. Why is she upset?" She looks up, seems to look at Jengi properly for the first time. "What did you do? What did you say to her?" And then, her voice softer now, looking down at the chair, at the fire, at the child's glittering eyes and her strange expression. She thinks about the nursery rhyme. "Oh ..." It seems to come to her. "She remembers?" And at first it's a relief. Soft laughter. And then, "Oh ..." She says again. "She remembers ..." Aunt looks down at the child. Locks her in a slow gaze.

Now tears are glistening on both Zettie's cheeks. By the firelight, Zettie's tears seems to Jengi like liquid gold. Surely, he thinks, this proves that the general's labs have been infiltrated? That Mamma Zeina's gathering is coming closer. Jengi blinks. The light shifts. Zettie is covered in snot and tears, the child is howling like an animal in pain.

Zorry tries to scoop Zettie into her arms, but their father strides out of the kitchen, stops her, roughly. "Don't you touch her. You've done enough. You and him." Father grimaces at Jengi.

"Get out of my house." He says. "Never come here again." Her father delivers these words calmly. This is so Zorry will understand he's for real.

Zorry stands up slowly to go. Her eyes travel over Zettie and her aunt. She nods curtly at her father.

"Come on Zorry," Jengi says. Holding his arm out. "We are doing no good here."

At the newly-mended front door, Zorry turns around once. Gazes at the cooling fireplace.

The last dipping flames curl around the rusted nails, the hinges of the leaning, singed chair. Everything seems to glow.

"Watch them sparks, Zettie," Zorry's parting words to Zettie. And now Aunt nods, pulls Zettie back and buries her face in the back of her neck. "You're too close to the fire, Zettie." She says.

That night, Zettie dreams. Her mother's chair is burning and the fire builds high and frightening until, just when the fireplace can barely contain it, then the chair gets smaller. Slumps and shrinks into itself. And then it's all gone. Zettie thinks. The chair. The fire. The rising. Blink. And now the fire is licking out of the fireplace, curling into the room.

The child wakes up howling.

Aunt is with the hens in the yard, out of ear-shot. In a bit, Zettie wipes her face with her sleeve. She thinks of something. When the ashes cool, Zettie says to herself. When the ashes cool down ... I'm going to find them chair nails. She plans ahead to sift the ashes for them later, when Father goes out for his next work rota, and whilst Aunt is in the allotment tending the roots.

Nails and screws from a chair can be right useful, Zettie thinks. Useful. In one way or another. She eases her feet down the bedside, splaying her small toes ready to meet the cold tiles. She pads over toward her bedroom window. She looks out.

Mamma said she would come to the fence.

Zettie looks out of her window for a long time, and then, "Mamma aint a liar." She says to herself. "That funeral didn't take. And Mamma said she will come."

THE GRAIN QUEUE

SINCE THE NIGHT OF the fire and the chair, something seems to have been released in Zettie. All the leftovers that no-one else can see a job for, Zettie finds. Together them throwaway things can be more, Zettie knows that. Wind worn glass shards. Bones of a cat. Grind 'em. The dried out skin shed by a lizard. Burnt things. Bloodied stones. All these things can make paint. The way Mamma Ezray used to make paint. Only Zettie thinks of things Mamma Ezray hadn't thought of.

She considers the nails and screws in the burnt up chair. Pulls them out of the cold ashes. With a thing like that Zettie can build something that stands, or something that can be fixed high and is hard for the Egg Men to take down, giving folks a chance to take a sideways look at it. Soon everyone will know what Zettie knows, that's the plan. They will know the new lizard's safe to eat. And that's when Mamma will come home. The thing has become very clear to Zettie.

Before sun up, Zettie is chalking lizards on the busted-in doors of the Sinta cottages. She's scratching lizards into the sides of broken bricks and on to the rubble of the tumbledown Sinta allotment buildings, mud daubed lizards along the tree trunks and low branches in the long copse which runs along the back of the cottages.

The child's gone mad, an effect of her medication, is the

general feeling in the Sinta households, as they scrub off the chalk swirling tails and chalk scales, the wide chalky eyes of the eating lizards. Mamma Ezray's lost youngest child has gotten their attention.

The sign takes a long time to finish carving with the small kitchen knife and, when it's done, then it's heavy to drag to the village centre, and much too heavy to climb the side of the village shop with. Also Zettie has a slight loss of nerve, looking up. In the end she leaves it tipped up against the side of the wall, in the dark alleyway beside the shop. But by sundown, Zettie has made around forty-seven small lizard drawings beside the grain queue, outside the shop. Nobody notices anything at first, just a small bent-over child, by the queue. Scribbling in the dirt with a stick.

"Sand paintings, Zettie? Have a slurp of rainwater from my flask, Zettie."

"The poor child. Are you lost? I've got some crumbs in my apron pocket."

"Oh wait, me too. Here, have these, Zettie. To keep you going, that looks like hard work."

By the time Zettie gets to the last lizard, then she's had a little practise. This one is the best one, she thinks. Staring hard at a wide eyed infant, peering at her over his mother's shoulder. And then she takes a small twig out of her apron pocket, sharpens one end. Plants the pointed end of the stick in the hard sandy ground outside the shop. Leaf for a flag, to warn folks it's there.

The leaf flag is soon ripped, the sharpened stick twisted and bent. Zettie's last lizard sand painting has been trodden in by one hundred Sinta mothers and their offspring and the feet

of more than a thousand edge farm fathers, all jostling and
irritable with hunger in the grain queue.

The grain queue dwindles as the general's curfew
approaches. The dark seems to come down around Zettie
softly.

Zettie is gazing down at the ground where her flag stood.
And then looking up toward the shop. Brief shrewd stare at
Gaddys, staring blindly out from behind her counter.

And then pushing out her small chin, Zettie pops her
thumb in her mouth.

I need paint, she thinks. Eyeing Gaddys' coiled hair. Paint.
And I need something good to paint on. Zettie looks down
at her skin. And then she knows it, knows it suddenly. Zettie
knows what to do.

Zettie runs home as fast as her small legs will take her.

Gaddys watches, nodding slowly. The child seems to her to
be fleeing. Well, that's a good start. Gaddys smiles.

It's time to get ready, Zettie thinks, running. Ready for
Mamma. Trees and shrubs are whizzing past her. She's
making tiny footprints in the dust road all the way home.

Mamma will be pleased when things are ... Ready. She
thinks. Mamma will see and know, Zettie tells herself. Zettie
has not dared to go back to the fence since that night. But
every night when the child dreams, Mamma is there. She is
waiting for Zettie to be brave enough, good enough, to come,
Zettie thinks. And then seeing Mamma Ezray, in her mind's
eye. The cobweb thin white fence to the killing forest pulses
and undulates behind her.

When Zettie reaches the stone wall outside her cottage,
she stops. And then, to avoid her father and aunt, Zettie slips

around it and into the shed at the back. Mamma Ezray's paint pots are still there, untouched since she left.

A strange feeling of delight is growing in Zettie, looking around at the paints. Mamma Ezray did not normally allow Zettie near her precious paints, except under careful instruction, when she might allow Zettie to mix some herself. Zettie's forgotten Mamma Ezray's training, of course (Mamma Ezray herself was trained by her father, the mapmaker). I can't remember, Zettie thinks. Skewering open a lid, finding the paint pot empty. Then again, some of the work is instinctive.

Red earth, mixed with a little moisture from the rain barrel, makes orange. The rows of leaf stems and the sap from the vines that creep around the back of the cottage, drape themselves over the shed roof like basking snakes, they make a blue-tinged dark green. As it turns out. There is some dried up, turquoise coloured paint at the edge of one pot lid, and on the ridged underside of another one, pink. The kind, Mamma used to say, that makes you think of seashells. Zettie has never seen a seashell. But on the back of her hand there is a deep, bright blue colour, when she looks. It's softly mottled with black. She must have picked it up by accident, messing with the pots.

The more that she explores, the more colours she makes.

Next morning, Zettie finds her way into the shed before sun up, when the air's still moist and cool and the hens are clucking sleepily in the henhouse. Zettie paints the scales first, arms and legs. She has no mirror, so her face is harder, must be painted by feel. When she's done with the scales, eyes and nostrils, more or less replicating the species colour of the lizard, she goes back and with a chunk of coal makes smudged black lines and circles, to indicate the special markings of the new lizard. The eating lizard. Zettie's feet seem to make their own way back toward the grain queue. Zettie looks down at them often, blue and green and grey, strange. She doesn't feel like herself.

"Wow! What are you doing, Child?"

"Eating lizard." She explains. Popping her thumb out and then in.

"Ah, Zorry. Lizards won't eat you. Don't be afraid of them little lizards."

"What's she doing?"

"Oh she's thinking about them killing forest lizards. I've reassured her. Mad little thing. Motherless thing."

"Oh those. Reckon they's pizen Zettie. Don't be touching those things, Zettie."

Zettie watches as the queue moves away. She feels her mother getting farther from her. It's a rising feeling of panic. Now Zettie moves to the front of the queue, blocks the door to the shop with her tiny body. And then lays down across the door jamb. Holds up the line. The villagers begin to step over the child.

"We get it, Zettie." An old edge farmer says, leaning over, scratches his ancient ear. Taps the side of his round nose. "Eating lizards. Spread the word, eh? Got it." Tugs his long silver-black straggled beard. Zettie sits up. She looks dangerously pleased and the old man glances briefly at Gaddys, gets up, wincing, from his crouched position. "Ancient knees," he says, making a distracting show of tipping sideways, leaning on the shelves. And then looking at Gaddys squarely, "I gave her a sweet. Guess she's crazy happy about that." Someone hisses at Zettie to scram. She doesn't see who it is.

"Do not feed that lizard child again." Gaddys stares the old man down.

There are whispers running up and down the grain queue all day.

CRACKDOWN

THERE WAS A BOMB last night. At sun-up Antek was one of those called up for rubble clearing duty.

"Foreign bomb." The tannoy said, on repeat. Its high pitched reproachful tone rising up over the barracks.

It's unusual to have a drone attack at the heart of the OneFolks' village but not unheard of. Whoever sent it apparently didn't know Bavarnica too well, and the officers' barracks even less well, Antek notes. The prisoners' wing was the most badly hit, and the side of batch forty seven's barracks a steaming pile of rubble and metal. The torn sides of the main building like a dollhouse. Meantime the batch 46 guards somehow had enough time to entomb themselves inside the steel bomb shelters. The general's top officers in their reinforced towers remained completely untouched by the blast.

The surviving prisoners, the walking wounded, are made to clear up and rebuild. That's Bavarnica's policy. Make them hate the bombs and the bombers and the foreign powers who sent them. "See what they do to you?" The message comes out loudly over the tannoy, clear across the barracks. "These foreign folks aren't anybody's friend. They are only bombs and death. Long death from which only the general can protect us."

Several of the officers hadn't been in reinforced towers at

all, but had been called to a single building for a meeting just moments before the blast. That building was simply scorched ground now. In addition, a handful of the batch 46 Egg Men had found, at the last moment, that their keys to the bomb shelters were missing. Antek's father was the only survivor of these. In any case, he'd headed towards the batch 47 barracks when he heard the siren, he was looking for his son when the drone hit.

Antek was called in late last night for an extra duty. He was to provide an hour of overtime to the general's wife, scrubbing the mould off the windows to her orangery and that's where he was when the first blast sounded. Antek hasn't seen his father for several hours. He sweeps up the bomb-dust, hoses down fires. Clears up the bodies before the rats and crows finish clearing up the bodies. Sweeps up fingers and toes, other body parts and, with the help of the prisoners, hauls out the dead from underneath the rubble. Drags them toward the gas-lit smoking pyres in the corner, where the old batch 47 barracks used to be.

From time to time Antek turns around and eyes his barracks. It's just a hole in the ground now, a pile of rock and dust beside that. The drones clean took batch 47 all out. If Antek hadn't been sent on his strange work rota before sun up, he knows he'd have been in the barracks too. Dead.

When the clean up was almost done and before the rebuilding had started, Gaddys came to examine the scene. She ticked boxes on a chart, mostly. Made red marks against a long list of names. Poked at pieces of rubble and eyed the broken buildings, sniffed.

You can't clear it all away, Antek thinks, sweeping, clearing, mopping, stacking and re-stacking. Pouring cement over scorched ground. There are always things remaining. A small brass button in the corner of a prisoner's half wrecked cell, non-uniform. The faded photograph of a long-ago child, laughing. Raising up her arms to some unknown new thing.

There are melted candles in the rubble of batch 47 barracks. An ancient postcard with rat-chewed edges, cafe scene with a musician, parasol and a woman. Hatless. Veil-less. These things had broken Antek up more than the blood and gore had, the burnt limbs. The dead remain not in grotesque butchered pieces but in their mementoes. The things they hoard and keep for years and will die to do so, thrown up to the surface by the bomb now. Like small dreams, sprouting out of the rubble.

Now Antek is standing at the very edge of the bomb crater which marked where the prisoners' cells had been. His eye is strung to the one green patch in the grey scene. It's on the other side of the crumbling wall to the batch 47 barracks.

Smoke still twists up from the remains of the building. There are grey mounds of rubble, and then, farther away, unfathomably green swathes of the killing forest appearing over the damaged fence just behind it. Antek eyes the fence carefully. Notes it's being rebuilt quite fast using what looks like swathes of cotton but on closer examination appear more like layers of cobweb. The fence seems to swell until the green forest vanishes once more behind the white veil of fence.

Night seems to fall quickly. The sky is now starless. One purple cloud of bomb-dust seems to him to open and swallow the old moon in a seamless gulp. And then give it all back, unfurling its lips and rolling out its long smokey tongue. Held the moon for a moment, held it there on the tip. Strange sky. Like a wordless warning.

A long, skinny cat skims past Antek's foot, too large for a Sinta domestic and too small to be from the OneFolks' village. Antek blinks, recognises the black markings, huge tufted ears of the caracal. Blinks again and it's gone.

"Did you hear?"

"Hear what?" Antek turns. He is gazing into the face of the only other surviving batch 47. Remembers the red-headed Egg Boy had a tendency to sneak out before dark. Nobody knew why but the batch 47 soldiers tended not to inform on each other, and apparently he wasn't home in time to be caught.

"The general's wife has been arrested." The red-headed Egg Boy says. Rubbing his luminous red hair between his fingers. The Egg Boy stalks away as quickly as he appeared. Disappears behind the rubble near the only remaining busted part of the fence to the killing forest. Antek waits a moment but the red-headed Egg Boy does not reappear. Antek quietly wonders how long he can last in the killing forest, batch 47 weren't trained for it. It doesn't bear thinking about too much. Then again, no need for an Egg Boy to worry about the snakes.

And in a moment, "You, Antek." A batch 46 Egg man taps his clip board. "We're rounding up batch 47. Any survivors?" Peers at Antek. "I mean anyone but you?"

Antek looks squarely at the man with the clip board. Brief glance toward the fence. "Just me." He says.

"Right." The Egg Man checks his clipboard, makes a mark on the page. Taps it with the end of his pen. "Right, Boy. You are on duty at the fence."

The Egg Man watches Antek go.

When Antek rounds the corner, he finds the next block is quite different, worse. Bomb rockoned buildings, smoke, rats scattering over the road, slipping in and out between the rubble. There is a small group of Sinta crouching in the ruins of their cottage, mostly old folks and children. There are several Sinta houses built on the periphery of the soldiers' barracks.

No-one turns toward Antek as he passes. They are counting their dead.

An ancient wooden rocking horse, peeling paint and one eye missing, is upturned in a pile of bricks. Its one remaining eye is wild and elated.

Antek looks away and down.

He notices that his boots are coated in brick dust. Something cold and slick's sliding in his gut.

Antek makes his way steadily toward his father's house. He wants to check in on his mother. This is what Antek tells himself. He gets as far as the gate outside the house. Pauses. The farmhouse wasn't hit, but it seems changed somehow. Firstly, there's a thick fence all around it, which is usually only used in the case of house arrests. His father's house behind the fence seems faded somehow. Smaller.

Now Antek turns and looks at the Sinta house next door. Zorry's house. There is a fence around that too. Glinting in the early light. Perhaps she will be there, he thinks.

The second fence looks sharp and new, set against the peeling paint of the cottage. Antek notes its recently broken gutters, boarded up windows. The fence like a cage that grows as the Sinta cottage sinks behind it, and the fence oddly tilting upward with the rising land. Making the fence seem larger than it really is. Incompetently made (Antek makes a quick and unforgiving appraisal: Misfit hinges. Lolloping gate. A steel trap of a latch that's sharp and rusting quickly). And the gate is properly stuck. It takes Antek a moment to realise that he really can't open the gate.

He goes back to his father's house.

Now he's gripping down on the latch, grabs the gate between his hands, strains against it. Hauls and twists and pulls at it again. Stuck. And then it's like he's holding one end of a rope and pulling it through space, not expecting anyone to be holding the other end of it. Antek sits back on his heels. He puts his hand to his chin, feels the soft groove of the scar there. This seems to release something in Antek. He remembers.

He must have been hiking with his father, as a small boy. Headed out for The Reach together. He looks up toward the mountain's sheer rock face. Remembered how his father used to hide from him in the rocks overhead, dip behind tufts of scrubby grass. Unravel and let go the boy's safety rope. What was the lesson? There was always a lesson. "Trust no-one." Father would say. "No-one, Boy."

Antek had fallen several feet down that day, and he can still recall his left cheek sliding down the rock. The boy had slipped down hard and fast, saved himself just two feet from the mountain base. Tumbled the last part and broke his left arm.

"Better than your head, Boy." His father got down safely moments later, stood over him.

And when he closed his eyes at night, in the weeks and months afterward, Antek's recurring dream: of the frayed end of the safety rope that was meant to hold him. The side of the mountain slipping away from him fast.

Antek holds on to the gate to his father's house. He stops pulling. He leans against the gate. I can't go home, he thinks. I can't go forward or back.

Antek slides his rusted flask up from the ground. He wraps the leather strap of it around his palm, slips away. The morning light dips and shudders. The dawn comes right before the dip, and then the general's sun rises. A search beam or a giant pumpkin. First light, Antek thinks.

On an impulse, Antek digs under the fence to the Sinta cottage, slides through the gap. He takes two or three steps toward the Sinta house. Raps on the front door which has been newly mended by somebody. In theory Antek knows he's entitled, as an Egg Boy, to do this. To be here. But it feels wrong to him.

Antek waits. Seeing from this close how Zorry's house decays. The curving wooden arches round the outer doorway and one hundred tiny loops the woodworm made. In patterns seeming orderly, strange. He realises the door is mended with rough hewn wood from a killing forest tree. There's a painted lizard on it. Orange paint. Like a warning.

Zettie pokes her small head out the window, points to the side of the house. "Father made Zorry live in the shed." She says. Intuiting what Antek wanted to know.

Antek raps abruptly on the shed door. One, two, holds his breath, *three*. Then he puts his palm against the door. He raps too hard then. Raps violently. Now he is concerned that he's scared her, caused Zorry to flee under or around the back of the shed. There's a long silence, but it's filled with life, that quiet. He knows that Zorry is inside, listening. Trying to figure the knock. Who it is. What it means. She sees the shadow of an Egg Boy in the glass pane of the shed door. Freezes. Egg boy, Antek thinks, looking at his own reflection in the mottled glass. He turns abruptly to leave.

And now mechanical sounds, at a distance. Metal loose in metal, low thrumming, insect sounds. They're rebuilding the barracks with machines now. The clean up must be over. Soon it will appear as though nothing happened there.

Zorry opens the door softly behind Antek. She steps out of the shed. Antek looks down at his arm and sees Zorry's hand there. Small shock of her touch on his skin. She says his name. And then,

"Are you the last of your tribe?"

Antek holds up two fingers. "Two." He says. "There are two of us." Zorry nods. "I thought I saw red hair at the edge of the killing forest," she says. And then, "What will you do?"

She looks at the side of Antek's head. Points. Your head wound is healing. Eyes the clotting wound knowingly. And then,

"What's that?" Zorry's eyes widen. She points to a place both above and behind him.

Antek turns. He looks in the direction that she's looking.

THE GREENING

ZORRY SQUINTS, COVERING HER face. And then curling on the ground, face tucked under her hands.

"What is it?"

"It's the greening," she says. And then, looking up, "Flood!" It's the last word Zorry gets out.

It crashes softly, hits mostly her curved spine first time. The back of her head. One rolling wave-like motion, breaks apart and spreads out like water running out from her on all sides. Hits the trees and then expands, billows and streams back, green spores smoking from it.

Fire and water, the villagers like to call that greening effect. It's rare and saved for the worst Sinta witches. There's not been a greening like this in the OneFolks' village in years. The rout will come after. Whatever poor soul was hit, they'll be dragged to the shop, stoned by every OneFolk farmer in the village, right there in Gaddys' yard.

Depending on where they stood, every villager had a different perspective. It was as though all the green spores in Bavarnica gathered up in a fury, came down on Zorry.

A Sinta in the field next door takes his hat off. He takes a sideways look at the baobab on the long horizon. He's not sure why. Church of the baobab has been banned for a hundred years, but it occurs to the Sinta farmhand: if the baobab were ever to walk again, and they say it has happened before and will happen again, then maybe that great event would be preceded by an occurrence like this one.

But the baobab does nothing. Dead black swollen limbs silhouetted against the dying sunlight. The air fills up with green spores. The farmhand sighs. He turns back to his work.

The second wave of greening seems to gather up leaves and debris, its tendrils smoking with spores, which slip away from the centre and spreading out more roots on each side. A stripe of green light slips over the farmhand's boot, a little sticks to the toe but it keeps on going, loops around and slipping back relentlessly toward Zorry. The Sinta farmhand hears the hoots and howls of relief coming from all sides as the green slip-stream moves over and away from his Sinta helpmates. He scowls, goes on digging. It takes a while to understand that the greening is looping, rounding, heading relentlessly toward Zorry's front yard.

Zorry squints and looks out from between her fingers. The greening rolls over eggs and chickens, keeps on coming.

"Keep still." Zorry hears her aunt's voice from the front door of the cottage behind her. "Keep. Still." She says, loudly. Her clear, authoritative voice reassuring Zorry. "It will just roll over you too."

She bustles into the yard toward Zorry. The greening ignores Zorry's aunt, runs right over Antek's boots and around his ankles. Antek hears it whipping near his ears, just above and behind him. Nothing seems to stick to him. Zorry's aunt seems to notice something, change her mind, yelling "Run!" Only it's too late for that now. It was always too late, Antek thinks. He sees Zettie's small face, she looks small and lost at the kitchen window. And now the sound of Zorry's aunt screaming. Choking, getting fainter, the wind is beating at his ears.

Antek looks down. Zorry is completely engulfed.

When the greening slips away from Zorry, she is panting, struggling, streaming eyes.

Now Antek and Zorry's aunt are staggering back towards the cottage, hauling Zorry, with some difficulty, between them.

Zorry jolts into life on the kitchen table. Heaves for breath and then seeing her aunt and Antek, she calms down enough to allow her aunt to check her over, look for signs of damage, patches of green. "Where'd it go?" Aunt says impatiently. "That damn greening. Better not gotten your insides ..." She blinks. "Zorry, if you breathed that damned thing in, then I'll kill you myself."

And now Aunt is dragging on Zorry's eyelids gently, checking the whites and the iris, the pupils.

"Nothing." Aunt concedes with relief, and no little amazement. "It didn't stick to you, Child." Hugging Zorry then, only Zorry's not speaking. She's moving her tongue against the back of her teeth, exploring the strange sensation.

"What is it? Speak, Child!" Zorry's aunt shakes her then steps back.

Zorry slowly unfurls her tongue.

The tongue is shrunken inward, long and pointed like a lizard's. It's a brighter green than before and it's grown to twice the size, so that it has to coil to fit into her mouth. The end has a small fork in it.

"It hurts." Zorry says. Feels the end with the tips of her fingers.

"Oh, the holy baobab wept Zorry." Aunt curses. "What in

the hell did they do to you, Child?"

"My tongue hurts," Zorry says again.

"I've heard of this. They say the pain doesn't last," says her aunt. Holding back tears.

There is a long, respectful silence.

When Father rushes in, cap in hand and breathless, looking from the wounded Egg Boy to his child, Zorry pushes out her tongue to show him. Father's eyes seem to roll into his skull. He passes out on the newly cleaned kitchen floor.

"It's not good." Zorry's aunt leans over. "Even your father is afraid of you now. Folks are the cruellest to the things they are most afraid of. I think we should hide you from the village."

Zorry blinks back tears. And then, "I know where to go." Wipes her arm across her eyes. Leaves a stripe of green on her face.

She slides down from the table.

Antek joins her at the front door.

They step carefully over Zorry's father, lying prostrate on the clean tiles. "Where are you going? Where are you going with that boy, Zorry? He is not our tribe!" Father's voice is getting louder and shriller, more choked. "Zorry!"

Zorry's father props himself up on one elbow. "Answer me! Where you going with that Egg Boy?"

Zorry turns toward her father briefly. "I'm going out." She says.

THE KILLING FOREST

ANTEK KEEPS LOOKING BACK, toward the fence. He
stumbles behind Zorry, catches his foot on a tree root, half
falls over Tomax and then, palms first, into a nest of nipping
saplings. His skin is itching where he landed. He sits up.
Examines Tomax's face.

Nothing. Tomax thinks. He doesn't recognise me.

There's a rhythm to the sound inside the tree behind
Antek, he listens to soft insect droning. Rolls clumsily out
of the nipping saplings. Traces the soft pattern of moss with
one finger. Notices the trails left by the insects. One thousand
crazy patterns in the bark.

"This one isn't a pizen tree."

"What?" Zorry scratches her head.

"It's not got a pizen. There are critters living in it."

"He's found a way to tell the killing trees from the regular
ones." Jengi says, sloping out from behind a high bush. "He's
been here ... What?" Turns toward Zorry, quick checking
gesture. "All of half a minute? How did we miss that?"

"Insects mean no pizen." Antek repeats, looking down. He
can't understand why the shopkeeper's assistant is here. He
turns back to face the tree.

Jengi smiles. "You're a fresh pair of eyes here, for sure."

"Ears," Antek says looking up.

"What?"

"I spotted it with my ears."

"Ah." Jengi taps his forehead. "Yes."

There's a gap in the trees at the edge. The fence is just visible through it. "That's where they've come in, the past three days."

"Who?"

Jengi turns slowly toward Zorry. "Egg Men, who else?"

"You three watch the fence. I'll try to get the long view." She turns toward Jengi, "He says it's not a pizen tree?"

"That's what the man said."

"Let's find out." Zorry climbs it.

The killing forest is noiseless. Listening. Snap of a twig overhead.

Tomax can't tell where the sound of his own breathing stops, Antek's begins. He watches the slow sap drip from a leaf in front of him, falling onto Antek's right forearm and appears to burn the skin there. He doesn't notice pain much, Tomax thinks. What's wrong with him? Gazes at Antek's left ear, examines the side of his head.

Antek doesn't like being watched.

He gets up. Moves around.

Jengi's leaning on the stump of a fallen tree, he's chewing a grass stalk. Watching the Egg Boy and the edge farm boy seem to circle each other. Antek is moving through the brushy scrub in a sun scorched clearing, just beyond Jengi's feet, trying not to step on dry bracken and failing. Tomax is scowling. The nipping saplings have moved closer to him. It takes a moment for him to notice, then he startles. "I don't like this." He says loudly. There's an answering bird call, at a distance. Warning hoot. Tomax feels something moving near his left foot. And then a gnawing sound in the scrub beside him. Shifts around on his haunches and then stands up, looking down. He can't see what it is.

"Rats?"

Jengi shrugs. "Scurvet more likely." He points to Tomax's arm, "You got bit already. You need to concentrate on where you're at instead of where you're going, Edge Farm."

Tomax looks down at his arm.

Everything about the killing forest disgusts and unnerves Tomax, he's felt itchy in his skin ever since he arrived. Felt the urge to run. "I shouldn't be here." He says.

Jengi notices there's a large gap in the fence running down the left side of the killing forest. Signs of force, bitten edges. That's new. "We may have been watching the wrong entry point."

Zorry catches his eye, looks where he looks. "Let's get further in."

"Not yet."

Jengi peers into the dark killing forest behind him, things move. "Somebody might be in the trees already." Any single one of the dark shapes behind them could be Egg Men, watching them now. Circling in.

Sound seems to rise in the forest. It takes a moment for Antek to tune in. To make sense of it.

Squawks, growls and bird sounds. He registers something large moving through the forest. Getting nearer instead of farther. Squints into the darkness. It comes to him.

"Egg man." He says.

All four drop.

The Egg Man's neck seems to bend a little, under the strain of his heavy skull, giving his shoulders a slumped crow-like appearance. The sleeves of his non-regulation coat are too short and his thick arms bulge out from under. The knobby bones of his back strain against the fabric and the stitches running down its spine tear away from their seams. The wind gets up behind him, blowing his coat tails a little. Edge farm soil dusts the leaves of the killing forest.

They see nothing at first. They see nothing for a long time, only the dark ferns, curling and uncurling, tree limbs bulging with moss, a few loping scurvet sniff the nipping saplings and move off. And then it's Zorry who notices. A rough outline, dark shape of a man. It's gone before it fully registers from eye to brain.

Antek hears a long, low insect droning. It's moving in a large semi-circle left to right. Sounds for all the world like drilling. Robotic sound, it's six, maybe seven feet away now, getting closer. Zorry lifts her nose, sniffs the air and then turning in one seamless motion, grabbing Antek's hair, the broken seam of Tomax's shirt by his throat, dragging them both stumbling to their feet and a piercing Sinta shriek that seems to lift to the tree canopy above them and be lost in the bird sound above, "RUNNNN!"

They reach the edge to the dark mouth of the killing forest. They pause, panting. There is the sound of the snake moving slowly around them again. Now they steer left and away from the sound. It takes Zorry a moment to realise that, once again, the forest has manoeuvred them deeper into itself and farther away from their exit.

The mouth of the killing forest gapes open in front of them. Leaves shift and rustle, separate. Zorry feels cold pooling in her stomach.

"Keep. Going." She says.

"No." Jengi holds her arm fast. "It's stopped, Zorry. Listen. Nothing's behind us."

She is panting. A moment later she shakes Jengi's hand off her arm fiercely. The two are eye to eye.

"It has steered us to here right from the beginning, Jengi."

"Yes."

There's a long pause. And then, "Zorry." Jengi says. "The danger's gone. Let's rest here for a while. Let's think."

He builds a fire with slow expertise, a plume of smoke twists up from between his hard palms. Soft crackle as the flames rise under his fingers.

"Remember." Jengi says. Eyeing the poisoned plant teeth which mark the edge of the forest's mouth. "The killing forest is designed to learn you. It saw us run. Now it knows where we're weak. It knows who's not watching all our backs and who is not watching his own. *Her* own." He gazes gently at Zorry. "Who wants to push on forward and who isn't feeling exactly at home in here." And then turning to face Tomax. "The forest is a mind. A predatory mind, iffen you ask me. It will find us out," he says. "Who we are."

The flames rise softly.

Zorry is examining the tree line at the edge of the forest mouth. Thinks she saw something move. "Look." She says. Pointing.

Once again she feels Jengi's hand on her hand. Soft electricity running down her arm. She pulls her hand away quickly.

"Shhhhh." Antek moves away from the fire, finger to his lips.

"Egg Man coming. Get down."

Zorry's voice appears to be coming from the tree canopy above them.

Tomax notices Jengi hasn't moved. He's stayed by the fire, prodding it softly. He seems strangely calm. Waiting. "Who is it? Who's out there?" Jengi says quietly. And then, just a little louder, "It's safe here. Join us by the fire?" There's a long unnerving pause and then the crunch, slide of Antek's father lolloping clumsily forward. The heavy stamp and slip of his good foot then the drag of the injured one, a misstep in his walking rhythm. Apparently the Egg Man didn't escape the bombing of the barracks, Jengi thinks. Antek considers this too. What it means. But he doesn't move from his hidden position.

Antek's father pauses in the dark shadow at the edge, where the firelight doesn't reach. They see his slumped shoulders and the slope of his head, just above the shrubs. He seems to examine the scene ahead of him and then change his mind. Turns on his heels.

Now the sound of him is getting farther away and in a while it's hard for Antek to locate his father's position at all. He's moving fast, injured or not, tripping over tree roots, Antek hears the crunching and snapping of twigs and bracken, the Egg Man's felling small trees as he goes.

Most of the trees in the forest are derived from the ancient cypress and sound carries in a cypress forest. Rises. Amplifies until it seems as though the whole of the forest echoes to the sound of the Egg Man's feet. And then Antek hears it. Just on his left. Snap. And then one careful footstep, slow crunch. His father has silently doubled back. Antek looks up, to see if the

others have noticed. No-one turns toward the sound. The Egg
Man is moving in on them, slower than before. This time Jengi
hears it. Slide of his knife from its sheath, metal against metal.
The Egg Man stops. Appears to change his mind once more.
Now they hear heavy feet, moving away.

Jengi sighs. He looks down at his knife sadly.

Tomax is lying face down on the forest floor. "Egg Man in
the forest, that's bad," he hisses. He inhales forest smells.
Sap from the nipping plant to the left of his head drips, some
falling on to the small hooked bridge of his nose, seeps down
his cheek and stings lightly. Tomax closes his eyes. "Damn.
Why did I come here?" He says quietly.

"Snake." Zorry whispers. Zorry feels something slithering
in the branches around her head and ears. She slips down
the tree. "More than one." There are receding circles in the
moist foliage around her shins now. She freezes. The snake
slips around her, and then moving off. They watch the grass
moving, smell the death smell of large reptile. It passes by
slowly. And afterward, a waft of soft rot and tin. Zorry climbs
up her tree again, more cautiously this time.

"Why does it have a light on its head?"

The snake pauses at the edge of the clearing, just by the
fence to the OneFolks' village. The fence billows. Seems to
undulate towards the creature. The snake recoils slightly. And
then, looping back on itself, makes its way slowly up a fruit
bearing tree, smelling its way forward blindly. Tomax eyes the
tree for a while. "I've lost sight of the snake." He says. This
seems to him to be worse. Tomax smells earth, fern, mould
spores. A six legged insect crawls over the thumb on his left
hand, bright shiny shell like a jewel, and he flicks it. It lands on

Antek's father, hidden from them by the roots of the tree that Zorry has climbed.

Sticky swivel of the Egg Man's eyeballs rolling in their sockets, eyeing Zorry and then Tomax. He fixes on Jengi. He sighs. He slowly gets up, moves toward the fence to the edge farms. When he reaches the fence he looks out over the tin roofs and the scrubby desiccated crops, the baobab trees bumpy silhouette against the desert. The general's lights are out, post curfew, and the remains of the old sun's natural light is casting shadows. A few scraggle-necked chickens peck in the dusty farmyards, a small child raises her head softly to look back at the Egg Man. He squints into the low light, turns back toward the killing forest thoughtfully.

Tomax tries not to breath loudly. Something's crawling slowly down his shirt neck. He hears Jengi move carefully through the brush until he's standing over Tomax. "Keep. Perfectly. Still." Jengi says.

Antek's father tuns his head slowly upward, takes a note of Zorry in the trees. She's shifted position slightly. He sinks just below the tips of a patch of saplings near the tangle of tree roots beneath her. Watches her from the weeds. Loops silently around and around the tree. There is no clear shot. Had he wanted one. "Good girl." He says, under his breath.

Tomax sits up. Examines the insect in the vice of Jengi's forefinger, thumb. Scratches his newly shaven head, and then examines it carefully with his fingertips.

"Thanks. What is it?"

"It's a killer."

"Look. Let's go back." Tomax says. Dropping the insect.

"Back where?"

There doesn't seem to be an answer to Jengi's question. And then, looking down. "I've been bit."

Thin black roots fan out from the red nip, like a small half moon or a fingernail mark. The skin is bumpy near the nip, and inflamed. Tomax is scratching it already.

"It won't be too bad," Jengi pronounces, after a brief checking glance at Tomax's fingers, wrist and palm. "You have to expect to get bit a few times in the forest. Tie it. Here." Pulls a rag out of his pocket, rips it roughly in half. Wraps it round Tomax's hand and secures it.

The lights of the OneFolks' village seem to Antek to be shrinking every time he looks back.

Jengi's fire is going out slowly. The branches are damp and smoke rises softly from it. Jengi claps his hands over the smoke, making shapes.

"What's he doing?"

"Smoke signal." Tomax looks at Antek grimly. "He's telling the edge farms to arise."

"How do you know?"

"It's what the last Digger tells the edge farms every night." Tomax says wryly. Tomax and Jengi are eye to eye for a long time. There's a flare and Jengi's face glows briefly, then the firelight dies away. Zorry slips down from her tree.

Jengi's face is in darkness when he speaks. Pausing over his words as though he weighs each one carefully. "Your father's batch of Egg Men were made for climbing, Antek." He says. "They were designed for pulling the fleeing Sinta out of their mountain hideouts and from behind tricky rocks. The general didn't want nobody making it over the reach to tell their story to the outside world, iffen there's even an outside

world left now at all. Which some Bavarnicans have their
reasons for kindly doubting." Jengi strokes his left thumb
with his right forefinger, he turns over his hand. Examines it.
"But the thing I been thinking about is ..." He looks up. "What
did they have planned for you, Antek? You seem to me to be
perfectly adapted to the killing forest." He lifts his hands,
palms up in a mock surrender. "No offence. So what did the
general want you to do here? I mean ... They going to throw
your kill switch on us or something?"

Antek looks down. He strokes the slightly raised scar on his
chin.

Now Zorry defends Antek. "He saved Zettie and he helped
me, he ain't got a kill switch."

"I don't know." Antek says, meeting her gaze. "I don't know
what I am. Who I might be. There are parts of me that are
run from Central Control." He turns over his hands. He looks
down at his palms.

"I should go back." His eyes are cavernous, strange, two
candles burned down to the wick, Zorry thinks. She feels a
wave of sorrow for him. He gazes up at Zorry. "I should get
away from you all."

Antek's father slips closer to hear. Hides behind a killing
tree. Small snake slips over his left hand and he eyes it briefly,
flicks it off.

The Egg Man rubs his hands together. The temperature
is roasting in the forest already, but the Egg Man can't seem
to get warm. He looks down at himself. He is hairless from
burns, his skin straggled with bruised veins. There is an oily
sheen of forest matter covering him from skull to boot.

An insect ticks and whirs in the darkness on his left side.

He turns toward it.

A biting tree branch near Zorry's right hand sniffs the air and moves toward her snake-like, slow. She steps away from it easily. Looks up. Soft light of moon through the branches.

"What's that noise?" Tomax asks.

"Howl of the one-eyed hyaena, last of its kind." Jengi scratches his chin. "A bit like me." Grins in the dark.

The branch of the tree stump Jengi leans on has rotted off and the stump is shiny with jewel coloured beetles. Jengi picks one up and lobs it. It clings to his fingertips and then flies from his hand. "Don't worry, Zorry knows how to handle those howling hyaenas."

The four listen to the muted, dying sound. You could think that you'd dreamed it.

Jengi scratches his nose, pokes the fire and adds fuel to it. The stick catches alight and now he throws it, burning, into the middle. Flames are coming up fast now.

"I have something to tell you. Antek." Jengi looks up. Eyes the dark trees around them. It's a brief, shrewd gaze.

"There's no general." He says.

"What?"

"He died thirteen years ago. Pizened. By Zeina's last assistant. Gaddys covered it up. And even if he hadn't been ... Pizened. For thirteen straight years there has been nothing to stop the Egg Men freeing the Sinta. Taking the flowers fund vans and stacking them with drought resistant seeds, driving them through the gates of Bavarnica. Ending this hell now, all in one night."

"So why don't they? Who knows about this?"

"A handful of people know."

"So why ...?"

"They're afraid of repercussions. Their past coming back to haunt them. They're afraid of letting the Sinta and the edge farmers get up off the floor."

"But if the edge farmers know the egg men helped, well then ... We would be the rescuers. Wouldn't we?"

"Aye. Your farms, your families would be safe from strong neighbours. Iffen you were on the right side when ..."

Zorry thinks of something Zeina once said, "And it will rain so hard that night that morning will come."

Jengi eyes the smoke, rising. Scowls softly. "Your people will be safe from all that's coming down the tracks. Safe from the future."

"So ... If what you say is true, that nothing's stopping them ...? Stopping us?"

"Just a gate." Jengi eyes him through the smoke plumes.

"You're saying an insurrection? A military takeover of Bavarnica, by the Egg Men?"

"I'm saying just the opposite, Son. I'm saying the Egg Men should lay down their arms. Dig their fields. Go back to their families. Back to living. All the Egg Men have to do to stop this evil from continuing is ..." He gazes gently at Antek. "Do nothing. Just stop."

"Not fight? Jengi. Asking an Egg Man to lay down his arms is like asking a Digger to. It ain't ..." Antek thinks about his father. "It's not written into Batch 46 DNA. They need something to fight. Someone."

Antek is staring into the middle distance, he's stroking the groove in his chin. Something is slowly filtering into his mind. "Something has gone." He says. He looks up. "I can't rightly say what it is. But ..." His hand falls away from his scar. "I have to try to find out," he says. He stands up. "I have to try to go back. Go back to the barracks and tell them. Tell them the general is dead."

Antek's father blinks softly. Surprised. He dips behind a killing tree, closes his eyes and leans there. *No.* He says gently. One word. He watches the general's sun dip behind the treeline. It goes out with a soft fiss. That means curfew. He looks down at his burns.

Insect sounds. Starting up on his left. It rises. The Egg Man lets the soft droning roll around him. Sinks back against the tree. He hears bird sound, squawks and hoots in the treetops above him. Ferns uncurl round his face. He looks down. Bends and flicks a slug off his shoe. He rubs the back of his neck. From here he can see the fire's last glitter. Small lights all down the branch beside Jengi's outstretched right arm, sparks dying one by one. The Egg Man's left leg is twisted and he moves away pained, at a lean.

Jengi looks up. Sniffs the air. "I can't smell Egg Man no more."

Tomax reaches out his hand, touches Antek's hand. "You keep looking at me," Tomax persists. "You remember me, Antek. Don't you? You remember something?"

Antek pulls his hand away once more. "I remember ... Some." Gazes softly at Tomax. Now there's a crackling in the trees behind him. He has a sudden intuition, "Father?" Antek asks the darkness. He whips his head around to see the exit to the OneFolks' village, small seam of red light. Blinks quickly. "I have to go back ... For them." Now he's scrambling blindly toward the red light and the exit to the village. Taking risks. Tripping on tree roots, getting caught in tree fingers outstretched toward him. Getting scratched up by the killing forest, hears Tomax and Zorry calling his name, again and again, he staggers onward. He's moving fast.

Zorry turns on Jengi fiercely. "They'll kill him. For what? For who, Jengi?"

"Aye. They'll kill him. Eventually." Jengi turns over his hands. Looks at the streaks of green on his palms, moss and mud. Zorry is angry. Angry suddenly. "His death will do nothing, *nothing*. Even together, we can't defeat the Egg Men. Not even a divided barracks. You don't have any answers. Mamma Zeina was right about you, you will kill hope with your next war." She gazes blankly out into the darkness. "You are ... Death. Jengi."

Jengi meets her eye softly. "Offer me an alternative, Zorry. Something better."

"Something ..." She looks out into the dark forest. "We need something *else*. Something we ain't found yet."

She gets up.

"Now where you going?"

"I'm going to find it. In there." She points toward the forest's dark mouth. Dark green mottled leaves move away from the entrance, as though to invite her in.

She turns back to look at Jengi.

"I didn't think you would use us." She blinks. "I didn't think you would ..." Now she has to force the words out, "I didn't think that you would sacrifice *him*, and Tomax ... sacrifice *me*?"

Jengi looks bleak. "Is that a statement or a question?" He goes on holding her eye. "This cause is all I am now, Zorry."

"Batch 46 are sharpening their knives, right now, Jengi. Getting ready to put their last son to death. Antek trusted us.

Ever think of that?"

Jengi can't answer. He notices, as if for the first time, how her eyes are mismatched. The thing he'd tried to forget. Lapis lazuli and silver, green and gold. They seem to him to change colour again and again. There is a long pause and then, "I see." She says. "We are all three *supposed to* die. Antek, Tomax, Zorry. A martyr for every tribe. Three Seeds, like the ancient book said. Well. No." She says softly, looking up. "I said *no*."

She draws back from the fire. There is a small patch of sky just visible through the tree limbs overhead, twig fingers part. There's a rustling of leaves, as though the forest were listening. "We are your stone seeds, and stone seeds *die*." Zorry laughs. A sharp bark of bitter laughter. Silence again. And then getting up abruptly. "I've gotta get out of here. Get away from you."

"Zorry. Where are you going?"

She turns to him, savagely. "I'm going to find every damned rain plant in this forest. I'm going to garden it and turn it, right here in the killing forest, then I'm going to plant 'em out there." She thumbs in the direction of the edge farms. The baobab.

"Sounds like a bold plan."

"Shut up. I'm thinking."

She squints, tries to make out a trail. There is something moving out there. A human shape, hoving in and out of view. And then it's gone. Gone as though she dreamed it.

"I'm going to find out what's in there." She peers into the killing forest's dark mouth. "What or who." She can see nothing ahead, not even her own hand in front of her face. "I'm going in."

Jengi watches Zorry walking into the dark mouth of the killing forest, neatly steering through the nipping saplings, ducking under heaving branches, right hand across the back of her neck. Palm down, to protect it from leaches.

She's moving fast. Moving fast away from him. Getting out of sight, sharpened stick in her right hand. Raised a little, readied. In case of snakes or scurvets, and at first it seems as though she's veering right toward the fence to the edge farm and then she swerves left instead. Heads down the smooth dark throat in the centre of the forest's mouth.

Zorry can smell hot soil, burnt tinder, tin and the slick trace left by a reptile. And then the unmistakeable musky aroma of the scurvet in the grasses around her. Now she's eye height with the stinging grasses. They slowly reach out tendrils for Zorry's small chin, sniff the air around the gentle incline of her nose. Everything in the killing forest is snake-like, she thinks, not for the first time. Even the plants. She blows softly on the plant nearest her left eye, to discourage it, and then watches it dip and waver, and then grow back closer still. Blinks. Zorry bites down hard on her bottom lip. She steels herself. Pushes on.

She hears human sounds, only not like human sounds. Human shapes hoving into view and then vanishing again. The forest seems to her to hold its breath.

"Hello." She says gently. And then, "Who are you? Are you for us?"

Us the word seems to her to echo. Something moves in the trees to her left.

Snake slides across her right foot. It seems to leave her alone, there's a rustling in the soft, curling ferns to her right,

"Who are you?" She repeats.

Silence.

"What did you want?"

Zorry thinks she hears the sound of falling water, somewhere to her right. And then bird sound, a little farther off. Soft hiss of someone putting out a smoking campfire. The branches seem to move around her.

Jengi watches as the dark mouth of the killing forest closes behind Zorry. He watches the point where she vanished for a long time after she's gone.

Antek's father slides out from behind a tree. He sinks down until he's sitting on its tangled, upturned roots. The snake slides slowly around his left leg. The Egg Man ignores it. He inserts one long, boney finger deep into his left ear. Pulls something out. It makes a slippery sound unplugging. "Tree slug." He says. Noticing the slug's poisoned sacs are empty, must have been unloosed in his left ear canal. This doesn't seem to bother the Egg Man over much. He flicks it. Scratches his ear. Steam goes on rising from the forest floor vent beside him. And now he's listening to the forest. Fussing sound, sighing of tree limbs, shaking of leaves as they rise and move away from his face.

He eyes the nip on his hand.

"Ouch." He sucks the hand. "Pleased with yourself?" He asks the tree, sarcastically. "Damn predator." He notices a praying mantis on his shoulder. Plucks it off. He examines its amazed face, softly turning it side to side, bites off its head. Chews it thoughtfully.

Crunch, *crunch*. The sound of splitting.

The forest is hot as sin but the Egg Man is still shivering.

His eyes are luminous, strange. Peering out through the nipping saplings. They dip and waver, sigh and move away from his face.

He waits 'till he's sure Jengi's asleep before he calls it in.

THE LAST REPORT

"WHO IS IT?"

"You know who it is." He pulls his ear lobe. Drags his sleeve across his face.

There's a silence at the other end of the line. And then, "What do you want, Egg Man?"

"I want what I always want."

"Remind me."

"I want ..." The Egg Man heaves off his right boot, a blue-shelled beetle tips out, scuttles into a fern. And then turning the boot over, examines its burnt sole. Sighs.

"I want a new plan."